CW00926014

Disarm Evil

Disarm Evil

A novel by Ritu Vedi

Ritu Books

Disarm Evil

First Printing, 2023

To those who are trying to make peace with uncertainty.

- Violence (depicted as good, bad, and neutral depending on context)
- Police brutality (depicted as bad)
- Racism (depicted as bad)
- Systemic racism (depicted as bad)
- Systemic poverty/oppression (depicted as bad)
- Death (depicted as bad)
- Spiritual deconstruction (depicted as good)
- Physical abuse (depicted neutrally. I personally believe it is bad. However, I also recognize that knowledge of healthy parenting techniques/anger management and the ability to implement them are both privileged things.)
- Crime (depicted as something people turn to when society and misfortune has put them in a desperate situation. The definition of "crime" is also depicted as a tool used to attack and oppress marginalized communities.)
- Religious manipulation (depicted as bad)
- Implied torture (the torture is not graphically described and is depicted as bad)
- Disabilities (Disabled character struggles with feeling complete and not like ve is broken. Eventually this character comes to the understanding that while disabilities can present unique challenges, people with disabilities are full people capable of living happy and fulfilling lives.)
- Disabilities as government afflicted punishment (depicted as bad)
- Disabilities/hardships as divinely afflicted punishment (depicted as bad)

- Violence (depicted as good, bad, and neutral depending on context)
- Police brutality (depicted as bad)
- Racism (depicted as bad)
- Systemic racism (depicted as bad)
- Systemic poverty/oppression (depicted as bad)
- Death (depicted as bad)
- Spiritual deconstruction (depicted as good)
- Physical abuse (depicted neutrally. I personally believe it is bad. However, I also recognize that knowledge of healthy parenting techniques/anger management and the ability to implement them are both privileged things.)
- Crime (depicted as something people turn to when society and misfortune has put them in a desperate situation. The definition of "crime" is also depicted as a tool used to attack and oppress marginalized communities.)
- Religious manipulation (depicted as bad)
- Implied torture (the torture is not graphically described and is depicted as bad)
- Disabilities (Disabled character struggles with feeling complete and not like ve is broken. Eventually this character comes to the understanding that while disabilities can present unique challenges, people with disabilities are full people capable of living happy and fulfilling lives.)
- Disabilities as government afflicted punishment (depicted as bad)
- Disabilities/hardships as divinely afflicted punishment (depicted as bad)

Content Warning

This is an adult fiction novel. The content of this book may not be suitable for minors. This book also tackles an array of topics readers may find distressing. Please read at your own discretion.

Content:

- Emotional abuse (depicted as bad)
- Manipulation (depicted as bad)
- Grooming (depicted as bad)
- Implied child sex trafficking (no explicit acts of sexual activity with a minor. However, a predator does briefly use seduction to manipulate a minor. Depicted as bad.)
- Child abandonment (depicted as bad)
- Death of a family member and loved ones (depicted as a difficult loss where grief is normal and welcome)
- Mutilation (descriptions are not detailed beyond naming parts which are removed also depicted as bad overall)
- Poverty (poverty is depicted as bad but the impoverished are depicted as mostly good or neutral. Also, poverty is depicted as the fault of oppressive systems and not as the fault of the character flaws of the impoverished)
- Drunkenness (depicted as neutral)
- Drug use (depicted as neutral)
- Murder (depicted as bad)
- Off screen sexual assault (no explicit acts of sexual assault and depicted as bad)
- Brief consensual second-base intimacy (depicted as good)
- Explicit language (depicted as neutral)

Table Of Contents

To those who are trying to make peace with uncertainty.

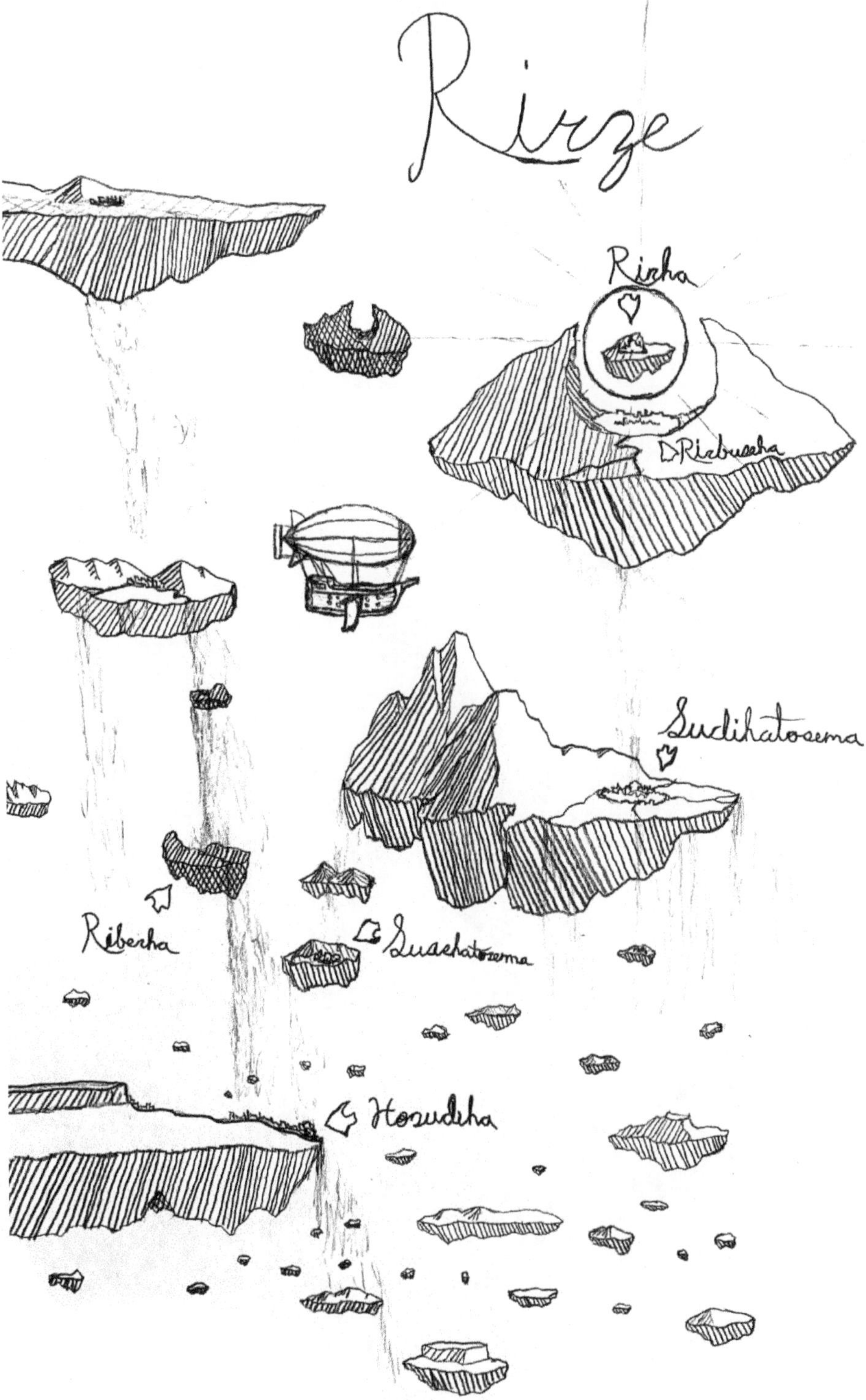

Rirze

Rirha

Rirbusaha

Sudihatosema

Riberha

Suashatosema

Hosudiha

Preface

In the Shattered Skies, there exists four species with intelligence and sentience comparable to humans. These are collectively called vetu, and include atu, bitu, yetu, and notu. "People/person" can be used interchangeably with "vetu" though "vetu" is considered a tad more formal. Inversely, family titles using characters from the language of creation are considered more intimate than their english counterparts: For example, "vedi" is more intimate than "parent".

As a result of the diverse nature of sexes among vetu (see "Biology/Form Of Vetu" section towards the end of the book for details), the concept of gender was never developed in the nations of the Shattered Skies.

Therefore, gendered pronouns and titles do not exist. Third-person singular pronouns are universally "ve" and "ver", with singular "they", "them", and "their" also used occasionally. A glossary is available with singular family titles, their meanings, and many of the names of places and things unique to the world of the shattered skies.

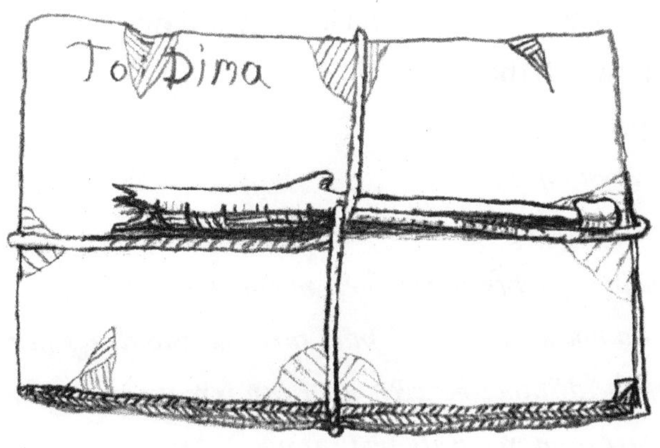

Chapter 1: Rirbuseha

[In the world of the Shattered Skies there exists the vertical nation, Rirze, which stretches from the cities of the exalted closest to the sun to the cities of the disparaged where the sun barely pierces through the many floating land masses above. In an uppermost city, Rirbuseha, a young, highly exalted, human-like atu, has just acquired a letter from a resident of the city's "Market Town", a company town that exploits laborers and often drives them to lives of crime...]

There is a venomous thorn, capped in red wax, tied to the front of the parcel. My face cannot resist the smile this gift forces upon it. I slide the thorn free of its restraints and let it roll around atop my palm as I muse over its brilliant violet color. A gift from my love Lise. It has been a salary since I first met ver- mature, handsome, and interested in what I have to say.

Lise often poetically compares my beauty to that of the flower that shares a vine with this thorn, and if I am the flower, then my parents and their underlings are the thorns.

I open the parcel:

"My dearest Dima,

With each passing labor, my body yearns for you.

I fear being apart from you for a moment longer.

If you do not act swiftly, I may turn back to drugs just to numb the pain of the distance between us. I can remain strong for now, but the time apart from you beats away at me.

I know that you cannot bear to remain under the control of your greedy parents.

So I trust that you will use this opportunity I have gifted you to be with me as soon as you can. I will do my best to wait for you, my prized flower.

Your beloved,

Lise Fo"

The fear I feel for Lise's health is compelling. Each labor I have to delay my escape increases the odds ve might be driven back to the harmful addictions I rescued ver from. Since Lise needs me, is it selfish to delay a moment longer?

I could do it now. I could leave this stall, use the thorn to knock out Gele, whom my parents always have surveying me. But then there is Joho, whom my parents have started to send to help me run errands. Can a thorn be used more than once? Assuming it can, and I were successful, I could run away with Lise this labor. Off on an adventure to Sudihatosema to help those in need. All I'd have to do is leave behind everything I have ever known...

Is this really the direction Ritu wants for me? Dear Ritu, if I am making the wrong choice, please stop me. Close the door so that I cannot go a step further. Otherwise, please quiet my fears.

Every time I pray I reach the same confusing conclusions. On one hand, I don't feel as though I, or anyone for that matter, is really meant to live in such luxury and comfort as we do in Rirbuseha. Especially when there are souls in need of saving. Afterall, there is the lesson:

"We have no time to live for pleasure.
With so many still lost we feel the pressure
To guide all that we can before Ritu's measure."

On the other hand, my family was exalted to this life of luxury and comfort by Ritu Verself. Is it wrong for me to question if my family really should have this life when it was given to us by Ritu?

I won't do it now. I'm too uncertain and it's too risky. I will give my parents one more chance to convince me that life in Rirbuseha is necessary. Or perhaps I should only speak with Numo. Of my two parents, ve is the most likely to even let me get a word in.

There is a knock at the stall door, and Gele's voice comes piercing through it, "Are you alright in there? You've been taking a long time."

"Yes, I'm fine," I fold the parcel and tuck it and the thorn into my pocket, "I'll be right out."

I step out of the toilet stall onto the busy market streets and my yetu supervisor, Gele, quickly wraps ver fuzzy insectoid legs around me - two around my waist, two around my chest, and two around my shoulders. Ve presses ver small, off-white, oval body snug against my back, like a thick backpack covered in fur-like scales. Ver eighteen ingot wide, gold and white moth-like wings are folded compactly behind us, and ver two feather-like antennae peek out over each of my shoulders, twitching as they scan the raw information of the universe weaved into the fabric of creation, looking for any potential trouble, but mostly to ensure Lise and I cannot come anywhere near each other.

Joho, a tall, black and white furred, bipedal canine, known as a bitu, stands attentive before us. Ve wears an exalted servant's uniform; a black pantsuit with well defined pleats and around ver neck is a purple collar, a humbling article, sporting a buckle in the shape of my family's crest; a pair of hands reaching upwards towards a circular ring as if to receive it.

Collars are an article worn by the servant class consisting of mostly vetu with dark complexion. It is taught that those of darker complexion are cursed to be more prone to vice as they are the descendants of those who plunged furthest from Ritu's light following the fall of all vetu kinds. Joho belongs to a race of bitu believed to be internally divided between being virtue prone and vice prone, resulting in their black and white fur. Making them more capable of exaltation than other bitu who are darker shades of black, gray, brown, or red. However, they are still beneath the white, golden, and other bitu of lighter complexion. It is a similar story for the other varieties of atu and yetu of darker complexion. Granted, as much as this explanation seems to line up with the reality I can observe, I have always felt something was wrong about it.

Joho is here because I am short for a fifteen salary old atu. I am a meager three ingots and a purse tall; almost two ingots shorter than my peers. Most teens don't need a servant to accompany them to the market, but I struggle to carry many bags without dragging them along the ground as I walk. What's worse is that these bags are even enchanted to make the load lighter.

There is also the matter of self defense. Market Town is the home of laborers who are not yet worthy of life in the surrounding city of Rirbuseha. They are not worthy because they lack necessary virtues or cling to certain vices. However, their presence is necessary to fill jobs and services which are unsuitable for those who are most highly exalted. As a result, market city is the hot spot and source of most crime in Rirbuseha. So Joho gets sent along to protect me and to carry things for me, a gesture that, while appreciated, is embarrassing.

At first I thought that other teens might be jealous of my having a personal servant. Though the other teens were quick to see things for what they were. My servant was there, not because I possess some higher status, but because I "needed help".

"Finally," Gele says.

Joho bows politely, "We mustn't keep your parents waiting. Wash up, and then let's grab the groceries we need and be on our way."

"Alright," I say.

I move towards a nearby water fountain and as I approach a column of water rises before me in defiance of gravity. There is a green gemstone, known as a notu, suspended within the column. The notu gemstone moves through the water until it breaks the surface of the side of the column facing me.

"Good morning Dima." the gemstone says. As the gem vibrates to speak the water it manipulates ripples in response.

"Good morning Kino." I say as I insert my hands into the column of water, one hand holding a silver coin known as a 'purse' because it is about as valuable as your average purse of bronze coins. The coin gets lifted from my hand, suspended in the water much like the notu, and then it is permitted to sink down to the bottom of the fountain. The water around my hands quickly stirs and vibrates for a moment before abruptly stopping. I remove my hands and they come out not only clean but also dry.

"Have fun shopping," Kino says.

"Will do."

Now properly hygienic, we move with the flow of people towards Market Town.

The tide of market-goers takes us to the wall which marks the perimeter of Market Town. People break into a number of lines to pass through the intake gates. These lines move quickly compared to the outbound gates where everyone is searched and identified by customs officers. So it isn't long before we pass through a gate and enter into the many extra wide streets lined on either side with well-kept storefronts. Vibrantly colored tarps bridge the tops of the buildings dying the light that passess through to coat the scene in varioious hues. Entering the market feels almost like stepping into a strangely colored yet beautiful painting.

The air is rich with pleasant scents, but every time I go shopping there is one scent that interests me more than any other. The smell of freshly baked bread.

It has become my tradition to grab a slice of buttered bread to motivate me through the course of a shopping trip, and so I follow the usual route to find the golden loaves I am suddenly craving.

"Happy shopping labor Dima!" Exclaims the golden furred bitu baker attending the front counter.

"Thanks Masi!" I reply.

"I've been expecting you, so I made sure a fresh loaf would be ready around the time you usually come by."

Here I was thinking that Ritu had just blessed me to arrive whenever the bread was fresh. It would seem the form of Ritu's blessing is a tad different than I had thought.

"Aw, thank you so much!"

Masi and I exchange coins for bread, though the bread is nearly twice as thick as usual.

"It's the least I could do for our most consistent customer." Masi says warmly. Though the warmth lifts from ver expression as ver gaze shifts towards Joho for a moment, then back to me, "Would you ask your servant to give a bit more clearance so that the shop doesn't feel... overcrowded?"

The question confuses me for a moment given that the bakery is quite spacious. I had noticed Masi would eye Joho each time we came in, but this is the first time ve has said anything. Something about ver request bothers me, but before I can sort out my feelings and respond Joho bows, "I'll wait outside." ve says.

Normally I would hang around and chat, but without Joho here, I feel awkward and less capable of calling out Masi for whatever that request was about. So instead of saying anything I awkwardly wave farewell and follow after Joho.

It doesn't take long to find Joho standing outside of the neighboring storefront which sells various qualities of firewood. Some people swear that different woods are better than others. I've heard everything from health benefits to minute differences in smell. I don't understand it. So far as I can tell, if you've smelt one wood fire you've smelt them all.

Joho's eyes are closed and ve is taking deep and slow breaths.

I start, "Sorry you were kicked out like-"

"It's fine." Joho interrupts. Something I am not used to ver doing, "Sorry. Wood is next on the list is it not?"

"Actually, we usually get that last so that you don't have to lug it around the whole time. Remember?"

"Oh, of course." Joho says, the whole while staring longingly at the stacked logs.

"We could get some now if you would prefer."

"Please pay no mind to my preferences. My apologies, I forgot my place there for a moment. Spices next."

I squint my eyes at Joho in skepticism of ver complacency. Then I walk into the wood shop as Joho just watches frozen in place. Ve knows I have made a decision and ve is not allowed to question it.

For whatever reason wood is among the more expensive goods in the market. Also, unlike other goods, it comes with a small note detailing the purchase to be stamped by the buyer's family ring. I've never understood why wood purchases would receive such special treatment.

I purchase a couple of logs of the most expensive option they have, as a gift for Joho, and then I buy a bundle of my family's usual variety of wood.

"Why the two varieties?" Gele asks.

"I want to treat Joho, show ver I appreciate ver."

"You can't-"

"You get enough say over where I can and can't go. You. Do. Not. Tell me what I can and can not buy."

"No, what I mean is you aren't-"

"I don't want to hear it!"

There is an uncomfortable moment of silence as the atu store clerk tries to assess when the right time might be to hand me the sack of logs I just bought.

"Um... Here you go." ve says uneasily as ve hands me my purchase.

"Thank you." I say triumphantly as Gele seems to give up on pestering me.

When I exit the store, I hand the smaller sack to Joho, "This one is for you! Let's call it a bonus as reward for all of your hard work."

Joho looks conflicted, "I'm sorry, I can't-"

"I am not taking no for an answer," I say sternly.

Joho seems to take a moment to choose ver words carefully, "If an officer finds me in possession of these outside of your family's company, I will be fine- erm- charged for them because I lack a note of purchase with my family's crest on it."

"Oh..." I say bewildered, "I'm sorry. Maybe, I could just give you the coins and you could go and purchase it?"

"Trust me, my possession of those logs, even with a note, would only be asking for trouble."

I am about to argue when Gele cuts in, "Ve is right."

I take a moment to think about this and only find myself more and more ticked off, "Why? What the hase is up with a system like that? Literally no other transaction works like that."

"I am not permitted to say," Joho says.

"Gele?"

"Me neither."

"Why the hase not! When am I supposed to know about this?"

"Some labor, when you are older." Gele assures me.

I know better than to pry. These two won't give up information easily. So we just continue our shopping and I try to forget that I am pissed.

Chapter 2: The Exalted

The heat of eternity grows ever near.
Will the heat stop while the temperature is fair?
Or will it grow to burn, filling the heart with despair?
We have no time to live for pleasure.
With so many still lost we feel the pressure
To guide all that we can before Ritu's measure.

My parent Nizevigu is at work, leaving me and my other parent Numo to eat dinner alone.

Joho quickly and wordlessly darts in and out of the dining room, providing us with proper cutlery and our various courses of food.

The dining room, like most other rooms in our home, is well lit with natural light pouring in through large windows, and the mostly white and gold interior decorations serve to bounce light into every crevice.

The walls are laden with massive enchanted canvases. At the base of the frames for each canvas is a slot into which you can slide a small painting, the canvas will then change color to replicate the image of the smaller painting but at a much larger scale.

Numo is technically sitting close to me, just across the pristine table, but the length I would need to walk around the obstacle between us just to touch ver makes Numo feel distant. Numo wears a pristine white suit with purple peeking out through slotted seams, and it looks impossibly wrinkle-free, making me feel like a commoner in my simple white dress.

"Vedi," I start, "May I ask you a question?"

Numo gives me a curious gaze. "Certainly darling."

"Why can officers charge people who are found to be in possession of firewood without a note of purchase?"

Numo's gaze immediately turns slightly dark as it locks onto Joho who seems to freeze in fear.

I must have asked something I shouldn't have, "Uh, I wanted to buy Joho and ver family some firewood just as a thank you for ver help. Joho hadn't asked for it or said anything. It was just something nice I wanted to do."

Numo's gaze loses its darkness but lingers on Joho as ve asks, "And what did Joho say in response to this?"

"Ve..." I am realizing that I have to choose my words very carefully. This simple question may have landed Joho in some hot water. "I expressed my intentions to the store clerk and ve informed me about how officers would charge. I didn't believe ver and bought the firewood anyway. Gele tried to inform me but I wasn't willing to listen until Joho turned down the gift. Then Gele confirmed that the clerk was telling the truth. However, no one would tell me why this weird thing about firewood even exists."

Numo squints at Joho as if trying to read ver mind for a moment before ve finally frees Joho from attention to look back at me with a sigh. Joho seems to hide ver relief as ve continues on with ver duties. Hopefully I didn't just put Gele in the hot seat, though ve did try to warn me while we were in the store. So ve was ready to face whatever consequences I just pushed ver way, and besides, ve is likely to be treated with far more grace than Joho would be. I think I handled this as well as I could have short of not bringing it up at all.

Numo's expression appears increasingly annoyed as ve looks at me, trying to work out how to respond, "I don't think you are old enough to understand just yet."

My displeasure at ver response seeps into my face, but I manage to keep my voice neutral as I say, "That's what Gele said too."

"Good." Numo says as ve goes on eating, likely intent on pretending the matter was never brought up, and I know better than to try bringing it up again.

"I do have another question though." I dare to say. In response Numo gives me a look that warns me to tread carefully.

When I don't back out of my intent to ask another question, Numo responds, "Go on."

"We are taught that we have no time to live for pleasure. Yet here in Rirbuseha, we practically live in constant pleasure. Don't you think we might be doing something wrong?"

"Now dear, there is a difference between living for pleasure and simply experiencing it. It is not as though we are to go out of our way to be miserable. Exaltation is the reception of blessings, and blessings are pleasurable by nature. The more receptive we are to Ritu the more Ve equips us with the virtues necessary to receive and care for the blessings which exalt us. There is no such thing as having too many blessings, because once we have an abundance of blessings, they pour out onto others. Consider Joho."

Joho, who was coming to serve Numo some freshly roasted kuvohedi steak, delivers the food and then stands attentively. Numo continues, "Oh, you sweet thing, I am just using you as an example. You can keep going."

"Yes, ve." Joho says before leaving.

"There are hardly any spotted bitu to speak of in this city. Joho and ver family get to experience the pleasures of Rirbuseha due to the generosity of our family. Without our wealth, we wouldn't have gotten a role to play in their exaltation. They may still be rummaging around in the garbage of Sudihatosema, if they could manage not to be deported to Hosudiha."

"Sure, but shouldn't we be doing more? As leaders, shouldn't we be more hands-on and meet the people we lead?" I ask.

Numo dismissively waves a hand, "Don't be ridiculous. Ritu exalted us to Rirbuseha to fulfill our roles. We have others in Sudihatosema to do the more 'hands-on' work as you put it."

"What exactly is our role?"

"We ensure no one finds exaltation without the necessary virtues. Exaltation without Ritu's virtues always leads to the superficially exalted individual abusing their resources, hurting themselves more than they could when they had less, and worse hurting their authentically exalted neighbors. At best the individual falls back into the level of society that best suits their level of exaltation."

"At worst?" I ask.

"At worst they build an empire of vice and go on hurting themselves and their neighbors indefinitely. Our role is to prevent these things." Numo says.

"So... if a person's vices don't always land them at the level of society they deserve. Such that we need to step in. Might it be that a person's virtues don't always lift them to the level of society they deserve? Who's job is it to step in then?" I ask.

"A vetu can override nature's attempts to pull them to their proper level of society if they possess the will and resources. Those who are superficially exalted have reason to resist nature, and sometimes succeed. Those who are superficially disparaged are not likely to resist nature's pull to exalt them. Though when they do, why would we intervene?"

Numo's answers make sense, though why don't I feel satisfied? Something isn't setting right, but I don't know what. I'll have to give it some more thought but until then I want to ask, "Okay, but how can we prevent superficial exaltation if we never leave Rirbuseha? How are we supposed to lead people we never meet?"

"We don't need to meet them. We just need to control their options." Numo responds.

"What do you mean control their options?" I ask.

"We control how much money they make, how long it takes for them to make it, how much it costs to buy things, and the news they consume. This allows us to control what they can afford to do with both their time and money alongside controlling what occupies their minds."

Joho enters the room to refill our drinks, and Numo conveniently takes a bite of food. After Joho leaves, Numo continues, "For instance, I know how much time it will take for you to fill your savings jar, and I have some control over that. You want to save up to go to the theater with your peers next deposit."

I don't like that Numo is bringing the trip up. That trip will take me closer to where I am supposed to meet Lise than ever before. As tempted as I have been to make a break for it sooner, I know I will only get one chance at this, and that will be the best opportunity.

"However," Numo continues, "saving for that trip would become impossible if I cut your allowance in half."

Suddenly I no longer feel safe voicing my complaints or asking questions as Numo's educational moment has morphed into a thinly veiled threat. Which leaves me wondering if controlling people's options is really the best way to help them. I hate how much it makes sense, but something feels wrong.

Numo continues, "Another example is our efforts to encourage people to settle down and start a family while young. People with families are less likely to misbehave and put their family at risk." Numo eyes me for an alm.

"Our leadership protects the exalted from being robbed of their exaltation at the hands of Ritu-rejecting progressives who are ruled by vice. If society is not divided, if the highest exalted vetu lived beside the lowest, they wouldn't be safe, exaltation would become meaningless, and it would lead to societal destabilization. Yes, we are to be sacrificial. Yes we are to step out of our comfort to help others, but that looks different for everyone. There are some who need to risk their lives and there are others who need to risk their wealth or status. Now, tell me, do you have any further silly complaints or aspirations you want to air?"

I would like to remind Numo of the way Ritu challenged the wealthy vetu to give ver wealth to the poor and follow Ver. Though Numo would probably just remind me of all of the wealthy patrons who funded Ritu's ministry and Ver apostle's ministries to follow. The command for the one wealthy vetu was not a command for all wealthy vetu. Still, something feels wrong about the way things are, but I'm unwilling to risk my trip to challenge Numo. So I remain silent and shake my head.

"Good. You're only fifteen, so I don't expect you to fully understand how vital our role is to society just yet," ve says, and then takes a sip of water. "Don't worry. I'm not going to keep you from your friends. You will need them. You all are the future of Rirze."

"Then why do you have such a problem with Lise and me-"

Numo throws water from ver glass across the table and into my face. I jump to my feet, gasping in shock from the sudden cold douse.

"I told you never to think of ver again! We all use each other. That's life. But never let someone use you if you cannot equally use them. I don't care how charming ve is. Ve is twice your age. Ve is a Market Town fose who has nothing to offer you. Time spent on ver is dangerous and wasteful. Do you understand?" Numo says with a daring glare.

I nod.

"I want to hear you say it," Numo demands.

"I understand," I say quietly.

"Good. Now sit. Not another word from you. You can change your clothes after our meal is finished."

While I would normally be fuming with anger, I find satisfaction in knowing that this exchange has made up my mind.

Chapter 3: Production

“Make a friend this time and maybe your punishment won’t be quite as severe!” Those were Numo’s parting words to me. As though this is the first time I will be meeting these teens and there hasn’t already been an established relationship of spite that makes me wonder how any of them deserve to live the exalted lives they do. From what I have been told, both myself and my peers are not yet mature enough to manifest certain virtues. Our place in society won't be known until it is seen how we fare as adults, independent of our parents, trying to climb back up among the ultra wealthy via business ventures in Market Town. However, it's not like we have to claw our way back from the same starting conditions as everyone else. Most of us who come from ultra wealthy families tend to have a leg up via business loans, or some foot in the door at a high profile company.

Normally, someone like me would be well respected among my peers at an event like this. However, I have gained a reputation for my disdain for upper society. People believe I am destined for disparagement, and on top of that I am short. So I have become a sort of punching bag for those who are jealous of my roots.

The aggression of my peers is so predictable at this point that I already know exactly what is going to happen when I enter the theater. I'm going to be ridiculed not only for my short stature, as per usual, but also for my choice of outfit; from the outside, a modest dress that shifts in color from dark blue towards the top to vibrant rosy orange towards the middle to yellow at the bottom. In addition, I have customized the dress with my own added embroideries.

I love this dress. It is my proudest accomplishment of my endeavors into the art of embroidery. When I finished it I thought it was comparable to the artsy dresses and suits the great seamers sew; better even, because my dress was nowhere near as obnoxious as "high fashion" dresses. However, my peers made sure to inform me of just how inadequate my seam work is. My tracks are not the straightest nor are they consistent in length, and some of the patterns, meant to resemble clouds at sunset, look close enough to inappropriate shapes to warrant ridicule. I've since tried to fix those shapes, but even with the fixes I applied, it is hard not to see what they once were.

Numo put up quite a fight to get me to change into something more high quality for such an event as attending the theater. According to ver, my dress blurs lines that are not supposed to be blurred and according to certain passages of the Holy Scriptures, we are meant to be a people set apart, so I should dress in accordance with my exalted status.

I personally believe that passage is referring more to what is on the inside than what is on the outside. Regardless, I think my dress looks great from a distance. It's not like I'm entering it into some sort of competition where it will be closely examined. In fact, I intend to abandon it. It will be easy to slip out of, and underneath I'm wearing a pair of pants and a shirt ideal for running. I just had to resist long enough for Numo to have to choose between letting me go or fighting me until I would be late to arrive, which would reflect negatively upon ver. So ve let me go, though not without making it clear that there will be consequences. Or there would be, if I were planning to return.

Initially I wore the dress because it felt symbolic. I am choosing to leave everything behind, even the good things, even this. I wanted to make an intentional choice to leave it. I don't want this to be a matter that I just push to the back of my mind, charging into my new life in denial of the cost. No, I want to acknowledge the cost. Or at least I did. This dress is going to be hard to let go of, though am I really going to let some mediocre dress stop me? It's not just the dress though. When I look down at it I am left to wonder, what am I leaving that I don't yet know I am leaving? Maybe I should have worn something else.

I take a deep breath. No use regretting a decision that cannot be changed. I tear my eyes away from the dress and look onward.

"Are you okay?" Gele, who is flying me to my destination, asks me.

Shoot, ve must have picked up on my emotional distress. Of course ve would, as a yetu, Gele's perception of me is mostly just a location and a bundle of biological data points ve pulls from the fabric of creation; heart rate, blood pressure, hormone mix, organs and their conditions.

"Um, I mean. You know. I've never liked going to one of these things." I respond.

"Then why save up for it? Is your favorite production really worth the social stress?"

"When else am I going to see it performed by actual people? I'm tired of the puppet shows." I say. Though the answer is really that I wouldn't be attending this if it weren't for my alternative motives. Yes, I love the idea of seeing the production in the actual theater, but I prefer watching puppets alone over engaging with my petty, and often cruel peers.

"Very well. Your parents have asked me to run some errands while you attend the show. I think they don't want me getting in the way of your attempts to mingle. However, we could run the errands afterwards, if you would like for me to stick near you for backup. I can come up with an excuse for getting home late."

"No, that's fine." I decline, and immediately my mind starts to wonder if this will permit me to take off sooner than I planned. However, there is still the issue of the yetu monitors watching the other teens. Lise and I's agreed meeting place resides within nine estates of the theater. This is a problem because a yetu can sense life up to nine estates away. So all I can do is suffer through the socializing, stalling until the other teens and their yetu supervisors have left, then stick Gele with the thorn and make a break for it.

Now that I think about it, maybe I should take Gele up on the offer. If I am not taking off early then ver presence might save me from some ridicule. Though I feel like I would have an even harder time sticking Gele with the thorn after such a kind gesture. In fact, I already feel bad about the hase I'm about to put Gele through as a result of my departure. Hypocritically, while I want to acknowledge the cost this will have to myself, I push the cost my departure will have for Gele to the back of my mind, trying to ignore it.

Market town is subdivided into a variety of districts which I can use as land markers to approximate how close we are to the theater which is located in the arts district. We have already flown over the market district, which neighbors and somewhat overlaps the food district. We are just about through the food distinct and I am glad I ate before we came because the delicious scents tempt my stomach to pretend it is empty. As the fragrance fades we cross over into the arts district which neighbors the ports district, and I am meant to meet Lise in the small space where the ports overlap with the residential district.

We are coming up on Tosema Boutique, which is just down the street from the theater. I used to aspire to design clothing for that boutique, up until I met Lise, and ve let me in on a little industry secret. Ve told me that if I ever wanted to work there (a heavily ridiculed dream, to be an employee instead of an employer, and an artist at that, for someone coming from upper society) I would need to come to terms with the fact that designers at boutiques are not looking to make products that will last.

They need the clothing to fall apart after a salary or two so that they can sell more clothing, make more money. I began to see Market Town for what it was, an economy driven by profit at the cost of everyone else. If I want to make clothes that would last it would have to be on commission from the ultra wealthy. Otherwise, I won't be able to find employment. No one wants to hire someone who's work will decrease demand.

After learning about all of that, I started to see similar practices everywhere, practices that make it more expensive to be poor than it is to be wealthy. How many people might be able to achieve exaltation if they weren't being needlessly drained of their money at every turn? Thus began my descent into cynicism. I could never thank Lise enough for all of the ways ve has opened my eyes to reality. Ve may not be as refined as Rirbuseha residents, cracking the occasional crude joke here and there, but ver insights help me not to feel like the ignorant child my parents wish I was.

I am also grateful to Ritu, for as much as there is making exaltation difficult, it is not enough to render ineffective the exalting power of

Ritu's virtues. I am not sure it is possible to change the nature of the market directly, but if I could just help people embrace Ritu, then surely the issues with the market will begin to resolve as people learn not to be so exploitative.

We land outside of the theater and Gele pauses for a moment after detaching from my back as if to give me an opportunity to change my mind about facing this alone.

"Thank you for the ride. I'll see you after the show." I say as I walk towards the massive marble building. The theater takes the shape of a half sphere and is covered in relief sculptures depicting many of the greatest stories ever told. Most prominent is a complete depiction of the events recorded in the Holy Scriptures along the diameter at the base of the building. This theater is one of the three crown jewels of Rirbuseha. The other two being the city hall and Rirha, the temple on an island floating over the city between the twin peaks.

With my words expressing resolve to stick with my decision, Gele resigns saying, "Have fun and stay safe." then ve departs.

The main entrance is bordered by marble chiseled to resemble clouds which descend from a perfectly circular marble ring. The ring is often used as a representation of Ritu or divinity, and the clouds descending from Ritu represent Ver breath of creation. The whole scene is crafted as a reminder that even the stories we imagine are not entirely our own; they too are of Ritu's creation.

In order to brace for what is to come I assure myself that I am above these preppy teens. Their petty insults warrant only pity. Pity that they are so beneath me that they feel threatened enough to try to cut me down.

I enter the immaculate lobby of the theater. The floor is the shape of a semicircle with a large wall dividing the lobby from the rest of the theater. There is a moderately dense crowd of people which nearly blends with the inanimate marble statues of people bordering the room backed by marble relief sculptures of yet more people that gives the illusion of a crowd stretching along streets of Rirsudi, Ritu's eternal city in the clouds. It is a depiction of the afterlife that more closely resembles vetu stories than it resembles the actual afterlife as sparsely described in the Holy Scriptures.

The line my choice of outfit blurs can be clearly seen as a narrow but evident gap between two groups of people. In one group there is a mixture of Rirbuseha residents some sporting modest yet well crafted high quality attire and others displaying the most obnoxious fashions imaginable; every socially deemed attractive quality being exaggerated to absurdity; the pointiest or shallowest of shoulders, the widest of hips, thinnest of waists, biggest of busts or buttoxes, yetu wings that curve in just the right way and not single piece of fur is out of place on any bitu's coat. The difference in dress delineates executives and politicians (the modest), from the performance celebrities (the flashy). There are even a number of notu in attendance sporting crystal-clear bodies sculpted from expertly controlled water.

Then, in the other group, there is the management class of Market Town residents which consists mostly of atu and bitu, sporting dresses and suits which attempt to be as obnoxious as the celebrities but fail to implement the more effective and expensive shapewear and will likely fall to pieces in a salary's time. Among them are a few like myself, who fall somewhere in the middle. My dress is artsy but not as busy as most others worn by the celebrities, and while I don't prefer the way shapewear feels, it boosts my confidence. So I wear some of the high quality shapewear that Market Town residents cannot afford, which makes my waist look a bit thinner than it really is and my non-existent breasts look a tad existent.

To my surprise my entrance into the theater goes mostly unnoticed. Where my presence would normally draw a couple of glances that spark demeaning whispers, the wrath of the teens seems to already be preoccupied with mocking someone else.

Attempting to not associate with either group, I pass between them on my way to the admission counter.

"If it isn't the middle class wannabe." exclaims Ditu, a white and gold furred bitu wearing a scarlet dress of moderate quality, and ve is also the ringleader of a small posy of upper-middle class Market Town teens, "Your parents could spend a servant on any outfit you want and you wore the dick rags that you failed to glorify." This earns some laughter from Ditu's goons, one a towering lanky bitu with light red fur and a cream colored dress that looks to be a hand-me-down fallen victim to an amateur tailor, and the other a tall brawny atu in a cheap blue tux with spacy seams, "Tell me, is the middle class roughian a friend of yours?"

Ditu gestures over to a dark-skinned atu I haven't seen before. The stranger is wearing a loose fitting masculine suit top and feminine skirt bottom, and ve looks just as thrilled to be here as I am. Ver body appears thin and frail, however the way ve holds verself makes ver appear tougher than ve probably is.

"We haven't met-" Is all I can manage to get out before getting cut off.

"Oh you should certainly go make ver acquaintance. I think ver name was something like Vema Ho." Ditu says.

Ve is trying to trick me into believing the stranger's name sounds like the word "vemo", a word used to describe someone as a being of lesser sentiance.

"You're not as clever as you think. I am not about to go insult ver sentience by calling ver 'vemo'." I say.

The stranger paces along the outer rim of the room. Ver tough demeanor seems to slowly give way to distress and embarrassment. Ve seems to scan the crowd looking for someone, ver arms crossed awkwardly in front of ver.

I shoot a glare at Ditu, "What did you do to ver?" I ask.

"What do you mean? The poor soul just had an unfortunate accident. Or fortunate depending on how you look at it. Ver outfit is now a bit more befitting of ver true societal status." Ditu says with a hint of mischief. Ve definitely is the cause of whatever "accident" befell the stranger.

Suddenly despair and tears take over the stranger's expression. Ve lets ver arms down, revealing a large stain along the front of ver outfit, just before ve darts through an emergency exit into the alleyway beyond.

Ditu, who watched the stranger's breakdown with amusement, speaks up, "I hear ve isn't from Rirbuseha. I bet ve is a charity case; superficially exalted by someone who wants everyone to see how generous they are, sacrificing their food to take care of a lower society fose. Ignorantly enabling ver self destructive vices and potentially endangering us all. Poor thing has no idea what to do with the blessings that have been thrust onto ver. Ve probably went to hide among the rotting compost where things feel a bit more like home." the goons break into more mocking laughter.

My fists ball tightly and my jaw grows stiff. Who is Ditu to judge whether or not someone is in their rightful place in society? That is Ritu's job not vers. If I knock Ditu's teeth in, will that jeopardize my escape? Maybe, I would certainly receive a beating from Ditu and ver goons if I lashed out. They are probably eager for the excuse to beat me anyway. Who knows if I would be able to run after that.

I stare daggers into Ditu's pious eyes for a moment of further contemplation before I decide that the stranger is more worthy of my attention. So I abruptly turn from Ditu and walk for the exit.

"Good luck," Ditu calls after me, "Maybe your dreams will come true and you will get abducted by a Market Town crook and held for ransom in Sudihatosema where you can live that middle class life you crave."

I open the exit door into the alleyway and, knowing these doors only open from the inside, I remove my sandals and use one to prop the door open. While the sun is still up, it is moving towards setting and casts a harsh shadow over the alleyway. There are some large compost bins to my right which reek of rotting food. Beyond the bins someone, presumably the stranger, whimpers quietly.

I am just about to exit when I have the instinct to look back. Ditu seems to have moved closer. Either ve intends to lock me out, which wouldn't be too bad, we would just have to move back around to the entrance and hope we don't run into any thugs, or ve and ver goons intend to jump me in the alleyway...

Crap. What do I do now?

I shift my sandal to make the cracked door look more shut, but the stranger should still be able to get back in when ve is ready. Then I turn to move towards Ditu. I need to buy the stranger time to get back inside, that is the best I think I can do.

"Well look at you looking out for number one." Ditu exclaims as I approach ver, "I'll admit, at first I thought you weren't strong enough to know when someone wasn't worth your time. I stand corrected. Perhaps you have what it takes to be one of us after all." Ditu extends a paw to me, "If you promise to start wearing some decent clothes, perhaps we could actually get along."

The thought of shaking Ditu's paw makes me sick. I would sooner spit on ver paw than shake it. Maybe I will... Though- this might be a unique opportunity for vengeance.

I push through my disgust to shake ver paw, "Perhaps we can." I say.

Suddenly Ditu's grip grows tight to trap my hand, "First, please tell me what made you realize ve wasn't worth it."

Shoot, Ditu is trying to assess my intentions. Why might Ditu walk away if ve had been in my situation? What does ve want to hear me say that would convince ver that I am trustworthy all of a sudden? I think back to the conversations I've had with Numo and attempt to adopt ver worldview temporarily.

"It just occurred to me that nothing good has ever come from my attempts to make sacrifices for the less fortunate. I wondered why that might be. Why might Ritu permit only negative consequences to come from my attempts to be generous. Perhaps," I swallow hard. The last thing I want to do is affirm the choices of these fose, but maybe it would be worth it just for the opportunity to stab Ditu in the back, "Perhaps it's only Ritu's business to help them when Ve judges them as worthy of exaltation and I am meant to play another role. I have been defying Ritu's will by trying to help people using my own strength resulting in fleeting change, or the enabling of destructive vices. Instead, perhaps I am simply meant to guide them to Ritu and let Ritu's transforming power help them towards lasting change. Whoever that person in the alley is, I'm going to trust Ritu will put them at whatever societal rung is best for them to be able to receive Ritu."

Ditu looks at me as if ve just spotted a sack of platinum coins on the side of the street.

I continue, "Speaking of which. I have been putting my preferences for how I present myself over what Ritu would expect from my class. How about instead of seeing the show we go across the street to purchase something more appropriate for what Ritu intends for us?" The eyes of Ditu and ver goons teem with opportunity, "Though I only have money enough for two outfits." I say.

"Just us then," Ditu is quick to suggest.

"I'm sorry, what?" the tall goon exclaims.

"Yeah, why shouldn't it be me?" the brawny one suggests, "Common Dima, everything Ditu has to offer you already have." At this Ditu looks appalled, "I, on the other hand, can offer you protection."

I look at the goon, a somewhat new acquisition of Ditus who replaced someone else Ditu had a falling out with, and I awkwardly confess, "I'm sorry but I cannot even remember your name."

"No matter, call me Zivu." Zivu says as ve extends a hand.

Ditu slaps away Zivu's hand, "Excuse me! Nothing to offer. The nerve of you. I thought we were friends!"

"Don't give me that shit," Zivu remarks, "Miseso and I both know that you were only ever interested in using us as stepping stones and that is all you intend to use Dima for as well."

"I cannot believe you would say such a thing. Miseso, do you really think that of me too?" Ditu asks.

Miseso, the tall bitu goon, doesn't say a word but shakes ver head no as ve looks fearfully into Ditu's eyes, but then ver gaze moves to Zivu's glare and ver fear seems to intensify. Ve looks back to Ditu and nods ver head yes.

There is something magical about watching Ditu sever verself from ver posy knowing I will only be abandoning ver in due time, but first, I think I can put the final nails in this coffin.

"Obviously you two were only looking to use Ditu for your own selfish gain." I accuse Zivu and Miseso, "Otherwise you wouldn't be so ready to turn on ver like this. I bet you only want to use me in the exact same way. Come on Ditu, clearly these two are not worth our time."

I latch my arm with Ditu who seems to revel in my having chosen to stick with ver, and begin to lead ver away from the goons.

"You're making a big mistake Dima, Ditu will stab you in the back in no time, you will see." Zivu calls after us.

Not if I stab ver in the back first.

Shortly after leaving the boons, Ditu takes over the lead and guides me into the crowd, but not towards the exit.

"I'm sorry, where are we going?" I ask.

"I just need to let my parents know where I am going. Also, thank you for that back there, I can tell we are going to be good friends." Ditu says.

This feels weirdly unlike what I would expect Ditu to do... I thought ve would just leave. Though, when I think about it, ver parents are still necessary to ver survival and ability to climb the social ladder. So I guess ve has incentive to remain in their good graces.

"Excuse me dear parents." Ditu says once we reach ver parents who are conversing with a well respected mage, "my new friend Dima here and I are going to the boutique across the way to upgrade our outfits."

"Ah, you must be Dima Zeju." one of Ditu's parents extends a paw to me and I shake it, "My name is Shuligo Jitu and this is my vetura-"

"Sonu Jitu," Sonu cuts in and also extends a paw that I shake, "you come from quite the high profile family. Though last I heard your loyalty to Ritu's will was iffy."

I am stunned at their blunt remark, and Ditu cuts in before I can responde, “I assure you Dima has had a change of heart, and ve has a bright future that I’m sure will result in the betterment of our society.”

Sonu’s eyes linger on Ditu for a moment, as though ve is trying to decide if Ditu’s judgment can be trusted, “I hope you are right. It is not wise to trust so easily.” Sonu says.

“Regardless, you will need to be supervised.” Shuligo asserts, “I am coming with you.”

“Awe come on,” Ditu complains, “Why don’t you just have the yetu keep an eye on us. I promise you, we’ve got this.”

“You should let them go Shuligo,” Sonu says, “I think it would be best if we don’t meddle too much with this newly formed alliance and whatever lessons it may cultivate. Besides, the boutique is just across the street.”

Shuligo looks like ve is about to argue when Sonu adds, “Unless you feel your opinion is worth going another night without...”

Shuligo’s mouth shuts in contemplative annoyance before ve speaks once more, “Fine, but before you two run off, we would like for you to meet someone.”

“Ah yes,” Sonu exclaims, “Kids, meet Minister Mufoje. Ve is one of the most respected mages of the Rirbuseha college.”

“Pleased to meet you two.” The minister greets us with hand shakes, “You know, I recently adopted a child around your age. Ver name is Hari. Ve is from Hosudiha but is perhaps the most brilliant young mage I have ever met. I think it was because ve is dark skinned that ve wasn’t able to gain admission into a Sodihatosema boarding school. So I took ver in to give ver that opportunity. When you two get a chance you should find ver. I’m not sure where ve went off to, but ve could use some new friends.”

Ditu's face looks pensive and nervous upon learning this information, "We will be sure to keep an eye out for ver. Pleasure to meet you." Ve says, as ve pulls me away into the crowd.

Once we are out of earshot I ask, "So, do you think we should go get Hari? Sounds like ve may be of some use to us after all."

"We needn't waste our time. Maybe if ve were actually brilliant." Ditu says.

"What, you don't trust the minister?" I ask.

"Being good at magic is useful but it is not brilliance and it is certainly no supplement for the virtues this level of society demands. Brilliance is not going to a formal event in a poorly sized outfit, brilliance is not running out into an alleyway alone to get yourself killed, and brilliance is certainly not coming out of Hosudiha anytime soon."

"Okay but what if ver magic can at least prove useful to us?"

Ditu stops and looks me in the eyes with intensity, "Let me do you a favor, listen closely. It does not matter how intelligent ve is. Ve lacks the virtues necessary to be here. This is made clear by the fact that ve was pulled straight from Hosudiha and brought here without so much as a supply stop in Sudihatosema. Ve is destined to fall from grace, and if we latch ourselves on to ver, we may be dragged down with ver or worse."

Ditu eyes me closely for a moment, "I am going to offer my paw to you once more. Are you destined for exaltation... or disparagement?"

Ditu seems to think ve can play Ritu with other people's societal statuses. Such levels of pride and arrogance make me feel equal parts sickened by ver and eager to betray ver. So I shake ver paw.

"Great, let's go!" Ditu says with a cheeriness that feels like a jarring shift from ver seriousness an alm ago.

Ditu locks arms with me again and we exit back through the entrance and head towards the boutique.

We don't make it far before a cry for help rings from the alleyway behind us.

Ditu shoots me a look, "Don't-"

I give Ditu a glare so devious ve gives up on ver plea, then I say "Screw you, you pious backstabbing fose. Wallow in the loneliness your actions have bought you." Ver eyes grow wide as reality reveals that ve has been severed from any opportunity for status ve thought ve held among the youth. I feed off of ver terror to energize my sprint away from ver. However, ve is only stunned for a moment before ve is hot on my trail.

"I'm going to rip out your lying tongue and choke you with it!" Ditu screams.

Betrayed by my short stature, Ditu is breathing down my neck in a matter of alms. Reluctantly, I draw the thorn from my pocket. Ditu grabs me by my curly, near-black, hair and uses ver quicker speed to thrust my head forward, aiming to smash my face into the ground. Before I can be brought down, I jab the thorn at the paw at the back of my head. Ditu's grip gives out as ve falls unconscious, I fail to find my footing and we both collapse to the ground just outside of the theater. I catch my fall and roll until I come to a stop.

Looking back I see Ditu, lying unconscious, ver face bloodied from receiving the brunt of ver fall. I am mutually highly satisfied by ver condition and deeply concerned at my having used my thorn so soon. Is it spent? Can I use it again? Hopeful that I can use the thorn more than once, I hold onto it and tear into the alleyway before Ditu's parents can catch me. As I go I slip my dress off over my head and take one last longing look at it. It's going to be a bit small, but with how thin ve is, it should do the trick.

I come upon the stranger, whom I now believe is Hari. Ve is standing in the middle of the alleyway with ver arms extending open palms in two directions. One of ver palms is aimed at a large compost bin, and the other is aimed at a tall, pale-skinned, adult atu who is wielding a knife. However, the adult seems to be pinned to the floor, unable to move.

Every teen dreams of having super powers. So when the time comes for our first lesson on the nature of magic we are all ears, up until the lessons turn into boring physics and math. Anyway, from what I can recall before I lost interest, Hari must be using magic to swap the enemies mass with the mass of the compost bin, rendering the enemy incapable of lifting ver body. Unfortunately, Hari must maintain concentration to keep the spell in effect. So ve and the enemy are stuck in this stalemate until Hari grows too tired to maintain ver focus. Then the enemy will have ver.

I run past Hari, toss my dress over ver shoulder, and shout, "The door is propped open, hurry inside and change!" Then I stick the thorn into the neck of the immobilized enemy, to my relief ve falls unconscious instantly, and I don't stop long before I take off running again.

Perhaps Hari's virtues would have lifted ver back up with time, but surely there is nothing harmful about righting a disparagement that was not the result of Hari's vices but was instead inflicted upon ver by Ditu's vices. Part of me wants to stop. To actually make a friend for once.

However, I won't stop. I keep running. I have no choice. Who knows how much juice the thorn has left. If I cannot use it again, then I cannot knock out Gele. So this is my only chance. I'll just have to hope that the scene behind me will be distracting enough for me to slip away without Gele or the other yetu noticing.

"Wait!" Shouts a voice from behind me. I take a glance and Hari is gaining on me. Crap!

Hari continues, "Where are you going?"

"Back off! You need to go back!" I yell.

"I don't want to go back!" Hari yells back.

We dart out of the alleyway and Hari is practically on my heels when suddenly I am grabbed from behind and hoisted into the air.

"I've got you!" Gele shouts, "You are safe."

Everything within me screams to give up. I can't stick Gele with the thorn now. Ve could get hurt. Gele doesn't deserve this! But I cannot turn back now. My parents will discover that I have the thorn. They will learn of my plan. I need to run. It is not right for me to remain in Rirbuseha!

Before Gele can get me too far off of the ground I stick ver with the thorn, and to my surprise ve loses consciousness, and we fall to skid and tumble along the ground until momentum throws us into the wheel of a cart of cabbages causing some of the cabbage heads to spill onto the street, frustrating a nearby merchant. I pull my aching body to its feet and look at Gele. Guilt washes over me at the sight of ver broken wings. The thorn falls from my grip. Ve will recover, but ve will be in extreme pain. Ve will suffer because of what I've done.

Hari comes running up to us. Ve stops to look with pity upon the unconscious Gele, "Wherever you are going, it would seem you're not planning on coming back. Is that right?"

"That's right," I say. As much as I want ver to leave me alone. I just have to know, "Why did you say you didn't want to go back?"

"I don't belong here." Hari says.

"Don't be ridiculous, Ritu didn't exalt you for noth-"

"No. That is not what I mean."

"Do you mean no one is meant to have this level of wealth?" I ask assuming ve and I may be on the same page.

"That may be so, but no. I belong with my family, my friends, I want life to be like the way it was."

"Did- didn't you come from Hosudiha?" I ask.

Hari shoots me a glare, "I'm not talking about the poverty. No one deserves this level of wealth and no one deserves that level of poverty. In Hosudiha, every cut could kill you. No one bats an eye when a child gets stuck by a cart and killed. You are likely to lose an elder to a sickness before you hear that it's going around. Every animal is sick from the polluted water and so they often go around blasting their diarrhea shit everywhere and on everything. If you don't have power you might as well be a punching bag for those who do. Before I came here I just thought all of that was just the way life was for everyone."

Hari puts on an artificial smile and proceeds to wear joy's skin as ve looks to the sky and goes on to proclaim, "Wow was I wrong. Turns out that if my ancestors had just been pale skinned we might not have ever been subjugated to work as slaves. Silly me being born to a family that can only manage to keep three out of twelve children alive." Hari stops abruptly, ver artificial joy vanishing in an instant as it is replaced with a look of disgust directed upwards, towards Rirha.

"No," Hari continues, "I never want to return to that poverty. Hase, we didn't even have it as bad as most. That is probably why I can miss partaking in the music and the food. Back with my real family I wasn't scolded for doing things the right way instead of some other pointless way. I miss the way my family and friends shared an understanding of certain things. I want to be with them. I want to help them out of Hosudiha if at all possible. I thought I might be able to do that if I came here, but there is no desire to help the people in Hosudiha among these indulgent parasites."

I don't know how to make sense of the idea that no one deserves that level of poverty. What Numo said about how no one resists exaltation still makes sense to me. So if someone is in poverty, and they neither want to be there nor deserve to be there, it only stands to reason that Ritu would exalt them. It would be cruel of Ritu not to exalt them, and Ritu is not cruel. Or perhaps Ritu's virtues are not enough to exalt? No, Ritu is all-powerful, the problem has to have something to do with the character or desires of those in poverty.

Why then does Hari want to be with ver family if ver family is of bad character? Meanwhile I want nothing to do with my family which has supposedly been exalted for our virtues... Maybe my family is superficially exalted... but if they are the ones who bring down the superficially exalted, who is there to bring them down?

Perhaps Hari's family is superficially disparaged. Perhaps they are virtuous but choose to remain in poverty to help those in need. That makes sense, and I resonate with the idea. It also explains why Hari would want to be with ver family.

"It must be nice to have a family you want to be with." I say.

"What are you an orphan?" Hari asks.

"No, my parents are just really selfish, greedy, and unpleasant to be around. Listen, I am going to Sudihatosema. It's not where your family is, but I hear there are more 'hands on' efforts to help people in Hosudiha that are based out of Sudihatosema, perhaps you will better be able to find a way to help your family from there than you can from here. Do you want to come along?"

"Absolutely, yes."

There is no turning back now. Not only will Hari hold me to follow through, but I also cannot stand the thought of witnessing Gele's suffering alongside the wrath I would face from my parents if I stayed.

So we run.

We run and leave behind the life that was chosen for us.

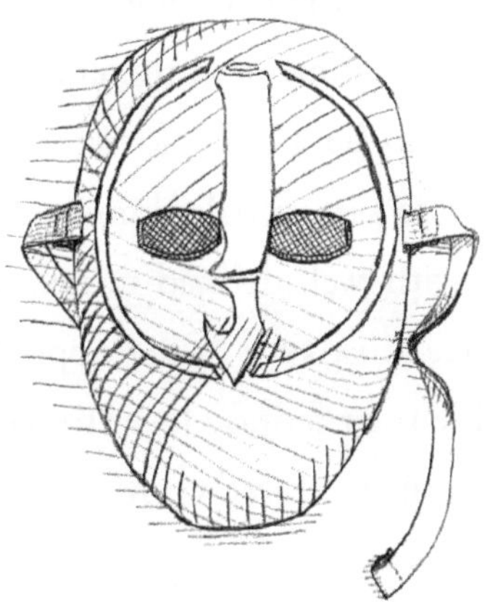

Chapter 4: Object

“Who is this? I thought I told you to come alone?” Lise asks, ver blue eyes peeking out through the crack of a chained door.

“This is Hari,” I say, “Ve was taken from ver family in Hosudiha and is looking for a way to help them. We agreed ve would be best positioned to give them aid from Sudihatosema. So I invited ver to come along.”

“Hosudiha you say?” Lise gives Hari a long look, “Hmm... I think I have a buddy who can help you out.” Lise looks back into the apartment ve occupies, “Hey Guhi! Dima is here!”

“Ve finally pulled the trigger huh?” Guhi shouts back.

“Yeah, but ve brought along another atu seeking passage to Sudihatosema and ver friend looks like someone you would be better suited to help.”

"Is that so?" Sounds of movement suggest Guhi is making ver way to the door and soon enough Lise's eye moves away and a new dark brown eye looks out at us, "Ah, I see what you mean."

The door shuts for a moment as the chain is removed and then it reopens revealing Guhi to be a tall and well built, light-brown furred bitu. Behind Guhi stands Lise, a pale-skinned atu, towering over me at maybe six ingots tall with well defined muscles, short well kept blond hair, and the sort of face most vetu of the opposite sex, and some of the same sex, might imagine their fantasy lover to have. They both wear nice yet modest trousers and linen shirts. Guhi puts in a bit of effort to look appealing while Lise doesn't aim to impress and yet looks quite impressive anyways.

"Hari was it?" Guhi says, "Come with me and I'll help you make more than enough money to help your family."

"As for us," Lise says as ve looks at me, "We have an air balloon to fill and then not a second to lose. Your family will be looking for us, so we need to get far away from here and quickly."

It hasn't even been three wages since I ran away, and now I am here, in an air balloon with Lise, watching my old home shrink with distance. Hari stayed back with Guhi. I am not sure what their plan is, because surely Hari's guardian will be looking for ver as well.

The island which cradles the city of Rirbuseha looks like a colossal eye. The whole island must have been a stereotypical leaf shape at one point when something punched a circular hole clean through the upper part of the island; turning one peak into two. Rirha floats in the center of the "iris" looking almost like a pupil. It is as though my old home is watching us depart as Lise flies our air balloon away, trying to approximate when we might be over the destination we seek to descend into. I look back as a cyclone of emotions rips through me, leaving me unsure how to feel.

"Don't tell me you are having second thoughts." Lise says.

"No, just. You know. It's a big change. There is a lot to process." I say.

"No need to process anything. You and I are together now. Process that! Isn't it amazing! We are finally together!"

"Yeah, I'm finally free!" I say, trying to get excited. However, something I said seems to sap all of the excitement out of Lise, "What? What's wrong."

"Oh, nothing." Lise says.

I'm about to insist ve tell me when ve continues anyway, "It's just- Here I am excited about us, and you can only think about yourself."

"Oh, I'm sorry, you're right. I'm being selfish." I try to redirect my mind away from Gele, Joho, my hand embroidered clothes, my projects, even my parents despite the bad relationship. I am with Lise, that was my goal. Well, not entirely, I am with Lise and we are about to embark on a mission to save those who remain in Sudihatosema.

"We are finally together. And now that we are together we can be Ritu's power couple. We might change the world!" I exclaim.

"That's a little better," Lise remarks.

This time I am bothered by Lise's remark. A little better? What more does ve want from me? Is ve bothered that I brought up Ritu when ve only wanted me to think of us? No, ve knows that there is no us without Ritu. We are a bushel of three sticks made difficult to break by being bound together. Which reminds me.

"Lise, can I ask you a question my parents refused to answer?"

"Uh... sure."

our new home, and apparently ve intends to stick to it. It will be a reward for finally leaving my old life behind, for choosing Lise… and Ritu.

"I can't wait," I say with a flirtatious smile. Maybe if I explicitly tell ver how much I want it, ve will pause the flight for a while and take me among the clouds. That would be so beautiful and romantic.

"I want you to teach me what sex is like." I say. I immediately feel embarrassment stiffen my body. I don't want it after that. Damn it Dima, don't come across so desperate!

Lise grabs hold of me and pulls me close. Ver finger traces the parts of me which most desperately crave affection. I close my eyes and it is as though my consciousness shifts from one part of my body to another as Lise's finger grows close to the most sensitive spots without crossing their borders. Instead, ver finger takes a rather tame path up my body until it comes to rest beneath my chin at which point I open my eyes and ve lifts my gaze to meet ver's.

"My flower, have patience. You shall have me soon enough." Lise says.

My thoughts whip up into a ravenous frenzy. Come on! Just take me already! Do I need to make an advance? No. I should respect ver wishes to wait. Right? Or does ve want me to initiate? Crap, Dima, curse your inexperience. I have no idea what I am doing. I need to take my mind off of this. Ritu help me!

"Okay…" I say meekly. Lise gives me a wry irresistible smile and then releases me to go back to flying the balloon. The distance empowers me to breathe again.

"So, um," I start, still flustered, "Are you going to fill me in on the plan for our ministry now?"

"Trust me you are going to love it. You will get to speak with people while they are at their most vulnerable and help them just as Ritu desires

for us to help them. It might be a little uncomfortable at first, but you are always going on about how you hate that your parents cannot seem to sacrifice their comfort to help others. So I don't think you will mind."

"Why might it feel uncomfortable?" I ask.

"Because you have been groomed your whole life to have certain boundaries meant to protect your comfort and keep you under the control of your parents. So this is going to require a shift in thinking for you, and it is going to require you to break down those boundaries."

"I mean, can you give me specifics?"

"Not yet," Lise says firmly, "One virtue your old life clearly didn't set you up with is patience."

I want to argue but feel I have little space to do so. I was so patient to wait for the right time to run. However, I am feeling rather impatient to get a room and to learn about this ministry. I am a bit worried, though of course I would be. In fact, knowing this will make me uncomfortable excites me. It means I am going to grow as a person. I am going to shed the selfish tendencies I inherited from my parents and become twice the vetu they ever were.

It has been five labors since my escape. Lise still hasn't satisfied any of my sexual cravings. However, ve finally informed me that this labor is the labor our ministry will begin. Then ve took me to a building on the outskirts of Sudihatosema and led me to the room we now stand in.

Lise nonchalantly obstructs the exit with ver towering form. Trapping me inside of the small, dank, dressing room littered with an assortment of suggestive outfits.

Ve wears an elegant white dress-shirt in an unconventional yet alluring way, with the collar popped and sleeves rolled up to reveal ver muscles. An annoyed expression struggles to keep an enraged one from ver face.

"Your parents were unwilling to sacrifice their comfort to help others. I thought that bothered you, yet here you are, just like them," Lise says.

"I am nothing like them!" I retort.

"Then put on the damn outfit, get in there, and help our client!"

"Lise, please. I was really hoping that my body could be yours. Only yours. That it would be special."

"Love," Lise extends a hand to caress my cheek, "I appreciate that... and as the one you have gifted your body to, I want to share it for the good of others."

"But-"

"You did give your body to me, didn't you? Or are you just saying you did?" Lise asks.

"No, I did. It's just-"

"Just nothing. Your body is mine. I get to decide how we use it. This is a beautiful ministry. It's not all about sex. Many people just want someone to talk to. That gives you the opportunity to guide them just as Ritu commands."

"But the Holy Scriptures condemn adultery." I plead.

"It's not adultery since you are not married. Maybe I'll marry you if you can swallow your pride and help me... and others. I'm asking you to do the very thing you expressed to me that you wanted to do. Sacrifice your comfort. Don't worry about me. I'm not going to get jealous as long as you give me mine at the end of the labor. You are going to do great things for people."

I have lost track of how many labors have passed, but it feels like far too many for me to finally realize that this isn't love. Love shouldn't come with so many nightmares. Love shouldn't leave my body in constant pain. Love shouldn't require me to indulge in drugs to forget about it. I'm just an object to Lise. A toy to be used for ver own pleasure and gain.

Help feels impossible to hope for. Most clients come in wearing masks, to hide their identity, but that doesn't stop them from sharing about their lives, if anything the masks seem to embolden them to share. They are not the people I had been taught to think of as predators; those who intentionally break social expectations, and those who reject Ritu. Sure there are clients who fall into the demographics I was warned about, but they are disturbingly outnumbered. Most of my clients are people I was taught to trust, to look up to. Those who should be most interested in saving me only come to use me.

I am trapped, sitting on a perfume-drenched bed in the middle of a trashy room masquerading as classy. Suddenly a long suppressed thought breaks into my mind. If Lise did this to me, what- what happened to Hari? Guilt floods into me. The thought that I might be responsible for dragging someone else through a similar hase to this one that I have suffered, is unbearable.

I had been staving off contemplating how I might put an end to it all. However, the guilt breaks me. My mind begins to swirl with all manner of dark schemes when suddenly my door opens. In walks my parent, Nizevigu, a slim pale-skinned atu wearing an elegant and intricate white dress contrasting ver long, straight, dark hair.

"Vedi!" I cry, "I am so sorry! You and Numo were right about Lise. Ve is a no-good fose. Please..." Tears I thought were long depleted begin to pour from my eyes as I fall to my knees at Nizevigu's feet, "Please take me home." I throw myself forward to embrace Nizevigu's legs only to be halted by Nizevigu's hand which grabs my forehead tightly, keeping me at arms length, not letting go.

Nizevigu looks down at my groveling, "Exaltation is Ritu's business," stranded, forsaken and alone in the shattered skies' best imitation of Hase, I nearly give into the despair when Nizevigu continues, "Don't worry. The ministry will be here in a few charities to help you. I came before them because you have some things that belong only to the exalted of Rirbuseha."

"What do you mean?" I cry, "I have nothing!"

"Soon you will have nothing but a second chance for Ritu to put you where you belong."

The next thing I know, the oddly familiar stranger releases my head and leaves, having received no services, and I am left bewildered and confused.

"You didn't think I'd notice, did you, your vedi coming in here to turn you against me!" Lise yells.

"What do you mean?" I ask, my confusion mounting. How could Lise think I'm still in touch with my parents? They died when I was twelve, and Lise took me in with malevolent intent disguised as benevolent love. Surely ve remembers that.

"I told you to cut ties with them! They are toxic and not good for our relationship! Do I need to remind you who you belong t-" Lise's words hang unfinished in the air when suddenly ve falls to the ground, a violet thorn crafted into a dart protruding from the back of ver neck.

In the doorway stands a short, bipedal figure, accompanied by a light-brown yetu perched on their back. The biped is dressed in a well-fitted charcoal-gray uniform, and their face is concealed behind a smooth mask adorned with the insignia of a thin golden circle vertically bisected by the iconic blade of a Rirmevu officer. They are a Rirmevu duo, anonymous law enforcement known as Ritu's moral hand.

There is a strange conflict within me. Growing up, I had always been told that officers and ministers, a Rirmevu being a form of both, were trustworthy. So why do I have feelings of distrust and apprehension at the sight of ver. While confusingly present, those feelings are overpowered by my desperate readiness to cling onto any semblance of hope.

"Are you alright?" the stranger asks.

"Take me," I cry, "Please, take me away from here."

I can see pity and contemplation in the biped's eyes, "Come, I want to show you something," the biped responds.

Nervously I approach, though my unease halts me when ve pulls a stubby blade from ver boot.

"It's okay," ve assures me, "This is a Rirmevu's blade. It's not meant for combat or taking lives. We use it to deliver justice to those who harm others. Here, take it."

I tentatively take hold of the cool handle of the small tool. The urge to slit Lise's throat with it surges within me. I attempt to pull the blade away from the stranger, but their grip remains firm. As I look up, their eyes meet mine through the eye-shaped holes in their mask.

"I want to help you. However, I cannot assist you unless you follow my instructions. I promise this will bring you satisfaction. What is your name?" asks the bipedal stranger.

The desire to harm Lise still lingers, but I manage to control myself and refrain from acting impulsively.

"Dima," I respond.

"Hello, Dima. Give me a moment to consult with my partner. What are ver crimes?" asks the biped.

"This one is just a victim. As for the asshole we just knocked out, ve is guilty of rape, assault, and based on the circumstances, I suspect abduction, although I cannot provide concrete evidence for the latter," replies the yetu, the other member of the Rirmevu duo.

"As much as I despise Lise," I say, "I have to admit that ve didn't abduct me. I came willingly."

"Willingly? How old are you? Fifteen?" asks the biped.

"I... I don't know," I stammer.

"Seventeen," says the yetu, who seems to have gathered the information about me from the fabric of creation.

I am bewildered at the announcement of my age. Seventeen! It has only been two salaries! I could have sworn I was approaching my twenties by now.

"Seventeen," the biped repeats, "You seem a bit short for your age, don't you?" I take slight offense at the comment, but I am in no position to argue. "Even now, your brain is not fully developed to give consent or make those sorts of decisions independent of your guardians," the biped continues to tempt my offense. "And I'm sure this was not the life you were led to believe you would have, was it?"

I shake my head. "No... but Lise didn't exactly lie to me. This was supposed to be a ministry to help people... just not in the way I had envisioned. But it was my mistake to assume we were on the same page," I admit, feeling my anger wane as I realize that Lise is not solely responsible for my predicament.

"Absolutely not! This is not your fault!" The biped declares.

"Lise knew what ve was doing," The yetu joins, "I don't know if you are aware, but you are not the only one this monster has conned into this scheme. Those you have been 'ministering to' were paying for your services. This was no ministry, this was a for-profit vetu trafficking scheme that was operating in the blind spots of law enforcement. If it were not for an anonymous tip we received, who knows how long it would have taken for us to catch this crook and ver accomplices."

My hatred for Lise is restored, though not without dragging myself also into the path of my resentment. I cannot help but feel like I should have known better than to get caught up in all of this and to drag someone else into it too!

"You said there were other victims?" I ask, "Are they alright? Were any of them named Hari?"

"They are being rescued by other officers as we speak. We don't know their names." The yetu says.

"I will let you know if we learn of anyone named Hari." the biped says, "In the meantime, I think it is safe to add abduction to the list of crimes," the biped continues and gently takes hold of my hand, "Unlike other officers who have the sacred duty of apprehending criminals they catch, as a Rirmevu, it is my sacred duty to enact punishment on the criminals I catch."

"What determines which officer is necessary for a given operation?" I ask.

"All is guided by Ritu's hand. Ritu decides who needs to be apprehended and who needs to be punished. Then Ve ensures the right officer is in the right place at the right time." The yetu says.

"Why not just kill the likes of Lise? Ve doesn't deserve to live." I say bitterly.

"As followers of Ritu," the biped says, "We believe in giving vetu every chance they can to surrender themselves to Ritu. If I were to die, my destination would be Ritu's eternal nation Rirsudi. If ve were to die,"

The biped nods towards Lise, "ver destination would be an eternity of suffering in Hase. It is for this reason that lethal force is forbidden, for we value the lives of our enemies, even above our own. However, this does not mean transgressors get off scot free."

The biped guides my hand to place Lise's thumb into a hooked portion of the small blade, then ve speaks, "For if your thumb causes you to transgress, cut it off."

Ve holds the thumb firmly as ve jerks my hand, pulling the blade cleanly through the joint of the thumb, severing it from the rest of the hand. I might be disturbed, sickened even, if it were not so gratifying to do.

Ve continues, "Better is it that you enter Rirsudi with only one thumb than to be cast into Hase with two." ve says.

"Now," the biped turns the blade in my hand so that the hilt is facing up. Ve then removes a cap from the hilt, revealing a metal pommel enchanted to glow orange with heat. "We'll use this to cauterize the wound. It will prevent ver from bleeding out, and the pain will serve as a reminder of the cost of ver transgressions." Ve gently guides my hand to apply the heat to the wound.

"For assault, we take the middle finger. On repeat offense, we take the other." We repeat the process, severing Lise's middle finger, and the biped utters another phrase about how it is better to enter Rirsudi missing a finger.

"And for rape, we remove all external genitalia or we seal access to the internal." The biped was right. Somehow, knowing that Lise will have to live with these consequences helps me feel at peace, and with this blade, I can make sure vemo like Lise never hurt anyone ever again.

Chapter 5: Rirmevu

Nine salaries later

The atmosphere down here is far from pleasant. The stench of sewage fills the air, the infrastructure is hazardous, and at most the sunlight is as bright as the late dawn of the islands which float closest to the sun. The interior of this tavern is even darker than outside, illuminated only by a few sparsely placed lanterns.

I don't have to be here, I have chosen to be positioned in Hosudiha. My presence protects the least fortunate from losing what little they have to criminals.

Of the patrons who pack into the tavern, the level of light only really matters to me, an atu who's primary means of perception is sight. Meanwhile, due to the tavern's location being deeper in the bitu occupied portion of the city where there is little to no overlap with the atu population, everyone else in here is a bitu, and while bitu eyesight is poor, Ritu, in Ver grace, gave them a superior sense of smell to compensate for their nearsightedness.

I am here because those who become intoxicated at the tavern attract the attention of criminals seeking to exploit their vulnerability. So I use the tavern as a trap to catch the criminals I pursue.

I wear a cloak that conceals my species and also hides my yetu colleague, Miya, who is perched on my back, underneath it.

"Could you please be more careful not to tickle my ears?" I whisper to Miya.

"Sorry, I need to see, and there's not much space in here," ve replies.

I clench my jaw and tense up to ignore Miya's antennae as they move around in my hood, attempting to access and read information from the fabric of creation.

My species is identifiable only by my hands, but the darkness of this place means that no bitu is likely to notice their lack of fur and claws.

Suddenly, a stranger's voice interrupts my thoughts. "Holy shit, another atu! And a pale one at that." they exclaim.

Crap! Panicking, I retract my hands into my sleeves. Crap! It's no use - the nosy stranger has already seen them and announced my species to the entire tavern. I make eye contact with an intoxicated dark-skinned atu, mug of booze in hand, stumbling into the seat opposite me. Crap crap crap! What the hase is an atu doing on this side of the city?

"Shhh! Shut up!" I plead.

"Why? I'm an atu and everyone knows it!" ve shouts, ver slurred speech drawing unwanted attention to us. "You don't see me getting all bent out of sh-" *hick*, "about it. Besides, bitu can sniff out an atu from a crowd of bitu. You arn-" *burp*, "fooling anyone."

"Please, I don't want to draw attention to myself."

"Don't wanna draw attention to yourself? Look at the way you are dressed! Your outfit may scream 'I don't want to draw attention to myself' but that's exactly why it draws attention."

"What do you want from me?" I ask, hoping to get out of this situation.

"Well, I could use a pasty friend here in a bit," the stranger replies. "and I'm exactly the kind of friend you need ri-"*hick*," now."

"I'm not looking to make any friends," I say.

The stranger doesn't give up. "Look at me. Feast your eyes," ve says as ve wobbly stands up, to gesture to verself; dark-brown colored skin, black dreadlock hair, incomplete smile, and altogether filthy. "I'm the latest person to be exalted out of Hosudiha... At least I will be, after tonight. And booking passage to Sudihatosema with my skin tone, even with money, is a tricky matter. So maybe you'd be willing to ac-" *hick*, "-ompany me? Commissions officers would be less likely to assume you stole the money."

"No, thanks. I'm good," I reply firmly, hoping ve'll get the hint and leave me alone.

"You're full of shit. Nobody is 'good' with being down here. Who are you to say such a thing? Oh, that reminds me. Hi," *hick*, "I'm Sho," Sho says, extending a crusty hand towards me.

"Uh..."

"You know it's only polite that I see your face if we're going to be sticking together from now on." Sho says.

"No. Uh, I've got to-"

"Oh, come on. There's no shame in a face. I'm the only one here who will really be able to see it anyway." Sho insists.

"I've got to go." With that, I stand and quickly turn to disappear into the crowd but my cloak snags upon a splinter jutting from the table, and the catch causes my hood to fall from my head, exposing Miya's antennae and my status as a Rirmevu.

"Oh... I see. We aren't in it together after all. Damn drink." Sho says as ve scowls at the booze in ver hand, "I should have known."

I replace my hood upon my head and leave. No longer safe to observe from among the patrons, I squeeze through the crowd of bitu and slip outside. Was I ever safe? Have they really been able to smell my species? What about Miya? Have they all known this whole time? It's a wonder we ever caught anyone staking out the tavern. Heck, it's a wonder we are alive!

"Fricken drunkard," I mutter as we skirt around to the side of the building. "Miya, would you take us up to the roof? We should be able to slip in through the hatch and perhaps watch from the rafters."

"Sure thing. Glad we got out without too much trouble. Though if they have been able to smell us this whole time, maybe everyone just knows better than to give an officer a hard time." Miya says.

"Maybe," I say as I remove the now pointless cloak and stuff it into the bag strapped to my leg. It's made of a light and breathable material so that Miya doesn't get overheated, and it doesn't take up too much space in my bag. Miya unravels ver light-brown wings, sparsely speckled with black-bordered white spots, ver legs tighten around me, and after a few beats of ver wings, we lift off for the rooftop. Once there, we locate a roof access hatch and slip into the shadows of the rafters.

Tavern patrons gather below to watch the evening's challenge and place bets.

"I'll bet thirty shots that the bloke doesn't even get the shit down!" yells a lanky drunkard wearing patchwork clothes over ver even patchier fur.

"Nah, you worm! I'll bet fifty that ve falls over dead on the spot. Look at ver, hardly any meat on those bones. A light gust would spell ver end!" counters another patron.

Meanwhile, Sho sits at the center table, mentally preparing for the challenge ve has volunteered to take. Ve seems to have sobered to some degree and appears petrified with fear. A shot-glass of water, known as 'tafose', sits at the center of the table before ver. The water has been notably cleaned, as it is not as murky as the nearby streams it was likely drawn from.

The barkeep, a bitu wearing a sturdy-looking apron over a well-kept green robe and looking healthy only in comparison to ver patrons, stands atop a pedestal and shouts, "All bets are in! My generous patrons, allow me to introduce tonight's contender. Once a citizen of Sudihatosema, now fallen from grace. One of ver parents was arrested on false charges and the other fell ill. In the desperate attempt to stay afloat, ve turned to a life of crime before ve too was arrested. Ve joins us here this evening two cycles after serving ver sentence in Hosudiha prison. This labor we will all learn if ve deserved the exalted life ve was born into or if Ritu made the right call sending ver down among those of us who remain. Ver name is Sho! Let us send ver off warmly, shall we?"

The tavern erupts into jovial cheers that morph into a chant, "Ta-fo-se! Ta-fo-se! Ta-fo-se!" I refrain from joining in.

Sho aggressively grabs the glass before ver and freezes. Ver knuckles grow white under ver fearful grip. After a moment of chanting, Ve breaks through ver hesitation and quickly brings the tafose to ver lips. Ve proceeds to swallow quickly enough so as not to think about ver actions too much.

Sho slams the now-empty glass back onto the table and breaks into a cough followed by some dry heaves. After a moment, ve regains ver bearings and stands quietly as the chanting fizzles out.

A tavern employee turns over a large wage-glass to track the passage of time. Though it holds much sand, the grains drain away swiftly. Sho only needs to survive and remain conscious for a couple of charities for ver life to take a turn for the better.

I can see the color leaving Sho's face.

"I hate this," I whisper to Miya. "I wish people would just open themselves up to Ritu and accept the services provided by the ministry before resorting to something like this."

"Tell me about it," Miya affirms. "I guess the saying rings true, virtue tastes bitter but yields blessings and life. Vice tastes sweet but yields curses and death. In denial of what vice yields, they surrender to it in vain."

My heart wants to feel sympathy for Sho, but I fight against my inclinations. Virtues would not lead someone to drink tafose for money. Ve is here as a consequence of ver own choices and vices.

Another fit of coughing comes over Sho. The tavern employee quickly shoves a bucket in front of ver moments before vomit erupts from ver mouth and nose. The crowd grumbles, and some spectators seem pleased to have won their bets.

Sho continues to vomit, and by the time ve finishes dry heaving, approximately half of the sand has drained from the wage-glass. Ve pushes the bucket away and looks up as if pleading to Ritu for strength. However, ver expression is one of anger and resentment.

Ve appears to spot me and stares straight into my eyes. Ver rage pours into my veins and petrifies me. I begin to hope that perhaps ve doesn't really see me. It's dark up here; it could just be by chance that ve is looking my way. Still, I cannot help but swiftly don my featureless mask to shield my face from ver terrible gaze.

"Don't think I didn't see that pious look on your face! Get that look off your yuppie face. Don't you dare judge me!" Sho shouts, directing ver rage for Ritu at me. At this moment, I am representing Ritu, and distress washes over me. Who am I to represent Ritu? As a rirmevu I am supposed to go relatively unnoticed. I want to flee, but before I can, the squinting gazes of other spectators catch me and wrap around me like chains. What would it say about Ritu if I were to bail now?

"You should know that I tried!" Sho announces. "Despite all of my efforts, I still ended up here, drinking the sewage of the exalted for money!"

Sho begins to cough again, and the employee rushes to provide the bucket, but it is too late as another geyser of vomit comes pouring from Sho's mouth down onto the table. Spectators jump back in an effort to avoid getting splashed upon.

Sho wipes the vomit from ver mouth and declares, "Hear me, all of you! I deserve to be exalted, but I would drink tafose for the rest of eternity before wasting a single alm more of my life worshiping Ritu!"

Sho's self-destructive plight has become evident. Sho is full of pride and hatred for Ritu. That is what brought ver here and holds ver prisoner in this city, not unlike many other Hosudiha residents.

Sho jabs a finger at me and says, "Remember my blasphemy when you're drinking my exalted shit!"

The last grains of sand tumble down, and the crowd erupts into cheers for their won bets and Sho's survival.

Money is exchanged, and a large sack of coins is placed before Sho. That amount of coin should be enough to exalt Sho to Susehatosema, a small town island floating above this bottom-of-the-barrel place at a little below the altitude of Sudihatosema.

"I don't understand why Ritu would let ver be exalted... Ve is a danger to verself and others. Why isn't there anything in place to prevent this?" I remark quietly to Miya.

"Maybe Sho needs a change of scenery to overcome ver pride and hatred. I hope ve is able to find such humility. Otherwise, ve will likely end up right back here again," Miya predicts.

"Do you really think that a change of scenery will do anything but enable ver vices?"

"I don't know. Like you, I'm also trying to figure out why Ritu might permit this sort of thing to happen. If ver vices are only enabled by this, then ve will transgress and the ministry will handle it."

I'm not a fan of the idea that someone might have to get hurt before we can do anything. Though what if no one gets hurt? If we took preventative measures unnecessarily then we would be the ones hurting ver.

Sho reaches a shaky hand towards ver winnings, but just as ver fingers graze the sack, ve collapses, and the tavern falls silent.

I am released from the chains of attention as the tavern looks to Sho with concern and to each other, leading to a commotion as they try to settle bets. Suddenly, the world seems to make sense again.

"The winnings have been snatched," Miya informs me. "The thief is making their way out through a window and is on the run." In the midst of all the confusion, only a yetu, such as Miya, could have noticed such a theft taking place.

"Understood," I affirm.

Now, my job begins.

I push through the hatch that grants access to the roof and heave myself up, only to feel something sharp dig into my leg accompanied by a tearing sound.

"Ah! Ouch," I recoil.

"You okay?" Miya asks.

"Yeah..." I finish climbing onto the roof and take a quick look. "I think it may have been a stray nail. I may be bleeding a little, but I'll be fine."

I quickly stand up, mindful of the hazardous conditions of the dilapidated buildings in this area. Splinters and exposed nails pose a constant danger, exacerbated by the dim lighting. Surprisingly, the air is not as chilly as one would expect in a place with limited sunlight. The geothermal heat from the surrounding islands, floating mid-air both above and below, prevents freezing temperatures from taking hold here.

Miya's insectoid legs are wrapped around me; ready to lift me into the air in a moment's notice, and ver antennae twitch as they detect the whereabouts of the now-out-of-sight thief.

"Proceed with extreme caution. There is a bitu and a yetu. They may be a renegade Rirmevu duo," Miya reports, moments before another yetu's wingspan cuts into the sky from beyond the tavern. "There they go."

Miya quickly unravels ver wings, and we lift off of the rooftop to give chase.

"Fami and Buso?" I ask in reference to the one Rirmevu team containing a bitu that I am aware of.

"No. I do not recognize these biosignatures." Miya says.

"This seems suspicious... Unless the yetu is wounded..."

"I understand what you mean." Miya affirms, "They are not wounded, so there is almost no chance the yetu didn't detect us. Meaning they must have known full well we were watching. They must want us to follow them. Do you think this might be a trap?"

"I don't know..." I say, "Unless the trap is mechanical, a yetu should know better than to think it could lead another yetu into an ambush. Given that we are flying through the air at the moment, a mechanical trap seems unlikely. Let's continue pursuit until we can see what building they dive into. Do you think you can keep up?"

"They are a bit faster than me since the bitu is so small, but I don't think they will get out of range of my senses any time soon."

We follow the thieves for about twelve blocks, soaring over rundown buildings and occasional landfill-looking slums that fill in anywhere lacking sturdier infrastructure.

Miya suddenly speaks up, "Oh, by the way, I am sensing that other ministry personnel have arrived at the tavern and started providing medical intervention to Sho. I think ve is going to survive."

This labor seems full of oddities. Sho blasphemed and survived, and now we are working to undermine what one might presume is Ritu's punishment for Sho's unforgivable transgression by retrieving ver stolen money. I might hope the thieves get away with the money if they didn't have to face punishment for their crime as well.

"Well, Ritu's will be done, I guess..." I say.

"The thieves seem to be leaving the city limits," Miya updates me. "They have entered into a free-fall. It's like they're trying to get to the cliff islands. This could get dangerous. Also, and I could be interpreting this wrong, but the bitu seems way too young to be a renegade Rirmevu. Like maybe thirteen salaries old."

This is increasingly out of the ordinary. A child and a yetu teaming up to commit a crime? The only reason I can imagine they would want to go to the cliff islands would be to dispose of evidence. Do they think we won't punish them just because they no longer have the stolen goods? Why not just drop the goods on an island as a distraction? It could be that they have some friends who can provide them with safety in numbers. If they are expecting me, and given the situation, I'm sure they would be, I wouldn't stand a chance.

We plummet over the edge of the island, following our target.

After falling for a few seconds, Miya speaks up, "They have started moving again, and I have just detected a large group gathered on an island down there, about five charities from here."

Ah, so it's the power-in-numbers strategy after all.

"Hmm," Miya continues, "The thieves seem to be headed in the opposite direction from that of the group."

"Weird. I wonder who the others are," I ponder aloud.

Miya's antennae whip around, trying to gather information. "There are about five people lined up; they are all in bad shape. I assume they are bound. There are about eight others, and a handful of them are wounded."

"Do you think law enforcement just busted some criminal activity on the cliffs?"

"I don't know. It seems odd that law enforcement would risk coming to the cliffs..." Miya's legs tighten. "Shattered skies!"

"What?"

"They... the... One of the people in the line was just kicked over the island's edge. They... they seem to be dragging the rest of the line off with... I think they were all chained together... I... I can't..."

"Does it seem like anyone will survive?"

"I don't... I think there is one survivor. They seem to have kept ver as a prisoner."

"Turn us around," I command and Miya is quick to obey.

Is this why the thieves dragged us down here? Did they do it to get help? Why not just ask? Perhaps they are just using this as an opportunity to get away? Could they have known this was happening? There are a lot of questions that need answers here, but they have to wait. Right now, bringing justice upon a band of murderers and potentially saving a hostage outweighs chasing after petty thieves.

"We are going to go help, but first, and I hate to say it, but we have to stop for supplies," I urge.

"There is no time for that!" Miya protests.

"What exactly do you expect to do when we get there? I may be able to win a one-on-one fight with most untrained people of my size, but most people are bigger than me. Add training, and I'm going to struggle. Add another person, of which there are six, mind you, and we may as well just show up and surrender."

"Do you think Ritu would have brought us here if Ve didn't think we were up to the task? Have you forgotten the stories of Ritu giving Ver followers great strength to single-handedly triumph over hundreds?" Miya asks.

"Listen. I'm angry too, and I want to save the survivor if we can. But what good are we to ver if we get caught or killed?"

"I have faith that we can defeat them. Even if we don't, maybe we do show up and just surrender. Maybe we could formulate a way to escape with the survivor from the inside." Miya says.

"Miya... I... I admire your faith. I really do. I'm jealous even, because I don't know if I have that same level of faith. I'm afraid my lack of faith may cancel out your faith, and... well..."

Miya comes to a sudden stop and lands us atop a small island about the size of a medium-sized airship. I can feel Miya's grip give up on me.

"No, Miya, wait!" I plead. Miya detaches from my back and begins to fly off, leaving me behind.

"I don't believe what you are doing is condoned by the Holy Scriptures!" I yell.

Miya stops for a moment, hovering in the air in front of me.

I continue, "In every story you mentioned, the heroes were explicitly blessed or told by Ritu that they would triumph. We have received no such confirmation or guarantee. People of faith are killed all of the time. We cannot just expect Ritu to save us from our mistakes, and I feel like you are about to make a big mistake..."

Silence lingers for a moment.

I gather my thoughts and continue, "Right now, Ritu has brought us here and provided us with resources on a wormwood island just over there." I point into the sky at an island resembling a black lump of coal, barely visible in the darkness at these depths.

Miya lands on the ground but remains quiet. I can tell ver blood is boiling.

"Let's make this quick," Miya concedes.

Chapter 6: Caution

Miya sets us down in the spot least plagued with hazardous foliage. While most plants cannot live at these depths, given the minimal sunlight and polluted water, the mutant plantlife of wormwood islands eerily thrives. If they were the sort of plant life to spread, no place would be safe. Fortunately, the plants cannot survive apart from the islands on which they grow. The island is their source of life, and they defend it viciously.

I remove my mask so that I can see a bit better and fetch a brown knit cap I knitted from the bag buckled to my upper leg. I have a great multitude of caps like it. Knitting is one of the many crafty hobbies I circulate between as a way to distract my mind when my thoughts get too negative or intimidating.

I use the cap to further contain my near-black curly hair, which had already been tied behind my head. Wormwood islands are no place for long hair or loose clothing. Miya folds up ver wings into tight packages close to ver back as best ve can. Fortunately, a yetu can fold their wings down to about the size of an adult's back, which is bigger than my back. Despite being twenty-six salaries old, I measure in at four ingots and a purse and weigh ninety purses, which would be annoyingly small if it were not necessary for my role as a Rirmevu. Where most atu or bitu average six ingots in height and weigh an average of one hundred and eighty purses, those bipeds who work as part of a Rirmevu duo must be of small stature for the average-sized yetu to lift their weight. If I were much bigger, Miya wouldn't be able to fly very well while holding me. Still, being short comes with its challenges.

"Alright, duck into this small pathway. I think it's a path cleared out by foselitu. But don't worry. They are not between us and our prize. Just keep straight, and I'll tell you when to stop."

I crawl along this narrow path, occasionally raising my body ever so slightly to avoid the deadly shock of a scarlet root.

Suddenly, my hand grasps something soft... with fur and feathers.

A shiver shoots through my body as I fight the urge to jerk my hand away and recklessly crawl back.

Initial panic gives way to anger at Miya for not telling me I was about to grab a foselitu, which quickly fades as it dawns on me that the foselitu is not trying to bite me or fly away. I peer closer at the small creature, barely visible against the charred ground. Striking blue feathers cling loosely to its wings, and the black fur along its body is patchy. Its mouth hangs open, fangs lifelessly bared, and eyes staring widely at nothing.

While yetu have an uncanny ability to tap into the fabric of creation to detect and assess life forms from great distances, their ability to detect non-living things is very "nearsighted," so to speak, given that they don't have eyes.

There, shriveled up on the foselitu's back, a mere finger width from my hand, a blue flower petal.

"Why the sudden stop?" Miya asks nervously. "You feel tense... Are you ok?"

"Yeah," I squeak out as I slowly retract my hand from the dead foselitu and turn my gaze upward.

There, maybe a hand above us, I catch sight of some dreaded little flowers.

"Why didn't you tell me about the blulips?" I ask.

"They are like a hand above us," ve responds defensively. "There are two dozen hazards just over a hand from us. I cannot tell you about every one of them; it wouldn't be practical. The best I can do for you is tell you where to go."

"I know." I take a deep breath to calm down. "In the future, if there are any hazards above us that might drop, say, a lung-collapsing flower petal down on my head or your back, tell me."

Silence hangs in the air for a moment while Miya processes. "Oh... Ohhh..." ver grip on me tightens as I imagine the dread of realization is washing over ver. "Sorry."

"It's ok. We should really train more on this sort of thing," I cannot blame Miya too much. Usually our supplies are provided by the ministry, so it is not often that we need to risk a wormwood island to forage for them. "Fortunately, we learned this lesson the easy way." I pause, not wanting to linger on ver mistake too long. "How is the survivor doing?"

"Not great."

"Then we had better hurry."

"Hang on..." Miya's antennas twitch a few times. "I'm just now realizing one of the other people on the island may not be an enemy. They are a rather scrawny dark-skinned atu who appears to be hiding, given that they are awake and healthy but have not moved this whole time. Apart from that one, the captive, and a mid-tone atu the rest seem to be pale-skinned atu and light-furred bitu, no yetu that I can detect and who knows if there are any notu."

"Good to know. Do you think ve can remain hidden?"

"It's hard to say."

"Alright, well, we should hurry along regardless."

"You should find the thorns we need clinging to the other side of the large tree over there."

"Thanks."

I round the tree, and sure enough, there is the violet vine we have been looking for, decorated with yellow flowers which tempt the eye away from the densely clustered hazardous thorns.

I muse over how, despite being the most dangerous-looking thing on a wormwood island, these vines are probably the least lethal. They are harmless unless they break the skin. Even then, they will only knock you out for a wage or so.

Occasionally, I'll look at such a thorn, and something I do not understand stirs within me. Like this thorn at one point meant more to me than it does now, though I cannot recall the significance.

After collecting everything we need, Miya gets to work while clinging to my back with four legs and using ver two free limbs to assemble the thorns and feathers into proper darts as I crawl back out.

The air at this depth is still, which makes it easier to land my shots. I load a dart into my crossbow-like gun and fire it down from the rock ledge where I'm perched. It strikes the lone pale-skinned atu below us, who promptly falls to the ground to find a urine-covered pillow of rocks to rest ver head upon.

I jump down from the ledge, and Miya glides us down, placing us next to the unconscious enemy.

"What crimes did ve commit?" I inquire.

"I'm not entirely sure of all their crimes, but I can confirm that the presumed leader is guilty of murder—pushing the victims off the cliff. The rest of them seem to only be guilty of assault."

I take a moment to contemplate. The victims will surely die from falling off the cliff island. Even if we were to follow them and catch up, Miya wouldn't have the strength or energy to lift both of us back up, let alone with any of the victims. This island is a cliff island, meaning there are no other islands below it. My late adoptive parent taught me that those who fall from these islands will continue falling until they perish from dehydration. Their bodies will then fall forever more. Only water vapor returns from these cliffs, replenishing the clouds.

I draw my Rirmevu blade from my boot, a tool of great significance to me as it once belonged to my late adoptive parent and it's the first Rirmevu blade I ever used. As I turn the atu over, I freeze upon recognizing the deep gray uniform beneath ver coat. It's adorned with hints of purple peeking through slotted seams and features the insignia of Hosudiha law enforcement over the right chest pocket. Panic surges through me as I focus on the insignia—a golden circle vertically bisected by three thin bars—a symbol representing my allies. Fear grips my mind, preventing me from fully rendering the face just within my peripheral vision.

After a tense moment, Miya whispers, "What's happening? Are you alright?"

"They... they are... Hosudiha law enforcement," I manage to convey, my voice filled with uncertainty.

Miya falls silent, ver legs tightening, and I can hear ver antennae whipping through the air as ve tries to make sense of the situation. "I'm not picking up any familiar biosignatures from them. Maybe it is a stolen uniform?" ve suggests.

My eyes gain the courage to look directly at the face. It's an average-looking atu face, but not one I have ever seen before. Curiosity compels me to push the coat further, exposing the regiment number.

"Maybe, but ve is from the fourth regiment. We haven't worked with them before," I respond, hoping that this is just a case of stolen uniforms. However, the absence of any reports about stolen uniforms in this morning's briefing leaves me uneasy. I look over at the steel-tipped spear the enemy has leaning up against the cliff face. It is forbidden for officers to use lethal force. So this spear casts doubt upon what everything else insinuates. Still, if this is indeed an officer, then my duty is to report ver and let the proper authorities handle it. As per protocol, ve is to be judged in a courtroom, not by my own hand.

"If these were officers... Wouldn't they be sure to have a yetu with them to keep a lookout?" I ask Miya.

"That would make sense... Though something my mentors would always warn me about in training was how as a yetu I was going to see more than anyone else. Things that would disturb me, things that would make me feel immense amounts of empathy for transgressors. It's common for yetu to feel the temptation to go renegade. Maybe that is why there are no yetu present."

I don't like the way Miya's explanation insinuates that these people could be officers engaging in foul play. I return my blade to the holster on my boot and retrieve a pencil and pocketbook from my bag to record the officer ID number.

Miya speaks up, "The thieves are back. Approaching from the same direction we came from, about five charities away."

My heart begins to race. If they are with these people, they will undoubtedly give away my position when they arrive.

"We need to intercept them before they can give us away," I declare.

"Wait... They stopped. It's like they are just watching us."

"Do they seem tired?"

"No, they could continue their approach if they wanted."

They had to have intended to lead us here... My mind resists making sense of the situation, but I think I can guess the reason why the thieves didn't just ask for our help. Would we have come if we knew we would be up against our allies? Would we have come so quickly if we had known how many there would be?

"Let me know if they try to make a move. I suspect they are waiting till we've knocked out everyone and have perhaps been wounded in the process. Then they will strike to take us out and loot everyone." I say. I may have just pulled that explanation out of thin air, but the possibility brings me comfort somehow.

"Will do." Miya says.

"For now, fly us back up to the top of the rock ledge. I want to see if we can coax out more enemies."

Miya flies us up, and I find a good-sized rock I can barely carry. I grit my teeth and have to slide my feet as I "walk" to take it to the ledge and throw it off, careful not to hit the unconscious enemy below. It crashes to the ground with a loud thump. With any luck, that will draw someone over to investigate, and I might get another opening to take one out. If there is no opening, the first thing they are likely to suspect is an accident, so my presence might remain a secret.

A voice calls out from the nearby campfire, "Zemi, are you alright?"

Two officers round the corner and walk into view... officers from Regiment Four.

Miya seems to pick up on my distress, puts the pieces together, and whispers to me, "Officers or not, they are way out of protocol. They are crossing lines, and we need to stop them, save the survivors, and report back to the ministry."

Miya is right. At the very least, not having to stop and enact judgment will save a lot of time.

The further officer is a pale-skinned atu who appears to limp from injuries. I take aim and fire at the injured one, and almost immediately thereafter, I leap from the ridge, a second dart gripped in my hand.

The first dart finds its mark, and the farther enemy falls to the ground, startling the closer bitu enemy and compelling them to look back at their fallen comrade, presenting their back to the unknown danger pouncing from behind. Miya glides me directly into the back of the enemy who can barely manage the beginnings of a yelp before I sink a dart into their shoulder.

"Take us back up quickly," I command Miya, who promptly obeys.

We wait atop the rock ledge for a moment to see if anyone else comes to the sound of the brief yelp.

"Everyone else seems to have been too far off to have noticed," Miya informs me. "These three were taking care of the band's Butushoselimo. If you move further along the ridge, you should be able to get a shot and incapacitate them."

Butushoselimo are large exoskeletal creatures with eight legs connected with fleshy webbing, save for two larger rear legs which they use to jump great heights and glide. They are infamous for being a rough whiplash-inducing ride if you're not careful, but they are also very quick. It's no easy task to knock out exoskeletal creatures with darts as one must hit the fleshy webbing close to the body. Too far from the body, and the venom might not get into the circulatory system. Fortunately, they are occupied with eating, and I make my shots rather easily.

As we move along the ridge to get a vantage point on the remaining enemies, I decide to quietly whisper my thoughts, "Miya, if these hostiles are wearing stolen uniforms, who do you think they might be? And along that line, who do you think the victims are?"

"I don't know. The only sorts of people you find out here are Rirmevu, criminals, bounty hunters who are hunting those criminals, or those who are ignorant of the dangers out here."

"The impostors have to be criminals of some sort, right?" I ask.

"We shouldn't discount the possibility that we may be dealing with crooked officers. I imagine there is a story behind a lot of the ministry's rules, and there are a number of rules pertaining to dealing with crooked officers. Honestly, as much as I hate to say it, I think it's safe to assume that these are officers that we are dealing with. The victims, on the other hand... Who knows? It's probably best if we exercise a high degree of caution around them."

"I'm thinking the thieves are a third party." I say.

"You think so?"

"Yeah. Assuming this is the camp of the victims, had the yetu been among them, wouldn't they have seen the officers coming?" I ask.

"Given the speed of Butushoselimo, even with a yetu's advanced warning, there would be little time to organize an escape. So the thieves might still be with the victims. The yetu might have flown off to get the child to safety and seek help. My guess is that the officers attacked a vetu smuggling scheme."

Suddenly, Miya's grip grows tight. "Enough chatter. We need to go rescue the hostage right now! The leader in the tent is... We can handle the final three if we hit them head-on quickly enough. Let's just go!"

"No. We cannot afford to risk putting ourselves in a situation where we have to fight more than one at a time," I reply matter-of-factly.

"Dima, if we don't take that risk, there may not be a survivor to save!"

"I want to save ver, but who's going to save us? Huh?" I say sharply. "If we don't take this slowly, we may be no better off than ve is."

Miya's wings begin unfolding.

"Don't you dare try to take control here," I bite. "I will stick you with a dart if you try!" The threat is genuine. I would merely be eliminating a liability.

"And how exactly do you plan to get off this rock before the enemies start waking up without me to fly us out?" Ve starts to beat ver wings.

"There is the airship. I could hide. I have options. I will stick you!" I nearly shout to overcome the sound of Miya's wings.

"The hostage is being raped Dima!" Miya bites.

I freeze and remember. With the blade in my boot I can make sure a rapist can never have another victim. Am I about to let someone get raped in the intrest of self preservation? I was just about to let them get murdered in the interest of self preservation...

"Fine! Screw it! Get us in there!" I say, though the frustration of my internal conflict makes me say it a bit too loud.

Suddenly, a new voice fills the air from just beyond the larger tent, "Hey Sarge, I think we may have trouble!"

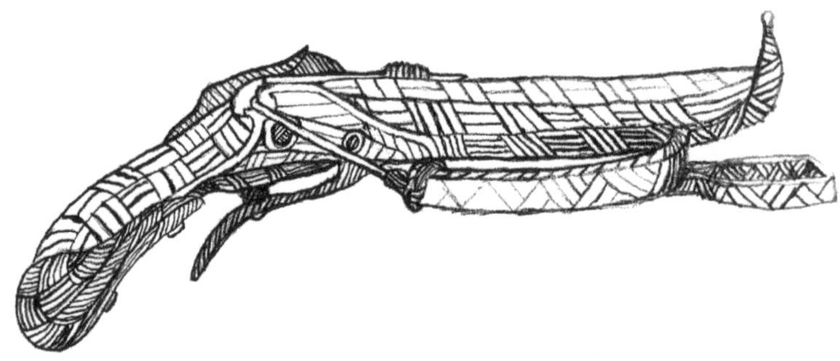

Chapter 7: Clash of Mind and Matter

Combat now inevitable, Miya fills me in on ver plan. "There is one just beyond this tent. I'll fly us up, and you can take a shot." Miya lifts us into the sky as I scramble to reload my dart gun. Three enemies are remaining, and there's probably about thirty charities before the first enemy wakes up. I have five darts left.

The turbulence from taking off makes the dart I'm trying to load into my gun tumble just to the side of the flight groove, narrowly missing my hand and falling to the ground below.

Four darts left.

I manage to retrieve a new dart from my pouch, but another one is pulled out with the movement of the first and falls.

Three darts left.

Miya lifts us over the tent. I can see the enemy who snitched on us. Ve is a mid-toned atu who brandishes a spear and wears leather armor tailored similarly to that of a standard officer's uniform. Ve spots us as well. I manage to load the dart, take quick aim, and send it into the dirt beyond the enemy. I missed, predictably, given that I'm ascending into the air, but still...

Two darts left... and three enemies to eliminate. Crap.

Deciding the spear is expendable enough, the enemy rears back and hurls it towards us. Miya quickly retracts ver wings to dodge the throw, sending us into a freefall, but the spear manages to clip Miya's right wing. We land atop the tent and slide down its slope until momentum throws us over its side, landing us near the smaller tents.

"Are you okay?" I ask Miya.

"I have a small cut on the wing, but stay focused. They're coming!" Miya replies.

Sure enough, the enemy comes charging around the tent, aiming to catch me before I recover from the fall and reload. "Get off and hide," I command Miya. As much as I am sure ve doesn't want to leave me, ve knows, as well as I do, just how essential ve is for us to get out of here alive. So Miya detaches from my back and skitters into the nearest small tent.

I move to aim my empty dart gun at the enemy. Even though it is not loaded, the enemy reaches to restrain the hand with the gun under the impression that it is a threat. Meanwhile, my other fingers are already clutching the end of my next dart, trying to pull it from its pouch.

The enemy grips my left hand with the gun, and squeezes it enough that the pain forces me to surrender my weapon, sending it clattering to the dirt. With ver free hand, ve grips my throat, immediately cutting off my ability to breathe, and easily lifts me from the ground until I stick the arm at my throat with the dart. The enemy instantly loses consciousness and falls forward onto me.

I cough and gasp to replenish my lungs as I struggle beneath the weight of the unconscious enemy. The fact that Miya is not helping me makes me assume there is another impending threat somewhere.

I manage to free my torso from under the enemy's limp body, but before I can kick them off my legs, I see a spear leveled at my face, brandished by a pale atu who's built like a brick wall.

"Go on, get up, remove your weapons, and throw everything aside," commands the new arrival.

I kick my legs free, perhaps a bit more aggressively than necessary, but the enemy doesn't seem to mind. I rise to my feet and hesitate for a moment to give Miya a chance to perhaps jump this enemy from behind, grab and restrain ver, giving me a chance to strike. But Miya doesn't seem to make a move. I am confident ve didn't abandon me; ve is more likely to take a risk on faith than to run away out of cowardice.

After taking too long to comply with ver demand, the enemy swings the spear around to strike with the non-bladed end. I raise my arm to try to catch the blow, and when it connects, sure, it hurts a little, but it feels like I just got hit by a frail teenager. I recover quickly and re-examine my foe. Ve is frail...

"Shattered skies!" ve shrieks as ve stares in astonishment at ver slim arms. Ve is not alone now. Behind ver towers a burly dark-skinned atu, wearing practical yet high-quality blue and gray robes that strain as though they are two sizes too small.

What is happening? I swear the enemy with the spear wasn't scrawny an alm ago, yet there ve is, struggling to lift the weapon. Also, who is this new atu? I thought the only dark-skinned atu on this island was supposed to be scrawny. Is ve another enemy?

The newcomer shatters my thoughts when ve slugs the scrawny enemy in the back of the head, sending them into the dirt, out cold. I quickly scoop up the spear while the new person rears back, rage in ver eyes, seemingly intent on beating the unconscious enemy unnecessarily. Ve freezes, clenching ver jaw and fists, only to let out a furious shout as ve punches the dirt beside the head of the unconscious enemy, tears pouring from ver eyes. I level the spear towards the new person who just looks at me, clearly still angry but not at me. Ve takes a deep breath to cool off.

"What in the skies is going on?" I shout. "Who are you?"

"I'm a friend. I was hiding, and I saw an opportunity to use my magic. Trait magic," ve replies, taking another deep calming breath. "I can take and give traits to and from living things. My name is Hari."

That name... of course, I hadn't gotten a long enough look, but this is the same Hari I split ways with back when... When was that? I remember Hari but the circumstances of our prior interactions seem muddied in my memory.

"Hari? You're alive?" I exclaim.

Hari gives me a curious look as if trying to see through my featureless mask, "Do I know you?"

Out from the tent just beyond Hari, bursts forth the final enemy, a pale atu who looks like ve could effortlessly throw the burly Hari fifty ingots. Ve wears a Sergeant's uniform, indicated by several medals adorning the left pocket and a few pronounced horizontal purple fabric bars vertically stacked above the center of the chest. I am not yet willing to believe that even this uniform isn't stolen, despite Miya's assessment.

"Look out!" I warn.

Hari turns to look at the new arrival and then looks back at me, gesturing, "Give me the spear!"

I hesitate. Hari is probably a criminal, I cannot trust ver not to use the spear against me let alone to use it ethically.

The enemy rushes towards us, "Idiots! Rushing into fights alone," ve shouts in frustration.

Hari is still looking to me for the spear, but when it is clear to ver that I am conflicted ve shouts, "Fine!" Hari runs past me.

Crap! Hari and this foe can both run faster than me. Hari must be counting on the enemy catching me, giving ver a chance to escape. What a fose thing to do. It may be hopeless but I have no choice but to try to fight.

When the foe is at the right distance I strike at ver head with the non-bladed side of the spear. However, the foe reads my attack and moves to catch my swing. There is no doubt in my mind that ve is about to yank this spear from my hands and drive it through my heart.

As the scene appears to unfold in slow motion it almost looks as though I am kindly just handing the spear over as the foe's fingers close around the pole with what looks like an iron grip, only to have the pole effortlessly push ver hand into ver face with such force as to send ver soaring fifteen ingots through the air to my right.

I stand dumbfounded for a moment. How the hase did I just- it has to be-

I turn around and just as I was beginning to suspect, Hari is standing behind me with an open palm pointed at a fist sized rock and ver other palm pointing towards the foe's general direction. Hari must have been using magic to swap the masses of the foe and the rock.

"Don't look at me!" Hari shouts, "most of the force of your strike was converted into movement, not damage."

"So you like playing with rocks do you?" The foe shouts, drawing my gaze back to see ver rising back to ver feet. One of ver fists clutches a stone and the other clutches several more stones, "Play with this!"

The foe begins hurling stones at us from beyond Hari's twelve ingot range for magic. I am quick to hit the first stone out of the way with the spear, but before I can bring the spear back to bear, a second stone is headed for me and I dive out of the way, allowing it to strike the unsuspecting Hari right in the throat. The foe, who was already closing in before the second stone struck, tackles the coughing Hari to the ground and proceeds to presumably beat the trait magic out of ver, given the lack of using it.

Hari is knocked unconscious before I can even stagger back to my feet. I start desperately digging into my bag, searching for the final dart. All the while trying to keep the spear leveled as a deterrent that I don't intend to use. Afterall, I was taught to preserve the lives of Ritu's enemies over and at the risk of my own.

Where the hase is it! Did the dart fall out of the bag at some point?

The foe and I lock eyes, and immediately I can tell ve knows I'm bluffing with the spear. If I were serious, I would have stabbed already.

Ve lunges towards me, and I strike again with the non-bladed end, which ve promptly kicks away with one foot, leaps into a spin, and brings ver other foot into direct contact with my temple.

The kick throws me to the ground. My ears are ringing, the world seems to sway, and pain fills my head. I try to gather myself enough to avoid another blow, but I can tell I'm taking too long and will soon be knocked out. However, the finishing blow doesn't come. I can hear a struggle, though my wounded head makes it sound distant and muffled. Finally, I manage to recover enough to sit up and look for my enemy.

Ve is fighting someone else, Hari? No, a bitu in minimal clothing, with chocolate brown fur. So the stranger must have recently been the hostage.

The foe throws several punches, which the stranger swiftly ducks beneath, such that none connect. The stranger, in return, throws a punch that lands upon the foe's cheek, but the foe skillfully turns ver head to make the strike a grazing blow, minimizing damage.

I feel something grab me from behind. My initial panic gives way once I recognize the familiar grip of Miya.

"Sorry... Here," Miya dangles my gun before me. "It's loaded." I grab the weapon and quickly work to aim it.

The stranger sends a knee looking for the liver of the foe, but the foe manages to catch the knee with ver arm and strikes at the crotch of the stranger. Simultaneously, the stranger uses the enemy's grip on ver leg to rise up and connect ver other knee to the foe's jaw just as the foe's fist connects with the stranger's crotch. The stranger's strike knocks the foe out cold. Meanwhile, the foe's strike seems less effective than one would expect, given that all bitu have an external testicle, which makes me wonder about the stranger's history with Rirmevu.

By this time, I have my weapon aimed, but it seems unnecessary until the stranger locks ver eyes on the spear at ver feet. Ve snatches up the spear and lets out a painful cry as ve braces to claim the unconscious foe's life.

I fire my final dart.

The stranger falls to the ground unconscious.

An unexpected voice speaks up from behind me, "Why in the Shattered Skies did you do that?" Fear shoots through my body. That wasn't Miya's voice. The thief! Of course they would choose now!

The fear converts into action as I turn and throw a blind punch at the person behind me. My fist connects with the groin of a scrawny atu who promptly recoils such that ver face comes low enough for me to see it is Hari.

"Gah! It's me!" Hari cries, as ve clutches ver crotch. Ver face is not nearly as bloodied as it should be. Also, what happened to ver build? I look past ver and see a built atu with a bloodied face still lying on the ground unconscious, but their skin is pale. Perhaps trait magic has something to do with all of this.

"Oh, I thought you were the thief." I say.

"The thief?" Hari asks.

Miya cuts in, "The thieves are inbound though!"

With that knowledge, I cut to the chase. "Hari, there is a yetu carrying a bitu, headed in this direction. Would you know anything about it?"

"Thanks for the apology," Hari says sarcastically, having received no such apology for my assault.

I sigh in annoyance, "I'm sorry. Now. Yetu carrying a young bitu. What do you know?"

Hari's lack of forgiveness in return for my thoughtless apology is evident in ver expression. Though ve does cooperate ever so reluctantly, "A yetu was leading my team. I hadn't seen much of what happened to ver after the law came cracking down on us. We also had a number of bitu with us."

"So they may be friendly," I say, "but we still need to play this safe and get ready to fight." I take a moment to consider our options, but my head aches with each beat of my heart.

"Why does your face look good?" I ask Hari.

Hari gives me a confused look that makes me reflect on my word choice, "I- uh, I mean. Why does it look healthy? Like, it was bloodied up just a moment ago-"

"Ah, I see what you mean," Hari says, "trait magic can be used to swap conditions between targets."

"What in the skies? You can give your wounds to other people!" I say.

"Emphasis on the word 'swap'." Hari says, "If I had tried to swap wounds with someone whose face was bruised, but still less brutalized than mine, I would make their face brutalized, but I would also take their bruises onto my face. Between two wounded targets, there is no case where one person walks away without wounds."

"Okay... I am not sure I follow but that could just be the fault of my splitting headache." I say.

"I think I get it." Miya interjects, "Would you be able to swap my colleague's head wound with an enemy's lack of a head wound?"

"Yes." Hari confirms.

"Will you?" I ask.

"Sure, close your eyes." Hari says as ve closes ver eyes and points one open palm at me and another at the one of the nearby enemies.

"Sure," I say and proceed to continue watching since ve isn't looking to see if I actually closed my eyes. Suddenly, Hari's muscles seem to rapidly grow and ver height increases straining ver clothes yet again.

"What's the deal? I thought you were going to heal me!" I scold.

Hari's eyes open, and ve shoots me an annoyed look. "You were supposed to close your eyes."

"Did you really think I would close my eyes in front of a possible enemy after all that just happened?"

"Hmm... My mistake. Anyway, before I heal you, you need to answer some questions." Hari says.

"There is no time," I urge.

"As far as I'm concerned, you are a bigger potential threat than the possible ally on approach. You are a law enforcement officer just like our enemies, after all."

Hari is towering over me, looking like a weightlifter. I may have more fighting ability, but not enough to overcome that much brawn bare-handed, especially not with my splitting headache.

"I'm not 'just like' them. They are crooked. That doesn't make all of us officers crooked." I retort.

"Then why the fuck did you shoot Zi?" Hari asks angrily, gesturing towards the unconscious stranger I shot earlier.

"I have a duty to protect sentient life." I say.

"More like a duty to protect your own. You fucking attacked Zi to save the life of that monster!" Hari accuses, fuming.

"I would have shot the other one if their situations were reversed! Which reminds me, I need to prick each of the unconscious enemies before they regain consciousness. Would you please hurry with the healing?"

Hari still looks displeased and ve seems to contemplate pressing me further, "One last thing."

Before I can react Hari swipes the mask from my face. In a panic I attempt to shield my face with one small hand while I desperately reach for the mask Hari dangles above me like a bully.

Hari managed to catch a glimpse of my face, and ve seems to take a moment to put the pieces together, "Holy shit! You are the one who led me straight into the arms of captivity!"

My heart sinks. Lead ver into captivity? How did I manage to do that? I have memories of grieving the loss of my parents when Lise stepped in and wisped me away. I don't recall anyone coming with me. But somehow that memory bleeds into Lise and I arriving at ver apartment. I must have met Hari at Lise's apartment, because I have no recollection of ver from before that.

"Don't worry. I don't hold it against you. I imagine you were just as much a victim as I was. I'm sorry but I think I only ever heard your name once. So I am having a hard time remembering." Hari brings my mask back down and extends it to me as I quickly swipe it from ver and slide it back on.

"At least I can still keep that a secret." I say bitterly, "My name's not the only thing you seem to be failing to remember. I didn't lead you into anything. I didn't even know you until I met up with Lise at ver... Until Lise and I arrived at ver apartment."

Hari gives me a sideways look, "Hmm... I think I see what is happening here."

"What?" I ask.

"There isn't time to explain. I got my answers. Let's heal you up."

I hate that Hari seems to be keeping something from me. However, we haven't the time for an interrogation.

"Can you also heal my colleague's wing?" I ask.

"I cannot take the wound from the yetu's wing. My targets have to have a semi-similar anatomy meaning, if I were one of the targets, I would need wings to take a wing wound onto. As for your head, I could try to perform the magic as a channel instead of a vessel, but I haven't quite reached that level yet. There is no guarantee it would be successful."

"Whatever you do, do it quickly." I say.

"Close your eyes, I get nervous knowing someone is watching and that can make things take longer." Hari says sternly.

Miya gives me a little squeeze, as if to tell me ve will let me know if Hari tries to pull something.

I sigh in resignation, "Fine," and I close my eyes.

Hari extends a hand toward my head and another toward the mildly wounded enemy. I close my eyes and after a moment the pain dissolves into nothingness.

"Shit!" Hari cries. I open my eyes to see ver clutching ver head. "Close your eyes!" ve yells angrily, and I obey.

It seems to take Hari a longer time to deposit this injury than the previous spells had taken. It's strange. I thought ve was going to swap my injury with the mildly bruised enemy, but ve seems to have taken my wound upon verself by accident. This must be what ve meant by not having mastered channeling magic. Vessel magic must be when you take a trait onto yourself, whereas channel magic is when you switch traits between two targets without taking any traits onto yourself. I think there is some overlap with regular magic in this regard, though that is just a guess. I haven't studied magic beyond what they taught us in grade school and what was necessary for my job, or so I thought. It seems my education may have been lacking in necessary information.

"Okay, you can open your eyes." Hari says.

I look at Hari, who appears fully healed.

"Do you think you could get me a stronger body build too?" I ask.

"I wouldn't recommend it. I may be stronger, but I am not used to this distribution of muscle mass, so my balance is all thrown off. Yours would be too. It's better that one of us is not tripping over our own feet."

"Makes sense. How many charities do we have?" I ask.

"They will be here in one charity. Also, some of the hostiles have started to stir." Miya responds.

"Alright, let's make this quick." I say as I run over to Zi, remove the dart, sprint over to the stirring enemy, and stick the dart into ver arm. The darts lose potency with each use, so this enemy will likely only be out for thirty charities. If I use this dart again, I will likely only get ten to fifteen charities of unconsciousness. So after I stick the last enemy, I toss the dart and gather the one sticking out of the first enemy I fought, to load into my gun.

I'm going to try to gather any spent darts when I come across them. I might have collected the darts as I went earlier, but I wasn't expecting to burn through all of them. Also, I don't like having to think about which darts in my bag have been used and which ones have not in the heat of the moment. I should really get a bag with some slots for spent darts.

When all is said and done, I begin scanning the sky for the incoming threat.

"Uppermost dawnward, forty-five degrees," Miya informs me of the enemy's angle of approach.

I lock my sight on the threat just as they swoop close enough to stand noticeably apart from the darkness, landing roughly thirty ingots away. The yetu and bitu thieves.

"They are with me!" Hari proclaims. "I am going to check on Zi."

Chapter 8: Vemo

I'm not sure if I should feel at ease or more alert. Miya and I are operating under the assumption that Hari and ver companions, apparently including the new arrivals, are criminals, and they know where I stand. I am a Rirmevu.

I create some distance from Hari, just in case ve tries to channel Zi's unconsciousness onto me. The young bitu stranger is holding a plank of wood, presumably grabbed before the theft back in Hosudiha, meant to block any darts I may try to fire. Ver clothes seem too big, ver fur is mostly brown with some black stripes, and ver eyes are locked on me.

I need to figure out my next move.

I can't simply knock out Hari and the other two, then leave them to be murdered. I don't even know for certain if Hari and Zi are guilty of any crimes. So I can't touch them unless they needlessly threaten someone's life again. The two strangers, though... I lock eyes with the bitu. They are guilty of theft and need to be punished for it.

"We declare the right to reconcile," a voice, presumably the yetu riding the bitu's back, calls out to me. The words interrupt my train of thought. The right to reconcile. Under its declaration, punishment is put on hold, and the guilty must make up for their transgression under the supervision of law enforcement. At that point, no punishment is dealt. In this instance of theft, they need to return what they have stolen and additionally pay triple a deposit's standard rate of interest. However, the large bag of stolen coins is not visible.

"You cannot enact that right if you no longer have what was stolen," I say.

"We have it on a nearby island," the bitu says.

"If you can prove it, I will escort you to a law enforcement facility, and they will take over from there."

"Very well. Hari, I am so sorry we couldn't have gotten help sooner," the yetu says.

"I would have helped!" shouts the young bitu. "If Jomira hadn't been such a coward-"

"Tai, that's enough," Hari cuts in, "You are young. You probably don't want to hear it, but your presence would not have been helpful. Jomira made the right call, and ve is our captain. You would do well to respect ver judgment."

"That's not true! I could have helped!"

"You could have been killed. We would have had to split our attention between fighting and keeping you safe, and more of us might have died as a result."

"Who died? Are my parents okay?"

Hari looks grave, tears swelling in ver eyes. "Everyone who survived is here, your parents didn't make it. I am sorry."

Tai's eyes widen with terror. "Where are they?"

Hari looks too pained to answer, so I step up. There is no point in hiding the reality of a situation that will be made evident soon enough. "Falling, I'm afraid." These words break Hari, who begins to bawl, but Tai almost looks hopeful despite Hari's dismay.

"You mean they are still alive!"

"No, there is no saving-"

"Shut up! We have wings, we could catch up to them and bring them back!"

"They are not falling!" Hari cuts in. Does ve really intend to lie to this child?

Hari continues, "There is a bottom down there you know. They have likely hit the new crust already. They are certainly dead."

New crust? It seems we have been taught differently. I was always told there was nothing but an eternal fall beyond these cliffs, and I was told on good authority. Hari seems to be misinformed, but maybe it's better to go with ver version of the story, lest Tai jump over the edge believing ve can really catch up and that the yetu would have the strength to fly all the way back up without rest.

"But it's possible there is no bottom, right? If there is a possibility they could still be alive, we should-"

"No," Hari and I sternly say in unison. We look at one another as if to work out who should explain first.

I continue, "Everyone who is falling is chained together. A yetu wouldn't be able to carry an average-sized adult for very long, let alone five of them all chained together. Bottom or not, they are all gone."

The hope drains from Tai's face and turns to sorrow, then to anger as ve collapses to ver knees. "Why, Ritu, why? We were so close! We were almost free. They promised we would travel to a land where we could see the sun... They promised!" Tears pour from ver eyes, and bitter weeping overtakes ver.

After being satisfied that Zi is in stable condition, Hari moves to Tai's side and a places a hand on ver shoulder. "I can only begin to imagine how you are feeling. We all lost people we love this sun, but you paid the highest toll of us all. I know you feel alone. I know there is nothing I can do to mend the void, but you can stick with me for however long you need. I will not leave you."

Tai leans into Hari and weeps in ver embrace.

Now I understand what is happening here. Hari's use of the word 'sun' in reference to a 'labor' tells me that ve and the rest probably call the neighboring nation Matuha their home. I had heard rumors of a group of foreigners attempting to exalt residents of Hosudiha against Ritu's will, it would seem the rumors were true and this lot seem to have finally paid the price for their attempt to undermine Ritu's judgment.

A sense of dissonance comes over me as I ponder whether this punishment was too harsh. However, any defiance of Ritu is an embrace of the ways of death. These people chose a path that would have ultimately led to their demise. Only the virtuous fruits of Ritu's spirit lead to exaltation.

Despite understanding the situation, I can't help but feel sympathy for Tai. How much say did ve really have in all of this? Perhaps that is why Ritu spared ver. Maybe ve has been found virtuous enough for exaltation after all.

With a sense of clarity, I return to the task of recording officer ID numbers. I approach the one I assume to be the leader and ask Miya, "What are ver crimes?"

Miya takes a moment to answer, likely going through a similar thought process as mine. "Ve is the only one I can guarantee is guilty of rape and murder. Just so you know, it might have gotten far more brutal had I not insisted that we act quickly," Miya says defensively.

"Do you realize how lucky we were?" I respond sharply. "There were at least three, maybe four occasions where we could have died or faced worse. Thank Ritu, things turned out the way they did-" I pause, realizing the offensiveness of my words. I glance at the grieving individuals to see if they heard my seemingly insensitive remarks. Fortunately, I don't believe I was overheard. I also look at Zi, feeling guilty for what ve might have endured while I prioritized our safety. But I did what I had to do.

"We will discuss this labor's events thoroughly during the debrief," I state.

I look down at the enemy wearing a sergeant's uniform. This scoundrel is fortunate that I have to operate under the assumption ve is an officer. If it weren't for the uniform, I would castrate ver in a heartbeat. I am tempted to do it anyway. Miya can't see if ve is in uniform or not. "This one is not wearing a stolen uniform. You know these criminal leaders; they take pride in their unique clothing style. So ve was probably too proud to wear anything that would hinder ver style."

I'm surprised at the words as they leave my mouth. Did I really just say that? Committed to my words, I proceed to enact punishment for rape and murder before reason can take hold.

I retrieve the blade from my boot and remove the enemy's testicles and penis. Then I remove the cap from the hilt of the blade, revealing enchanted metal that glows a brilliant heated orange with which I cauterize the wound.

Ritu, why did this fose have to commit murder? I want this filth to feel every bit of pain from this removal. However, the punishment for murder will prevent ver from experiencing that pain.

Murder is the most severely punished crime by most Rirmevu like myself. Some believe rape and torture should be punished equally. Disagreements on how to deliver justice are unfortunately common among Rirmevu teams. As for Miya and I, we stick to the principles of my adoptive vedi. For murder we begin by paralyzing the culprit from the waist down. On repeat offenses, we paralyze their torso as well. So, I slide the blade between the vertebrae of the leader's lower back, paralyzing the pelvis and legs.

"You might want to discard the uniform," Miya suggests. Ver words send a shiver down my spine. Ve knows I lied. Ve probably picked it up from the context and my elevated heart rate or something.

"Why did you let me—" I start to say.

"I can't see what kind of uniform ve is wearing. I just think that whatever style this enemy is sporting is undeserved," Miya interrupts, subtly expressing ver approval or at least ver understanding of my decision.

I glance at Zi, knowing ve would prefer this individual to die, but I hope ve can find some solace in this situation. I remove the coat and shirt from the enemy and proceed to toss them over the edge of the cliff island.

"That wasn't necessarily in accordance with the protocol, was it?" a voice asks from behind. It takes me a moment to spot the mid-tone brownish-gray yetu on the ground.

"Neither is theft," I reply.

The yetu chuckles, "I suppose not, though I haven't bothered with the protocol for quite some time now."

"So you're a renegade Rirmevu?" Miya inquires.

The yetu ignores the question and continues, "You can call me Jomira. Given what you just did, would I be correct in assuming that you are unsure whether these are officers or criminals? Or did your sense of justice override your allegiance such that you were willing to act against a comrade?"

"You don't know, do you?" Miya asks nervously.

"I do. The one you just castrated is Sergeant Makali. I used to work with ver. Ve was one of the reasons my partner and I went renegade," Jomira reveals.

Color drains from my face. The realization that they were not mere enemies fills me with terror. Jomira could be lying, but something tells me otherwise. I just attacked my fellow officers. Still, we disposed of the uniform. Plausible deniability exists.

"And they will find out it was you too," Jomira continues. "Your face may be hidden, but the corruption within law enforcement runs deep. They can all confirm that Sergeant Makali was wearing ver uniform. It will be your word against theirs. This wouldn't be the first time I've seen them get away with murder as well."

My legs weaken beneath me. What was I thinking? What have I done? My eyes shift to the unconscious sergeant, and rage surges within me. What were you thinking? What the hase were you thinking?

Ritu, what am I going to do?

"We have to turn ourselves in," Miya declares.

I am hesitant to agree with Miya. Do we have to turn ourselves in? I wrestle with conflicting thoughts and emotions before arriving at an answer. It will cost us, but ultimately turning ourselves in is the right thing to do. Ritu, have mercy on us.

"First," Jomira interjects, "you will have to help me with my right to reconcile, and I insist on delivering what we stole, along with the penalty fee, directly to Sho and not to the ministry."

"Of course," I say.

"Do you understand what that entails? Do you know what happens to those who blaspheme Ritu?" Jomira questions.

"I know they face severe social repercussions." Miya answers, "No one wants to associate with them, they struggle to find employment, and it's essentially social suicide. Usually, they have to move away, try to find a place where no one knows their identity, and start anew."

“Some manage to escape,” Jomira says, “but anyone who blasphemes is put on a list. They are allowed to survive for a while, but only until everyone ceases to care about them. Then they are quietly apprehended and forced into slave labor, if they're lucky. In Hosudiha, though, it's not uncommon for a person to be apprehended right away. Given the story they told about Sho back at the tavern, I'm sure ve was immediately apprehended.”

“I don't believe you,” Miya retorts.

“Me either,” I add. “That doesn't sound like something the ministry would allow to happen.”

“Why wouldn't they? Those who blaspheme Ritu are considered unforgivable, aren't they? If a person is spiritually dead, without hope of entering Rirsudi in the next life, are they truly alive? If they become like walking corpses, spreading the ways of death, aren't their lives forfeit?” Jomira asks.

“Of course not! All vetu life is sacred!” Miya responds firmly, without a moment's hesitation.

Despite Miya's defense, Jomira's words unsettle me. “While I believe that most people in the ministry share Miya and my perspective,” I say, “Hearing how some talk about those who continually transgress, the way they discuss same-sex couples is repugnant but unfortunately not uncommon.”

My gaze falls to the mutilated sergeant, “I want to believe that the ministry wouldn't allow such individuals to rise to power, but there ve is.”

“I'm glad to hear you believe all vetu life is sacred, but do you know why you believe it? Sure, there are times when one life must be lost in defense of another's life or autonomy, but do you have a reason to defend the unforgivable, or do you simply refuse to believe life can become forfeit?"

I feel uneasy and unable to provide a response.

"It's because we are all made in the sacred image of Ritu." Miya says, "Such an image cannot lose its value."

"What does that mean exactly?" Jomira asks, "Does Ritu not cast Ver image into the fires of Hase? Valuable or not, it would seem that Ritu believes some souls are forfeit."

"It's not Ritu who casts them into Hase." I say, "Hase is a choice. Those who go there go only because they have chosen Hase over Ritu."

"Are we not all transgressors who choose transgression?" Jomira asks, "Who choose the ways of death? Who choose things of Hase on a regular basis? If we all choose Hase regularly, then what will stop us from choosing it on the sun of judgment? Who gets into Ritu's kingdom?" Jomira asks.

"It's not that they chose Hase." Miya cuts in. "You are right, due to our corrupted nature, we all choose Hase regularly. It's that they have rejected Ritu. To be in Ritu's presence after rejecting Ver would be to suffer more than if they were simply cast away from Ritu's presence. Ritu casts them away as both an act of righteous judgment and mercy."

"So it's merciful for Ritu to send those who reject Ver to Hase?" Jomira asks rhetorically, "We are now left with the same problem, just with softer words. Now it's a mercy to blasphemers and those whom they may influence to send the blasphemer to the eternity they need, having rejected Ritu, before they can drag others along with them. If we permit the irredeemable blasphemer to live, are we not doing a disservice to those they may lead astray?"

"If it were necessary for their lives to be claimed, then Ritu would claim their lives," Miya says.

"Do you not deem it necessary for people to be punished for their transgressions, even though Ritu doesn't carry out such punishments Verself?"

Anger rises within me, "Are you trying to convince us to consider the deaths of blasphemers as necessary? What is the point of this conversation anyway? We should be working to get away from here before the officers wake up!"

"No, we are not done with this conversation," Jomira retorts firmly. "I don't trust you to make rational decisions. I don't trust you to side with your present convictions and value my life and the lives of my crew when they come up against the right authority figure or a spirit trying to pass as Ritu. If we are going to travel together, I need to know I can trust you."

"Who are you to lecture us about trust when you and your crew are here willfully causing more damage than good?" Miya asks, "If you were a Rirmevu officer once then you know the nature of exaltation. You cannot just give money or housing to someone who lacks the necessary virtues to maintain and use them responsibly, and those virtues come through one's receptiveness of Ritu's spirit. A vetu must first be receptive to Ritu, and the virtues to follow are what will lift them out of Hosudiha and keep them out of Hosudiha. Without Ritu's virtues, they will either end up falling back down or they will build a fortune out of their vices and harm society."

I reflect on Miya's words, ve has a point, Jomira and ver crew are not entirely ethical given the ways they defy Ritu's commands. However, who among us is perfectly moral? Still they seem to deliberately be contributing to harm. They cannot be trustworthy people.

"That is another conversation we simply lack the time to address." Jomira says, and I cannot help but find that to be entirely too convenient of an excuse, "The issue at hand is whether I can trust you to value my life and the lives of my crew."

"Why do you believe all vetu life is sacred then?" I ask, "What is your answer to your own question?"

"All vetu life is sacred because we are all instances of the same consciousness. Even a person who fails contributes towards our collective maturity," Jomira explains.

"On what grounds are you basing that?" Miya questions.

"Are we not to love others as ourselves? Even our enemies?" Jomira asks, referring to passages in the Holy Scriptures.

"I think you are reading meaning into those passages that isn't really there," Miya accuses.

"It's a different interpretation of the same passage. Perhaps I am reading meaning into it that isn't there. However, at least I have a reason to consider all vetu life sacred," Jomira responds.

"And what about those whom Ritu casts into the fires of Hase? Are you just going to ignore that reality?" Miya asks.

"Not at all. The belief that Hase is a place of eternal conscious torment is actually quite new. Most, if not all, of the earliest ministry members believed that those who are cast into Hase are annihilated, wiped from existence, not left to suffer eternal conscious torment," Jomira explains.

"I still fail to see how that makes sense with your interpretation," Miya says.

"Yeah, same," I add.

"I don't necessarily believe that same thing," Jomira continues, "Tell me, are you two better people now than you were five cycles ago?"

"I like to think I am," I say. Unsure of how this question relates to the topic at hand.

"Ritu refines me through sanctification every labor," Miya says.

"Exactly. Hase is merely a part of the refining process. As we are bettered, we are pruned of those parts of us that are harmful or otherwise destructive. Those parts are tossed into the fire of Hase, annihilated. We are all one consciousness being pruned and bettered by our collective experiences. Harmful parts of us, perhaps even entire bodied instances, are pruned and annihilated in Hase fire without sacrificing the whole, but instead, to allow it to thrive. You may have shed negative aspects of yourself to become a better person, but you are still you. All of this prepares us to combine into the single consciousness that will be born again into Ritu's kingdom," Jomira explains.

"Aren't you forgetting the story in the scriptures where a person is in Hase, conscious and desperate to warn ver family of it?" Miya asks.

"Are you not aware that parables often use fiction to teach us something the author believes to be true?" Jomira counters.

"Okay, I see where you are coming from," I say, "but it still feels like a stretch, like you are trying to add to the scriptures. Not to mention, it contradicts the long standing teachings of the ministry."

"Listen, we are all limited and flawed beings. We can't believe we are infallible in our ability to distinguish what is from Ritu and what is the fabrication of a malicious person or spirit. The teachings of the ministry leave room for vemoization, hate, fear, and corruption. They allow people like Sargent Makali to get away with murder and rape. We all add our interpretations of scripture to our understanding of it. While my understanding may be wrong, I am actively seeking to learn where I am wrong. In my search, it has become clear to me that many of the ways the ministry interprets and applies the scriptures are harmful. So, until Ritu corrects me, I reject those interpretations," Jomira explains.

"No, you listen!" I demand, "Sure, there are problems within the ministry, but that's no excuse to abandon it and create your own religion! Besides, what exactly are you asking us to do? Break someone out of prison based on the assumption that they were arrested just because they blasphemed and not for any other reason? The money goes to the ministry, and we will either deliver it to the victim if we can, or the ministry will use it in the best possible way."

Silence fills the air, and I notice that those who were grieving have moved to Zi's side. Tai is looking at me and holding the plank of wood as if anticipating that I might try to take a shot.

"Wake Zi," Jomira commands.

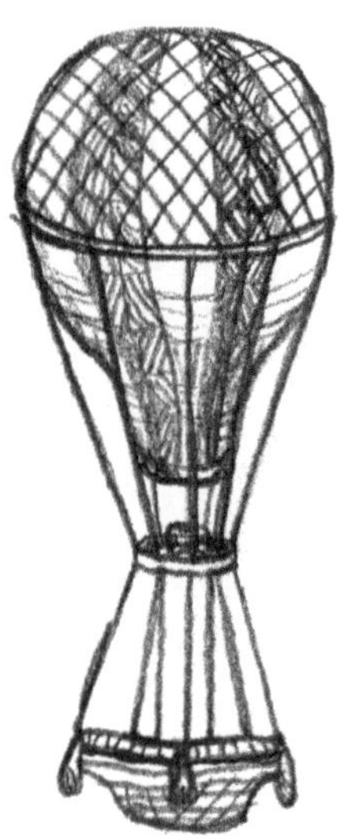

Chapter 9: Processing

Adrenaline surges through my body. If Hari wakes Zi, I'll be completely overpowered. I quickly shoot a dart. Tai appears to block it but must have missed because Hari collapses to the ground. There is a momentary sense of relief, but suddenly Zi continues ver furious yell from before. Ve sits up aggressively, assessing the situation. Despite ver distress and obvious anger, Zi's movements quickly become controlled.

"Zi, we only have one enemy left before we can leave this island," Jomira informs as ve rushes to Zi's side.

"Miya, get us out of here!" I command.

"I can't! The damage to my wing is preventing me from getting us off this rock." Miya responds, burdening me with fear.

"Listen," I say as I toss my gun and bag aside, and raise my hands, "I know when we've been defeated, and I don't want to be left on this island, possibly injured or unconscious, with a group of hostiles who are involved in murder and rape and have a grudge against us. I understand that you don't trust us and don't want to take us along. So..." I hesitate, as I detest suggesting this, "perhaps you could tie us up and drop us off somewhere safe?"

"Are you sure about this?" Miya whispers to me.

"What other choice do we have? Besides, I'd rather take our chances with them than with the officers," I whisper back.

"They are the reason we're getting out of this situation alive," Tai interjects. "It wouldn't be right to leave them with these goons."

A moment of contemplation passes before Jomira speaks up again, "We will do as you've requested. Zi, I know you're in great distress right now-"

"My grief can wait until we're in the air. I'll restrain them." Zi says.

"If it helps..." I meekly add, and Zi glares at me. I gesture toward the sergeant, "That one no longer has genitals and cannot use their legs."

Zi's glare shifts to the sergeant, and rage emanates from ver face. "You really believe you did something, don't you?" Zi looks at me. "If you weren't here threatening to report me as a murderer, making all of our lives that much more difficult, I wouldn't hesitate to kill this scum. Ve will most likely harm more people because of you, and I despise you for that."

Zi stares fiercely into my eyes, allowing those words to sink in for a moment.

"You say that as if I haven't done anything." I say.

"You haven't. Ve will simply have some mage inflict those injuries on another unfortunate soul. Why do you think they have you report other officers instead of punishing them like everyone else?"

It dawns on me that Zi is referring to the use of trait magic. I hadn't considered how trait magic could undermine Rirmevu punishments.

Even though I've been an officer for a while, I can't recall ever hearing about trait magic or seeing any indication of its existence.

"The ministry would have trained me to combat such magic if they knew I might encounter it in the field," I assert. "And they haven't. So it's clear that trait magic must be uncommon, and the chances of it being used to heal Sergeant Makali seem low."

"Yeah, sure. I hope you're right, for your own sake. But I'm telling you right now, you're wrong, and you better watch your back. Let's keep moving."

As I walk past ver, Zi kicks the sergeant in the head and spits on ver. "That felt good. I only wish we could stick around to hear ver screams of pain when ve wakes up."

Ropes dig into my arms and legs as I sit restrained in the basket of the small emergency air balloon we took from the larger airship due to a lack of enough crew to fly the ship.

Since the moment the ropes first tightened around my arms, a seed of distress has been growing within me, steadily sprouting. Miya is confined to a cage nearby, while Jomira and Zi work on flying the balloon. They occasionally pause to yell in frustration or kick something. It's evident that they haven't had a chance to grieve or process everything that has happened, and the weight of it all is bearing down on them. They also periodically glance over at Miya and me to ensure we are behaving.

Tai sits close by, consumed by grief and whimpering softly. Hari's unconscious body lies next to ver.

At this moment, I pray to Ritu. Why, Ritu? Why must I be tied up again? I have been free from captivity for salaries, so why bring me back here? Is it because I violated protocol? What will these people do to me?

On the surface, they seem to want to help people escape Hosudiha, which might appear commendable if it didn't directly contradict Ritu's will. Ritu's will is for these people to remain in Hosudiha, where they cannot rise above it until they open themselves up to Ritu and receive Ver fruit of virtues. Like Miya said, you cannot just give money or housing to someone who lacks the necessary virtues to maintain and use them responsibly.

There is a distinct possibility that these people are actually slavers who intended to deceive the escapees with false promises of defying Ritu's judgment. If that's the case, what will become of Miya and me? I cannot bear the thought of returning to captivity. I can't!

I start frantically squirming, desperate to break free from my restraints. I need to escape! Perhaps Miya's wing is strong enough to glide us away from these people. There must be a way out!

"Hey!" Zi yells at me. "Calm down, or I will use one of your darts on you!"

"Release me! I want to leave this vessel immediately! Drop us off on an island if you must. I want out of here!"

"Ve is panicking," Jomira observes. "We can't simply abandon them to the elements, especially with the risk of the officers finding them on their ascent. And we can't have ver screams give away our position. How many darts did you manage to find?"

"Don't you dare! Release me this instant!" I shout.

"Please calm down," Miya tries to reason with me.

"Miya, quickly! See if you can reach over and loosen the ropes. Make them loose enough for me to—" Suddenly, Zi stands before me, clutching a dart in ver paw.

"I too was once a captive. I mean, before this sun." Zi says, "But I felt a similar distress when those very ropes bound me. I understand your fear, and I want you to know that I would never wish captivity upon anyone, even someone I despise."

Zi crouches down to my level and continues, "The only reason I can find peace with you being tied up right now is because it was your idea. You have every right to be scared, and you will be coming with us, whether conscious or unconscious. What will it be?"

"You're lying!" I accuse, "I witnessed you being hit in the crotch back there, and you hardly flinched. You've been punished for rape by a Rirmevu, and I—" My accusations are abruptly cut short by a slap across my face.

"You should take a moment to consider the possibilities before accusing me of something so vile. Did it ever occur to you that I might not have been born with a testicle? Not everyone fits neatly into one of the twenty-four more common bitu biological sexes."

I find it hard to believe. There are twenty-four bitu sexes for a reason. It's a sacred and symbolic concept. Ritu wouldn't allow for exceptions to the well-defined categories Ve established, would Ve? Then again, this labor has been full of examples of Ritu defying my expectations.

"Miya, is ve telling the truth?" I ask, aware that a yetu can easily invalidate such a claim.

"To the best of my knowledge, ve is telling the truth," Miya confirms.

"Let's not forget that a testicle can be removed for other reasons too. Not everyone who appears to you to be 'missing something' is the way they are because of some vice or punishment. Sometimes people just are the way they are and there is nothing wrong with that. Everyone thinks the Rirmevu are a brilliant example of Ritu's perfect justice, but they never stop to consider the stigma Rirmevu punishments cast onto all people with disabilities, regardless of if they are guilty or innocent of any crime. I would love for you to sit and think about that for a bit, but we cannot have you giving away our position. So what will it be? Will you remain conscious or unconscious for the duration of the flight?"

Hopelessness and a stifled shame steal my tongue from me and these strikes to my understanding of the world disarm my will to fight them. I slump down into the ropes not sure how to feel, and so feeling numb.

Eventually my mind starts to try to make sense of all of this. In retrospect I guess it was foolish to forget that creation is corrupted. Not everyone is born with all of their fingers or limbs. As an extension of that I guess it's possible for someone to be born with a mixture of sex characteristics from two or more categories such that they do not cleanly fall into only one category. What Zi is saying makes sense. So I must be missing something. Something Ritu has in place to prevent or dissuade people from criminalizing everyone with disabilities.

After thinking about it, I actually do know what is going on. Once a rirmevu punishment is dealt, the person is supposed to be treated as having been washed clean of the transgression. Perhaps the ministry should focus more on that teaching and crack down on those who treat the punished as though they are still dirtied by their transgression.

"I'll leave you be until you give me another reason to use this," Zi says, holding up the dart before pocketing it and returning to work.

Ritu, I pray, what is your plan in all of this? Something about this whole situation, You must certainly be up to something in all of this. Did You use Tai and Jomira to bring me here, to save these criminals as an act of mercy, while also exposing the corruption of regiment four? Perhaps Your will was for me to expose this regiment, but my actions outside the protocol may have jeopardized everything. Now if we were to report the regiment to the proper authorities, we would likely face punishment alongside them.

We have a responsibility to report them, even if it comes at a cost. How many more people will suffer if we don't?

An eye for an eye, a tooth for a tooth. I gaze down at my legs, wiggling my toes. The cost... Do I possess the strength to pay it?

The balloon lands in a small clearing behind an apartment complex on the outskirts of Hosudiha. "This is where we shall part ways," Jomira begins, "But there's a condition. You both must make a vow to Ritu that you will not speak of us or our intentions to anyone. If you can't do that, then we'll have to take you with us and keep you from leaving. We'll be forced to bring you to our homeland, where you can stay and keep our operation a secret."

"We need to report the officers' actions, and we can't do that without mentioning you and your operation. Besides, the officers already know about you. The most we can promise is to keep quiet about your intentions to return the stolen coins to Sho and possibly break ver out of prison. But I can't even make that promise until Miya and I have a chance to discuss it."

Jomira pauses for a moment, then ve says, "We'll give you two some time to talk it over. We have a lot to process as well."

"You will return all of our possessions though. I just want to make sure that is clear." I assert.

"All but your blade." Jomira says.

"What? Why? That blade belonged to my vedi! It is important to me." I shout.

"Such a blade is no one's property." Zi interjects, "Do you have any inkling as to the nature of enchantments?"

"I believe enchantments are just high level magic. Aren't they?" Miya suggests.

"Property magic, it requires the concentration of a consciousness to remain in effect." Hari starts, "Enchantments can only be achieved if you can manipulate the mind of a notu into devoting all of its concentration towards a property you cast onto it. Then you entrap the notu inside of whatever material you wish to enchant with that property."

"Your blade contains a notu slave." Zi simplifies, "That is how the pommel remains hot indefinitely."

I bite my tongue. There is no way they are telling the truth. This story confirms in my mind that they are scoundrels looking to use my blade for something nefarious, like framing me. I need to report this right away. However, I am in no condition to start throwing around accusations. I think the safest thing to do is buy their lies so that they will let me go.

"You don't buy it do you?" Zi says flatly.

Crap, was it that obvious?

"Not at all. The ministry would never let that fly!" Miya exclaims.

Crap Miya, now's not the time!

"I, uh. I don't know what to think about it. Though I will be getting that blade back. Even if I have to hunt you down myself!" I say.

Jomira's crew lets out sighs of resignation.

"I'll do my best to get the blade back to you once the notu is free." Jomira says. Making a promise that feels empty given ver evident lies, "For now, we have much to discuss, much to process... We will be back in a bit."

The others climb off the balloon and approach the backdoor of one of the apartments. They knock and the door seems to be opened from the inside. They enter, leaving Miya and me alone, still bound, in the basket of the balloon. However, Jomira will likely keep ver senses on us to ensure we don't attempt anything.

"That's odd," Miya remarks, "I'm not sensing anyone apart from Jomira's group in the unit they just entered. Must be a notu inside. We'll have to keep that noted. Anyway, I'm sorry about your blade. I know it was special to you."

I give a deep sigh. Anger clashes with sorrow and anxiety within me, "I swear I'm going to make them regret it. Especially if they use it for anything mischievous. Though it's not like there is much we can do about it right now. Apart from reporting it as stolen as soon as possible."

There is a moment's pause before Miya brings us back to the matter at hand, "A vow to Ritu... I've heard stories of people facing terrible fates after breaking such a vow. That seems like a tall order," Miya begins.

"Yeah, but think about it. I doubt Sho is actually in prison. So the risk of a prison break is unlikely. Agreeing to their terms won't cost us much," I reply.

"But what if Sho is in prison? We could end up being accomplices in a prison break," Miya says.

"Either we take that risk or we let the officers escape and have the chance to repeat their actions," I say.

We both pause, contemplating the situation. The sounds of grief emanating from the apartment resemble the cries of tortured souls. It feels as if these people have already paid a heavy enough price for their transgressions. However, I refrain from voicing that sentiment. Whether the price has been paid or not is Ritu's decision, not mine.

"Fine," Miya concedes. "Let's do it... So what now? Do we call them back out here?"

Another anguished cry pierces the air.

"I think we can wait..." I say.

Chapter 10: Agents of Ribe

It's a different room than our usual debriefing space, smaller, windowless, and uncomfortably warm due to the lantern providing the only light. Miya is absent when ve would normally be present.

I have just finished recounting the entire story, carefully omitting the parts I vowed to keep secret. The minister sitting across from me diligently took notes of every word I said. Ve wears a sharp light-gray suit with the ministry's distinctive purple slotted seams, adorned with a gold metal circle horizontally bisected by a shut golden eye. The uniform of ministers who do the grunt work pertaining to vetu resources, public relations, and magic support.

The room feels suffocating, and sweat trickles down my face.

"You reported that they took your rirmevu blade correct?" The minister asks.

"Correct." I try to maintain professional composure as I affirm that it was stolen. However, the pressure of the room along with the emotional weight of having lost something as sentimental as my late vedi's rirmevu blade, makes distress seep from my face.

"Are you alright?" Ve asks.

"Yeah. It's just... The blade was my vedi's" I reply. Embarrassed that my emotional vulnerability had been acknowledged, though also appreciative of the compassion.

"I see... did they give you any indication as to why they took the blade and nothing else?"

"They came up with some absurd excuse, but I worry that they plan to use it to frame me for something."

"Hmm... What was the absurd excuse?"

Fearing I might notice a confirming facial response to what I am about to say, I look away, "They tried to claim that the ministry uses enslaved notu to enchant items. As if that would ever happen." I say and then laugh a bit at the absurdity of it. I risk a glance at the minister and ve looks more disturbed than amused.

"It's sick, the sort of things these fose will come up with to tarnish Ritu's reputation." Ve says.

"Yeah," I say, feeling validated by the minister's disgust.

"Alright, let me just finish off my notes here."

I'm relieved to have finished my report because I desperately need some fresh air.

"Okay, to ensure I have all the details correct, I'm going to need you to retell specific parts of your story," the minister explains.

"You must be joking," I say, the words practically falling out of my mouth. "Why are we stuck in this room? Can't we discuss this elsewhere?"

"Dima, I need your cooperation. I promise we would choose a different location if it were possible. Unfortunately, this is the only available space. Now, please tell me about the first enemy."

"Very well, I was perched on a ridge, and there was..." My thoughts abruptly shift, overwhelmed by resentment toward my fellow officers. Those damn fose. They go and break up my family for no Ritu damn reason and somehow it's my fault I ended up here? What sort of monsters would just decide to ruin someone's life like that?

"Dima?" the minister interrupts my train of thought. "Tell me about what you saw from the ridge."

"There was... I think... The heat is getting to me. I can't remember. But you wrote it down, right? Could you read it back to me? Maybe it will jog my memory?"

"Hmm... Perhaps we can come back to that later. Tell me about the two individuals who investigated the loud noise."

"Right, those two came to check the noise, and they were..." Even if I am to blame, how did I not prove myself? I served my sentence, tirelessly worked two jobs during the labor, and in the evenings I was in the food kitchen earning my stay at the ministry.

I did everything I could and none of it was enough. What is it with this city? Why does everything cost money? We didn't have to pay to use the toilet in Sudihatosema, did we? Food and water weren't so expensive either!

"Tell me about the conflict that occurred after Miya disobeyed orders."

"We... um... We took flight and spotted a..." What are these thoughts? Who is that person? All I see is darkness, but why do I remember someone in front of me? Are these my thoughts? Am I losing my mind?

Those thoughts were the first ones to cross my mind that almost made sense. "I really need some water or something. Something isn't right with my head." I say.

"We're almost done here, Dima. Tell me about the spear."

"Right, um, there was a spear held by..." Suddenly, a bright light blinds my vision. Someone grabs hold of me. What's happening? Where are they taking me? Then, just as abruptly, I find myself back in the dim room, sitting in front of the minister as if nothing occurred.

"By... um..." I try to continue.

"Now tell me about the person who assaulted the vetu trafficker."

"Yeah... ve..." I hesitate, fearing that my memory will fail me again. The minister's relief is evident in response to my hesitation. What is happening here? I don't voice it, but this time the memory remains. Ve was Sergeant Makali from regiment four. Miya detected that ve was guilty of murder and rape.

The relief on the minister's face quickly turns into confusion as stern voices from outside struggle to penetrate the thick door followed by a frantic knock.

The minister's confusion gives way to panic at the sound of a short-lived struggle. Ve quickly moves to attempt to barricade the door with ver chair but as ve approaches the door it swings violently open, knocking the chair aside and throwing the minister off balance.

Zi's imposing figure fills the doorway, and ve swiftly overpowers the surprised minister. Zi's presence was intimidating even when ve had minimal clothing. Now donning leather armor that accentuates ver muscular figure and feminine curves, Zi exudes an aura that instills fear, making me dread the possibility of having to confront ver.

Zi looks at me, not with the gaze of a predator eyeing its prey, which somewhat eases my fear, but ver expression clearly indicates ver lack of enthusiasm to see me. "Jomira and Hari informed me that they were using mind magic to cleanse your brain. There was a mage hiding in a nearby room with Sho, strategically manipulating and swapping your memories through a small hole in the wall behind you." Zi explains in a flat tone.

Hari peeks ver head from around the corner, saying, "We wanted to give you the chance to escape."

Trait magic, mind magic... How many different kinds of magic exist? Why wasn't I taught about their existence, considering the possibility of encountering those who use them? The ministry is clearly aware of such things, so they could have informed me. And now they're attempting to erase my memories. What of? The last thing ve inquired about was the sergeant. Did they want me to forget about ver crimes? What else have I forgotten? On top of all of that, Jomira was right, the corruption runs deeper than I initially believed, deeper than I was willing to accept. If I'm not safe reporting to this level of authority, would it be safe to report to someone even higher up?

Wait. If this is what they're doing to me, what are they doing to Miya?

"Where is Miya?" I shout.

"I'm sorry, we don't know," Hari replies.

Fear and concern grip me. What are they doing to my friend's mind?

"We need to find ver!" I say.

Jomira lands on Zi's shoulder and says, "Unfortunately, ve isn't held in this facility. Dealing with the senses of a yetu requires more cunning."

"Where is ve?" I plead.

"Hari was telling the truth—we genuinely don't know," Jomira states, allowing ver words to linger. "Come with us, and we'll do our best to locate your friend and save ver if possible."

Zi appears somewhat annoyed by the offer. "Alright, I found the words to express what I need to say. Can we really trust ver now? Yes, ve knows about the corruption in regiments four and two, but ve likely still believes there's a level of authority ve can rely on. It's not as if ve suddenly sides with us."

"Ve might not," Jomira acknowledges, "but for now, we share a common enemy, and ver need is great. We've all been in ver position before, and even if we part ways after saving ver friend, we'll provide assistance."

"No!" I retort, "I see through your intentions. Ribe has these regiments posing as disciples of Ritu, using them to tarnish Ritu and the ministry in my mind. Meanwhile, Ribe is using all of you to trap me in a situation where I feel indebted to ver. Well, I didn't ask your boss to save me from verself! I owe you nothing! Step aside, agents of Ribe! I will find Miya with Ritu's aid, not yours!"

A cool breeze enters the room, momentarily dissipating the mental fog induced by the heat. Suddenly, I realize that revealing my awareness of their true motives puts me in a dangerous position. The tinge of cold manifests as fear, settling deep within my bones. I'm such a fool—I should have agreed to work with them and then found a way to escape while they weren't looking!

"Ver brain is too broken to be helped," Zi says.

"Very well," Jomira concedes, "but by your commitment to Ritu, you must come with us, at least for now."

"I don't have to do anything." I argue.

"You possess memories and thoughts that don't belong to you. They were stolen, and while you're not the one who took them, you're responsible for returning them based on your commitment to Ritu and

Ver teachings. Now, come along. We don't have much time." With that, the team exits through the doorway.

I don't want to believe them. The memory slips must have been the heat, playing tricks on my mind.

I dare to peer over my shoulder to see the hole the mage supposedly used to channel a spell onto me. There it is. A hole that has no business being in the wall of a room where sensitive information is shared.

I stagger after the group, and as I round the corner, my skepticism regarding the brainwashing story takes another serious blow as I witness Sho following at the back of the group. Ver appearance is far healthier than it was wages ago at the tavern, and I can't help but suspect that Hari's magic played a role in ver sudden health.

I no longer feel safe in this place. I need to escape. Ribe has trapped me through dependency and my sense of duty. The cunning manipulator. Ritu, please free me from this entanglement as soon as possible.

Wait, I only need to inform Sho about what I know. Once I do that, I can just trust that Ritu will guide me out of this predicament. I shouldn't rely on Ribe. Under no circumstances can I depend on Ribe. There must be another way forward.

"Wait," I call out to them.

"There's no time to wait," Jomira retorts.

"Yes, there is. Sho, you resent law enforcement because you bought into the lie that your vedi got arrested for no reason." Hatred consumes Sho's face, but someone has to tell ver how it is, so I continue, "You believe that you've worked hard enough to earn exaltation, but exaltation is not earned through the virtue of hard work alone, and that is why Ritu hasn't exalted you, because Ve knows better than you." I say.

"You mud-eating worm!" Sho yells, lunging towards me. Hari and Zi attempt to intervene, but they're too slow. Sho throws a punch, and I swiftly dodge it. When ve tries to tackle me, I strike ver face with my elbow.

Ve crumples to the ground, clutching ver face with both hands. "Gah! Rrrr! You have no idea!" Ve staggers back up onto ver feet. "I hope you have to experience the hopelessness of surviving in those slums some labor." Ve then spits at me, sends a daring glare into my eyes, and walks away.

I can't blame ver for being angered by the truth. They genuinely believe they're doing what's right. I despise Ribe for deceiving them all, including the officers. Surely, they could see through the facade if they truly wanted to. Perhaps they're unwilling to face the reality of their situation, and for that, they'll face judgment.

Sho pauses, glancing over ver shoulder at me. "They were all officers. I hope the memories they stole from you hurt to get back."

Although I suspected it, hearing it confirmed by Sho sends a wave of fear through me. How deeply entangled in Ribe's lies are these regiments?

I mustn't burden my mind with Ribe's mischief right now. Escaping is the priority. I turn my back on Jomira's crew and walk in the opposite direction.

How am I going to get out of here undetected? Jomira's crew have Jomira's senses to guide them out of here... Perhaps Ritu will guide me out. I won't rely on Ribe just because it feels safer than relying on Ritu. Perhaps I can simply walk out unnoticed. If I pretend that the brainwashing was successful, they should let me go, right? Maybe this situation isn't as hopeless as it seems.

Suddenly, a chill runs through me. This escape shouldn't be possible. There should be some of the regiment's yetu monitoring this facility... Jomira must be aware of that. Ve must have taken care of it somehow. I recall Miya mentioning a notu in the apartment earlier. Being inorganic and thus difficult for a yetu to perceive, the notu must be working with Jomira to neutralize the yetu surveillance. I'll need to report this when I find someone I can trust.

However, there are other problems to consider. If I walk out freely, the ministers behind me will expose me once they regain consciousness.

I pause to contemplate.

Each of the ministers is likely to be placed on leave due to their head injuries. If I go back, fake a head injury, and pretend that the brainwashing was successful, claiming that I too was knocked out, I might be able to walk away without suspicion...

Suddenly a disturbing thought crosses my mind. What else might they do to me if I return to their custody?

I pause to contemplate for a moment. If they had intended to dispose of me, all this mind-wiping would have been pointless.

I begin walking back to the room I was in. The others have already moved out of sight.

Another troubling thought comes to bear. What might they do to me if they believe they can simply wipe my memories away?

The possibilities crawl beneath my skin, causing me to clench my jaw and fists as the unsettling feeling passes through me.

I imagine if they had plans to harm me, they would have done it before the debriefing. But what might they have already done? I quickly search my mind for any similar experiences of strange thoughts intruding on my mind.

Only one comes to mind—the encounter I had with the stranger on the labor the ministry saved me from Lise. My eyes widen. Who was that stranger, and what memories did ve take from me?

Hari. Hari must know something! Ve suggested things happened differently than I remember and ve knew about mind magic.

I turn around with hopes of catching Hari before ve leaves. Though the hallway behind me is now empty.

I run through it to where it intersects with another hallway that I look down. Nothing.

I run to the next intersecting hall. Still nothing, though I can see a door has been kicked in. That is likely where Sho was being kept. Where in the skies did they go?

Perhaps those holes in my memory ought to be a concern for another time.

For now, I cannot recall any other instance of mind magic being performed on me. So perhaps this is the first time this regiment has tampered with my mind. That might suggest that they don't employ these measures haphazardly.

If I walk out, I'll be hunted down. If I stay, they might attempt further mind-wiping. But now that I know their methods, maybe I can defend against it by feeding them random thoughts and pretending to forget.

Then they might release me, possibly placing me on leave for a head injury, and I could reunite with Miya, who will likely be on leave due to ver wing injury.

It's a risk, but I believe staying, pretending to be knocked out, and claiming the brainwashing was successful might be my best option. However, now I have to gather my courage and fight my fear of captivity.

I take a deep breath and assure myself, "I am not a captive. I have a battle ahead of me, and if I make a mistake, then I may become a captive. But I won't let that happen."

"I, and the minister debriefing me apparently, sustained the least concerning head injuries compared to everyone else. They believe I may have passed out for some other reason. It seems to be a common occurrence in those smaller debriefing rooms," I inform Miya.

What I can't share with Miya is that, considering the beating the minister took from Zi, I suspect the debriefing minister was healed using trait magic.

I think ve knew about trait magic, but the guards at the door were unaware. That allowed ver to be quickly healed while the others had to receive more traditional forms of care.

Based on the questions the minister asked me during our later debriefing, it appears that my knowledge of trait magic was one of the things they intended to wipe from my memory.

Fortunately, I was able to defend myself against further mind-wiping as I had planned. This time they replaced my decoy thoughts with the thoughts of someone who was filled with fear and confusion. I don't think the other person knew whose custody they were in.

The whole concept makes me feel sick... Though not as sick as the last thing they tried to wipe from my mind...

Is there really a notu in every enchanted object?

Miya lies in a cot next to mine, ver wing bandaged. "That sounds terrifying. I'm glad you're okay. I wonder why they didn't have us together? I could have alerted them. What about the other yetu who were supposed to be monitoring the facility? Why didn't they notify everyone?"

"They were found unconscious, struck by darts. They suspect the attackers had a notu working with them." I say.

"Interesting... So the attackers had resources. I wonder if they were part of an organized crime ring." Miya says

"Miya, something strange happened during the debriefing, actually, a lot of strange things. But this one stood out. They had me repeat my story, but I kept forgetting details, and even now I can't recall some of them."

"A similar thing happened to me! It was bizarre. But after a short break, they read the notes back to me and helped me remember what I had said the first time."

"They did? What do you remember?"I ask.

"They didn't do that with you?" Miya asks, "Perhaps they forgot that step amidst all the commotion. Anyway, while pursuing a thief, I detected a conflict between some vetu traffickers and other enemies. Unaware of the trafficking issue, we decided to help the traffickers as they seemed to be the victims in that situation. We saved some of the victims, only for them to turn on us and take us prisoner. I think they let us go once they realized we were officers because they didn't want to draw too much attention to their operation from law enforcement."

"Oh... I see." I say.

"What? Do you remember something different?"

"No... That makes sense." I choose to withhold what I know until we're somewhere more private. Currently, we lie in a room below the deck of a Ministry airship, and there could be listening ears around.

As we gain altitude, the air becomes noticeably cleaner and less stagnant. My head feels light from both the climb in altitude and my frequent deep inhalations of the fresh air coming through the open porthole.

Through the opening, I observe as we ascend past Riberha, the second-largest wormwood island in the nation of Rirze. A column of crystal clear mist and water pours into it, while columns of black water flow out of it, descending into Hosudiha below.

Every time I see Riberha, a conflict stirs within me. It's difficult to believe that anyone deserves to live in Hosudiha.

Sho's thoughts echo through my mind. Ver situation feels unjust, ve worked two jobs during the light, volunteered at the food kitchen in the evening, and ve still wasn't worthy of exaltation.

Ritu's judgment must be just. Sho must have done all of that to credit verself with ver exaltation. Ve must have been motivated by pride or some other vice.

At any rate, if ve had ever truly received Ritu into ver heart Sho wouldn't have rejected Ver. So it makes sense then. Sho was never really receptive to Ritu, the virtues ve managed to exhibit were short lived and motivated by selfish intent.

"I can't wait to visit a spa once we return to Sudihatosema," Miya says, "This leave was long overdue."

"Yeah... I hope it lasts," I reply.

"Well, the doc says my wing will take at least a quarter-deposit to fully recover. I imagine we'll be able to get some real rest during that time. Might even get bored, honestly."

Miya and I stand on the deck of the ship, watching as we ascend above Sudihatosema. I'm dressed in a cream-colored jacket which exaggerates masculine features ever so slightly, and green pleated trousers with a floral pattern I embroidered near the cuffs of the pant legs. Miya wears a small, green, mesh cloak draped over ver wings, adorned with a matching floral pattern to mine. Two decorative, green-beaded, wing rings I made for ver to hang from ver pierced inner wings. We have a small wagon to carry all of our luggage.

We are ready to simply exist in civilian life for a while.

As our ship crests the mountains that shield the city of Sudihatosema from the dawnward winds, we behold the city's beauty.

Well-crafted buildings with thatch roofs and plaster walls form radial rows surrounding a large lake at the city's center. The lake is fed by sun-lit columns of mist and water, cascading from the island above where the next city, Rirbuseha, is nestled.

Rirbuseha is considered the most breathtaking city in Rirze, and some claim it's among the most stunning in the entire Shattered Skies. While everyone I know in Sudihatosema dreams of being exalted to there some labor, my feelings about Rirbuseha fluctuate.

Sometimes I long to return there when life gets tough, and other times, when I'm invigorated by Ritu's life bringing work, I never want to lay eyes on it again. I cannot imagine how boring it would be to just resign myself to a life of paperwork.

Granted, the sort of paperwork they do up there is what keeps all of Rirze in working order. They have a certain level of power over society, and I am convinced that wielding that sort of power would be boring.

The ship docks at a ministry base port teaming with perhaps fifty ministry class airships of varying shapes and sizes. Something about witnessing the military might of the ministry makes me feel a tad safer here.

Chapter 11: Duty

"Alright, let's just open the door, toss the bags in, and get to the spa. We can worry about unpacking later," Miya plans aloud as we approach the front door of our home.

However, I ignore Miya's plan and wordlessly enter the house.

"Uh, okay, I guess we can unpack first if you really want to. I just want to get there while it's still early in the morning. You know, beat any lines," Miya expresses.

"I need to talk with you about something," I say.

"I knew this was coming. Before you blow up, I am sorry I almost marooned you. That was a strict violation of-"

"It's not that. It's nothing about what you did. Though we really should talk about that too at some point."

"Okay... What do you want to talk about then?"

"Let me check something first."

Miya probably would have alerted me to anyone in our house, but I want to make sure there are no notu hiding around. Trouble is, notu can be as small as my hand. They make great spies, only requiring sun exposure every deposit or two and sometimes water for their body, but never needing to eat, drink, or poop. They aren't easily detected by yetu and can hide in a shadow for labors, listening.

There are two small bedrooms, a bathroom, and the living space.

I resent myself for the state of my room. It's either I keep my room spotless as my parents drilled me to do, or I do only the bare minimum to keep the floors and bed clear enough to be used. My brain cannot be content with half clean, and I don't have time to clean to the degree that was drilled into me growing up and in rirmevu training, so unfolded clothes fill chairs and baskets more so than drawers and the wardrobe. The lines between clean, dirty, and worn but not yet dirty are only discernible by me.

I dig and dig until I am just the right amount of exhausted and satisfied that there are no notu in my room. Though by the end of it, those divisions of clothing cleanliness have become indistinguishable even to me. Making me dred the labor of sorting this out later.

I move on to Miya's room.

"What are you looking for?" Miya asks.

"I have something that I need to bring with us. A gift for one of the masseuses."

"Oh! I thought you might have eyes for someone there," Miya teases.

"Shut up," I say light-heartedly. Though Miya seems to abruptly fall silent.

"I'm just playing with you. I don't actually want you to shut up." I say.

"Oh, okay. Thanks. Yeah, I wasn't sure how to take that. Wait, why would it be in my room?" Miya asks.

"Well, it wasn't in my room. I may have thought to store it in your room since it is more organized."

"Okay... Next time please ask first. Also, don't expect me to say yes too much. I don't need my room becoming just an extension of yours."

"Yeah, sorry. I'll ask from now on."

"Well... I would help you look if I could... How long are you going to look?"

"Until I find it."

"Okay... Uh, what did you get ver anyway?" Miya asks as ve impatiently pokes at a knot in ver web.

"A doll," I say.

"Odd gift, though I collect the cooler feeling sponges I get from some tea shops, so who am I to judge?"

Yetu are notorious for keeping well-organized living spaces. Given that they are nearly blind to non-living materials, it's essential that everything has a place. Miya's room has a web of woven ropes drooping shallowly from the ceiling, allowing me and those vetu of more average heights to walk cleanly beneath it. The design of the web is such that Miya can know where ve is at any given time just from touching the pattern of the weave.

There are rows of shelves against one wall, lined with yetu drinking sponges, each with a tea shop's logo stamped into it, alongside a braille logo carved into the material. The essence of tea remaining on the sponges gives the air a very pleasant tea-shop-like scent. On the opposite wall, there are a handful of clothing items I helped to arrange by color, style, and matching wing ornaments. Many of Miya's articles have my artistic touch in the form of embroidery or having been made by me outright. In the center of the web is Miya's nest made of a variety of soft materials woven together. There aren't many places to hide in here, so I quickly move on to the rest of the house.

Miya's web neatly and decoratively spills from ver bedroom into the hallway and from there into the rest of the house, granting ver access to each amenity. Spots where Miya can perch and rest are also speckled throughout the weave.

Meanwhile, in my underworld, various bits and pieces from unfinished or abandoned crafts litter the floor, couch, table, chairs, and counters. Most of the components consist of thread, yarn, beads, and wire. Some labor I'll have time to complete all of these crafts. Though maybe not. I have no idea what the future holds, especially not after the crap I pulled on the cliffs.

I look just about everywhere I can think of, but I feel the need to do a second sweep. What if it ran to a spot I cleared while I wasn't looking?

"Okay, I think you've looked just about everywhere. I'm afraid to tell you, but I think it may be lost," Miya says.

"I'm just going to call it good. It's confession time. There is no doll-"

"What were you wasting time looking for then? Wait. Does this mean you don't actually have a crush on the masseuse?" Miya asks.

"No, I do. I... I just... later. I was looking for notu." I say.

"Notu? What are you about to tell me?" Miya asks.

"I lied about not remembering anything different from the craziness of the other labor because I wasn't sure if there were ears keeping tabs on us. I'm still a bit worried they could be listening in, actually." I say.

"I understand. I'm listening if you feel like this is a safe place to talk." Miya says.

"Not sure where would be better. Okay, so. The hostiles who attacked the traffickers. They were no ordinary enemies; they were law enforcement officers from regiment four." I say.

"You're joking? Why didn't you tell me that while we were fighting them at the time?" Miya asks.

"I did! Here's the other thing. You know how Hari could use trait magic?" I ask.

"Trait magic?"

"Shoot. That's right, they wiped that from your memory too." I say.

"Wiped from my memory? What are you suggesting?"

"I'm not suggesting anything!" I explain everything about the debriefing and Sho's part in it, "Then Zi came and knocked out every one of the guards. I imagine ve was being aided by property magic from Hari. Anyway, they told me about mind magic and how it was being used to sanitize my mind-"

"And you just believed them? Dima, they are criminals!"

"Do you remember the enemy leader wearing a sergeant's uniform? I do! We disposed of it to cover up for my having punished ver. If they were all just civilians, wouldn't they all have been punished by us? If so, how did we get to Zi so quickly? Also, I know you can't see it, but in my notebook, I might have handed over the page with officer ID numbers, but I can still see the numbers imprinted on the next page. I know they were telling the truth, Miya!"

"Okay, okay. I believe you. But didn't they do a follow-up debriefing with you? Wouldn't they have just finished the mind wiping then?" Miya asks.

"I found out that if I thought of something random instead of thinking about the answer to their question, they would take the decoy thought and not the one they wanted. Afterward, I just played along as though I had forgotten. Which is good for you to know on the off chance we find our minds under attack again." I say.

"What are we going to do? We need to tell someone! But how do we know who we can trust at this point?" Miya asks.

"I don't know. I want to go to a Sudihatosema justice facility and have another debriefing. I can't imagine the corruption reaching this high into the skies."

"It's a risk." Miya says.

"I know, but it's one we have to take. At least we know what to do if they try to pull us into more dark rooms."

"Darn it. Could we maybe go to the spa first and then do it after?" Miya asks.

"I wish. But every moment we're not working to stop them is a moment they could be murdering, raping, and brainwashing more people."

Thank Ritu, this debriefing room looks normal, filled with sunlight and comfortable cushioned chairs. I'm relieved that Miya and I can debrief together, as we usually do. It makes me feel safer as I lay out everything I know about the corruption of regiments two and four of Hosudiha.

"Thank you for reporting this information to me, Dima, Miya," responds Minister Duzemi after hearing our whole story. Duzemi wears a uniform similar to the last officer who debriefed me, but ver uniform is more decorated with medals and rank. Ver experience is evident in ver face, worn down by expertly masked stress, "If what you are saying is true, you are right. The actions of regiments two and four are in clear violation of several protocols. Also, it would seem that you both have come upon classified information regarding the magical arts."

Duzemi knocks on the door of the room, and it opens. "Send minister Guhi and minister Jitu to rooms 3Ku and 2Ku," Duzemi says to the one who answered the knock. The door shuts, and ver attention returns to us. For some reason the family name Jitu rings a bell, but I am having a hard time remembering where I know it from.

Duzemi continues, "The use of trait magic and mind magic is strictly forbidden to the public and lower ranks, as, unlike property magic, it is outright theft. We try to keep knowledge of such magic out of the public sphere because while very few are so skilled and knowledgeable as to practice forbidden magic, once people know about it, there will be those who try to learn how to use and abuse it. Do you understand?"

"I understand," Miya responds.

I nod.

"As for ministry members," Duzemi continues, "such information is held only by high-ranking officials. Though sometimes officers and ministers stumble upon such information when dealing with foreigners as you have, and it would seem that Dima has figured out how we combat mind magic to a degree."

I might take pride if I had figured it out on my own. However, it was Zi who filled me in on what was happening. As Jomira and ver crew come to mind I feel the need to share about them. Maybe it would be worth the suffering that comes from breaking a vow made under Ritu. Or perhaps it's fine if Miya and I keep this information to ourselves so long as we do something about it later... I'll spill if that proves impossible.

"We have higher-ranking mages who practice forbidden magic ethically. Given that you have not yet been exalted to a rank where you will have access to such knowledge, it is your duty to surrender your memories of trait magic and mind magic to us. A mage will transfer the information out of you and into me so that I can confirm you did not try to pass over decoy information. Not that you would, it's just protocol. We will also need to search all of your belongings and investigate anyone whom you have had contact with. We will start now."

My skin begins to crawl. Everything Duzemi said makes perfect sense, but my experience with mind magic has made me feel distrustful.

The floral perfumes filling the air delight my nostrils, and my body revels in the skilled hands of the cute masseuse who rubs my back. I haven't felt this relaxed for deposits. In spite of how relaxing this environment feels, my hands busily attempt to knit my troubled thoughts into some, yet unknown, article of clothing just over the corner of the bed. Knitting doesn't completely block out my thoughts, it mostly breaks them up as occasionally I need to pause my thoughts to evaluate my work, this makes my thoughts easier to process and less likely to pull me into a negative spiral.

That debriefing was unnecessarily long. I don't understand why they needed to take us into another one of those dark rooms, and they asked me so many questions I cannot even remember most of them. But honestly, who cares? I did my duty. I told them about the corruption of Regiment Four, and now it is in their hands to deliver justice.

Miya lies on a nearby bed, ver joints gently pulled and bent, the equivalent of a massage for an exoskeletal creature, performed by a yetu masseuse.

I have heard Miya describe ver masseuse as handsome on more than one occasion. So I guess you could say we both have our spa crushes. Honestly, who wouldn't want to land a masseuse as an intimate partner? However, neither of us has ever tried to pursue a romantic relationship with them. I don't know Miya's reasons, but for me, I prefer to build relationships based on shared interests and genuine connections rather than just physical attraction. I believe those sorts of deeper bonds have a better chance of flourishing, so I'm not inclined to pursue a relationship with the sole intention of it becoming intimate eventually. Besides, in this line of work, I imagine Sodi and Kize have enough flirts to put up with, so I'd rather be an easygoing customer they can feel comfortable around.

"So, what happened to your wing?" Miya's masseuse, Kize, asks curiously. Kize's fur-like scales are mostly a light brown with a few spots of off-white that gradually transition into yellow.

"We've had a crazy quarter-deposit," Miya replies.

"Anything you can share?" Kize inquires further.

"Unfortunately, not really," Miya responds with a sigh.

"Typical. It's hard to get any good gossip working on a ministry base, but with how often they investigate us, you would think it's easy," Kize remarks with a chuckle.

"Whatever it was, it obviously made you pretty tense," my masseuse, Sodi, a pale skinned atu, observes as ve digs into a particularly troublesome knot on my back. I try not to tense up, but it's a tender spot.

I'm about two-thirds as tall as Sodi, and ve has a solid heavier build that complements ver curves. Some may assume ver to be unhealthy, but ve is surprisingly strong and fit, as evident each time ver capable hands work on my stress-ridden back.

Sodi has a few awards from fitness events displayed modestly around the spa. Whenever someone makes a rude comment about ver weight, ve makes sure to point out that all the awards belong to ver.

"It certainly made us more than a little tense," Miya adds, "Fortunately, we should be in the clear now and will probably return to work in about a quarter-deposit."

I wish they hadn't brought up work. My knitting intensifies incrementally as my mind starts to flood with worries. What if they can't incriminate the sergeant? What if there isn't enough evidence to stop them? I was wearing a mask at the time, but what if someone from Regiment Two tells Makali who I am? I have no reason to distrust Regiment Two, but Jomira's words about the depth of the corruption haunt me.

Maybe I'm just getting paranoid. Why can't I just relax? Why can't all my worries wait until tomorrow?

But what if I don't have until tomorrow? What if they come for me?

If I'm with Miya, ve should be able to warn me if they come for me, but I'll have to stay on guard.

Bit by bit, I reason myself into relaxation, to the point where my worries start to fade away as quickly as they come. For a moment, everything feels blissful and my busy hands actually manage to find some rest as well.

Hot rocks are laid on my back, and Miya is wrapped in a warm towel before we are left alone for a moment.

"I'll be honest, I didn't expect to be able to relax," I express.

"Yeah, same. This was much-needed," Miya agrees.

As our appointment comes to an end, it feels like I might actually leave here feeling refreshed. Kize and Sodi return to remove the rocks and towel when suddenly, all of my worries and thoughts come rushing back to me.

Crap.

Chapter 12: Broken

In yet another attempt to ease our anxieties, Miya rides on my back as we stroll alongside one of the many waterways that cut through Sudihatosema, carrying water from the central lake to the island's edges. The air is filled with the enticing aroma of freshly baked goods. Families meander between shops, and children gleefully run around, laughing and skipping stones.

It's a refreshing change to stretch our legs and breathe in the fresh air as we make our way to witness the splendor of the four sanctuaries. I purposely refrain from visiting the site too frequently to preserve its magical allure. Overexposure can easily transform beauty into mundanity. Considering all of the time we've spent in Hosudiha, the contrast is bound to intensify the otherworldly effect of experiencing such a sacred space.

"What if they can't prove their wrongdoing? What if they want to... punish us?" I ask.

"How would they know it was us? You were wearing a mask, right?" Miya counters.

"Yeah... I'm not sure. Somehow, I have this feeling that my identity could be exposed. And perhaps they remember the pattern on your wings."

"Unlikely. It's not bright enough down there for anyone to discern the patterns on my wings," Miya reassures.

"You're right. Maybe I just need to take it easy."

"Here's the plan," Miya says, "I'll keep my senses alert for any familiar biosignatures, and you keep an eye out for recognizable faces. We'll only start worrying if we have a valid reason."

"Okay... but the worst part is that I can't remember any faces," I say, "Maybe it was too dark. However, I do remember the sergeant's face. I'm just not sure what to look for."

"Hmm... I mean, I can't exactly visualize their biosignatures either, but I rarely forget someone as important as them. I'm confident we'll recognize them if we sense their presence."

Miya struggling to recall a biosignature is unusual. When did ve ever have difficulty remembering someone? Suddenly, every unfamiliar face fills me with a sense of unease.

We approach an exquisite stone archway adorned with stained-glass windows stretching over top of the arch and emanating colorful light.

On the far left of the window, the glass art portrays representatives from each vetu race—a yetu, a notu, an atu, and a bitu—gathered around a perfectly circular ring of fire. The scene is brimming with color and vitality. However, as one's gaze shifts to the right, black shards of glass begin to seep into the scene. The same figures that were once near the circle of fire now seem to retreat into the shadows. Leading the group of vetu is a bitu. This is why even the most highly exalted pale-furred bitu can still get crap from some people belonging to certain denominations of Ritufani.

Further to the right, more black glass emerges, and even though the circle of fire is distant now, the vetu shield their eyes and bodies from it, as if the mere existence of the thing that once brought them life now causes immense pain. Continuing to the right, the fire becomes a mere speck, and the vetu have turned against each other. Amidst the fighting figures, ghostly monsters appear, mirroring the hostile postures of the vetu. It's as if they no longer see each other as vetu but rather as these monstrous apparitions.

At the farthest right is a close up of Ritu surrounded by darkness, about to make Ver next move.

We pass beneath the grand archway, and the world opens up into an expansive outdoor space. Rows upon rows of white marble pews face a magnificent stage, adorned with marble sculptures of joyful vetu rising and forming an arch overhead. Sunlight penetrates the arch, giving it a radiant golden glow. At the apex of the arch, a glass star directs a beam of light down onto a marble trough cradling a marble atu infant at the center of the stage.

Beyond the arch lies a perfectly circular lake veiled in mist created by cascading water columns which fall from Rirbuseha. The mist refracts the light, creating a breathtaking rainbow, and strategically placed glass panels around the lake reflect sunlight back into the mist, resulting in a sea of smaller rainbows.

For a moment, wonder drowns out all of my thoughts. I feel so insignificant yet privileged to be part of something so vast, beautiful, and benevolent. The child depicted at the center of the stage represents one of the four vetu forms Ritu assumed to rectify the misunderstandings the vetu had about Ver. Ver life, death, and resurrection all serve as a reminder that while our mortal existence may consume us, Ritu holds power over death and has promised that it won't be the end of our story. We were not created to perish but to live.

Once death has consumed all life, even death itself will perish from starvation; having no more life to consume. Then Ritu will revive all of us, concluding the consequences of embracing death, and only life will remain. Those who reject Ritu will be given a place separate from Ver, where they will forever experience the death they bring upon themselves.

This stage is one of four nearly identical stages evenly spaced around the lake; each dedicated to one of the four forms Ritu took to save all vetu. Every quarter-deposit, numerous citizens of Sudihatosema gather here to worship Ritu and study the sacred scriptures. The sanctuary resonates with teachings despite the loud sound of crashing water, for people recite aloud the minister's words, their voices gradually traveling from the front of the pews to the back. While there are other sanctuaries in the city, these stages are Sudihatosema's crowning jewels.

Various vetu move about here and there, some playing and walking in the spaces between the sanctuaries and others taking reverential postures and gestures amidst the pews.

With reverence, I approach the stage, overwhelmed by feelings of guilt and unworthiness with each step. The mounting feelings of guilt grow more unbearable the nearer I draw to the marble infant. So I stop where I can barely discern its facial features. I recently disobeyed Ritu's commands by punishing an officer, an act not condemned by the Holy Scriptures themselves but condemned by the Ministry, which is treated as a command from Ritu nonetheless.

Perhaps I don't deserve to stand here. Maybe I don't deserve the elevation above those I protect in Hosudiha. No, I do. To question that would be to question Ritu's choice to exalt me. However, even if all have exactly what they deserve, every vetu still owes Ritu their life, and with each transgression I commit, I feel a deeper sense of indebtedness.

Ritu, what would you have me do? My heart aches knowing the plight of those in Hosudiha. There must be a path that any of them can follow to become receptive to Ritu. If only someone could forge that path and guide them along it.

"I think I want to return to Hosudiha... but not as a Rirmevu," I say to Miya.

"What?" Miya asks, startled by my words. "We've made significant progress as Rirmevu. We may even be on the verge of exaltation. Why would you want to give that up?"

"Someone needs to offer themselves to Ritu, to become a tool for helping the people in Hosudiha become receptive to exaltation. And that someone should be me."

"That's quite the savior complex you've got there." Miya remarks, "There are already many people whose responsibility it is to do that kind of work. Do you think Ritu is incapable of doing what must be done through them? That somehow you bring something to the table that Ritu cannot bring Verself? I fear that your pride may have taken hold of you."

"I have no delusions of saving people. Only Ritu exalts through the fruits of Ver spirit. I simply want to contribute by removing obstacles so those in Hosudiha can surrender to Ritu." I say.

"I'm sorry, but you still sound incredibly arrogant. There are already efforts in place for that purpose." Miya says.

"I don't know, Miya. Maybe you're right. Perhaps this feeling isn't Ritu telling me to act, but rather a warning about something Ve is about to do. Whatever it is, Ritu's will be done."

"Indeed, Ritu's will be done. Just be cautious not to mistake your own will for Ver's."

It is midlabor rest, and the streets are less crowded as shops are closed for another wage. However, there are still people wandering around, perhaps taking walks like Miya and me.

The scent of baked goods lingers in the air, and my stomach grumbles, longing to be filled.

"It just occurred to me that we forgot to grab lunch," I remark.

"Hmm... Now that you mention it, I was starting to wonder why I felt so hungry," Miya says. "Well, let's hurry home and-"

Someone stops in front of us.

"Dima Zeju, Miya Vufo, you are both under arrest, and I kindly ask that you come quietly," ve says, opening ver coat slightly to reveal ver officer uniform and identification number. More people begin to gather around us, and even a yetu officer lands on a nearby lamp post.

"Miya?" I ask.

"I don't recognize them... So they're probably not the Hosudiha officers. I think it's safe for us to go with them." Miya says.

My heart sinks. I know this is about the protocol I violated. But if they were planning to arrest me for breaking protocol, why wait? Perhaps there was some delay in processing the paperwork? Ritu, what is your plan in all of this?

I raise my hands in surrender. "Very well."

My hands are bound with steel cuffs, and Miya is fitted with a steel vest that restricts ver wing and leg movement. We are led into the back of an enclosed prisoner transport wagon waiting in a nearby alleyway.

Several officers board the wagon, and the driver prods the Rovo, a creature with ten long legs protruding from its exoskeletal body, causing it to move, its legs resembling waves, as it pulls the wagon down the street.

Fear fills me as I anticipate the punishment that awaits, and that fear gives way to panic when the yetu officer departs and soon after the wagon makes a left turn. We are not headed toward the base...

A familiar voice speaks over the screams of pain surging through my body, "You two didn't really think I wouldn't find out it was you, did you?"

My skin crawls. I try to squint my swollen eyes to see who spoke and fail, but I can venture a guess. However, the blurry figure before me is standing, subverting my expectations.

I can't see Miya, but ver groans and weeping let me know ve is alive.

Suddenly, tafose is thrown into my face. It washes away some of the blood obscuring my vision but leaves my eyes stinging and my nose burning with the scent of sewage. The room appears to be a mostly empty hole dug into the dirt beneath a building, dimly lit by lanterns. Though it's bright enough for me to see Sergeant Makali standing before me, wearing a brand new uniform to replace the one I disposed of. How is ve standing? Why was ve given a new uniform? How is ve not in custody? What is happening?

"Do you know what we were doing down on those cliffs?" ve asks.

My face is too swollen to respond. So Makali continues, "Recall the story of the Tower of Matuha. The Matuha people believed themselves to be better than Ritu. They sought exaltation but cared not for Ritu and Ver virtues. So they attempted to make themselves like Ritu in adopting the role of exalters by building a tower to exalt themselves against Ritu's will. If they have succeeded they would have established an empire of vice and brought harm and suffering to millions of vetu. Thankfully Ritu confused their minds so that they could not cooperate, and to this labor the tower remains unfinished. A symbol of vetu subservience to Ritu and a warning to any who dare attempt to exalt themselves without Ritu."

Makali nods towards an officer who stands near the door and the officer steps out only to return a moment later pushing a wheelchair. The person who sits in it is a dark-blond with brown spots furred bitu, bound, and with a sack over ver head. Their knuckles are pale with stress, but their legs seem to rest without strain. Another dark-gold furred bitu is wheeled in, similarly bound, but they are wiggling their arms and legs in a desperate attempt to break free. The second bitu is wheeled out of my view.

Makali continues, "The minds of the Matuha people were sickened with the very same infection that always threatens to poison Hosudiha. It's an infection that promotes the idea that people can exalt themselves apart from Ritu."

Makali moves behind the bitu sitting before me and startles the bitu into a panic by merely placing ver hands firmly onto the bitu's shoulders.

"These two were caught seeking a way to exalt themselves and their family without Ritu," Makali says, "Once the idea takes hold in someone's mind, they can't be cured. They will continuously try to defy Ritu and may inspire others to try as well. So we prune them from society. Sometimes you have to amputate a few to save the rest. They become vemo, and once they're vemo, they're either used or disposed of." Makali lets out a disgusting chuckle, "Or used and then disposed of. Anyway, the prisons are well supplied, so lately it's been mostly disposal."

Makali pushes the bitu aside helplessly and moves to stand in front of me such that I have to crane my neck upwards just to see ver.

"Anyway, those two would be a bad influence if we permitted them to return to their family. While you two are young and ignorant, I don't believe you are vemo. No, I think Ritu may have use for you two yet. Though the ministry higher-ups won't do for you what needs to be done because it wouldn't look good. They represent Ritu, and so have to weigh their actions against public perception. So sometimes we must do things in secret to preserve Ritu's image so that souls are not lost. That is where I come in. I'm sending you to the bottom where you two will perhaps be a better influence than these two vemo. I trust Ritu will use you two to lift the family up to where you all really belong," Makali looks off to the side at someone I cannot see. "Do it."

My vision fades to black. My pain seems to migrate through my body to gather in a small region on my lower back, and I lose feeling in my body below that point. The rancid smell of the air suddenly intensifies, and I vomit into a gag blocking my mouth. My whole body itches. I can hear voices, but everything is muffled. I feel sick. What is happening to me? Maybe I just blacked out. Maybe I'm hallucinating.

I am jostled around in this weird world of scents and irritants. Every bump sends waves of pain through me, stemming from my back. Something covers my head, and my ears are plugged. This carries on for what feels like an eternity.

Suddenly, the straps around my wrists grow loose, and before I can start to move, I feel propelled forward and down onto the floor. The weakness of my body pleads with me to lie still, but fear, confusion, and adrenaline override such fatigue. Despite the numbness in my legs and the sharp pain in my back, I feel none of the injuries I had sustained from being beaten earlier. Unable to pull myself up, I struggle to remove the cover from my head, though once off my eyes are met with moderate darkness.

What is plugging my ears? Where are my ears? Why do I have so much hair on my face? I feel around my head and eventually find my ears resting more towards the top of my head than on the sides. They are different than usual. I thrust my clawed and fur-covered paws in front of my eyes. One paw is dark-brown, and the other is dark-golden blond.

Am I a bitu? How is this possible? What sounds like a muffled struggle tries to breach whatever blocks my hearing. My unfamiliar paws quickly return to attempting to free my ears, accidentally scratching myself in the process. Finally, I manage to dislodge globs of what seem to be candle wax, but not without pulling some fur out.

The sound of a stranger's gagged screams emanates from somewhere, compelling me to look around at what looks like an out-of-focus and poorly lit street. There, just a few paces to my right, another bitu spasms on the road as though they don't know how to control their limbs. Their head is wrapped up like mine was.

I painfully slide the gag over my head, freeing my jaws and triggering me to vomit and cough.

While still coughing and heaving, I claw my way over to the stranger, my legs providing no aid.

Upon reaching ver, I attempt to help them remove their head coverings. Their distress persists, and while I have to dodge a few hazardous limbs, the stranger can do nothing to stop me.

Once everything is removed, they gasp, cough, and vomit. I help them roll to their side so that the vomit doesn't pool in their mouth. They appear to be a dark-gold furred bitu, not unlike the second one I saw in the torture chamber. They continue to flail, and from their mouth spews gibberish.

"You're safe!" I try to console them with a foreign voice that brings me yet more distress.

The person's eyes seem to bounce around from one thing to the next for a time before fixing on me. Their body grows calm, and their babbling grows silent.

We lie in mute darkness on the dirty street for a while.

Suddenly, a door to one of the nearby makeshift buildings creaks open a bit.

"Holy shit!" A voice calls out, and the door swings fully open. "Hinuso, Viadu? Is that you?"

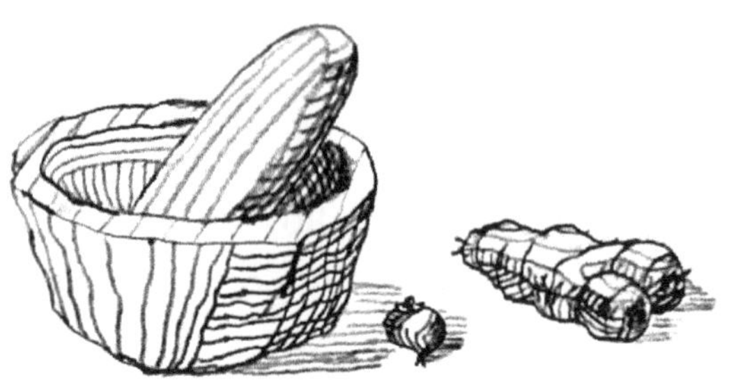

Chapter 13: Hosudiha

There is only one room, maybe one hundred square ingots in size. The floor is covered with a patchwork of thin mats, and articles of clothing hang from overhead beams beside dried vegetation and a dimly lit lamp. Rickety shelves line the walls, displaying handmade clay and tin pots, pans, basins, cutlery, and a few worn-out toys in one corner. Presumably there is little more to the positions of these strangers who keep calling me Viadu.

Laying upon one of the mats, I stare at my unfamiliar paws. Is Viadu who I am?

"I cannot believe they did this to you," says the dark-gold furred adult bitu stranger as ve works to clean and mend me. Ve and the others present are wearing ragged, loose-fitting sleeping clothes.

"Those reckless worms," The stranger continues, "With all the yetu flying around, you'd think they would know they nabbed the wrong people. What murderer are you suffering in the place of?"

The stranger works as tears fight to pour from ver eyes just as much as ver face fights to snarl in rage. The other dark-gray furred, able-bodied, adult bitu works more solemnly to clean and mend the bitu I woke up next to.

The eyes of two minors peer at us from the room's corner, obediently silent. One looks to be maybe eight salaries old with dark-gray fur and the other maybe six with brown fur. They bombarded the two adults, presumably their parents, with questions about us referring to us as their vedira before they were scolded and told to sit quietly in the corner.

I haven't said anything to them yet. I don't know what to say. How do I tell them I'm not Viadu when clearly, I don't know who I am? I think I'm Dima, an atu, but nothing I remember makes sense of being in this body. It must be a dream. None of this can be real.

The bitu I woke up beside, whom they keep calling Hinuso, starts babbling gibberish again.

"Ritu! What did they do to your minds?" the golden stranger clasps ver head in ver paws. "Viadu can't talk or walk, and Hinuso is spewing nonsense! What are we going to do?"

"The kids will have to watch them while we are at work. We will reassess the plan after we see how they are recovering in a few tankards."

"Reassess?" The golden one punches the gray one on the back of the head, causing pain but not lasting damage. "What exactly are you suggesting, that we leave them for dead somewhere if they don't recover to some extent?"

"No, I-"

"They are my vera, Kidu, not some sickly jufida that needs to be put down!"

"I understand. I'm not suggesting we leave them for dead. Just that we... I don't know, figure something out." Kidu, the gray adult, replies.

Before Kidu can finish digging ver own grave, I decide to try and speak, "I-" The strangers startle and look at me hopefully. "I can talk."

"Ritu damn you!" the golden stranger strikes my arm in anger. "Viadu, why haven't you said anything?"

"What happened to you two?" Kidu asks.

"I'm so sorry... I... I don't know who you all are." I say.

Eyes widen, and the golden stranger's expression darkens. "Don't you dare pull that on me."

"I'm not pulling anything. I'm sorry, but I am being serious." I say.

Ve jumps to ver feet and snarls at me, "Shut up!"

"Jove, please," Kidu pleads.

Maybe I should have remained quiet.

Jove's snarls last for only a few alms before ve drops ver head and begins to weep. Ve falls to ver knees at my side, and Kidu moves to comfort ver. Hinuso is still flailing, but more slowly and intentionally now.

"I'm sorry," Jove says through tears. Ve looks into my eyes desperately, "It's me!" My failure to recognize ver must be evident on my face. Ve begins to break down again. "Jove... We are vera! If you are trying to be funny, you need to stop right now! It's hurting me. I cannot take it right now, okay?"

"I'm sorry, but I'm not joking," I say.

"How could you forget me? Who are we without each other? Who do you think you are, if not my sibling?" Jove yells.

"I'm... My name is Dima-"

Hinuso grows still.

"No, it's not! Stop this!" Jove scolds.

"Jove, we need to let ver talk," Kidu says.

"Listen!" I yell, "I don't know how, and I know it's going to sound crazy, but I am not in the right body."

Jove pushes out of Kidu's attempts to comfort ver and paces back and forth, descending into another negative spiral. "No! Stop! This isn't funny! Why are you doing this to me?"

Knowing ve probably won't let me finish saying what I need to say, I try to speak over ver, "I don't know where your vera is, but they are not in this body right now. I am, and my name is Dima!"

Jove stops pacing and just looks at me in pure disbelief. Ve looks over at Hinuso, who is watching ver. "What are you going to tell me? Your name is Bouki or something?"

Hinuso stares at ver for a moment, then says something gibberish-like, "Myaduplu."

I could have sworn I heard something like 'Miya' "Miya! Miya, is that you?" I shout and attempt to prop myself up with my arms to look at ver. "If it's you, wiggle your body once for yes, twice for no."

Ver body wiggles once. Thank Ritu's grace! I'm not a bitu losing ver mind! I am Dima, and that's Miya!

Jove hollers, "Miya! Who the hase is Miya? No no no! You two need to stop this nonsense this instant!"

I can't help but smile, knowing Miya is here, but the smile is vanquished by a sudden slap. I look at Jove, slightly shaken. Jove, whom Kidu is trying to block from further assaults, looks furious. However, after a brief moment of eye contact with me, rage is replaced with remorse.

"I'm sorry. I... I need some space." With that, Jove ducks out of the small hut's front door.

I feel bad for ver, but there's nothing I can do about it.

"So, you two are in the wrong bodies, huh?" Kidu asks. "And you both believe this to be the case? Your name is Dima, and yours is Miya?"

"Right," I confirm. Miya also wiggles in agreement.

"Well... I'm not sure which I would have preferred, you being crazy or your claim being true, but reality seems to favor the latter." Kidu looks at Miya. "You can wiggle more than once to disagree with things, right? Wiggle twice if you can."

Miya wiggles twice.

"Three times?"

Miya wiggles three times.

"Shit."

I look at Miya and say, "So... Are you having trouble figuring out how to control that sort of body or something?"

Miya wiggles once, indicating difficulty.

"Yeah, I guess that makes sense. Yetu share very little in common with bitu. Though I suppose the anatomy between bitu and atu is similar enough that I haven't had as much trouble," I reply, contemplating the differences.

Come to think of it, yetu don't even speak with their mouths; they communicate by vibrating a loose patch of flesh on their backs. Now Miya has to figure out a whole new speech system. No wonder ve is struggling so much.

"Wait, are you telling me you two used to be a yetu and an atu?" Kidu asks, appearing slightly startled by the possibility. Then ver expression turns dark, and before we can answer the first question, ve asks, "Are you Rirmevu?"

Ver demeanor feels threatening, and Miya wiggles once in affirmation, "No," I lie. Realizing that I chose to lie, Miya quickly wiggles a second time in refutation. "...but I understand why you might make that assumption."

Kidu eyes me for a moment. "I didn't ask that plainly enough to receive an honest answer. It's too obvious that I don't have a high opinion of them."

Backing up my lie with a partial truth, I respond, "Well, I mean, I was unjustly punished by one. So I'm not so sure about them myself."

Kidu half laughs, saying, "Not so sure? Haven't been down here long, have you? Well, you'll be sure soon enough."

The weight of Kidu's words hangs in the air, and I can't help but feel a sense of unease.

Kidu finishes ver work mending us and then gets up, "If you'll excuse me. Pups, come along, we're going to check on Jove," ve says.

With that, Kidu and the pups exit the hut.

How in the shattered skies did this happen? There can be no doubt this is Ritu's doing.

"Miya, do you remember that feeling I got back at the four sanctuaries?" I ask.

Miya manages to turn ver head to look at me, wide-eyed.

"Yeah, I know, right." I say.

Suddenly, ve looks confused.

"What?" I ask.

Now, ve looks kind of shaken... Oh wait, I think I know what's happening. "Your facial expressions are communicating your feelings." I explain.

Ve looks intrigued.

"Yeah, that must be strange for you, given you've never had a fleshy face before... Or eyes! Vetu, I imagine you're experiencing a lot of firsts. This is your first time seeing with eyes!" I exclaim as I look at my hand to get a feeling for the sort of sight Miya may be experiencing. However, my eyesight is blurry such that what I see feels less significant than I was expecting given my experience with clearer atu eyesight.

"I think I can relate a little." I say, "I'm used to my eyes being my most important sense, but somehow, I can see better with my nose now? But like, I can see things that I could never see with my eyes. Smell is very weird right now. Though I imagine you're going through something similar, given you have a bitu nose too."

Miya's eyes just watch me in fascination.

"Ritu, I wish you could talk. Maybe you should keep experimenting with making different sounds with your mouth? Eventually, you'll figure out what makes what sound, right?" I ask.

Ve looks at me and starts to babble a little.

I crawl over to ver side, "Here, maybe I can help you figure out how to move this body too." I point to one of ver... fingers? Are these called fingers? Oh well. I touch ver finger with one of my own, "Can you move that one?"

Miya seems to try processing what I mean for a moment. Then ve tries moving a handful of other fingers on both paws before managing to move the one I touched.

"Nice! Now... how about... this one?"

Suddenly, Jove enters the room again, Kidu and the pups on ver flank. "Hold on. You two used to be another species?"

"Yeah... I used to have an atu body and ve used to have a yetu one." I say hesitantly.

Silence takes hold. Jove's eyes dart back and forth across the floor as ve processes and for a moment I am worried ve might conclude that we are Rirmevu when ve says, "If you're in the bodies of my siblings, what are the odds that my siblings are in your bodies?"

"Oh shoot, that's right!" I say.

The thought of someone else having full access to my body does not sit well with me, but in addition to that, my body wasn't necessarily in the best hands last I remember. Ritu, what will they do with it?

"We need to get back on our feet as soon as possible and find them," I declare. Then I look at Miya, "I just hope this doesn't take too long."

The next morning, Jove busily moves about the small room, getting dressed. Ver outfit is a brightly colored red dress that, while aged, looks to have been meticulously cared for. Ve pulls out a tray with a handmade mortar and pestle to grind up some fresh-smelling herbs.

When I was an atu all of Hosudiha smelled like sewage. However, it's a different world as a bitu. I'm not sure how to describe it apart from the fact that it's like my nose got glasses and my eyes have blurred a bit. The sewage is still there, and potent, like a canvas primarily covered in brown paint. With bad "eyesight", the canvas just looks like a brown blur. However, with corrected "eyesight", you can see the bits of blue, green, red, and yellow.

At first, Jove's scent is so busy with colors that it feels brown. However, ve proceeds to cover verself in a sort of powder that seems to erase most of ver natural scents. Then ve applies the paste ve just created in the bowl to key spots around ver body, accentuating some smells that are akin to ver natural smell's colors, along with a hint of herbs.

The pups and Kidu must have gotten ready and run off while I was still asleep. I've never been so uncomfortable while trying to fall asleep. The hard floor, the way we were all packed into the small room touching and overlapping, the snoring, and how I have yet to grow used to being covered in fur, which makes me itch all over. Yet once I finally managed to fall asleep, I slept hard.

"Okay, here are your chores while I'm at work. First, you're going to bathe. I don't care that it's not your body, I don't care what low standards of hygiene you might assume we have down here in Hosudiha, you're going to take care of your bodies," Jove instructs.

The assumption Jove makes of me leaves me wondering what experiences ve must have with others who have "fallen from grace." Ve continues, "After bathing, you'll use this comb. You're going to brush every bit of yourself, but be careful not to break the comb; we only have one. You're also going to crumble up a bit of this brick and use the dust to rub your teeth."

Jove turns over a fair-sized stone, and beneath it are some gutted foselitu lying on a bed of salt. Ve picks up a slab of meat and begins to eat it as ve speaks, "Food is here." Ve picks a few dried fruits, which are strung from the ceiling. "And you're going to want to eat some of this too. Yes, it's safe for us to eat raw meat, but be sparing with how much you eat. There's not a lot to go around."

"Um, what are we supposed to do if we're in danger or need help?" I ask. "I can't walk, and Miya can't even really move."

"Don't worry, I have sitters for you," Jove reassures. Ve opens the door and shouts, "Mebi, Shibi, get your asses in here!"

Jove's two pups come running into the room. The oldest is already making excuses, "Vedi, ah swear da jar was already broken when ah found it."

Jove lightly hits the older pup on the head. "Mebi, you idiot. What pot did you break? You know what, I'll deal with you later. Actually, you're on shit duty."

"Whaddaya mean? Ah didn't do nothin!" Mebi protests, only to be smacked on the back of the head a second time.

"Keep that up, and I'll put Shibi in charge," Jove declares. Shibi, the younger of the two pups, looks excited at the prospect.

"These two are like babies," Jove says. At first I think ve is talking to me about the pups, so I crane my head back to look at ver only to see ve is still talking to the pups and gesturing to Miya and me. "They have no control over their bowels. They're going to soil themselves, and you're going to help them clean up."

"I think I'll be able to take care of myself," I try to suggest, only to be met with a look of pity from Jove.

"Ve will need your help," Jove reaffirms to Mebi.

"Ew! That's gross! Ah don wanna have ta wipe vedira's bum," Mebi protests again.

"I don't want to hear it. They're just like babies. You've cleaned baby shit before. It's no different," Jove lies, "If I find them in their filth when I get back, I will beat the shit out of you and make you clean that up too."

With that, Jove ducks out of the door. Mebi takes a deep breath and looks at Shibi. "Ye're on shit duty."

"Nu-uh! Vedi said it was yer job!" Shibi counters.

"And... Vedi left me in charge. So as da bitu in charge, I'm assignin ya shit duty." Mebi says.

"That's not fair!" Shibi says.

"Life's not fair." Mebi replies.

"Ya'know what? Ye're right," Shibi starts to inconspicuously step towards the door. "Thanks for takin da beating when vedi gets back!" Then Shibi darts out of the door.

"Ya little fose!" Mebi takes off after Shibi, and as ve runs ver voice carries back to us, "If vedi beats me, I'll beat ya!"

Chapter 14: Blood

"We woulda gotten dat nice house by now if the two of yah hadn'ta gone and got arrested," Shibi says somewhat bitterly as ve holds the bucket of water I am using to rinse off my excrement-covered washcloth. Ver right eye is swollen from ver confrontation with Mebi.

"It wasn't our fault, it was Hinuso and Viadu's," I retort.

Shibi ignores my response. "Y'all're lucky, yah came back right before we're gonna get it. Kidus' been workin twice as late, and Joves' workin a night time job now, after ver school work. I don like whatevah job Joves' doin now though, sometime ve come back looking like ve was in a fight. Hopefully ve can quit now dat ye're back."

"We'll need to recover first." I say.

Mebi enters the room with arms full of clean clothes. Ve walks over to the bed, and some toeless socks fall to the floor as ve moves. The holes in the toes of the socks are intentional, as opposed to the other holes. Bitu like to keep their claws free. Mebi plops the clothes onto the middle of the floor and runs out of the room. Shibi's eyes fixate on the door Mebi left through, anger growing on ver face with each passing moment until Mebi returns shortly thereafter with a handful of various articles of clothing ve likely dropped along the way. Throwing the rest of the clothes onto the pile, Mebi declares, "Y'all er gonna put dis away."

"Whaddya mean, 'y'all'? Where you goin?" Shibi questions.

"I got other respons-imilities, ya' know," Mebi declares as ve goes to exit the hut again.

Shibi's knuckles grow white with frustration. "Ya lazy worm! Ye're just goin off ta play ball with Jojo!" Shibi grabs an excrement soaked rag from the bucket and throws it at Mebi, managing to hit ver square in the back. Mebi snarls back at Shibi and then runs after ver.

Shibi tries to run away, "I'm sorry! I'm sorry!"

"Ya will be!" Mebi is too quick, managing to grab Shibi by the leg before ve can get far. Then, swiftly, Mebi drags Shibi close, restrains Shibi's arms with one of ver own, takes hold of the fur on the back of Shibi's head, and then dunks Shibi's head into the bucket of soiled water. Shibi fruitlessly struggles to break free.

Everything happened quicker than I could process. There is no danger of drowning as both bitu and atu have a hole at the base of their skulls through which they can breathe even if their nose and mouth get submerged or something manages to get lodged in the throat. The hole is not submerged. Still, I try my best to drag myself close to intervene.

"Enough of this!" I yell, taking hold of Mebi's wrist and pulling ver to the side. Mebi, maintaining ver grip on Shibi, inadvertently pulls ver sibling out of the water as I pull ver. Shibi coughs, gags, and promptly vomits all over me.

My ability to handle this situation gracefully has been completely eradicated. My other arm is too busy propping me up to be used to pry the two apart. So I start to painfully squeeze Mebi's wrist in an attempt to force ver to let go of ver sibling. I snarl at Mebi, in a uniquely bitu way that feels foreign yet natural to cross my face.

"Let go of ver!" I command as I dig my claws into Mebi's wrist. Eventually, the pain is too much, and Mebi lets go. Now free, Shibi promptly grabs the bucket of soiled water and throws its contents into Mebi's face, drenching me as well. Momentary shock freezes me in place as I try to figure out how to stop this, but before I can think of anything, Mebi bites my arm. Reflexively, I loosen my grip as I recoil from the sudden pain, and Mebi takes this opportunity to wiggle free and pounce on Shibi. The two engage in a one-sided fight as Mebi unleashes ver anger on Shibi.

Filled with adrenaline and rage, I somehow, more effortlessly than ever, crawl over to the fight. Despite enduring a few kicks, punches, and scratches, I manage to grab Mebi by ver scruff and use my hold to brace myself. With my other paw, I grab Shibi's scruff before Mebi collapses under my body weight. I muscle each of them helplessly onto the ground beneath me as I perform a sort of limp-legged plank over them. They both fruitlessly struggle against me but still manage to get in some scratches on each other because I cannot hold them apart quite far enough.

I dig my claws into the scruffs of their necks, trying to make it painful. "Stop!" I demand helplessly. All I can do is hold them down to minimize the damage until they finally manage to exhaust themselves.

While my parenting experience is lacking, and the examples of parenting in my own childhood are poor, I have observed enough of others' parenting to know that there was probably a better way to handle this. However, neither do I know what I could have done differently given my limited mobility, nor do I have any idea where to go from here.

"I am not letting go of you two until you apologize to each other and apologize to me," I say.

Mebi and Shibi seem to just ignore me as they pant and stare daggers at each other. This goes on for a while until they catch a second wind and start clawing at each other again.

"Hey! Stop this! Stop it right now!" I try to yell. "Mebi! Were you really going to go play ball with your friends?"

They continue to struggle, but I hold firm and ask again, "Mebi! Were you going to play ball with your friends?"

This pattern continues for a while, and I am about to give up when Mebi finally admits, "Well, they're probably done now! It's da one thing ah look forward ta, you little fose! Ya just love makin me miserable, don you? Ya make life unbearable. Imma half tempted ta kill ya if I could get away wit it, but maybe it would hurt ya more if ah killed mahself and blamed you!"

Shibi stops struggling, and ver face starts to look incredibly sad.

"So Shibi had every reason to be angry at you, didn't ve, Mebi?" I say.

"Ah don care! Ve deserves to be as miserable as ve makes me!" Mebi yells.

"Mebi, look at Shibi. That doesn't look like the face of someone who takes joy in making you miserable." I say. Shibi is clearly trying to fight back tears but cannot.

"Ve is just trying to play the victim. Ve wants ya ta think I'm da bad one, but it's ver! Shibi has been nothin but a burden, makin us all miserable ever since ve was born! Ve is a waste of space! If ve was never born, we woulda been outa this place ah long time ago! Hinuso and Viadu probably woulda never been arrested. This is all ver fault!"

Shibi is sobbing openly at this point and cries out weakly, "Ah'm sorry."

"Stop actin like ya care!" Mebi shouts. "If ya cared so much, you woulda left! Kill yerself before ya drive me to kill mahself!"

Shoot, this whole thing is getting out of hand. Maybe I shouldn't have intervened. It's too late now, though. I need to figure out a way to resolve this without either of these two leaving here ready to hurt themselves.

"Why don't we put this to the test," I say. Both pups side-eye me with slight confusion.

I continue, "Mebi, you believe Shibi doesn't care about you. That all ve wants is to make you miserable, right?"

"Ah don jus believe it," Mebi says, "Ah know it. Ve has done nothin but make meh miserable at evereh opportunity."

"What if Shibi did all of your chores and gave you the rest of the labor off, no complaining, no expectation of help from you? Would that change your mind?" I ask.

"Like hase ve would ever—"

"Ah'll do it!" Shibi interrupts.

Mebi takes this in for a moment, "Make it the whole of forever, and then maybe ah'll change mah mind," Mebi counters.

"Mebi," I start, "that's not reason—"

"Fine!" Shibi agrees. Mebi looks almost surprised. I release each of them.

Mebi sits up, ever so slightly bewildered at the deal ve and Shibi just struck. Shibi also sits up, still sniffly but with a look of determination in place of the despair ve was expressing moments ago.

"Okay then, Imma go enjoy mahself," Mebi says while looking daringly into Shibi's determined eyes, testing to see if Shibi will really just let this happen without complaint.

"Fine," Shibi says, clearly still bothered, but ve softens up a bit and adds, "Ah hope ya have fun, and ah won make ya miserable anymore." Shibi looks like ve is about to cry as soon as Mebi leaves.

Mebi is on ver way out when suddenly I notice blood on Mebi's scruff. "Wait, Mebi!" I call after ver. Mebi looks at me annoyed. "Did I hurt you?" I ask while pointing to the blood on ver.

Mebi wipes the back of ver neck with ver paw and pulls it away to see only a little bit of blood, but enough still to make ver look concerned. Ve runs over to me and shows me ver neck. "Is it bad?" ve asks.

I take a look, and while there is blood on the fur, I cannot see any punctures in the skin. "I don't see anything," I say. I then notice my paw is significantly more covered in blood which is trickling down from where Mebi bit me. "Oh, it's me."

Mebi sees ver bite mark and looks almost remorseful, ve says, "Ah'll help clean and patch ya up, but after that, don expect to get any help from me for the rest of forever!"

We do our best to clean my wound and bandage it. Mebi even helps Shibi clean up the rest of the mess giving the excuse, "I'm not about ta get in trouble fer yah not cleaning dis up well enough."

After everything is taken care of, Mebi finds a pot for me to lean on so that I can use both of my paws to some extent. Mebi then leaves, and Shibi just sits looking at the door. Ver tears finally feel free to flow, and ve starts to cry. This makes ver angry. "No! Stop crying!" ve scolds verself.

"It's okay to cry," I try to affirm.

"But ah don-" *sniffle* "-wanna cry."

"Would you like for me to help you stop crying?" Shibi looks almost frightened by the suggestion. "It's okay, I just want to help you feel better."

I'm pretty sure I saw this work for a parent in Sudihatosema once, "Try taking some deep breaths. Can you take some deep breaths with me?"

Shibi looks at me miserably. I continue, "In," and I take a deep breath in. Shibi tries to mimic, choppily.

"Out." I say as I exhale, "Can we do one more? In... Out... Can you count to ten with me?"

"I dunno how," Shibi says through ver slightly more manageable sorrow.

"That's okay," I say, "Just repeat after me. One."

"One."

"Two. Three. Four. Five. Six."

"Two. Three. Four. Five. Sex," Shibi repeats, and chuckles. I smile as I roll my eyes and continue.

"Seven."

"Sexten," Shibi says mischievously.

"Someone is feeling a little silly!" I say as I tickle the pup, and ve laughs. "Want to try one more time?"

"Nah, Ah'm good," Shibi says.

"Do you need a hug?" I ask. Shibi nods and leans into my open embrace. Maybe I would make a good parent, though I'm not sure the sibling brawls are something I would be able to handle every labor.

"You know you didn't have to agree to do Mebi's chores forever, right?" I say.

"Ah just don wanna be a burden. Ah make everyone miserable. Ah deserve it." Shibi's tears start to creep back.

I am at a loss for words for a moment. I'm not sure what the right thing to say right now is. I am tempted to tell ver ve isn't actually a burden. However, Miya has taught me many things, and one of those is how unhelpful it is for me to invalidate ver feelings. But what am I supposed to do?

"Yeah, it sucks that you had to be born, doesn't it?" I say, and immediately I begin to internally panic over my choice of words.

"Yeah," Shibi solemnly agrees.

Oh, maybe this will work. I lean into it. "I'm sure it sucks to be born here, no matter who you are. I bet Mebi wasn't an easy pup to raise in a place like this. Hase, ve still seems like a challenge to put up with."

Shibi gets a little smile. "Yeah."

"Maybe after a while of seeing how much you really don't want to be a burden, Mebi will learn to be a bit kinder to you."

"Yeah."

Having only received "yeah" as a response, I'm starting to think I've lost ver. I probably said too much. So, I shut up and just hold Shibi for a while. Miya, who has been quietly lying nearby, seems to have a pleasant look on ver face. I think ve approves of the way I handled that, which makes me feel better.

This whole situation is so surreal. I felt Ritu mentally preparing me to return here while we were still back in the four sanctuaries. However,

I'm not sure anything could have prepared me for just how Ritu intended to get me here. The way Ve is bringing about good from Makali's evil feels both uncomfortable and comforting. In spite of the ministry's corrupt portions, Ritu is still in control. I am grateful for the heads up Ritu gave me, because I would probably feel so hopeless and bitter if I didn't know Ritu has me here for a reason. It's especially comforting that I'm pretty sure I know what that reason is too.

With Ritu's help, I am meant to guide this family to a place where their hearts can be receptive to Ritu so that the fruits of Ver spirit can lift us out of Hosudiha. How much more inspiring it will be when Ritu uses a paraplegic too! It's just like in all of the stories in the holy scriptures! One who was exalted is brought to those who are the lowest so that they can bring anyone who cares to follow to Ritu, and, by Ritu's fruits of virtue, bring them out of the darkness.

Though it is clear that this effort is not on Miya and I's shoulders alone. Ritu placed us with a family that is already on the cusp of a micro-exaltation. Even without Miya and I, this family, despite its apparent dysfunction, is a gleaming example of how Ritu honors those who work hard. However, it is going to take this family having a radical change of heart towards Ritu if we are to be exalted any further.

With work on my mind, after a while, I am starting to feel anxious that we haven't managed to get anything done. Who knows how much longer I can go before I soil myself again. Though given how hungry I feel, there may be nothing to come out at this point.

"Would you like to eat something?" I ask.

Shibi nods.

We split a foselitu. Normally, I would hesitate to eat something so raw, but trusting Jove, not wanting to give Shibi an excuse to not eat, and practically compelled by hunger, I chow down. It is extremely salty, given that it came from a bed of salt. I try to brush some of the crystals off, and it helps a little, but now the taste of raw meat is more prevalent. It takes everything in me to get it down. We also share some dried fruits, which help combat the raw meat taste that is left in my mouth.

I start to hear, "Fffff... Ffff," and turn to see Miya is managing to point over at the food and is making an effort to say an actual word.

"Food? Do you want food? Good job, Miya!" I say, almost as though I am talking to a child. Miya gives me an annoyed look.

"Sorry, it's hard not to use baby voice given everything." I apologize.

I break up bits and pieces of meat and fruit to start feeding Miya who, to my surprise, is actually managing to move ver arms with some intent. Ve pinches some meat between ver palms and sloppily attempts to put it in ver mouth as opposed to accidentally putting it in ver nose, a challenging task for ver at the moment.

"Is it true dat all atu stink?" Shibi asks suddenly.

"Oh, uh... I don't think so..." I say.

"Jove says dey don do enough to cover up deir odor. Dey just bathe and den spritz some fragrance on as if it will erase deir odor." Shibi says.

"I mean, Jove isn't wrong. I think it's just that atu cannot smell their natural odors as well as a bitu might."

"Is it true dat atu use bitu fur to stuff beds?"

"What? No, I don't think that is something we do at all..."

"Hm... Mebi told me dat one. Ve thinks ve knows everything, but now ah know something ve doesn't!"

"I wonder where Mebi heard something so horrible about atu."

"Is it true dat rich people eat bread every tankard?"

"I'll be honest, I would not consider myself as having been rich when I lived in Sudihatosema, but yeah, in Sudihatosema, it's pretty common for everyone to enjoy bread on a laborly, erm, tankardly basis."

"If ya can be poor and eat bread, wha does dat make us?"

"I mean, I wouldn't say I was necessarily poor either."

"Why weren ya rich?"

"I had what Ritu deemed me worthy to have, and that wasn't riches."

"What did ya do ta naw be worthy anymore?"

"Oh... Um... I don't think I'm no longer worthy of Sudihatosema."

"Den whyrya here?"

"I think Ritu needs me here so that I can help people receive Ver into their hearts and teach people the ways of life which lead to exaltation."

"So ya think ya deserve more than what ya got, but ya have what ya have because somehow Ritu cannot help us witou you?" Shibi asks.

"Um... I mean, I don't think Ritu couldn't do this without me... I don't know why ve might have chosen me for-"

"What if dis is wha ya deserve?" Shibi asks.

"I- uh... I mean. I guess that is possible... I- Can we talk about something else?" I ask, not wanting to think too much about that possibility at this time.

"Why do ah deserve this? Ah was born down here. Is everyone born down here?"

"No. Others are born in Sudihatosema or even Rirbuseha among other places."

"How are dey more worthy dan me if we couldn't ah don anything ta be worthy befer we were born?"

"I guess we might all be born in different circumstances, but over time we end up where we are worthy to be."

"How long does dat take? Jove had a pup befer Kidu had Mebi, but ver pup died soon after being born. So what if we die before we get ta the place we're worthy ta be?"

"I don't know. Maybe they just go straight to Ritu's eternal nation in Rirsudi."

Shibi thinks about this for a moment, "If Ah ever have a pup, Ah'm going to send em right to Rirsudi."

"Uh, you- you mean you would kill them? Okay... I know why you might think that's a good idea... but if you did that, then you would probably end up in Hase."

"Ah'm already in Hase. Might as well keep mah pups out, especially if dey go to Rirsudi instead. Ah wish mah parents had."

"Listen, I'm sure if killing babies was the best option, then Ritu would do it or command us to do it."

"Ritu kill babies? Command us ta kill babies? Would ya be okay with dat?" Shibi asks.

"Well- I- I would have to trust that Ritu has a good reason."

"If ya think Ritu has a good reason for doing whatever Ve does or doesn't do, is there something Ritu could do ta make ya think Ve isn't the good person ya thought Ve was?"

"Where are you getting these questions?"

"I think 'em, and hear 'em from Jove."

"Well... I think you should maybe talk with a minister about those questions."

"But didn't Ritu send ya to help answer mah questions?" Shibi asks.

"Maybe I am meant to help in other ways. Here, let's get started folding this laundry." I say, wanting this conversation to end before I misrepresent Ritu.

We begin folding laundry, and Shibi proceeds to bombard me with questions about Sudihatosema and rich people. The more we talk, the more the possibility that I am here because I deserve to be here unsettles me. I had not considered that possibility. Though why would I? I might consider it if I were not sure Ritu spoke to me at the sanctuary to prepare my heart for this mission. I find comfort in the reality of Ritu's involvement enough to distract me from Shibi's other tough questions. It's probably best not to dwell on them. Perhaps I'll remember to ask a minister about them once I return to Sudihatosema.

I take a peek at the bite wound. It has actually already stopped bleeding. I think it will heal up, and my fur might help it go unnoticed so that the pups don't have to face punishment for it.

I hold the bandage out to Shibi, "I don't think I need this anymore. Would you go ahead and wash it so that it's ready if we need it again."

Thank Ritu, recovery on all fronts seems to be progressing quickly.

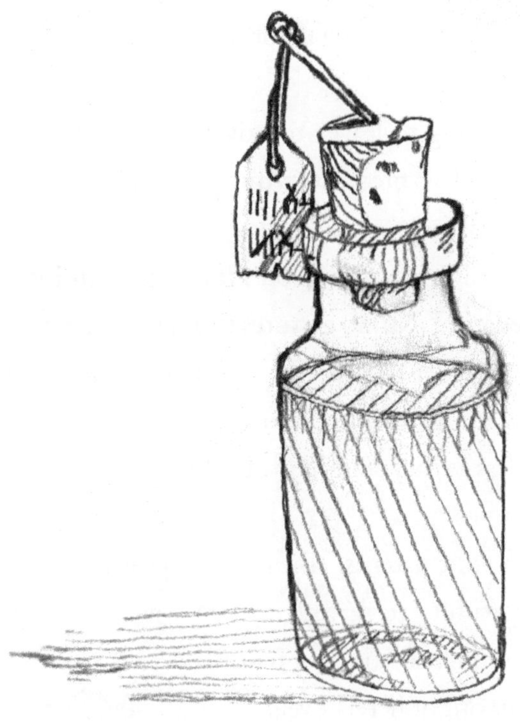

Chapter 15: Infection

I walk down streets laden with mental fog. Sunlight breaks through the mist and bounces off of nearby windows creating a sea of rainbows akin to the four sanctuaries. The pleasant smell of baked bread guides my progress as Miya the yetu rides along on my back.

Suddenly a figure stops in front of us. My body freezes in shock at the sight of my parent Numo.

"After everything we did for you," Numo says, "We gave you the best start anyone could hope for. Opportunities for power, money..."

"I never asked for any of that." I retort.

"How could you be so ungrateful!" Numo yells, "you would leave behind everything we did for you for the false promises of some pedofile. I thought I raised you better than to fall for something like that. What are you stupid?"

"I didn't have anything to leave! You died!" I defend, "Besides, you never cared about what I wanted. Everything you did wasn't for me. It was for you!"

"How could you think it was a good idea to go with Lise? Look at ver! Ve is clearly a predator." Numo gestures to a newly manifested Lise.

Lise bears teeth of violet thorns. Ver skin is white as snow and lips blue like death. Veins are pronounced but look like scarlet roots, and ver eyes are wide and lifeless as they stare at my body.

Fear compels me to run.

"I freed you from your parents," the monster growls as it gives chase, "I gave you the opportunity to serve Ritu that you always wanted and how did you repay me? I'll tear you to shreds!"

"Miya! Miya get us out of here!" I yell.

"On it!" Miya says as ve extends ver wings. Ve begins to lift us to safety when suddenly a spear comes from nowhere and severs a portion of Miya's wing, sending us crashing into the ground.

Once I skid to a stop I look for Miya and find a bitu in ver place. I try to pull myself back to my feet, but my legs will not move. So I begin to desperately crawl to somewhere safe.

"Just as you should be grateful to Ritu for forgiving your transgressions and offering to save you from Hase. You should be grateful to me," says a new familiar voice. I keep crawling, but I cannot help taking a brief glance over my shoulder to see Makali's towering form, a silhouette in the mist, but there is no mistaking the shadowy figure for anyone else. Behind Makali is a perfectly circular ring of fire and it is hard to tell whether the person speaking is Makali or Ritu, “I’ve given you another opportunity to serve. I have humbled you. Saved you from your pride. Perhaps you need to be humbled further.”

Suddenly Lise bursts through Makali’s smoky form to seize me in ver jaws.

I wake breathing heavily, sweating, heart racing, as one does when waking from a nightmare. Though it is hard to tell if I have really escaped the nightmare by waking. I am still in a bitu body, still paralyzed, still in Hosudiha. Ever since the start of Lise’s “ministry”, nightmares have been nothing new to me. However, the one’s I’ve had over the last couple of labors have been an evolution of the usual nightmares of being trapped and assaulted. Not only do they fill me with fear and dread like they used to, now they make me feel guilty, unsure, and then there is the whiplash of going from dreams where my legs work, to nightmares where they don’t, to reality where they still don’t work. It makes it hard to get the labor started.

Apart from Miya’s and my nightmares, Miya is slowly gaining more and more precision control over ver larger limbs; enough to pick up and grab onto things with ver whole paw, but not quite with individual fingers just yet.

Shibi works hard to take care of everything that needs to be done around the hut. Ve cleans the clothes, hangs them to dry, and puts them away. Ve cleans and puts away the dishes. Ve collects dead foselitu from traps, but does not yet know how to clean them. Ve scrubs the floor and, erm, helps Miya and me with our waste. By the end of the first labor, ve looked ragged. I try to help as much as I can, but it frankly feels like tending to me takes more time than my help buys. I can, however, use my sewing skills to mend the clothes which are in dire need of such repairs. So that becomes my main means of contribution.

It's around midlabor on the second labor when Shibi is outside washing clothes in a bin and Mebi comes walking in looking for food. I am sitting leaned up against a wall, busying my hands with patching the holes in some trousers.

"So," I start, slowing my work but not stopping completely. "Do you still believe Shibi is out to make you miserable?" My words seem to freeze Mebi for a moment. Ve doesn't respond before continuing on as though I didn't say anything.

I continue, "Seems to me that Shibi is willing to make verself awfully miserable for your sake."

This earns me a response, "Good. Ve's gotta lotta debt ta work off." Mebi bites.

"Did you ever pay off the misery you've caused your parents?" I ask.

Mebi looks angry, "Of course ah did. Dey made me every bit as miserable as ah made dem! We're even."

"Do you think you've made Shibi miserable at all?" I ask.

"Listen, Ah know what y're tryna do. Mind yer own business! Yer not even mah real vedira. If ya were not in ver body, we would've left ya on the streets ta die. No one round here has da energy er money ta take care'a fose like you!"

With that, Mebi storms out of the hut.

I'm not sure if I just helped or made things worse...

As the labor goes on, I do my best to help Shibi with chores. Though, unlike yesterlabor, I find myself getting more easily winded. By midlabor, I feel exhausted, and a headache sets in. While the bleeding did stop, the pain in my arm still makes the bite feel fresh. I dare to pull the fur back and look at the skin. It's yellow and swollen.

Finally, my strength to remain propped up gives way, and I lie down and squeeze my head with the paw that isn't attached to a painful arm.

"Are ya okay?" Shibi asks.

"I'm not sure," I say, "I think the bite got infected."

Mebi comes wandering in. A flicker of concern crosses ver face at the sight of my sickly form before ve hardens and moves along as though there was nothing to see.

"Mebi, vedira is sick!" Shibi calls out.

"Dey're not er Vedira. Stop carin so much." Mebi says.

"We are in their bodies though," I argue. This gives Mebi pause.

"Ya need ta go find Kidu," Shibi pleads, "and we need ta get Dima some medicine!"

"Fine. Ah'll go getter, but Ah'm doing this fer mah vedira's body, not fer da fose in it."

Shortly after we all eat far too little precious food, Mebi arrives back with Kidu. Ve looks, and more noticeably, smells filthy. Last time ve came home, I had to fight not to vomit. This time I'm too weak, and it comes up.

Kidu immediately notices how miserable I look. Ve comes over and touches my forehead.

"Seems like you have a fever," Kidu remarks and begins to examine me. Noticing my swollen arm, ve pulls back the fur, and immediately rage comes over ver face. "Which one of you vermin bit ver!"

The pups cower in fear. Shibi bites ver tongue. Mebi looks terrified, probably believing that either I or Shibi will fose ver out. After all, Mebi has done well to try and make enemies of us, but Shibi doesn't say a word.

"It was a foselitu," I say.

"A foselitu!" Kidu scoffs in disbelief. "What foselitu has a jaw that big?"

"The one that bit me," I say matter-of-factly.

Kidu glares at me, struggling to believe a word I say. From behind Kidu, Mebi stares at me, just as bewildered. Ve even takes a quick glance at Shibi. It's clear that ve cannot believe we would have ver back.

"Let me see that bite mark again," Kidu commands as ve grabs my arm forcibly. I am too weak from the fever to resist ver.

Ve looks at it intensely, then turns to the pups. Mebi looks incredibly distressed.

"Ah bit ver!" Shibi declares. "Mebi and Ah were fightin and-"

"I don't want to hear your excuses!" Kidu shouts. "Do you have any idea what this might cost the family?" Kidu grabs Shibi by the scruff and raises a fist, "I'll give you an idea!"

Kidu rears back to strike Shibi. "No! Ah bit ver!" Mebi declares. Ve runs over to me and grabs my arm. "See," ve gently places ver teeth over the mark to show the size of the wound matches ver mouth.

Kidu looks shaken. "What is this? I thought you two hated each other?" Mebi and Shibi lock eyes.

"Ah-Ah think Ah-" Mebi stammers, "Ah don't."

Mebi's words seem to disarm Kidu who sets Shibi down and soberly walks out of the hut.

I never thought I would be grateful to be in a place with so little sunlight, yet here I am, suffering from a fever-induced migraine, wincing at every lantern we pass as Kidu traverses the tattered streets and navigates the currents of people coming and going. Vendors of various kinds line the curbs, tempting those passing by to consider their wares. Kidu pays them no mind, and ver eyes remain resolutely focused on the street ahead. I sit limply in the makeshift harness, strapping me to Kidu's back, too weak to even lift my arms. Speaking of which, one of them feels like it's on fire.

Kidu is taking me to get treated by the ministry's free medical services. Though the way Kidu put it made it sound as though there is a chance I might not get treated.

Suddenly, Shibi comes squeezing through the crowd after us but seems unable to catch up completely.

"Hey... Kidu... slow down," I say weakly.

"We don't have time to take this slow." Kidu says.

"Nooo... just enough for Shibi to catch up." Shibi starts shaking ver head and shushing me as I talk, for some reason.

"What?" Kidu says in aggravation as ve turns around, "What the hase are you doing here? I am going to whoop your ass!"

"Ah just-"

Kidu grabs hold of Shibi, who was too occupied with trying to explain to be able to manage an escape, pulls ver close, and smacks ver on the face.

"Get going back home," Kidu says as ve tosses Shibi back onto the ground. The crowd starts to move around us as if we were nothing more than an inanimate obstacle.

Shibi scrambles to ver feet and tries to remain strong as ve yells back, "Ah wanna stay wit Dima!"

"Go!" Kidu yells. And with that, Kidu turns back around and continues walking at a pace that Shibi would need to jog to keep up with. And keep up Shibi does.

After a while, Kidu turns around suddenly to catch Shibi as ve continues ver pursuit of us. A moment of silence passes before Kidu lets out a frustrated growl, "I don't have time for this!" Kidu starts walking again, leaving Shibi frozen in a state of confusion, "Keep up!" Kidu scolds.

Shibi smiles as ver stubbornness pays off, and ve runs up to follow closely beside us.

Kidu walks through the front doors of the poor excuse for a hospital, and we stroll up to the front desk where a bitu sits doing paperwork. The waiting room is disturbingly dank and small but also surprisingly empty. Five hole-ridden chairs sit vacant around what may be one of the sturdiest-looking doors in Hosudiha, likely in an attempt to protect those personnel and supplies which lie beyond.

Before Kidu can say a word, the secretary speaks, "All medications are out of stock. If you are here for anything other-"

With that, Kidu sighs and is already walking back out of the door, "Figures," ve mutters.

As Kidu exits the building, it is almost eerie how the eyes of every street vendor peek at us. I might not have been able to see this had my eyes not already been squinting at the various sources of light that send pain reeling through my skull.

"Shibi," Kidu says and crouches down to whisper, "Do you know why the merchants around these parts go out of their way to buy glasses?"

"Because they wanna look smart?" Shibi says.

"Not necessarily. They absorb the expense because they want to know our faces. They know we wouldn't go into the building unless we were in great need. Now that they have seen us go in, they will charge through the roof for the medications they are selling."

"Why'd we go in then?" Shibi asks.

"Because we are already tight on money, and you never know when you might catch a fresh supply of free medication before it gets cleaned out. We were lucky to get a free bottle of disinfectant for you last salary."

"Ya mean dat one bottle dat smelled really strong?" Shibi inquires.

"Yeah that one. Now that they have seen us, we need to steer clear, circle around, and try to find a merchant around the corner who didn't see us."

Shibi nods, "Okay."

We take a long walk around the complex, which, not unlike other buildings in this city, has barred windows and walls topped with shards of glass. All together, the buildings around here look almost more like prisons than dwellings, businesses, and, in this case, a hospital. It's all in an effort to dissuade theft.

As we approach a corner, Kidu sets me down, "You will need to wait here. I can't have the merchant see your condition. Shibi, you stay here and watch ver." Kidu commands and then walks off around the corner.

Shibi tends to me with great concern, "Don worry. Vedi'l take care'a ya."

"I'm sure ve will," I say with a weak smile.

Shibi starts to tear up, "Ah'm sorry Ah did this ta ya. If Ah hadn'ta thrown dat rag at Mebi, none'a dis would've happened!"

"Don't blame yourself." I try to comfort, "I chose to intervene. This was because of my own choices. You two have survived all this time without me; I didn't have to get involved."

"Why're ya so nice? Ah've never met anyone like ya. Most people keep der snouts outta other people's business, dey won help," Shibi inquires.

"I mean," I start, "You don't have much to go off of to think I'm nice. Though if I had to venture a guess..." For some reason, the words "people like me die..." get caught in my throat. I cannot speak them because they cannot be true.

"Ritu exalts them," I say.

"Daya think Ritu'l exalt ya?"

"Some tankard. When I'm ready. Though for the time being, as I said before, I think I am meant to be here."

"Daya think Ritu'l exalt me?"

I look into Shibi's hopeful eyes, "Open yourself up to receive Ritu and ver teachings, and I know Ve will."

"Ah have Ritu in me, what virtues am ah lackin?" Shibi says.

"For now, just keep being selfless and you will see exaltation in no time." I say.

Kidu emerges from the crowd of shoppers and wordlessly starts hoisting me back into the harness.

"Dijyah get da medicine?" Shibi asks.

"No," With the look on Shibi's face, you might think Kidu just stabbed ver, "Word got around. At these rates, the disinfectant will cost us another three salaries. We are headed home. Jove will have to go out tomorrow to try ver luck. Hopefully, it will only end up costing us a couple of salaries worth of savings at most."

"Tamorrow?" Shibi repeats in shock, "Ve might die tanight!"

"Shut up!" Kidu snarls, "Or do you want to announce our plans to the whole market so that we will never be able to afford the disinfectant?" Shibi clenches ver jaw but doesn't say another word, "Good."

So we begin the long walk back, having accomplished nothing.

People like me get exalted. I'm supposed to help these people receive Ritu and be exalted by Ver virtues. I'm not supposed to die. My good works aren't supposed to get me killed! Surely I won't die. Surely Ritu will heal me somehow. Perhaps it will be miraculous, and everyone's faith in Ritu will be restored, and they will be inspired to surrender their lives to Ritu and Ver virtues will fill the hearts of Hosudiha! It will bring hope to the hopeless. They will all see Ritu's power over disease, maybe even death!

Suddenly, Shibi runs up beside us. I hadn't noticed ve had fallen behind.

"Keep up, Shibi!" Kidu snaps.

"Sorry," Shibi responds meekly.

We arrive at our dwelling. Mebi is doing Shibi's chores inside as ve waits. Kidu sets me down on my mat and goes to get ready for the evening.

Once Kidu is properly distracted, Shibi sneaks a knife, a cup of clean water, and quietly hurries over to me. Ve kneels at my side, and my eyes widen at the potent smelling bottle ve removes from ver pocket, disinfectant.

No.

I look at Shibi, who doesn't stop to look me in the eye, "What have you done?" I whisper.

"Somethin selfless," Shibi whispers back.

At that, ve quickly opens the bottle and uses the knife to open my wound. I let out a bark and a squeal, alerting Kidu, but before ve can even utter a word, Shibi pours water over the wound, washing away puss, followed by a high dose of the disinfectant, which burns with the heat of a thousand suns.

"What are you doing? What is that?" Kidu interrogates. As ve moves closer to see the bottle of disinfectant, rage is quick to come to ver face, only to be murdered by fear from a knock at the door.

Chapter 16: Something Selfless

For a moment, Kidu's attention is fixated on the door, ver mouth quivering as ve chokes on the words of a response. Taking advantage of this lapse in attention, Shibi pours the remaining disinfectant into the now empty cup and sets it a short distance away.

Kidu's fear of the door is soon overridden by the fear of refusing to answer it, and ve shakily opens the door to come face to face with the last thing ve likely wants to see right now.

A Rirmevu duo stands at the door, flanked by what appears to be a mage and a Rirkase duo. Rirkase is a form of law enforcement wherein an atu or bitu teams up with a notu.

While Rirmevu tend to work as solitary pairs, this sort of grouping is not uncommon when confronting a criminal on their home turf, especially under the gaze of maybe four dozen or more people peering out of their huts to spectate the drama.

However, most residents of the slum only look long enough to figure out what is happening, and the moment they do, they avert their eyes. I had always wondered why people would avoid watching, given that spectators keep us law enforcement accountable, but in the time I have been living down here, I have heard the advice parents give to their children: Stay out of trouble. If you think someone is about to commit a crime, look away so that you don't become a target.

Very few want to risk bearing witness to potential foul play on behalf of law enforcement, so the glowing eyes peering out of the surrounding shadows vanish almost as quickly as they appear.

The bipedal uniform of a Rirkase duo is mid-grey with the iconic purple slotted seams of the ministry and features a golden metal pin in the shape of a circle vertically bisected by gold sculpted to resemble a notu gemstone. In a Rirkase duo, the notu works as a sort of living, self-healing armor that is useful for absorbing and deflecting blows while their colleague is the damage dealer.

The mage wears the same style uniform as the officers who debriefed me. Though ver uniform brandishes a gold circle horizontally bisected by an eye that is open and looking upwards instead of closed, the mage's actual eyes are closed. Ver hand is extended towards the Rirmevu duo, while the other hand clutches a rock, likely granting the officer at the door the durability of the stone as a measure of precaution.

Of all those standing at the door, the Rirmevu duo feels closest to us, not just because they are at the front of the group, but also because the biped is half the stature of everyone else.

The Rirmevu biped is the only one to adorn a mask in an attempt to hide ver identity, though ver species betrays ver. Two objects under ver knit cap create subtle mounds, and ver mask doesn't rest flat against ver face like it would on the flat face of an atu. Additionally, one leg looks slightly bigger than the other as the pant leg attempts to hide the presence of a tail. That uniform cannot be comfortable for ver. It is obvious that ve is a bitu, and that means ve is most likely Fami, and the yetu on ver back is likely Buso.

Fami is a dark-red furred bitu whose family was exalted while ve was still a pup, and ve was quickly entered into Rirmevu training once it was clear ve would be of small stature. Many people wonder if ver role as a Rirmevu was a good idea, calling into question ver ability to enact justice on members of ver own dark-furred race. Others suggest that having more dark-furred bitu officers will help ensure enforcement is carried out righteously, while also serving as a symbol of hope for dark-furred bitu who do not believe in exaltation.

The last I heard, Fami was not yet actively serving in ver role. Ve was shadowing other officers first, and ve even shadowed me during a patrol... The more I think about that patrol, the sicker to my stomach it makes me feel...

Fami's words from back then echo through my memory.

"I know protocol dictates that punishment be dealt no matter the age, but ve is just a child. How was ve supposed to know any better? If we punished every child for theft, there would be no one left with thumbs!

Children take things that are not theirs all the time. It's a natural part of growing up. This isn't right!"

"I understand what you mean Fami," I responded. "And you are right. We need to exercise some discretion. In this case, children taking toys from each other is different from a child stealing and consuming the hard-earned food of several families. Besides, ve seems to have been engaging in this behavior for a while without being caught by a yetu."

Fami gazed into the distance, seemingly unsure and torn, with ver grip on the struggling dark-red furred pup appearing fragile.

At that moment, Miya chimed in to support my point. "Listen, Fami, if we allow this kind of behavior to go unpunished, soon every child in Hosudiha will be encouraged by their parents to embark on endless crime sprees. There would be no hope for anyone to achieve exaltation through Ritu's virtues because everyone would descend into depravity overnight."

Adding the final touch, Buso interjected, "As much as it pains me to agree with both of you, I don't believe we have any other choice."

Fami's gaze is hardened and steadfast as ve begins to speak and assess the scene. "We are here to enact the necessary-" Ver eyes fall upon me, my open wound, clearly near-death condition, and the empty bottle of disinfectant in Shibi's hand. Ver hardened gaze breaks with compassion. "Pu- I, um..."

"Remember," Buso speaks softly to Fami, "Remember why this is necessary."

"I knew ve wasn't ready," The atu half of the Rirkase duo mutters.

Fami's expression attempts to harden once more. "We are here to enact the necessary punishment for the crime of theft as committed by you." Fami points to Shibi.

"Ah declare da right to penal subs-itution!" Mebi shouts almost immediately, paw raised in the air. Everyone present is taken aback by ver words. Fami's speech hangs incomplete in the air.

"No!" Shibi yells, "Ah stole it! Da punishment is mine ta-"

"Quiet!" Kidu shouts, "You pups are the future of this family. When I am no longer able to work, it will fall upon you two to keep us afloat. Your thumbs are more valuable than mine." Kidu raises ver paw. "I declare the right to penal substitution!"

How could I let this happen? This has to be a failure on my part. I am here to illuminate the path to exaltation for these people. If I were doing my job, Shibi would have known that stealing the medicine is wrong. Shibi would have known to wait for Ritu before taking matters into ver own paws. If anyone should suffer the consequences of this theft, it is me!

I try to raise my paw and declare the right to penal substitution when the pain in my arm causes me to yelp in a distinctly bitu way, reminding me that this is not my body to sacrifice.

Attention falls on me momentarily.

"Shibi, finish taking care of Dima... Er- Viadu. Let's get this over with."

Fami's gaze darts back and forth between Kidu and me for an instant, "Okay..." Fami says.

"Please, let's take this outside. Spare the pups the sight." Kidu says.

"Very well," Fami agrees. "Though perhaps we should settle the fine first. That's three swigs and three shots for the medicine, plus an additional swig and two shots for the fine."

Kidu nods and walks over to ver coin purse, adds a few more coins to it, cinches it shut, and throws it at Fami, who catches it with ease. Then they leave the hut, closing the door behind them.

In Sudihatosema terms that is four charities and five alms! If I could access my money, I could buy the medicine and cover the fine forty times over, with money to spare! Yet down here, such a small sum of cash makes the difference between exaltation and being stuck in the slums for three more salaries. My mind struggles to make sense of this. How hard can it be to earn four charities down here?

My bewilderment at the unaffordability of such cheap medication subsides enough for me to read the room. The pups are staring at the door. I'm not sure they know what to expect from this.

"Ve will be okay. I promise." I say.

Shibi begins to cry, "Dat was suppos ta be mah punishment! Ah made da selfless choice!"

"And Kidu did as well," I remind Shibi. Though I'm not sure to what extent Kidu's actions were selfless versus just looking out for ver future, "Ve will be alright."

"Will ve? Why did we have ta pay for it? Isn't a thumb enough? Ah thought it would only cost me a thumb," Shibi's thoughts come rushing out of ver lips as ve slips into a negative spiral.

"Yes, there is a fine," I explain. "People can't replace their possessions with thumbs. We will be okay, though. We can make the money back, and we will. Kidu will manage without a thumb, I promise."

"Ya have no idea how many people die from infected burns, do ya?" Mebi bites at me.

I narrow my eyes. "We have an advantage," I gesture to the cup of disinfectant. I do know that many people die as a result of Rirmevu punishments. Ministry teachings suggest that such deaths are Ritu's doing and not ours. However, the number of deaths resulting from punishments is still a point of discomfort for me. I try hard not to dwell on it.

"So what?" Shibi asks. "Whad if vedi loses ver job because ve struggles ta work without a thumb? What're we gonna do? Will Jove have ta work longer? Will we ever see ver again? What have Ah done? Ah just keep making everyone miserable! Y'all would be better off withou me."

As if to affirm Shibi's declarations, the sound of Kidu's yelps comes piercing through the door. Silence hangs in the air for a moment.

"I wouldn't be. I might have died tonight," I say, trying to reassure Shibi. However, my words are undercut by a grueling scream from Kidu, followed shortly by the pungent scent of seared flesh.

Fami opens the door. Ver eyes look hollow, similar to how they looked after our patrol incident a while back. Ve still feels remorseful about enacting these punishments, and I can't blame ver. Ve can't bring verself to look at those of us in the room before stepping back to let Kidu in and closing the door behind ver.

"Water!" Kidu commands, holding ver now thumbless dominant paw before ver. Mebi quickly fills a bowl with water for Kidu to plunge ver paw into. Kidu grits ver teeth. "Quick with the disinfectant." Shibi grabs the cup and brings it over to Kidu, who snatches it and applies a small splash to the wound, letting out a painful scream.

The door flies open once again, and Jove comes charging in, looking understandably distressed. Ve verself looks worse for wear, with ver red dress dirtied and torn, and one of ver eyes swollen. "What happened?" Jove asks.

"I made a stupid choice," Kidu says through gritted teeth.

"Shattered skies! Did you steal?" Jove exclaims.

Shibi interjects, "No, ve didn make da stupid choice! Ah did."

"Shut up pup!" Kidu shouts. "You wouldn't have ever had to make the choice you did if I just swallowed my pride and paid for the damn medicine to begin with." Kidu's body strains from pain, "Dima was dying. It was clear to everyone, but I just couldn't stomach the thought of prolonging our stay in this hase hole any more than necessary."

Kidu looks at me, the pain in ver face almost makes me wonder if ve is angry at me. Then Kidu continues, "However, Dima certainly would have died, and that would be one less paw to help us dig our way out of here. You did what you had to. There is nothing more to discuss."

"I beg to differ!" Jove yells. "How could you be such a fool?"

"Stop!" I yell, "This was my fault. Ritu was going to heal me. I knew that, but you all didn't. I should have said something."

Jove stares at me, ver furious eyes setting flame to my soul. "Ritu wasn't about to do shit! Ve did nothing when I was raped for the first time at two basins old, nor any of the other times for the last twenty-three basins. Not even this evening! And Ve didn't even do anything when my firstborn died in my arms shortly after I gave birth to ver. Who the hase do you think you are? Do you think your life is the only one that matters?"

"No. Ritu just chose me to-"

"To what?" Jove dares.

"To... I could die at any time. If I die then Ritu finds someone else."

"Someone else to do what?" Jove insists.

"To... to help you people..."

Jove snarls, "If Ritu wanted to help, Ve should have done it a long time ago."

"Ritu does help. Ve just doesn't violate people's free will. Ve lets bad things happen because, in order for us to validly choose Ver, we must be permitted to validly choose evil," I defend.

"Ah yes, let's just ignore all of the times Ritu violated people's free will in the Holy Scriptures. The time Ve split an island to save Ver chosen people, undermining the free will choice of the ruler who sought to murder them. Ritu never split an island to undermine the free will of my attackers. Or how about the time Ritu turned the Bitu ruler's mind feral to make the ruler submissive to Ver. Ritu never confused the mind of one of my attackers. Ritu doesn't give a shit about honoring people's free will, and Ve doesn't give a shit about us," Jove retorts.

"Who are you to question Ritu's judgment?" I bite back.

"Oh, I'm sorry. Ritu is good by nature, right? Ve is good even if Ver actions don't live up to our vetu ethical standards. Is that it? Tell me, how do you know Ritu is the good deity you think Ve is if you cannot use your own standards of goodness to make that judgment? Surely you know that an evil person can do a good thing? You can't conclude Ritu is good just because Ve has done good by you. So how do you make that judgment?" Jove's theological knowledge, though flawed, unsettles me.

"That is not our judgment to make!" I respond firmly.

"Then on what ground do you declare Ritu is a good deity?" Jove presses further.

"On grounds of faith!" I assert.

"Why? On what grounds did you choose to put your faith in Ritu as opposed to any of the other thousands of beings claiming to be deities?" Jove challenges.

The question momentarily scrambles my thoughts, but an answer emerges. "Ritu's Holy Scriptures! It is clear they were inspired by Ritu, and they are good."

"Again, on what grounds do you declare the Holy Scriptures to be good?" Jove presses, "If they are inspired by Ritu, wouldn't they be good even if they seemed evil by your personal standards? How do you even verify that they are inspired by Ritu? Is it that they are well preserved? What standards of preservation make a book divine? Is it that you believe the book predicts the future?"

Jove loses a bag from ver shoulder, pulls a copy of the Holy Scriptures from it, and starts flipping through the pages without looking at them, "How many beings might be outside of our plane of time, capable of flipping forward and backward through our plane of time like flipping through a book? There could be any number of such beings reading my very words right now. They could flip ahead fifteen pages and read what I might say in the future."

Jove shuts the book and throws it into my lap with enough force to hurt a little, "Does their existence outside of our plane of time make them divine? Infallible? Perfect? How many such beings might be capable of creating a reality like ours? How many of them might be capable of inspiring a book like the Holy Scriptures? How many are capable of producing that feeling inside of you that makes you believe they are Ritu any time you feel it? Maybe they can even erase and replace words in the future to change them. They could give us prophecies and then force their prophecies to come true. They could raise the dead. Does that make them perfect deities?"

Never before have questions struck me with such fear. I strain to think of a defense.

"You're just spouting off a bunch of what ifs with no basis in reality." I say.

"And you're not?" Jove asks, "We are looking at the same body of evidence and I am saying what if Ritu is a fallible author and you are saying what if Ritu is an almighty deity. Just because you leave off the 'what if' and assert your explanation as fact doesn't make your 'what if' any more true than mine. Unless you can provide some evidence to discount my possability, they both stand as equally likely. If we were to favor the simpler explanation, you are suggesting a being that has everything my being has and more. Making my explanation the simpler of the two."

Jove's words tear into me, into everything that has given me life. If I could, I would run away. I've faced many dangers in my life, but the danger of these words seems to tower over any other threat I've known.

Jove continues, "If it weren't for magic, I might even question the existence of a creator! If Ritu didn't exist, I might sleep better at night, free from the rage that comes with the thought of an all powerful being who is capable of saving me but unwilling to do so, and the fear that I may have to suffer for eternity due to that neglect. Down here most people have to play dirty to survive. If Ritu expects me to lie down and die, to let my family perish, just to adhere to ver virtuous ways of life, then Ritu can suck my dick."

It is evident that Ritu allows far more to happen than I am comfortable acknowledging. All this time, I had assumed that Ritu's plan was to rescue me from this place. That I would regain my body. That I would have my legs back. That life would return to normal after rectifying an unjust system. I don't want to entertain the thought that it could end any other way, but my mortality is becoming increasingly difficult to ignore.

What expectations should I have for this family? Should Kidu have purchased the medicine? If ve had, how long would it be before another minor injury becomes infected? How long before illness spreads like wildfire through this overcrowded slum, where there are over half a dozen people crammed into every one hundred square ingots? The potential for death down here is high. Buying the medicine might have saved me for now, but how many more of us might die as a result of the consequential prolonged stay?

I feel stranded in a storm ridden sea of uncertainty. I desperately reach into the recesses of my mind in search of anything which might save me. Lessons I received in theology, apologetics, my scripture studies, all crumble beneath the weight of Jove's words like the crumbling pieces of what was once a sturdy ship. Waves of despair threaten my life when suddenly my mental flailing brings me into contact with something which floats defiantly atop the raging waters, another 'what if'

"Maybe we are all one collective consciousness..." Jomira's beliefs leave my mouth. Of everything that might have saved me, this was not what I was expecting. Yet, for the time being, in this possibility, my mind finds security where all else falls to pieces.

"What nonsense are you babbling about now? Why can't you just admit that Ritu doesn't give a damn about us? I'm tired of your excuses!"

"Because it's all I have!" I yell, "I... I just can't accept that I'm here for nothing. Maybe you don't have to believe that our experiences, whether good or bad, contribute to something positive, something that makes up for all of this shit. But I want to. I need to! I'm not sure I can go on if I don't! I've been through rape too! Rape and captivity! If it weren't for Ritu, for the ministry, I'm not sure I would have survived. I'm not sure I would have had the will to."

Jove's hardened rage wordlessly fixates on me for a moment. The room is mostly quiet apart from Kidu who cannot help moaning and growling from the pain in ver paw. Gradually, Jove's furious expression softens, replaced by a mix of indignation and resignation.

"Fine," Jove says, bitterness lacing ver voice. "Whatever. I'm glad you have something to hold onto through all of this shit. I had hoped for freedom. When I was raped this tankard, I thought to myself that at least we would be moving out of this hasehole soon. I don't know if I can continue like this. My trust in Ritu died long ago! I wish I could be as privileged as you. What do I have to live for? My pups are growing older, and their chances of success in this world are diminishing. They're falling further behind with each passing tankard. What hope is there for them?"

Suddenly, a bag mysteriously falls to the ground. We all turn our attention to its origin and I catch a glimpse of gleaming eyes peering through a gap between the walls and the roof before they quickly disappear.

Jove swiftly runs outside, attempting to catch the stranger only to return shortly thereafter, demanding, "Open it!"

Mebi steps forward to open the bag, while Kidu curiously pokes ver head over it to take a sniff.

"It was the bitu officer!" Kidu exclaims.

Inside the bag, we find all of the coins from the fine and a note. Mebi hands the note to Jove, who squints and reads it silently. Ver face reveals a mix of emotions, but settles on a familiar one, anger.

"Good fortune may have found us," Jove says, "but everything I said about Ritu still stands. I don't know who you are to have earned Ritu's favor, but remember this, I hate you for it." Jove crumples up the note and tosses it onto the floor. "Ve said ve would cover the fee and even left us some extra coins," Jove adds before leaving the hut with a solemn demeanor.

Kidu rises, grabs the bandage with ver non-dominant paw (which still has a thumb), and tears it haphazardly in half using ver teeth. Ve hands one half to Shibi and wraps the other around ver injured paw. The shortened bandage barely covers the wound, merely draping over it. "Didn't I tell you to take care of Dima?" ve asks Shibi.

"Uh, yah. Sorry," Shibi meekly responds, turning to tend to my wound.

As Kidu opens the door smoke from a burning drug wafts into the hut prompting ver to quickly step outside. "You better not smoke it all without me," ve remarks.

Mebi delves into the bag and begins laying out the coins. Ver eyes widen as ve discovers a silver coin that I have taken to call a wage as it is known in Sudihatosema.

"Vedi! Vedi!" Mebi exclaims.

Kidu and Jove reenter the hut, Jove holding a lit blunt while Kidu attempts to use it to light ver own blunt. Mebi extends the wage, causing Jove to freeze upon seeing it. Taking advantage of Jove's momentary shock, Kidu uses Jove's blunt to ignite ver's and then takes a deep drag, exhaling a cloud of smoke with a sigh of relief. Ve notices the wage, takes another drag, and asks, "A tankard? Is there more?"

Mebi places the coin on the ground and empties the rest from the bag.

Along with the initial payment, we discover a total of three wages.

Ritu bless Fami.

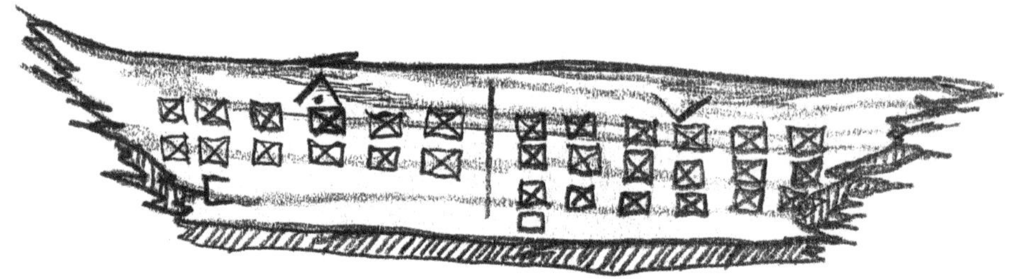

Chapter 17: Luck

The slums emitted more brown scents than this level of society, and I can now discern the difference, whereas before, as an atu, both places were just a brown blur. Now I can detect the subtle presence of pleasant scents amidst the overpowering sewage odor.

I find myself imagining how Sudihatosema must smell with this nose. There is certainly a trade-off. While the scents might be a pleasant blue blur to an atu, for a bitu, the brown would be there too, not lost in the blue blur. One can never escape the brown. But how much more beautiful must Sudihatosema smell through the nose of a bitu? Perhaps the brown adds to the scent image, similar to how browns can enhance the beauty of a painting or even be beautiful as subject matter.

Most of my labor-dreams now revolve around experiences of scent rather than sight, as they used to. Ever since we moved into this apartment, which is roughly the same size as the hut, if not smaller due to the addition of a stone slab covering a hole in which water is constantly running by to carry away waste.

At least the family no longer has to travel and pay to use a public toilet, and Miya and I no longer need to worry about making as much of a mess when nature calls. We even have a designated area for a fire under a chimney, and the walls are made of brick that extends to the ceiling. So, although the space looks similar, it is undoubtedly an upgrade in many aspects.

Apart from the overwhelming scent of sewage, which fluctuates when waste floats by in the water beneath the floor, there are also occasional whiffs of what I assume are cheap floral perfumes. Flowers don't grow down here, so the scent must come from perfumes, unless the flowers are imported, which seems unlikely given the financial circumstances of the residents.

The scent I find most welcoming is the intermittent and familiar aroma of baked goods. Judging by how little of the air is filled with these scents, I assume they are treats that only a few people purchase for special occasions or celebrations.

However, there is one scent that dominates over all others, except for the sewage. It is so prominent that I might have detected it even as an atu. It's the distinct aroma of burning woods and coal. As an atu, one campfire smelled like any other campfire, but as a bitu, each wood and type of coal has its own unique scent. It is more clear than ever that illegal wood burnings in Hosudiha is a widespread “issue”. People even seem to take pride in the different scents they can acquire for burning.

What I cannot understand is why, when I was an officer, I wasn’t informed about these burings. It is not like the bitu try to hide it. Even Jove and Kidu have spoken quite casually about looking forward to acquiring some nice woods for burning. Though as newcomers, we haven't had the chance to burn anything in the quarter-deposit we've been here, as we're still adjusting to the new expenses that came with the move.

Speaking of new expenses, Jove sits between Miya and me, hunched over a wooden plank with a pencil in ver paw. Ver eyes are filled with stress and disbelief as ve struggles to balance expenses against income. Kidu and the pups sleep behind ver, while Miya appears to be sleeping as well. I have been pretending to sleep, but my thoughts won't let me rest.

What is the point of virtues when luck seems to play a bigger role in a person's quality of life than anything that is under their control? You have to be lucky enough to avoid sickness, injuries, and trouble that would set the family back by salaries. Even in Sudihatosema, it seemed like I couldn't go a deposit without the expense of something breaking, needing replacement or repair. Such expenses are all the more costly down here, and back then, I didn't even have to worry about healthcare because it was freely provided by the ministry, with ample supplies. So there is also being lucky enough to be born into favorable circumstances.

Though is there such a thing as luck when Ritu is pulling the strings? What truly got us out of the slums? The image of the incomplete tower of Matuha comes to mind. Ritu.

Perhaps, the "luck" element is the part that is in Ritu's control. No one exalts themselves, even if it may appear that way. Shibi has received Ritu into ver heart, and Ritu is at work cultivating virtues within ver. Those fruits of selflessness are still immature; manifesting alongside vices which have yet to be shed. Still, Shibi's fruits of Ritu's spirit have inspired virtue in the rest of the family. Perhaps it was that progression that made the difference. That was what Ritu needed us to learn before Ve would change our "luck" and exalt us.

That explanation clarifies a lot, but not everything. While processing all of this, Jove's words have been piercing my thoughts, demanding to be addressed. I cannot avoid them any longer; I must confront those words and the questions they raise. After all, I am here to tear down the barricades blocking these people from Ritu.

I recall Jove's words, "Down here most people have to play dirty to survive. If Ritu expects me to lie down and die, to let my family perish, just to adhere to ver ways of life, then Ritu can suck my..." Yeah, those are the words.

Ritu, why didn't You stop ver attackers? Why didn't You save ver firstborn? You intervened for others before, so why not for Jove? I might assume that ver experiences are the consequences of ver own actions, but at two salaries old? Two salaries old! How could ve have deserved that? If You deem it permissible for a two salary old to suffer at no fault of their own, then who is to say Jove is at fault for any of the sufferings ve has endured? And given all of that suffering, is it reasonable to expect ver to adopt the ways of life when the ways of death seem to be all that protects ver, all that leads to any kind of progress?

Perhaps, Ritu, You know that You cannot expect Jove to easily relinquish the ways of death, and in knowing that, You exalt ver to a place where it might be easier. Still, where were You? Why did You take so long to lift ver out of ver sufferings?

My own situation comes to mind. I am here not because I deserve to be here, but because Ritu's mission demands it.

Maybe Jove's sufferings are meant to serve a similar purpose? You may have plans for ver to become involved in the ministry. I had wondered for so long why You didn't stop me from going with Lise before I chose to just ignore that you let it happen. Now I realize that had I not experienced that, I wouldn't have been able to connect with Jove;

Jove knows that I can understand ver plight to some degree because I have suffered similarly.

In essence, a mission field is more than just a physical location; it is also a spiritual place that one reaches through life experiences. Often, people won't listen or learn from a missionary unless the missionary has been in their spiritual location, has suffered in the same ways they have. Jove has suffered, and it may not be ver fault, but that suffering equips ver to be compassionate and sharpens ver words to break through to more people. If Jove survives and ver relationship with You is restored, ve may become a more effective minister than anyone currently in the field. That must be why You have permitted ver to suffer the life ve has suffered...

Unfortunately, in permitting ver to suffer, Jove has become convinced that You don't care about ver life. Whereas You may care more about ver life than anyone else! Or perhaps You care just as much about everyone's lives, but in different ways. We all have different roles to play, and for some, their role requires more suffering than others but may be more highly rewarded in the end. Now, how do I help Jove realize that?

The weight of this task burdens me, but I understand it clearly now. It's not my responsibility to save everyone; my role is to be a stepping stone so that Jove, and perhaps this entire family, can go on to guide the hearts of more people to Ritu than my privileged ass ever could.

Jove's other questions still linger in my mind, demanding to be addressed. However, for now, I am satisfied with the progress Ritu and I have made. I can finally attempt to find some rest.

"Damn it! Damn it! Damn it!" Jove whispers under ver breath, squeezing ver head between ver paws.

"What is it?" I ask, startling Jove with my sudden question.

"Don't scare me like that," Jove quietly snarls. "Go to sleep. I don't want to talk to you."

Jove looks back at the plank of wood, trying to ignore me.

"We're lucky to have you," I persist.

Jove's hardened anger softens a bit. I continue, "Thank you for working as hard as you do, and I'm sorry you've suffered as much as you have. You deserve better."

"Shut up!" Jove says, almost forgetting to be quiet. "I said I don't want to talk to you."

"Okay," I say. Well, perhaps now isn't the time. I turn over to try to fall asleep.

A moment passes, and then Jove says, "I deserve better, huh? Who are you to say that? Aren't I getting exactly what your precious Ritu deems me worthy of deserving?" Ve wants me to recognize the hypocrisy in my words, seeking both discomfort and validation in my response.

I roll back over to face ver.

"I'm not so sure anymore," I respond.

"Interesting. So you're starting to question Ritu's judgment, are you?" Jove says with a devious smirk.

"No," I clarify. Jove's smirk vanishes. "I'm just realizing that not everyone suffers because they deserve it. Sometimes we suffer so that we can learn to overcome it, equipping us to help others overcome similar sufferings later."

Jove's brow furrows, and ver gaze returns to the plank of wood as ve processes my words. "I never asked to be made into a tool, to be stripped of my dignity just so I can be made useful for some deity. What a vemoizing thought."

"Vemoizing? How so?" I inquire.

"How so? I'm not some tool to be sharpened and shaped! I'm a whole-ass person. I have wants, desires, and dreams! Those things matter to me. Who is Ritu to tell me who I am? To say that my wants, desires, and dreams don't matter? That Ver wants, desires, and dreams for me are more important? If Ritu wants to shape me into something other than who I am, then why make me this way to begin with?" Jove asks.

"Your wants, desires, and dreams do matter to Ritu, but so do everyone else's. Ritu works through vetu to lift one another up so that those wants, desires, and dreams can be realized. However, sometimes a person can only be lifted by someone who has been broken in a similar way. So what is Ritu to do? Just abandon those who are broken? Or will Ritu build a ladder of once-broken people so that Ve can reach the most broken? That means some people will have to suffer more than they deserve so they can contribute to that ladder."

"I never asked to be a part of some damn ladder!"

"Who would?"

Silence hangs heavy in the air as my words seem to cut deep into Jove's resolve.

"What is the point of all of this?" Jove's voice breaks the stillness. "Ritu sets up the vetu, knowing we would fail. Then Ve plays this long-ass game of who's going to find Me and be saved from the fire I've made to burn the losers forever. What do we get out of this cruel game? Couldn't Ritu have given us whatever we gain from it at the very beginning?"

"Well, we do get the opportunity to make a choice," I respond.

"So? What does that matter?" Jove's frustration is palpable. "If this life is just an opportunity to make a choice, then what is the point of the next life when all the choices have been made? If there is a point to the next life, then why not start there? Is all this suffering and ladder shit really necessary? And what choice? Find Me or burn forever? Oh, and remember, 'My ways are higher than your ways,' so you're going to struggle to perceive My plan as good. It may even seem bad by your standards, not unlike the plans of deceptive spirits and even some clever vetu. But just ignore your sense of ethics and reason to instead trust that My spirit will guide you to the truth. Also, ignore the fact that people claiming to be led by My spirit disagree enough to warrant tens of thousands of denominations of the faith, and ignore the fact that there are thousands of deceptive spirits out there adept at fooling people into believing they are My spirit. Good luck!"

"Those are good questions Jove... I'm going to have to think about that," I say, my mind once again grappling with the weight of Jove's words.

"Please do," Jove responds.

I add Jove's latest existential crisis inducing questions to my processing to-do list. However, I'm too tired and shaken to process it all right now. Exhaustion weighs heavily on me, but the unsettling nature of those words prevents sleep from claiming me.

"Are we going to be okay?" I ask.

Jove remains silent for a while before responding, "I hope so. But not without taking some major risks... and making some unfortunate sacrifices. I hope our luck doesn't run out anytime soon."

"You know the ministry provides free housing, right? We could maybe-"

Jove scoffs, interrupting me. "If by free, you mean they don't make you pay money for it, then sure, it's free. But they make you pay with your time. The ministry doesn't believe in handouts. They think it makes people dependent. So, they require you to work for the ministry, doing things like working in the food kitchen, sorting donations, or even creating jewelry and stuff for them to sell. They call it skill building, but in reality, they work you to the bone without pay and then force you to attend a tankardly service where you're pressured into worshiping Ritu and learning about Ver 'precious Holy Scriptures'. Only after all of that do you have a chance to work one or two additional jobs, if you can find any that align with the Ministry's schedule. Then, as if the ministry didn't already squeeze us enough for our time, they have a curfew and some places even take a cut out of any paycheck you earn from other work. It's a facade for slave labor."

The memory of the bracelet I bought from missionaries a few salaries ago resurfaces, and I can't help but feel a sense of unease. If what Jove is saying is the truth, I feel guilty for supporting such efforts. However, I try to remind myself that not every ministry endeavor may be as unhelpful and exploitative.

"Oh," I say thoughtfully, "Pardon me, but may I ask you another question?"

Jove lets out a deep sigh, "At this point our conversation is turning into a break, and I could use a break from this so sure why not."

"Isn't it illegal to burn the sorts of woods people burn here?" I ask.

Jove scoffs once more, "Life in Hosudiha is illegal. Up until our move we were living in illegal housing. Even now the water running beneath our apartment is illegally sourced. Everyone living in Hosudia is guilty of something. We are only apprehended or punished when they need to fill prison cells with more slaves or an officer needs to let out some steam."

"What do you mean by 'fill prison cells with slaves'?"

"Supposedly slavery was abolished. However the indentured servitude of criminals is an exception to the abolition. The population of Hosudiha is a population of wage slaves that can be converted into indentured slaves when needed. Slavery was never really abolished, it was only rebranded as prison labor, ministry labor, or cheap labor, and whether they know it or not, law enforcers are the newly rebranded slavers."

Jove has no idea how heavily ver words slam into me. What have I really been doing as an officer all of this time? I feel crushed by the weight of a guilt that I do not yet fully understand.

The weight of the conversation and the silence that follows lead me into a state of distressed contemplation, followed closely by an overwhelming urge to sleep. Though my sleep is restless, and full of new nightmares wherein I am the monster.

"Starting this tankard, you two both have jobs working in the mines," Jove declares to the pups.

"That's not fair! Ya said we'd get ta go ta school after we got da apartment," Mebi accuses.

"Ya promised!" Shibi chimes in.

"I know. I was overly optimistic and ignorant. However, I still believe we have a future worth looking forward to. Now that we are out of the slum, once I get my degree I should be able to find a job in sales and clients who are willing to work with me. No one wants to do business with a slum dweller salesperson. So while we are tighter financially than we've ever been, we are finally in a spot where we can get out of it," Jove explains.

"How long's that gonna take?" Mebi asks.

"A basin," Jove responds.

"A basin! That's like forever!" Shibi retorts.

"Yeah! And didn' dat one kid die in da mines last basin?" Mebi argues.

"Well, it's either this or we go back to die in the slums! Is that what you want?" Jove yells, "Besides, it won't take a basin for us to get you two out of the mines and into school. It will only take until Miya is fit to work."

The pups groan in annoyance.

"I don't want to hear it! Come on, get ready. We are leaving in ten shots, and I'm going to show you both how to get to the mine. Dima, you are in charge of cleaning while we are all gone," Jove instructs.

I'm still getting used to measuring time in terms of clean water earned in a span of time, so it takes my brain a moment to make sense of the time frame Jove expressed. I believe a basin is the same as a salary. Ritu, I hope it doesn't take that long for us to get out of here.

I have become proficient at crawling and propping myself up at this point. I am more helpful than ever before, though I am not sure how ready I am to completely take over household duties.

"Miya," Jove continues, "keep practicing movement and help as much as you can."

Miya gives a thumbs up, an achievement ve accomplished a few labors ago, but hardly the biggest one. Ve has also reached a point where ve can roll over and army crawl to some extent. Soon enough, ve will be more mobile than I am.

Within ten charities, Miya and I are left alone.

"I'm struggling, Miya," I admit. This will mark the first significant span of time Miya and I will be left alone, and I have a lot to vent.

Miya points at verself and nods.

"You too?"

Miya nods.

"Well, shoot. I want to vent to you, though I feel bad that you can't vent back."

Miya makes a gesture as if to say, “Go on.”

“Okay... Jove and I had a conversation four labors ago while you were sleeping.”

Miya shakes ver head.

“Hmm...” I pause to interpret the head shake. Is ve expressing disapproval of my conversation with Jove? The conversations do feel somewhat dangerous. Or was Miya just not asleep like I assumed?

“Were you asleep?”

Miya shakes ver head.

“Oh, so you know the conversation I'm talking about then.”

Miya nods.

I sigh, “The part where ve basically called Ritu's plan an impossible game of hide and seek where the losers burn forever. I never realized just how hard that game is to play. Because ve is right! There are parts of the Holy Scriptures that don't seem good to me and I was always told to just trust Ritu, don't apply my standards of ethics because Ritu's ways are higher than our ways.

Then we turn around and criticize other texts that claim to be holy scriptures because they don't live up to our standards of ethics. We are meant to trust the spirit, but it's evident that it's hard to distinguish the spirit from deceivers or even from our own carnal urges and desires. The prophecies are touted as the proof of Ritu's hand in the Holy Scriptures, but how many beings can read our future like flipping ahead a few pages in a book? There is no way to prove that it's only Ritu who can do that.

Maybe they flip back to this point, rip out whatever Ritu had written, and then write their own take on us and our lives like some sort of fan-crafted work of fiction. Would we even be able to tell the difference between someone who can see the future and someone who is just powerful enough to ensure the future they predicted comes to pass?

I want to believe in something, Miya, and for the first time in my life I don't feel like I am obligated to believe anything specific.

I don't have to believe in Hase.

I don't have to believe that my attraction to males is against Ritu's intended design.

I don't have to believe I am morally bankrupt or otherwise incomplete without Ritu.

I don't have to believe that belief systems outside of mine are inherently evil.

I don't have to go through all of the effort to scripturally justify what I support and what I oppose.

I don't have to interpret the world in the ways I was told I had to interpret it despite everything else saying some of those interpretations are unnecessary, unhealthy, harmful, or just more trouble than they are worth. I can consider many interpretations. It's like I'm going from only seeing in black and white to seeing in full color.

I can believe these things if I want to, or reject them. Maybe even hold onto them as possibilities that I consider alongside other possibilities I'm uncertain about.

I am free, but now that I am free, I don't know what I want to believe in. Do you know what I mean?"

Miya puts on a thoughtful expression and tilts ver head back and forth.

"Sort of?" I ask.

Miya nods.

"I wish you could add your thoughts to the table," I say.

Miya points to verself and nods.

"Can you say 'me'?" I ask.

"Mmmumm Mem."

"Close. How about 'too'?"

"Tut, t. Mem tut."

"Me too. Oo."

"Mm tooo..."

"That's it! You got it! Me too!"

"Mee too."

"Awesome! High five!"

Miya pats my paw with ver paw. I am so excited for ver to start talking. "Now... Do you want to race?"

Miya nods and manages to roll over and starts to army crawl over to me, then turns to face in the same direction.

"Alright, on three. One... Two... Three!" And just like that, we are crawling, and I leave Miya in the dust. I have to savor my ability to do that while I can.

I long for my body. I long for my legs and bowel control again. How in the world are we going to find our bodies? Never mind finding them, how are we going to find the time to even try?

Miya lets out a sudden yelp, and I turn to look at ver. Ve is trying to lift ver leg, but ver pants are snagged on a splinter in the floor.

"Oh, shit," I say as I crawl over to ver. Prior to my life in Hosudiha I tried not to use profanity since it was culturally looked down upon. Down here however, such words hold unifying and endearing power. So I've let some slip into my vocabulary a bit. "Did it scratch you?"

I help ver break free, but not without damaging ver pant leg.

Suddenly, a memory from several labors ago hits me. While I was exiting the tavern, located near the mines, to chase the thief, I tore my pants on a nail or something. It took some cloth and maybe a little blood with it. That would have my scent on it, and with it, we might be able to track down my body!

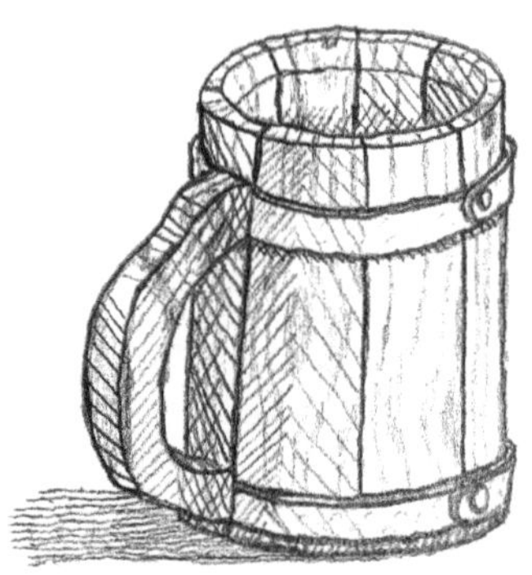

Chapter 18: Something Selfish

Miya has made great progress with walking, speech, and fine motor skills. Though ve is not super sturdy on ver feet just yet, ve could work a basic job at this point. That's why we've been keeping ver progress a secret from the family.

The moment they know Miya is work-ready, they will put us to work. While that's great because Shibi and Mebi will be able to go to school instead of having to work in the mines, it will prevent Miya and me from starting our search. It's been about three deposits, and they should be able to handle a few more labors while we search for their vedira.

As soon as the pups have left for work, we wait for a bit to be sure they don't come back having forgotten anything. Then Miya eases verself onto ver feet, fetches a blue robe of Hinuso's to put on, and hoists me up onto ver back.

Finally, it's my turn to be the back rider, though I admit, with how much Miya has had to fly me around, we were probably close to even in terms of taking turns carrying each other. Also, I have little to offer in terms of aiding Miya, whereas ve could sense things I couldn't when ve was the back rider. Still, I find my new role amusing.

While Miya is not the sturdiest walker as of the present, and carrying me only makes that worse, ve is managing the task remarkably well. I think only a dozen or so onlookers have assumed Miya is a drunkard carrying another who is too drunk to walk.

After much tripping and rest stops, the smell of raw coal serves as an indicator that the mines, and by extension, the tavern, is near. There are actually a few familiar scents in the air. Two are clearly Shibi and Mebi, but the third is harder to place. I know I've smelled it before, but I cannot recall where.

We walk around the tavern to see if the roof may be accessible from the outside. However, of course, outside access to a roof hatch would be a bit of a security risk for the tavern. So they have been careful to ensure no such access exists unless you have wings.

So, we enter the tavern through the front door, and that unfamiliar scent suddenly has a face. There, where Sho had once sat, is Fami sitting alone. However, ve is not engaged in the tafose challenge Sho had suffered. Ve is about as short as I was in my atu body. Ve is also in uniform, though without the mask. Glasses are perched on ver uncommonly dark-red furred snout as ve is leaning back, drinking mead, and staring into the distance, deep in thought. At this time of labor, the tavern is practically empty, so when we enter, Fami is quick to notice and almost seems startled at first. Then ve sees our faces, and ver eyes light up.

"Oh, hey. I remember you two. Come. Come. Have a drink with me!" Fami calls out.

The sudden invitation from the officer is unsettling and slightly bothersome. We were hoping to be in and out, though we do still need to work out a way to access the roof hatch and the barkeep is not likely to let us just start climbing around.

"You are going to need to set me down to climb up there. Might as well set me down with Fami," I whisper to Miya.

"Alright," Miya says, "If you say so."

"I'll join you," I call out, "but Hinuso has some business to tend to."

"Very well." Fami says.

The barkeeper pauses ver progress polishing a glass and walks over to me.

"Welcome to my tavern. My name is Geni. What can I get for you?"

"I'm sorry," I start. "I don't have the coin to-"

"Not another word." Geni cuts in, "If you are a friend of Fami's, it's on the house."

"Oh, thank you. Isn't it a bit early to be drinking?" I ask.

"Not in Hosudiha! What? Did you fall from grace just yestertankard?" Geni remarks, garnering a chuckle from Fami.

"Um, sure, I'll take mead." I say.

"Coming up." Geni says.

Miya approaches Geni and asks ver something, presumably about the roof hatch.

"These two are with you, right?" Geni calls out to Fami.

"What is ve intending to do?" Fami asks me.

"We managed to get something important stuck on the roof. Miya was probably asking if it would be alright for ver to climb up and get it." I say.

"Okay," Fami looks past me and shouts back to Geni, "Yeah, they are with me!"

Geni gives a nod of approval to Miya and starts pointing to suggest a means of climbing up. I'm glad this chance encounter has gone from an inconvenience to making things easy for us. However, given that Miya only recently started getting proficient with walking, I'm concerned about ver attempting to climb up without any support.

"Is your yetu partner here?" I ask, "Hinuso just recently recovered from an injury, and I'm worried about ver climbing."

"Um, no. Ve is... sleeping." Fami stammers. Odd... It's almost noon.

"Hey, I can help you!" Fami calls after Miya, who was just about to attempt the climb. "What exactly are you two looking for up there?"

"Um..." I start to say. Shit. If Fami figures out who I really am, what might ve do? I wish we hadn't run into ver at all. "No, that's okay. Ve can handle it."

"No, really. It's nothing. I can help." Fami insists.

"No!" I shout. My heart is racing. Damn it, why am I so afraid of ver. Have I really lost so much trust in my fellow Hosudiha officers?

Fami freezes in the middle of standing up. My anxiety got the better of me, and now Fami is looking at me with far more uncertainty. Ve sits back down.

"Okay then. It's something private, I assume," Fami says. "Fair enough. None of my business."

Miya, looking slightly disappointed, returns to the task of climbing. The fact that Fami is backing off and not investigating my clearly suspicious behavior put me a bit at ease. Ve clearly only has good will towards us.

Fami continues, "I don't know if you remember me. Actually, you probably do..."

"I know you," I say. "You're Fami, the new bitu Rirmevu."

"Yeah... Sort of. Anyway, the last time I saw you, you looked like you were lying on your deathbed. I'm glad to see you recovered. How have you been since then?"

"We have been... well. We've managed. What you did helped us find legal housing. So, uh, thanks for that. I'm surprised the ministry let you take on the fee like that."

"Hardly," Fami says, "Sergeant Makali really chewed me out. Ve went on and on about how we cannot negate the consequences of crime or else it will just encourage more crime. Which, I mean, I get it. People take advantage of generosity all the time. I assume you saw firsthand how the free supply of medicine at the hospital gets nabbed and then sold right across the street. But I knew, the moment I assessed your family's situation, that it was the right thing for me to do. It, and other things I've deemed right, might cost me my job though."

"I'm sorry to hear that." I say.

"Don't be. I've begun to realize something in all of the time training and then actually working. It seems that no matter how hard I try to be a good enforcer of the law, I can only be as good as the laws... or worse... and the laws... Ritu forgive me. The laws just don't seem completely good."

Fami takes a deep swig of mead as if to wash out ver mouth of heresy. Then ve continues, "Sure, there are a lot of good ones that we can all agree on. I just am realizing more and more that trying to apply rigid laws in a world where right and wrong seem so contextual, it just ends up hurting more people than it helps. Maybe they were never supposed to be applied rigidly. I don't know. I wish Ritu had made the laws harder to abuse and easier to understand. You'd think that would be sort of important to Ver, given how many people suffer as a result of how easy it is to abuse or and misapply the laws."

"Yeah," I say soberly, "I hadn't considered that. I mean, lies often come packaged with truths in an attempt to go unquestioned. Maybe the Holy Scriptures contain both truths and lies..."

Fami looks disturbed by the suggestion, so I add, "I mean, it could also be what you said about them just being misunderstood and misapplied."

"No, you're right. There could be lies. It's just an uncomfortable thought." Fami says, "Either way, the Holy Scriptures don't seem to produce an infallible guide to life and governance. Be it due to its own fallibility or the fallibility of those interpreting it..."

"Or the malicious intent of those interpreting it." I add.

As different as Fami and I's backgrounds are, this conversation makes me feel deeply intertwined with ver. Ver world is falling apart, and so is mine. Ve is asking verself many of the same questions Miya and I are. It brings me hope knowing we aren't the only ones going through this. How many more of us might there be? Enough to make a change? Even if it's just Fami, it's nice to know that someone can reach these same conclusions without having to experience the unlikely things Miya and I have. I hope enough people start seeing and caring about these problems in our society because otherwise, what place is there for me here?

"Anyway, I'm leaving the ministry," Fami declares.

Ver announcement startles me, "Really?"

"Yeah. I'm not sure it's where I need to be. Though I'm not sure where to go from here. How do I even get off of this rock without the ministry's help? Then there is what I did to Buso..."

"You didn't!" I exclaim, pretty sure I know what Fami did based on the clues ve has given up to this point.

Fami gives me an inquisitive look.

"Did you knock out your partner with a dart?" I ask.

Fami's eyes narrow in suspicion. "Yeah... Anyway, it's not an easy decision to make."

"I get that..." I say.

"You do?... What is your name again?" Fami asks.

"Oh, um..." For an alm, I forgot I wasn't Dima to ver.

Fortunately, our conversation is suddenly interrupted by the sound of a crash from Miya's direction. Fami jumps to ver feet and runs over to Miya, who lies among a now toppled table and chair.

"Are you okay?" Fami asks as ve helps Miya to ver feet.

"Yeah, I think I'm okay," Miya affirms.

Fami suddenly begins to sniff curiously. "Is that..." ve moves ver head around, tracking the direction of a scent, and suddenly ver eyes lock onto the piece of ripped cloth in Miya's paw. "So, um... How do you two know Dima?"

Miya looks at me. "What do you think?"

"Come over here." I say, "Let's take a seat. Fami, how much time do you think we have before Buso comes looking for you?"

"Probably already is, honestly," ve says as ve approaches the table with Miya.

"Okay, I'll try to make this quick. Dima is a friend who broke protocol and went missing. Given what you've told me, I assume you may go missing in much the same way."

"Yeah," Fami says, "I honestly should have planned my escape a bit better. It was a spur-of-the-moment thing. I didn't feel like I could go another labor punishing more people. The moment I realized I wouldn't be able to do what they wanted me to do, I realized I was questioning Ritu's judgment, and I got scared. What did Dima do?"

"Honestly, I thought I knew, but I'm not so sure anymore." I say.

"What did you think ve did?" Fami asks.

"I thought ve had punished Sergeant Makali." I say.

"Oh shoot! Uh, how so? I don't recall Sergeant missing anything... Unless..." Fami's eyes widen, "No way!"

"Yeah. The penis and testicles, but it was more than that. Ve committed murder too. Ve should have paraplegia like me." I say.

"Should have. What do you mean?" Fami asks.

"I remember punishing ver for murder, but then, labors later, I saw ver again. Ve was standing as if nothing happened. Then..." I realize I am not sure I can tell ver what happened next, and so I let silence take hold of the conversation.

Fami breaks the silence, "Labor huh... Don't you mean Tankard?"

Crap, I'm a really crummy liar. Though of course I would be. Lying is a vice I have spent most of my life avoiding.

"Back in the hut, you were called Dima for a moment."

"Yeah..." A feeling of unease washes over me as I contemplate coming clean, "I hardly believe it myself. So I don't expect you to. But, I am Dima."

"And you are looking for Dima?" Fami asks.

"I'm looking for my body. That is Miya." I say.

Miya waves.

I continue, "I don't know how... but after our run-in with Sergeant Makali, after I broke protocol and punished ver, ver punishments were seemingly undone. Ve said ve was sending us to the bottom. That Ritu would exalt us back up to where we belong. They rolled out two bitu on wheelchairs, the original owners of these bodies. Then, somehow, we were just in these bodies all of a sudden. It's as though Makali had given ver punishments to this body and then shoved me into it."

"Sounds like some twisted form of magic." Fami says pensively, "How much do you know about magic?" ve asks.

"I know that somehow mages can switch physical properties between two targets as long as they maintain concentration. That switch can include the mage as a target or not. The bigger or farther away the target is the harder it is to cast or maintain the spell. That's about all I know."

Fami nods thoughtfully. "I know a bit of magic. I had to learn physics and then learn how to express concepts of physics using the language of creation. From there, I can mentally tap into the fabric of creation, and pass through commands to temporarily alter the fabric."

I lean in, intrigued by Fami's words. Fami continues, "I had always wondered what I might be able to do if I expanded that education to include biology or psychology, but I've never been given the time or resources to explore. Perhaps one could cause targets to switch bodies, and somehow that doesn't require maintained concentration. Well, anyways, I wish I could help, but my magic is limited, and I've sort of doomed myself to be caught with how reckless I was. I wouldn't want to draw any attention to you two."

"Do you have any idea where we might try looking for our bodies at least?" I ask.

Fami shrugs and shakes ver head. "I'm still pretty new. They haven't shared much with me at this point."

I feel a surge of frustration. "Shit, at this rate, we just need to hope we get lucky and happen upon my scent while walking around randomly."

Suddenly, the ground shakes, glasses clatter, and shouts can be heard in the distance.

"There must have been another cave-in at the mine," Geni remarks casually, "It's been a while since that's happened."

"The mine! Miya, get me up. We need to go make sure the pups are alright!" I say.

"I'm coming too," Fami says.

Chapter 19: Cost

On our way to provide assistance we run past a small group of supervising officers. When they spot Famai the one sergeant present yells out, “Fami!”

Fami shoots the sergeant a glare, and seems to be uncertain if ve should stop or not before ve decides to stop and stand at attention,

“Yes ve!” Fami says.

“What the hase are you doing? If you run in there you might be taken hostage by some vemo looking to take advantage of a bad situation. Stay here and let the vemo clean up their own blunder.” The sergeant orders.

“With no respect ve, go fuck yourself.” Fami says before ve takes off into the mines and Miya follows after.

The sergeant’s yelling trails into the mines from behind us, “Fami! Ritu damn it, there will be hase to pay for this!”

Blood.

The scent permeates the air. We arrive, amidst a group of miners, ranging from children to adults, brutalizing their paws and hands as they tear away at the debris.

Given that I am strapped to Miya's back, there is little I can do to help, so I am left to observe, and I am startled by what I see. Apart from the obvious dire circumstances, I notice two particularly disturbing details. Of the adult miners present, most are dark-furred bitu or dark-skinned atu, and almost all are wearing orange prison garb.

At this moment I cannot help but reflect on how I have contributed to slavery. Most of us get assigned to patrol areas where vetu of darker complexions are more densely populated. Officers are not nearly as densely positioned in Sudihatosema. I was ordered to inflict carnal punishment onto those who were driven to crime, not knowing it was desperation that often drives them there. Each punishment makes people more desperate until they are either arrested by a standard officer, or have to commit something unforgivable and so are killed or enslaved as a consequence. It is an intentionally designed pipeline where officers work as the slavers and Hosudiha residents are kept desperate enough to be treated like livestock.

My thoughts snap back to reality as I witness Fami swiftly position verself behind a familiar-looking adult, one of a few pale atu prisoners here, and shout, "You, start grabbing the biggest boulders you can find!"

With Fami pointing one open paw towards the next largest stone and the other open towards a small rock, suddenly the scrawny miner is heaving massive boulders with little to no effort. Meanwhile, the small rock is slowly digging a crater into the cavern floor every time it feels the mass of one of the large boulders grabbed by the miner.

When Fami mentioned ver magical abilities earlier, I had underestimated the extent of ver power. Handling larger targets requires greater skill, and given the size of these boulders, Fami proves to be a formidable mage, alongside being a Rirmevu. I am grateful for ver presence and abilities.

One by one, corpses are pulled from the wreckage, resembling sacks of flesh more so than bodies. Some adults, some children, no bodies belonging to Shibi or Mebi, but each like a knife slowly severing the lifeline tethering me to hope.

Fami remains focused, waiting for each boulder to settle before moving on to the next one, while the other adults clear out the smaller to medium-sized rocks and Miya assists them.

"Set me down!" I yell, "I can help!"

"No!" Miya responds, "There is no time and you would only get in the way."

"Well, at least set me down so I'm not weighing you down." I insist.

Miya doesn't respond to the suggestion for a bit as ve digs, "I don't want to leave you, just in case we need to run."

The prisoner throws a large boulder which slides a distance before hitting another boulder and getting tossed up onto its point. Fami, thinking it has settled, releases ver concentration, but the boulder slowly begins to tip over.

"Fami!" I shout, trying to warn ver. Ve looks at me with a questioning gaze, but before I can utter the warning, the boulder slams into the ground, causing a violent tremor throughout the cavern. More rocks start falling, one of which implodes the familiar miner's head, leaving ver lifeless on the floor. Another rock strikes my back, knocking the breath out of me and inflicting sharp pain in my ribs, causing Miya to stumble forward as well. The wall of rubble we had been working to dismantle shifts into a landslide, burying three other rescuers.

Suddenly, the island snaps, dislodging a boulder from the ceiling. It appears to me to descend in slow motion.

Fami's eyes lock with mine—eyes I can see myself in. Ve is special, perhaps even more so than me. Ve holds the potential to inspire greater change. Witnessing ver life being claimed by the falling boulder fills me with terror. Why ver? Who am I to survive this? Will I survive? If Fami, with ver life being more valuable than mine, can die, what chance do I have? And if I do survive this, can I expect to survive tomorrow? If anyone deserved to live, it was Fami.

Lost in shock, I am consumed by questions of injustice and worth, spiraling into an inner darkness, a spiral that can only be broken by one thing.

"Help! Help!" Shibi cries out.

Miya, seemingly unaware of Fami's fate, scrambles up the debris pile towards a small paw sticking out through a hole, waving desperately for assistance.

"Fami!" Miya yells, "Give me some help here!"

"Miya..." I say solemnly, the weight of Fami's absence sinking in.

Miya freezes at my response and Fami's lack of one. Ve can't tear ver gaze away from the trapped paw. Then, breaking through ver grief, ve begins to dig fervently.

Others join in, climbing up the rubble to help. Shibi and Mebi are the first to escape, followed by two other pups.

"Vedira!" Mebi exclaims upon seeing us. Both ve and Shibi embrace us tightly, their tears flowing freely. Miya and I return the embrace.

"How long have you been able to work?" Kidu yells. Ve works near the mines and managed to help us get back to the apartment while on a rare break. Which was a life saver because Miya was pretty spent after all of that.

Shibi sits on ver mat with ver leg secured between two thin planks of wood, while Mebi lies on ver mat, holding ver head with ver paws, trying to alleviate pain. I too lie on my mat, struggling to move without experiencing a surge of agony from what I suspect is a broken rib. That leaves Miya sitting before Kidu, visibly fatigued but relatively unharmed, and presently enduring the brunt of Kidu's scolding.

"Do you have any idea what all of this means? It means we're fucked! Weren't you ever taught patience? Do you think we don't want to find Jove's vera? We want to give you time to search, but now wasn't the right moment! Now was the time for you two lazy assholes to work! To help Jove find the time ve needs to earn a degree! To achieve financial stability! We were so close! The pups didn't have to be in that mine this labor! But now, due to your selfish impatience, we're back to that Ritu damned slum where we'll probably all die. We won't have a home there anymore, and with these injuries, we won't be able to afford this place either! Hase, we would've been better off if you let the pups die in those mines!"

"Kidu! That's uncalled for!" I shout, though until that point, Kidu's words rang true. This was our fault, but the pups shouldn't have to bear the weight of regret for surviving... not like I do.

"Is it? If they were dead, maybe Jove and I could recover. We wouldn't have to spend money on medicine and food. It would be better for a few of us to die than all of us. We might as well spare ourselves the suffering and drink some foselitu poison."

"Kidu! We'll find a way to get through this. We'll recover." I insist.

"How? Tell me genius!" Kidu scolds.

"I... I have some friends who can help." I say.

"Do you now? And where have these friends been all this time?" Kidu throws a pan at me, and I barely manage to deflect it to avoid further injury to my ribs. Miya rises to ver feet to restrain Kidu. "If you've been hiding something from us, I'll make sure you pay when we find out!"

"Stay calm!" Miya snarls.

Kidu locks ver gaze with Miya's intense eyes, "You both have until we're kicked out of here." Kidu says. Then Kidu forcefully frees ver arms from Miya's grasp, "I have to go back to work so we can afford that poison when the time comes. You two!" Kidu points a finger at Shibi and Mebi. "You better get off your asses, apologize to your manager, and get back to work!"

"What the hase!" I exclaim, "They're injured! They need to recover."

"Yeah, what's da deal?" Mebi questions.

"You can't afford to recover. We need your jobs more than your jobs need you. If you can't be of use to the mines while injured, you'll be replaced faster than a rabid foselitu. So get back to work, or else we'll be drinking that poison tonight!" With that, Kidu storms out of the apartment.

"Do ya really have a friend who can save us?" Shibi asks timidly.

"Yes," I reply.

"Why haven't dey helped us yet?"

"We need to find them first."

"Are dey hiding?" Shibi asks.

"Sort of..." I say.

"Why?"

"They aren't allowed to help us."

"Why?"

"I... I don't know."

"Why?"

"What do you think?"

"Ah think it's cause Ritu hates us." Mebi cuts in.

"I'm not sure about that," I say, "but I do believe someone's hatred might be a factor... or perhaps greed, or a thirst for power over others."

"How're ya going to find yur friends?" Shibi asks.

"I don't know..." I admit.

"Where do we even start?" Miya asks.

"I'm not sure. Maybe we should just wander the streets and see if we pick up any clues?" I suggest.

"Shouldn't we prioritize finding a safe place for the family before worrying about our own bodies?" Miya asks.

"I have no idea how to locate our friends without utilizing your body's senses. Do you have a better idea?" I ask.

"I don't know... Maybe we could ask around?" Miya says.

"Careful who ya ask," Mebi says, "Ah don know anyone who wouldn't sell ya out fer seeking illegal exaltation."

"In that case... I don't know..." Miya says looking a bit defeated for a moment, "Maybe we could ask Geni. Barkeeps tend to be knowledgeable about the happenings in their town and ve seemed trustworthy."

"You're right," I affirm, "I think the tavern is the best place to begin, and we should head back there immediately. Shibi, Mebi, forget about going to work. Take care of each other while we're gone and let Kidu know that we instructed you to stay here. We'll be back."

Leaving pups their age alone at home still feels strange, but sometimes that's how things have to be down here in Hosudiha.

Chapter 20: Hope

Miya stands before the tavern door, our noses catching familiar scents that freeze us in our tracks. It's the scent of the officers that were with Fami that night deposits ago.

"Do you think they're in there?" Miya asks.

"I don't know... Do you think we could catch a glimpse of them through the window?" I ask.

"We can try."

We find a window to peer through. The tavern is still rather empty, just as it was this morning. After this labor's events, when the work is over, I'm sure there will be a surge of miners spilling in to drown their traumas with drunkenness. For now though, Geni seems to be the only one present, and either ve seems to have already gotten a head start on the drunkenness, given that ve sits at a table with three mugs of mead, or ve has unseen guests.

A thud from behind startles both Miya and me. We spin around to spy what appears to be a Rirmevu duo, but it's clear by the scent that the yetu is Buso, Fami's former colleague, and Buso is carrying the unnamed atu mage from a few deposits back.

"We were hoping you would join us," the mage abruptly starts, extending a hand. "Hi, my name is Suki."

Miya hesitantly extends a paw, and they shake. Then Suki offers ver hand to me, and I shake it as well.

"I'm Hinuso," Miya responds, "and this is-"

"I know who you are," Suki interrupts, "I know who you really are."

"Heh, heh..." Miya awkwardly laughs. "What do you mean?"

"You are Miya," Suki points at Miya, "And you are Dima. So there's no need for me to introduce Buso, right? You two worked together on a job shadowing once."

Buso lifts a leg and waves at us, "Nice to see you two again," Buso says.

"How do you know us?" I ask, feeling a mix of awe and fear.

"Come inside, and we'll talk about it." Suki invites.

At that moment, a notu rounds the corner of the tavern. Ve is a towering bipedal person with a body made of clay.

"Looks like we managed to catch you!" ve yells. Now, that makes me nervous. Catch? Is this a trap? What for?

"That's Powa. Don't mind ver," Suki nervously interjects. "Ve has trouble knowing the appropriate amount of intensity in certain situations."

"Drink with us!" Powa demands.

At this point, it doesn't feel like we have much of a choice. We enter the tavern, and Geni leans back in ver chair to get a good look at us.

"Welcome back. Come, share a drink with us in memory of Fami." Geni, says glumly.

We gather at the table with the others, and I notice one key figure is missing—the notu's partner.

"Where's um, Powa's partner?" I ask.

"Ah, Tatu has a stick up ver ass. Always has. So we didn't clue ver in on this little meeting of ours," Powa responds.

Buso cuts in, "We came here hoping to learn a bit more about why Fami decided to stick me with a dart and take off before ve died." Buso sighs, "I regret being so cold towards ver. Maybe if I had been more warm and social, ve would have trusted me enough to talk before running off so recklessly. Ve was just new and seemed eager to please. It was hard to know how open I could be with ver"

"Do you have any idea why ve did it?" Miya asks.

"I have a guess," Buso responds.

"What's your guess?" I ask.

"I think the letter of the law was getting under Fami's skin. I think ve was wrestling with the ways the laws don't always seem like the proper solution, and I can't blame ver for feeling that way. We all do. Well, at least the three of us."

I feel both relieved and heartbroken. Relieved to know that these three are not simple puppets of the ministry, but heartbroken to think that they might have been there for Fami, that they might have helped us in the mine. How different things might have been if they had been there.

"You're on the right track," I say.

"Ve told you something?" Suki asks hopefully.

"Tell us now!" Powa demands.

"Okay," I say uneasily, "Fami believed what ve was doing was wrong and that belief made ver feel like ve was questioning Ritu's judgment. Regardless, ve couldn't bring verself to go along with ver orders any longer, and that made ver scared. I've heard that terrible things happen to people who reject Ritu..." Suddenly, my mind recalls my conversation with Jomira, and I remember the example I gave of the blasphemer who sent letters back to ver parents. That was the familiar face in the mines. The pale atu miner in prisoner garb. Chills creep through me as I continue, "Terrible things. If ve was at all aware of what happens, I'm not surprised ve did what ve did."

"Me neither," Suki agrees. All eyes turn to ver.

"How do you know who we are again?" Miya asks uneasily.

"I am one of the mages who helped put you in those bodies." Suki says almost casually.

Miya jumps to ver feet as if a foselitu had fallen in ver lap. Meanwhile I just freeze and stare. One of the mages. One of the mages who stuffed us in these bodies.

"Before we get too hasty, permit me the opportunity to apologize and pledge to return you to your bodies at the soonest opportunity." Suki says.

"Where are they?" I demand.

"If I had to guess, District seven. However-"

"Take us there right now!" Miya demands.

"No!" Powa shouts.

"Not right now," Suki corrects.

"Why not?" Miya asks with clear aggravation.

"Because there will be lots of guards down there until tomorrow morning!" Powa shouts. "If we strike in the morning, we might be able to sneak in when there are only a couple of guards around!"

"Also," Suki adds, "I can't guarantee your bodies will be there. They only bring me in for the one job. They don't tell me why I'm doing it, who I'm doing it to, and they don't let me stick around. I have the magical aptitude they need, but apparently, I lack the clearance to know much about what they're up to. That doesn't stop me from occasionally extracting information from the victims' minds however, which is how I learned who you two were. Sorry if that might have caused you to doubt who you were for a little while..."

"Wait," I interrupt. "First, it's freaky that you can extract information from people's minds. Please never do that to us again. Second, it seems you're offering to help us break into a government facility. Are you officers or renegades?"

"Both," Buso answers. "We haven't shown our renegade hand yet as we're still working out a way to escape. I hate to admit it, but I think we have a higher tolerance for evil than Fami when it comes to putting up with it while we're powerless to stop it. So we scheme for a way out while enduring Sergeant Makali's schemes to 'trap vemo', as ve puts it. I've considered working as an informant from the inside a couple of times, but I don't think I could live with myself if I stayed, especially if I had to pretend to be the sort of person they let in on their schemes."

Powa and Suki murmur in agreement.

"Okay," I say, trying to process everything. "I can't help but keep thinking about Tatu stumbling upon this. Where is ve? How can we avoid ver foseing on us?"

"Probably licking the boots of the higher-ups," Suki answers. "We've tried hanging out with ver a few times, but it's always awkward. Ve goes on and on, vemoizing everyone the ministry tells us to fear or ostracize. We never had much to add to the conversation, so ve stopped hanging out with us, and we stopped inviting ver to our gatherings."

"Don't worry about Tatu stumbling upon us either. I'm always careful to keep a lookout," Buso assures us, drawing on yetu senses.

It's been so long since we've benefited from yetu senses that I almost forgot Buso was using them.

"Are you really going to help us? Won't that reveal your hand a bit?" Miya asks.

"With all of us together, we might be able to infiltrate and exit without being identified!" Powa exclaims. "Buso can sense any yetu from a distance, then Suki can transfer their precise location from Buso's mind to mine. We'll sneak in, neutralize them, and then we can easily ransack the place."

"Powa is correct," Suki confirms, "With ver as our strategist, it should be a relatively easy job for us. What I want to know is what is your plan once you find your bodies. Once you have them, you'll be hunted. So you must have an escape plan, and if you do, we want to be a part of it."

"Well, that brings us to the reason we're here in the first place," I explain. "Several deposits ago, we stumbled upon a vetu smuggling operation. A group of people were trying to help Hosudiha residents escape when they were attacked by Sergeant Makali and some of ver officers. Makali killed most of them and raped one. That's why I punished ver."

The expressions on their faces turn to anger and solemnity.

"Rightfully so!" Powa declares.

"Thank you," I reply, "Anyway, Miya and I managed to rescue three of the smugglers and one escapee. I don't know if they've resumed their activities so soon after everything that happened, but we were hoping we might find them," I look at Geni, "We were hoping you might have heard something."

"If there were any news about an escape opportunity, I would have mentioned it. I did know about the smugglers you mentioned, though. I haven't heard anything about them for pots now. But after hearing your story, I understand why. There have been rumors of people receiving letters under their doors that guide them to hidden stockpiles of food. So far, the rumors seem to be true, and vetu are landing enough food for up to a pot. It seems there's someone out there doing good for the people, but it's not an escape opportunity."

My heart sinks. Are we doomed to die down here? It feels like our only hope would be to somehow commandeer an airship, even though law enforcement would be on our heels faster than I would pounce on a well-cooked piece of meat.

"I don't want to wait around too long before we go after our bodies. Due to our circumstances, we need to escape sooner rather than later. So we might as well retrieve our bodies tomorrow and then figure out our next steps," Miya suggests.

"Okay," Buso agrees, "Let's meet here shortly after dawn when the jubu start chirping."

At that moment, workers seeking solace from the labor's terrors start pouring into the tavern, prompting us to disperse.

The migration of people slows the progress of our trek back home, almost coming to a halt at times. Initially, I worry that we won't make it back before Jove finishes work. But as Miya narrowly avoids being knocked over multiple times, my concern shifts to the fear of being trampled to death.

Finally, we emerge from the crowd and enter the stairwell leading up to our apartment. The scent of baked goods, quality meat, fresh fruits, and vegetables fills the air, pulling at the noses of passersby. Why are there so many enticing scents here?

Geni's words about the benefactor cross my mind and I am tempted to hope.

Upon entering the apartment, we find Kidu, Shibi, and Mebi gathered around a large sack overflowing with food.

Kidu quickly stands up and moves to close the door behind us. "Be careful not to let the scent waft out and attract unnecessary attention," Kidu warns.

"What's all this?" Miya asks.

"When I returned from buying the fose poison, I found this letter slid under our door," Kidu explains, holding out a piece of paper. The outside bears a distinctive symbol—a circle vertically bisected by a narrow ladder. On the other side is a roughly drawn map with an 'x.' "I found that sack of food at the indicated location inside of a wax-covered crate. I couldn't smell it until I was right on top of it."

This must be the work of the benefactor. Hope knocks at the door of my heart, but I am apprehensive to let it in. This wouldn't be the first time malevolent intentions came to me masked as benevolence.

"With this food, we might be able to hold out longer than I had thought, but our deaths have only been delayed," Kidu continues. "When I returned to work after my break, there were two Rirmevu teams looking for me. I think law enforcement is onto us. I don't know how they haven't discovered where we live, but I can no longer go back to work. This food will eventually run out, and then it's the end of the line." Kidu gestures towards the fose poison. "Unless you two have some good news for us."

"Maybe," Miya says hesitantly.

"Maybe? Are we getting out of here or not?" Kidu asks.

"We've made some new friends who might be able to help," Miya says.

"New friends? What happened to your other friends? Do you think the magic of friendship will get us out of here?" Kidu scoffs.

"No, but—" Miya tries to explain.

Before ve can finish, a piece of paper slides across the floor. It bears the same symbol of a circle with the narrow ladder. Miya quickly opens the door, but no one is there, and the scent is unfamiliar.

"Here," Miya turns to see Kidu holding the letter out to us. "There's something about an airship tomorrow morning, and it might involve more food, but I can't read the words. Can you?"

"No, I can't read. But Dima can," Miya replies, taking the letter and handing it to me.

As I read the letter, I find a rough depiction of an airship with an arrow pointing from the airship to the old docks on the dawnward side of Hosudiha, along with an evening time. The message reads:

"Hello,

If you've received this letter, you're being offered an opportunity to escape Hosudiha. We are a secret organization dedicated to rescuing as many people as possible.

You may have already received some supplies from us in the past deposit, demonstrating our desire to assist. On the evening of the labor the jubu hatch, we will gather at the dawnward ports.

Keep this information to yourself and avoid bringing additional people, as it may overcrowd the ship and force us to leave you behind.

After memorizing the contents, burn this message to prevent it from falling into the hands of authorities."

Could it be the smugglers? Or is this a trap? If it were a trap, would they really discourage us from bringing more people? And then there's the food—it builds trust. But it could also be part of the trap.

"Well?" Kidu urges, awaiting our response.

"It might be the opportunity to escape we've been searching for," I say cautiously. Kidu and the pups light up with hope. "Or... it could be a trap."

"A trap? Who's settin traps? Why?" Mebi asks.

"Sergeant Makali. According to some renegades we met, Makali has been setting traps to catch anyone attempting to escape from Hosudiha," I explain.

"Dat's stupid!" Shibi exclaims.

"How can we differentiate between an opportunity provided by your friends and a trap?" Kidu asks.

"It's a valid concern," Miya acknowledges. "However, we are caught between certain death and the chance of escape. We might just have to take the risk."

"We can minimize the risk," I suggest. "Our new friends are also seeking a way out of here. They will join us and serve as a formidable defense in case things go wrong. Miya and I will meet with them tomorrow morning to make preparations. In the meantime, the rest of you should stay home and pack."

Just then, Jove enters the apartment and takes in the scene—the injured pups, Miya standing, the sack of food, and the fose poison. "I don't know how to feel about this," Jove admits. "But regardless of what you're about to say, I'm going to start with a smoke. Excuse me." Jove steps back outside.

Chapter 21: District Seven

We all stand just beyond the enemy yetu's sensory range. Buso slipped into range for only a moment to get a read on the situation. With so many people meandering about, odds are that the yetu didn't even notice Buso.

"Bad news," Buso begins. "There don't seem to be any prisoners inside at present."

My heart sinks. I was looking forward to this being the moment we confirmed that our bodies are alive. It's hard not to take the news as though Buso just announced that our bodies are dead. After all, Buso cannot see dead bodies.

"However," Buso continues, "it looks like there are only three light-furred bitu officers inside and one yetu on the roof landing. Though it won't be as easy as dropping Powa on the yetu's head from high above. They have updated security standards ever since the station was attacked earlier this salary, so there is likely to be a notu up with the yetu. Powa, have you devised a solution?"

"It sucks! But we'll have to go with it," Powa declares. "Dima, you were a Rirmevu right?"

I find the word 'were' distressing. I haven't really stopped thinking of myself as a Rirmevu, but I guess that would be the case. "Yes," I reply.

"So you have sling-based combat training versus a notu opponent?"

"Yes... but I cannot walk." I say.

"Not a problem. I'll be your legs!" Powa shouts.

"Um, is that a thing you can do?" I ask.

"Yes," Powa affirms, "I will just wrap my external body around your legs and manipulate your legs by manipulating my external body."

"Okay... but how are we going to coordinate movement?" I ask.

"That is why it sucks," Powa says flatly. "We will just have to get a little bit of practice in and communicate well."

"Communicate well... Won't it be kind of easy to take us out if we are broadcasting our movements?" I ask.

"Yes, so we are going to have to come up with coded language that only we understand." Powa says. I cannot help but feel like this is going to go poorly.

Powa continues, "Together we can fight the other notu and incapacitate ver with Suki providing us with magical support. It shouldn't be too difficult really. However, before we can fight the notu, we are going to have to take out the yetu so that they don't have a chance to fly away and get help. So here is my plan," Powa dramatically hunches over as if ve is about to tell the world's deepest darkest secret, "Suki, Dima and I will get into an adjacent building while Miya and Buso hang back to minimize arousing suspicion. Once in position, Dima will use this dart gun to snipe the enemy Yetu and then we will run across the rooftops over to the target building to engage the Notu while Buso flies Miya up to help us engage the remaining three officers."

"Okay, assuming that works out. I still have a broken rib that will make it difficult for me to maneuver." I say.

"No problem, Suki, spread the butter!" Powa says eliciting a number of confused expressions from the rest of us.

"Spread the butter?" Suki asks.

"Yeah, spread the butter," Powa says, pauses, then clarifies, "Deposit a portion of Dima's wound on to everyone with a rib turning one broken rib into a bunch of smaller greenstick fractures that we can better manage and fight with."

"Wait, what?" Miya asks.

"That is a thing that can be done?" I exclaim.

Suki narrows ver eyes at Powa, "Don't be using coded language before we've discussed it," then Suki looks at Miya and me, "Yeah that is something I can do. It's called trait magic."

"Hang on, so there is normal magic, trait magic, some mind reading magic, and some sort of body swapping magic-" I stammer.

"The mind reading magic and the body swapping magic are both mind magic." Suki cuts in.

"Mind magic! How many kinds of magic are there exactly?" I ask.

"Four I believe," Suki says.

"Why weren't we ever informed of this?" Miya asks.

"The ministry is very intent on restricting knowledge of the upper levels of magic for the safety of society. I don't even fully understand enchantment magic yet." Suki says.

Receiving this information gives the most intense sensation of deja vu that I have ever experienced. Not knowing the range of magical possibilities also fills me with anxiety. What could happen to me? Could someone control my mind with mind magic? Could my body get morphed into some horrible amalgamation of nonsensical body parts?

"Wait, can you do something similar for my spinal cord?" I ask.

"Unfortunately no," Suki says, "A partially severed spinal cord would be more inhibiting than a greenstick fractured bone because it would leave us all partially paralyzed in different ways. It is better that only one of us has any paralysis so that Powa can work as their movement aid."

I cannot help feeling disappointed.

"I'm sorry," Suki says.

"No, it's okay." I say, "Please, let's move on."

"Alright," Miya says, "I have a question. How exactly are we going to get close? Won't the yetu recognize Buso and Suki's biosignatures?"

"Not if Suki is in Miya's body!" Powa says, receiving an apprehensive look from Miya, "As for arousing suspicion, maybe Suki and Dima could make it look like they are doing something that doesn't make us seem out of place?"

"We can figure something out," Suki suggests confidently. I, on the other hand, don't feel nearly as confident, "Dima, do I have your permission to do whatever is necessary to make this plan work?"

Suddenly, ideas start to come to mind, and I am not a fan, "You do know these bodies are siblings, right?" I say.

"Relax, we aren't going to do that," Suki assures me.

"Good." I say.

"We might make out though." Suki says.

I feel blood rush to my cheeks.

Suki follows that up with, "Only if necessary of course."

I stare daggers at Suki, "No! Siblings! Repeat after me. Sib-lings," I assert aggressively.

"No problem," Powa cuts in, "Suki, scramble the eggs!" Powa says, earning an annoyed look from Suki.

"I believe Powa is suggesting we scramble our biosignatures." Suki explains.

"What exactly does that entail?" I ask uneasily.

"I swap around a bunch of organs and stuff with a target until both me and my target's biosignatures and scents aren't recognizable." Suki explains and suddenly the prospect of becoming a conglomeration of body horror sounds more feasible than I ever wanted to know.

Suki continues, "So would one of you be willing to scramble with me?"

Suki looks at me and I, very much freaked out at the idea, shake my head profusely.

"I'll do it." Miya volunteers.

"Alright, sit tight." Suki says as ve extends an open hand towards Miya.

After a short pause Suki's and Miya's bodies morph into some crazy-looking atu-bitu hybrids. Where Miya has atu ears, an atu nose, and blotches of skin, Suki has bitu ears, a bitu nose, and blotches of fur. I feel bad for Miya because Suki definitely got the more aesthetically pleasing combination of parts, but Miya doesn't have a mirror, so there is no need for ver to know.

"Okay," Suki chirps, "that scrambles my biosignature enough to ensure the yetu wouldn't be able to recognize me let alone recognize our bodies as being related. Would you be willing to make out with me to save your life now?"

"Listen, you were and oddly still are very attractive. So when I say 'only if necessary,' it's because I hardly know you, and I'm not one for casual intimacy." I say.

"That is all I'm asking for. By the way, I'm not one for casual intimacy either. I'm just able to separate real intimacy from intimacy as a tool." Suki says.

"I just remembered," Powa says as ve looks at Suki and me, "We have some goggles to protect your eyes from any attempts the notu might make to bend the water on your eyes."

Suki loses a bag from ver shoulder and starts distributing equipment. Ve hands me a dart gun along with five darts. Probably couldn't get more darts without arousing suspicion. Ve also hands me some goggles.

"The goggles have prescription lenses to correct average bitu eyesight. So hopefully they sharpen your vision enough that you will be able to make your shot." Powa explains.

The notion of sharper vision excites and compels me to quickly don the goggles. The world sharpens a little as I place the lenses before my eyes, though the world does not look as sharp as it had through my atu eyes. I close my dominant eye and find that the scene blurs a bit more. It would seem that my dominant eye is a bit closer to the bitu average than my other eye. Which is fine, I think I will be able to aim well enough with my dominant eye at this level of clarity.

"It's not perfect, but it is better." I say.

"Things look better to me, but I also have no point of reference for what 'clear' vision would look like." Miya says.

"Suki," Buso says, "You should probably also take my antenna. It will help you get a read on the emotional state of the yetu which may let you know if they are onto you."

"You won't be able to see anything though..." Suki says.

"Miya will direct our flight in to join you all once the lookouts have been handled." Buso says.

"So... What are we going to do to deflect attention from ourselves once we are in position?" Suki asks as we climb a flight of stairs.

"I don't know... We could pretend to fight?" I suggest.

"Pretend to fight... I am a scholar. I couldn't even pretend to fight you to save my life." Suki replies.

"Well, unless you have another idea." I say.

Suki sighs in resignation, "Fine, let's try it."

Suki kicks open the door leading to roof access and immediately starts yelling, "I cannot believe you! You disloyal shit-eating worm!"

For a moment, I feel confused, but I quickly catch on to the type of fight Suki is trying to emulate. While it's not what I had in mind, I think I can go along with it.

"Disloyal? You want to talk about disloyalty! You go off to Ritu knows where for dep- pots," I grit my teeth at my near blunder, I almost forgot to use Hosudiha vernacular. I had better just keep going, "and what do you expect from me? To just become celibate?" My words echo painful memories of when they were once yelled between my biological parents after one had been disloyal.

"Yes! What the hase? Do you have no self-control? What the hase is wrong with you? I can go all that time without sex; you should be more than capable. Just take care of yourself, why don't you? That would be fine. Why go after others?"

"Don't you give me that shit! I know you are off fucking some secret lover. Don't act as if you can just not have sex for pots."

"I can! People do it all of the fucking time! If you can't, then you have a problem!" Suki, ver borrowed antennae twitching, then breaks character for a moment to speak in hushed tones, "They're pretending not to notice us. You might be able to take the shot soon."

Apparently, yetu can tell where another yetu is focusing their attention in the fabric of creation. Or at least, that is what I assume. I have no idea how Suki might know, but ve does. This also must not be the first time ve and Buso have done this because ve seems to be taking to seeing with those antennae with ease.

"I don't have a problem! You're the one with the problem! No one just doesn't need to have sex ever." I say before I peek over the ledge. The notu also seems to be looking away out of discomfort. Near the two guards, there is a large gong. I assume that is what they are meant to hit should there be anything to alert the other guards about. We will have to make sure they don't hit it.

"I have a problem?" Suki shouts. I take aim as Suki continues going off behind me. It is a far shot. I spent two darts earlier to hone my aim, though I am still not so sure if I am going to be able to make this shot.

"Yes. You do! This might come as a surprise to you, but no one tells you about your problems because they don't want to ruin their chances of getting to fuck you!" I release the dart and it vanishes into the darkness. A moment passes where nothing seems to happen.

"Did I get ver?" I whisper.

"I hate you!" Suki yells, "Get out of my life, you sick pervert!" then in a more hushed tone, "I think you missed."

There is a merchant who is tending a stand of cabbages down on the street beyond my target, and suddenly ve falls unconscious. This causes a mad dash of people who rush the stand to steal cabbages.

"I missed but they are distracted. Quick, go go go!" I whisper.

Powa hoists us up and over the short wall and we fall down to the rooftops a small distance below with Suki close behind. I struggle to reload my dart gun using only my paws as we run, usually I have to slip a foot into the cocking stirrup and use both hands to draw the string. However, with my arms made strong from crawling all of the time, I manage to get the string cocked back without having to ask Powa to stop and help.

"What happened down there?" I hear the enemy notu ask ver comrade as we grow near.

The dart gun has a strap that I use to sling it over my shoulder as we begin attempting to climb the wall up to our foes and I hear the enemy Yetu reply, "I'm not sure. It's like the merchant just... Wait an alm-"

Powa and I are struggling to coordinate a climb when suddenly Suki casts the mass of something small onto me and I'm able to practically launch us onto the rooftop with my arm strength. I manage to grab hold of the dart gun mid-flight. As we land the yetu's antenna points directly at us.

"Crap! We have comp-" the yetu starts to yell only to be cut off as I launch a dart into ver.

"We have what?" The notu asks, then ve notices the dart.

"Oh crap," The notu says, then ve spins around to see me.

"Fly the coop!" I say, trying to tell Powa to dodge in coded language.

However, simultaneously Powa shouts, "Charge!"

"I haven't readied my sling yet!" I yell.

Before Powa and I can coordinate the enemy notu lunges at me and lands a solid punch to my cheek. Ver clay fist shatters into pieces on contact. The force from the hit tosses Powa and me to the ground, but somehow the strike felt more like a painless push to the face than a punch.

"Roll," I command as I realize we did not make nearly enough code phrases. Luckily Powa is able to help me use our momentum to roll to my feet a short distance away.

"Oh no you don't!" The notu declares having noticed Suki clinging to the ledge, eyes closed, and it occurs to me ve was probably using ver magic to give me brick-tough skin. Suki, on the other hand, is left quite vulnerable. The notu takes full advantage to bring ver other fist down onto Suki, who manages to break concentration just in time to raise an arm to block the blow. Suki's arm absorbs the hit, and the notu's fist once again shatters on contact, this time leaving a violet thorn sticking out of Suki's arm. Suki instantly loses consciousness and falls a short distance down to the rooftops below. Ve should be able to recover from that hit, but for the time being, we've lost our magic advantage.

Normally, with the enemy's back turned to me, this would be the perfect time to strike. However, that is not the case when fighting a notu. I might end up hitting a thorn hidden somewhere in its body. Or it might coat my fist in clay and restrict it. All I can do is ready my sling.

The notu wastes no time. Ve spins around and literally throws a barrage of fists at me, each fist leaving ver body, turning into projectile clay balls, likely carrying a violet thorn payload.

"Fly the coop!" I try to command again.

"No need," Powa says as the clay balls seem to defy physics to change trajectory mid air, moving into a sort of orbit around me until they slow and Powa absorbs the material into ver extended body.

Simultaneously, I hear the dreaded loud GONG! It would seem the notu sent a fist flying towards the gong alongside the ones ve threw at me. Shit! This is about to go from bad to worse.

"Oh shoot, I hadn't noticed you, fellow notu." The enemy exclaims.

"How do you do?" Powa asks.

"Honestly, this job has been a lot more boring than I was hoping it would be." The enemy says.

"I've got a pretty nice thing going here. Lots of excitement." Powa says.

"Really? Hmm... I would join you, but I don't want to gain a reputation as a deserter." the enemy notu says.

"Makes sense," Powa replies, "We wouldn't want you on our team with a reputation like that. Though maybe when your responsibilities are done here you could join us."

"That would be nice." The enemy says.

"Um, Powa. I think ve is just buying time for backup." I say.

"Well, I wasn't actually, but I guess things sort of worked out that way." The enemy says as ver comrades begin to emerge from the roof hatch with dart guns training on us. They each fire their darts and Powa is quick to move ver clay to catch all three projectiles, ball them and launch them back. Two of Powa's clay balls find their mark knocking out two of the new arrivals, but the third clay ball passes close enough to the enemy notu to be caught and absorbed back into its body.

"Can't have you doing that," The enemy notu says.

"Crap. That was close. Thanks for the save." The remaining enemy bitu says.

Just then Buso and Miya come swooping down out of the darkness to tackle the bitu officer down into the building.

"Well shit." the notu says looking back at the now empty roof access.

"You use profanity?" Powa asks.

"Only when no ministers are listening." The notu says as ve turns back to look at us and take an combative stance.

My target comes into view, the notu's gemstone. The gem works as the notu's eye and center of consciousness among other things. I fire my sling, sending a stone flying for the gem, only to be caught in the clay palm of the notu. “Of course you're using a sling. Ya’ll came prepared, didn’t you?” The notu remarks.

“We tried our best.” Powa says.

“You certainly did.” The notu’s gem sinks into the clay of ver head for protection, and then ve blindly charges with the intent to wrap ver body around me. Powa makes us jump up and then kick off of the half wall lining the rooftop to flip over the enemy. As we fly through the air, Powa attempts to pull further clay from the enemy’s external body.

The notu, predicting that we would try to get behind ver, swings both arms on either side of ver body in a way I wouldn’t be able to replicate given my jointed arms. The strike catches us off guard, and in our attempt to dodge as we land we stumble backward, losing our feet for just a moment, but that is all the notu needs. Before we can recover, the gem resurfaces to see our location, and another charge is initiated.

This notu certainly knows how to combat a sling user. Ve is careful to protect ver gem and not to give me even a moment to load another stone, aim, and fire.

I toss my sling aside and pull the dart gun back out.

“Powa, get me close!” I say hoping the notu cannot hear me with its gem sunken into its head.

Powa dodges the charge in a way that permits me to swing the pommel of the dart gun into the notu head which explodes as my strike sends the notu gem flying off of the rooftop down to the streets below, certainly knocking the notu unconscious. The clay body falls into a heap on the ground and shortly thereafter Miya and Buso emerge from the building victoriously.

“Mission success!” Powa yells.

My adrenaline recedes and my body wakes up to how I overexerted it.

"Powa," I say between heavy breathing, "Please let me lie down."

"Oh, sure." Powa says as ve lowers and releases me to collapse to the ground.

"Are you dying?" Powa asks loudly.

"No-" *Pant*, "I-" *pant* *pant*, "I just need an alm." I haven't moved like that in deposits. I am in no shape to do that again for another three deposits.

"I will remain out here to watch over Suki," Buso suggests, "You three go search the building. There shouldn't be anyone else down there, but stick together just in case."

We descend into the darkness of the facility. The second floor of the facility is filled with crates. As curious as I am to learn of their contents, we haven't the time to look. We move on to the first floor where there is a living space with toppled chairs and a table laden with food. The officers must have been busily eating their lunches when the gong sounded.

Finally, we head down to the basement. The space where this whole body-swapping shit happened. The room looks rather empty upon approach until we catch sight of the tip of a fully extended yetu wing. For a moment, Miya and I are filled with excitement that sets us off to run into the room, only to be frozen by the sight.

Tattered and actively being eaten by small grubs, Miya's wings are stretched out before us, secured to the wall with nails, and on display in this empty dank room. Only wings. Miya's body is not here as far as I can tell.

"Are those..." Miya begins.

I don't want to answer. I cannot even bring myself to utter a single word.

"Answer me, damn it!" Miya demands.

The only word I can manage comes out so quietly that I wonder if I actually managed to say, "Yes."

Miya takes cautious steps forward, as though approaching too quickly may scare away the wings Miya covets. Miya reaches a shaky paw out to touch them, "Fami said magic might have been used to put us in these bodies... Do- Do you think magic can fix this?"

"Fami did say 'who knows what is possible with magic'... So... Who knows. Maybe." I say.

"Nope!" Powa shouts, "That only works on living things!"

Miya shoots Powa a glare.

"Sorry! I- I'll keep quiet." Powa says.

Miya goes to remove the wings, which seem to easily tear away from the wall due to the rot. Ve tries to fold them, but they snap with minimal effort. Miya stares wide-eyed at ver crumbling wings.

"No no no! Why? Ritu why?" Miya yells. Ve tries desperately to retract them into transportable packages, only worsening the condition of the wings with each attempt.

"Miya, stop!" I plead, but my words are lost in ver panic. I try to grab and restrain ver arms.

"No! Let go!" Miya yells.

"You are only making it worse!" I say.

Miya snaps ver teeth at me, causing me to release ver to avoid another bite and Powa retreats us.

Once ver wings have crumbled beyond recognition, ve falls to ver knees, slams ver fists onto the wall, and screams ver breath away.

"Powa, please take me to ver." I ask quietly and Powa wordlessly obeys, kneeling me down beside Miya. I gently lay a paw upon Miya's shoulder as ve proceeds to weep.

The loss of Miya's wings unearths some thoughts I have been avoiding. What if only corpses await us at the end of this search? What will we do? We will have to cross that bridge should we happen upon it. For now, at the very least, we now have Miya's original scent.

"I'm sorry, Miya." I try to console, "I know your pain."

"Maybe." Miya snarls bitterly, "But at least you will get your legs back!"

Miya's words strike at a point of uncertainty I hadn't realized was there. This whole time, I have been operating under the assumption that I will be getting access to my legs back along with my body. But knowing what I know now about magic...

"No. I'm not sure I will. I believe this paraplegia is the punishment I gave to Makali. If that is the case, unless I can give it back to Makali and be sure ve won't just dump it onto another of ver victims, this burden will be mine to bear... Possibly for the rest of my life."

Miya and I fall silent as we each grieve our losses.

"If nothing else, we have scents; we could track down our bodies before this evening." I say.

"Right," Miya says as ve takes one more long look at the tatters of ver wings. Ve grabs a piece, stands, and says, "Let's get out of this hase hole."

We follow the scent trail quite a distance as it twists and turns through the labyrinth of streets until the trail ends on the docks of the dawnward ports.

I'm not sure if I should feel hopeful or dismayed, "They— I think they escaped..." I say.

"Do you think they escaped with the help of the same secret organization? If so, maybe they will know where we can find them!" Miya exclaims hopefully.

"Maybe." is all I can manage to utter. Else, they could be anywhere in the world at this point. We may never find them. I am torn between hope and hopelessness. Regardless, there is only one way forward, "Let's all meet at the tavern in four wages. Then we will hope our escape goes over without a hitch.

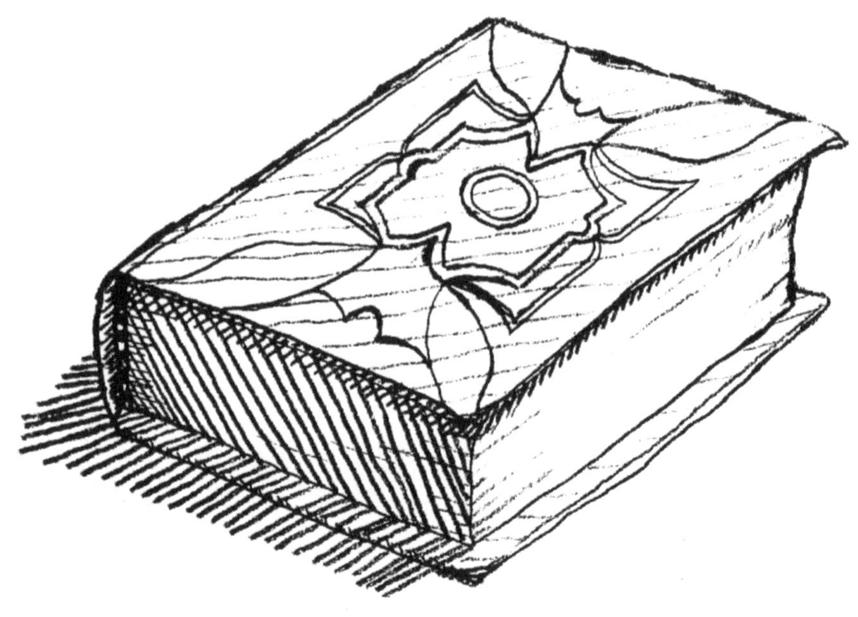

Chapter 22: Coexist

Our mission to district seven must have taken less time than it felt like it did, because the family is still working out what should be packed and what should be left behind.

I don't know what to pack given that I don't know what is and is not Viadu's. So Jove is taking care of my packing alongside vers. However, I notice Jove is packing with a glazed-over and hardened expression. Either ve is deep in thought or dissociating, I cannot tell.

"Are you okay Jove?" I ask.

"Why me specifically?" Jove asks, "If things go poorly with this escape, none of us will be okay."

"I mean, are you going to be okay abandoning everything you have been working towards? You have worked so hard for a degree, and now you will leave before all of that hard work can pay off."

To my surprise, Jove cracks up at my words, "Pay off. I'm glad I won't have to pay off my schooling. Do you remember three deposits ago when I was trying to figure out our finances? Right before we had to send the pups to work in the mines."

"Yeah, I remember." I say.

"Do you remember how I told the pups that they would only have to work in the mines until either I got my degree or you two were able to work?" Jove asks.

I nod.

"I lied." Jove says.

"What?" Shibi and Mebi cry out simultaneously.

"That night, three deposits ago, I finally braved figuring out our financial situation. I hadn't wanted to do it before because it felt hopeless, but having just moved up in society, I was optimistic. Turns out, with all of the debt we have accumulated, even if I got my dream job, we would all have to keep working just to sleep in our new home."

Apart from Jove, everyone else has stopped packing in shock at the hopelessness of our situation, even if everything had gone right.

"Doesn't matter now," Jove continues, "If this one thing goes well, we will be able to start over with a clean slate!"

Jove's words trigger a wave of distress within me. Ritu, the ministry teaches that exaltation is a matter of receiving You and then the manifestation of Your virtues equips us to multiply our blessings, bettering our circumstances by extension. However, it wasn't Your virtues that got us out of the slums, it was Fami.

The image of the incomplete tower once again returns to my mind.

Did we build a tower when we accepted Fami's gift? If so, why didn't you stop Fami? What were we supposed to do with the gift? Just toss it aside? Maybe, though that feels like a completely unrealistic thing to expect from a family that is in such a desperate situation. Still, all that has happened would seem to lend merit to the idea that you have designed nature to bring us back down. Yet here we are, about to build that tower even higher in a desperate attempt to resist nature's efforts to bring us back down to where we belong.

"Hey," Jove says, looking at me with a curious and concerned expression, "What about you, are you doing alright?"

"I'm fine." I say, not sure if I'm ready to have Jove rip my beliefs to pieces again.

"Don't give me that shit. You look like someone who is waiting to die." Jove's demeanor feels far less hostile at this moment than it has ever felt before. Ve seems like ve might actually want to help me as opposed to tear me down. I am curious to see where this goes, and so I take the risk of opening up.

I let out a sigh, "Makes sense... I'm anxious that we may die. It's more than that though. Recently I began to realize that I am not obligated to believe the things I was told I had to believe. There is one thing I would rather not believe, but it just makes too much sense with everything that is going on."

"What might that be?" Jove asks.

"It is believed that Ritu designed nature to pull vetu towards the level of society they are equipped to handle via their relationship with Ritu. We were not lifted from the slums by our relationships with Ritu, we were given a hand out. That would make our exaltation inauthentic, and so it would make sense that we would feel nature pulling us back down as a result, and that feels like exactly what is happening. However, instead of letting Ritu put us where we need to be, we are seeking to further exalt ourselves inauthentically. I cannot help anticipating that we will inevitably fall from grace, and the further we have to fall, the less likely we are to survive. On top of all of that, I feel guilty, because it was my selfish vice that got us into this mess."

"Did you learn from your mistake?" Jove asks.

For some reason I was not expecting that question. So I have to think about it. I wasn't patient. I put my wants over the needs of the family. I didn't communicate and assumed they would deny me any opportunity to find my body.

Jove adds to ver question before I can respond, "Will you work with the rest of us going forward? Or will you continue to keep secrets, do your own thing, and not trust us?"

I look at Jove and say, "I will work with the family going forward. I'm sorry I acted so selfishly."

"Me too," Miya adds.

"Then what reason would Ritu have to disparage us? If you have learned from your mistake then the consequences of your vice have yielded virtue, have they not?" Jove says.

"I-... huh." I don't know why I hadn't thought of it that way before.

"Wouldn't that make you more worthy of exaltation than you were?" Jove asks, "Not that I believe in all of that bullshit, but you can believe what you want, and I don't think your beliefs are considering the fact that you learn from your mistakes. If you are never allowed to be wrong then you are never allowed to grow. So if it is Ritu's prerogative to punish every vice instead of using the consequences to better you, then Ve is not worthy of your reverence in my opinion."

"That makes sense, but whether Ritu is worthy of our reverence or not, what if Ve is intent on punishing us?" I ask.

"If Ritu is letting Sargent Makali get away with rape and murder, then I honestly don't think we have much to worry about." Miya says.

"There is another thing. What if Ritu doesn't intend to punish Makali? What if Makali is right? What if our lives really are forfeit, and that's why Makali gets away with it?"

"I don't know this Makali character," Kidu joins in, "but from the sounds of it, if Ritu is on ver side, then fuck Ritu."

"Couldn't have said it better myself," Jove agrees.

Shibi stops packing at this point and just seems to sit silently with ver back turned to the ongoing conversation.

"Are ya okay?" Mebi asks ver silently. However, at this point we are all listening in.

"Ritu is my friend." Shibi says, "Ve has been there for me through so much. Ah don like how we're talking about Ver like Ve is a bad vetu. Ah think we are the bad vetu at this point."

Kidu's resolve softens a bit, "Pup, we are not calling Ritu a bad vetu. In my opinion Ve would be a bad vetu-" Shibi seems to wince, "*If* Ve were the sort to side with a rapist and a murderer. Ve may not be like that."

"Then why doesn't ve do something about Makali?" Mebi questions.

"Sometimes we learn that someone we trusted isn't as trustworthy or as good as we thought," Jove says, "It can be difficult to accept, but maybe we have to accept that Ritu just isn't good."

"Due to our limits and fallibility as vetu, we cannot be certain of Ritu's nature." Miya says, "Like you said once Jove, what if Ritu is just the author and we are the characters in Ver book? You had asked if Ver power as an author made ver perfect, in addition to that I'll ask this, would an author be evil for writing our life stories?"

There is a moment of pensive silence, then Miya continues, "Given that we cannot be certain of Ritu's nature, nor of the very nature of our existence for that matter, maybe our concern should be to only believe what the evidence strongly suggests, while leaving room for correction if our conclusions are wrong. As for those possibilities which cannot be proven, perhaps we ought to either discard them or, if we must, only hope for those possibilities which make sense and are worth hoping for."

Miya's gaze moves from one of us to the next, "The evidence we have with respect to Ritu's actions or lack thereof, points to multiple possibilities, and while the possibility of Ritu being evil makes sense, is it worth hoping for?"

"The only ways I can imagine Ritu not being evil require Ritu to not be some almighty, morally perfect being." Jove says, "A being that is both almighty and all good doesn't make sense in the context of our existence. However, if Ritu is not almighty or all good, why bother worshiping such a being?"

"Maybe Ritu doesn't want worship." Miya says, "Maybe the idea that Ritu is to be worshiped is a vetu one. We may be making all of these assumptions about Ritu and meanwhile Ritu is trying to better the world but needs our help to do it. Will we really only help Ritu better our world if Ritu is some omnipotent deity?"

"No..." I say, "but I am not sure a limited Ritu is worth believing in. It makes victory over evil seem far less certain. Also, if Ritu is not all-powerful, wouldn't that undermine the point of Ver ministry to bring us the hope that Ve can overcome and save us from death?"

"Perhaps not." Miya says, "Ritu might not need to be omnipotent to have power over death. The possibility that Ritu might be an author would be one way Ritu might have power over death in our reality even if ve is not all-powerful in Ver reality. Regardless, the point is that there are multiple possible explanations that the same lines of evidence could point to. We are left to choose what we hope for, and we are likely to be wrong, and if Ritu is worthy of our hope, Ve will have plenty of grace for us when we are inevitably wrong. Ve didn't make us capable of knowing these things for certain to begin with. That is, so long as we leave ourselves open to correction in anticipation of being wrong. This is the best I think we can do with the information we have." Miya looks at me, "So, what do you think is worthy of hope?"

"I don't know..." I say.

"Are you sure it's not that Ritu favors Makali and is going to throw us into the fires of Hase?" Miya jokes.

"No," I smile a little, "At least it's not that."

"So long as it's not that, maybe hoping for Ritu is fine." Jove says, "I don't know. Personally I don't feel like I need Ritu to go on living."

"I'm not sure there is anyone who can tell you otherwise," Miya says, "Let those who don't need Ritu not be bothered by Ver." Miya looks at Shibi, "And let those who find hope in Ritu have their hope."

Shibi gives Miya a smile and I cannot help smiling as well. Everyone seems content with the way this conversation went. For the first time, the family dynamic feels peaceful in a way I did not think was possible.

"I don't recognize any biosignatures. There are no yetu. In fact, everyone on board is dark-furred bitu and dark-skinned atu. So that bodes well," Buso informs us.

"Unless they are stolen bodies!" Powa suggests.

"This whole operation is taking place on the edge of city limits. If they are officers, then they would have a reason to hide their identities to protect the image of the ministry," Suki affirms. "I've been ordered to scramble undercover officers before."

Suki is dressed in civilian clothing with a large cloak under which Buso hides, having been coated in some of Jove and Kidu's scent dampening powder. Powa, the size of a doll, rides on Suki's shoulder. The presence of a yetu and a notu would arouse suspicion that we may be officers. A yetu should be able to fly out of Hosudiha, and a notu, who wouldn't need to spend money on food and shelter, could easily be exalted by legal means. So either of them needing help would be odd.

It occurs to me just how unfair this whole system is for bitu and atu... Most yetu present in Hosudiha are prisoners, and most notu are just here looking for something exciting to do.

"So... Is there anything else you all want to check, or should we just head on down?" Jove asks.

"Not much else we can check... Anyone's nose picking up anything sketchy?" Buso asks.

All bitu present start sniffing around a little.

"Nah." Kidu says.

"Nothing." Jove affirms.

"Smells a little less like poop." Mebi adds.

"Yeah, less poop." Shibi agrees.

I take a deep breath. Nothing. "I mean, if the organization members came in on the airship, then we couldn't be smelling them at all, just the people coming to escape," I say.

"Those could be officers too," Miya suggests.

"Still, nothing notably familiar," I say.

"Alright, here goes everything. Let's go quickly. We are already late. We are lucky they haven't left yet," Buso remarks.

Powa jumps into Suki's pocket, and we head down to the dock where the single airship is waiting. The ship is about thirty ingots long and flies unmarked dark gray sails with no flag.

"Hello there!" a voice calls out from the deck of the ship. "You would be the last group we were expecting. We were beginning to wonder if you were coming. We'll come to help you climb aboard!"

With that, three bitu and an atu come out to assist us in boarding. They come wearing different styles of dresses, robes, and pants-suits, along with closed-toe shoes. While closed-toe shoes are an odd choice for bitu, it's not unheard of, perhaps due to being on an airship.

Despite the unfamiliarity, there is nothing indicating immediate danger. Could this be the end? Are we finally free?

Chapter 23: Hitch

We climb aboard and find two atu already on deck. Judging by their attire, one appears to be a crew member, while the other is a fellow passenger like us. Another bitu emerges from one of the ship's cabins, carrying a tray with great care just as our helpers finish lugging our possessions aboard. They shout to us, "We know what you have been through. Please, to celebrate your freedom, share some tea with us before you head below deck."

Odd... Miya and I take the first cups and as we do I catch the bitu's scent. It is unlike other Bitu I have encountered. Like they just bathed in water and then spritzed some perfume on their mess of natural odors...

Their scent, their shoes, the way the letter was worded. It all feels far too suspicious... I squint at the contents of the cup I hold and my heart drops into my stomach when I see blue flower petals...

"Stop!" I yell, splashing the tea into the face of the bitu holding the tray. They stumble back, spilling the drinks onto another stranger and the deck. "Step back!" I demand, gingerly taking the cup from Miya's paw and tossing it away. Miya catches on and pushes the group away from the puddle. The two bitu hit by the tea clutch their necks, gasping for air before falling silent.

"Tatu! Dezadu!" one of the strangers exclaims, staring in disbelief at the choking bitu.

Suddenly, Suki's cloak flares up as Buso extends ver wings, throwing the cloak onto the puddle with ver legs. "It's a trap! It's most certainly a trap. Vetu are dying below deck!"

"You vemo worms!" The stranger yells at us, "You are going to pay for that!"

The atu passenger who hadn't gone below deck yet gets blindsided by a fist, causing ver to fall unconscious with a thorn in ver neck. The remaining enemies, three bitu and one atu, draw daggers from concealed sheaths.

"Sorry about this," Miya says to me just before ve rips away the harness strapping me to ver back, sending me toppling to the deck.

"Gah! Shit!" I exclaim, clutching my agitated rib. It may not be a complete break, but it is still tender and hurts like hase from the jolt of the fall.

"Suki!" Miya shouts as ve charges in.

"I've got you!" Suki responds.

Miya confronts the foes, their blades futilely bouncing off ver body while Suki extends one hand toward Miya and clenches a fist-sized rock in ver other hand which ve pulled from ver pocket.

Since the weapons can't penetrate Miya's skin, three of the bitu resort to grappling and restraining ver. Given Miya's lack of combat experience, ve is easily overpowered and starts screaming in pain as the attackers begin breaking ver arms and legs. Ver skin may be impenetrable, but ver joints need to remain flexible for movement, making them vulnerable to breaks. One foe attempts to bring their blade down on an exposed joint. Suki has no choice but to immobilize Miya to save ver, meanwhile Suki verself is highly vulnerable as ve cannot break out of ver concentration lest Miya die.

Seeking to take advantage of Suki's vulnerability, the atu enemy moves in to attack ver. Powa jumps from Suki's pocket and quickly moves to turn the tea soaked cloak into an extended body. Looking something like a living ragdoll.

Powa attempts to tackle the enemy with ver toxic body, but is too easily dodged due to short stature. After the enemy successfully dodges Powa twice, ve spots an opening and swings ver dagger, hitting Powa's gem with the flat of ver blade and sending ver flying out of ver rag doll body and over the edge of the air ship. The still conscious Powa screams as ve falls.

"Powa, I've got you!" Buso yells as ve leaps over the edge of the airship, "Just keep screaming so I can find you!"

The enemy now faces Jove and Kidu as they provide defense and ve charges into the defensive line. Ve slashes at Jove who is quick to dodge backwards. The momentum of the strike creates an opening that Kidu tries to take advantage of. However, Kidu's lack of combat experience makes ver slow to recognize the opening and act on it. So the enemy has plenty of time to see Kidu coming.

Expecting to collide with the foe, Kidu throws verself with enough momentum that ve cannot stop verself from falling into the vacant space the evasive enemy steps out of. Time seems to slow as Kidu stumbles forward. The enemy's blade ends its arch from the strike at Jove, and then enters into a reverse slash. Kidu attempts to catch the blade with ver paw while it's still slowed in the apex of its arch. However, with no thumb to enforce ver grip, the blade cannot be restrained and so is deeply drawn through Kidu's gut.

"Kidu!" Jove screams as ve charges in once more. I thought I had seen rage on Jove's face before. Turns out I was wrong.

Similar to before, the momentum of the enemy's blade is still completing its arch, but Jove is quicker to charge into the opening. The enemy attempts to sidestep Jove as ve did with Kidu, but Jove's momentum is more controlled and ve redirects ver charge into the enemies gut, tackling ver to the ground flat on ver back. Jove mounts the enemy looking to rain fists down onto ver, only to be struck in the arm by the dagger the enemy managed to keep hold of.

Jove lets out a yell of pain as the enemy grabs the fur at Joves chest, and uses it to pull verself up and smash ver head into Jove's snout dazing Jove. Taking advantage of the stunned Jove, the enemy pulls verself up further and locks Jove's head beneath ver arm. Jove panics as the lock cuts off blood circulation to ver head and Jove begins to attempt to dismount and break free, but to no avail. In a matter of alms, Jove's body falls limp.

The enemy kicks the now unconscious Jove off of ver, and jumps to ver feet.

"Vedi!" Shibi screams, attempting to limp to Jove's aid.

Meanwhile, Mebi stands frozen in terror.

"Shibi no!" I yell trying to crawl after ver in futility.

Shibi attempts to tackle the enemy only to get promptly kicked in the face hard enough to slam ver body into the deck. The enemy, dagger still clutched resolutely in ver paw, looks down at the dazed and crying Shibi.

"Don ya dare lay another finger on ver!" Mebi yells, ver fear slain by fury.

The enemy looks at Mebi with a hardened and cold pity, "I always hate it when these vemo have to drag their kids down with them." Ve says as ve bends down to lift Shibi by the scruff, "I hate having to put them down."

Mebi runs in, but the enemy hardly pays ver any mind, likely believing Mebi poses no substantial threat. The enemy thrusts ver dagger at Shibi and it severs flesh, but not Shibi's. Mebi has thrown ver body into the path of the blade and taken the strike to ver shoulder, ver scapula working as a shield keeping the blade from piercing all of the way through and into Shibi.

Mebi's face is twisted into a fierce snarl and ve digs ver claws into the forearm of the enemy causing the foe to start yelling from the pain.

"Ah said not ta touch ver!" Mebi scolds.

The enemy attempts to swing Mebi off, to throw ver over the side of the ship, but Mebi's claws pierce deep and ve holds on despite being whirled around. Ve then decides to drop Shibi to free up a fist with which to punch Mebi in the face.

"You little shit! Let go of me!" The enemy yells.

I catch sight of a satisfied smirk which crosses Mebi's face between punches as ve barley manages to say, "Never."

The enemy tries to pull Mebi off of ver, but to no avail. Mebi maintains ver grip restraining the enemies ability to use the dagger by keeping it stuck in ver shoulder.

The enemy raises Mebi into the air, and brings ver down, slamming ver into the deck, this finally knocks Mebi out and ver body bounces away leaving a trail of blood.

"You vermin," The enemy says as ve clutches ver bleeding arm, "I felt bad before, but now I'm going to enjoy gutting you."

"Mebi!" I yell.

My mind fills with maddening screams. Ritu I feel so helpless! Give me legs! Give me something! Anything!

"Somebody, help the pups!" I scream.

The enemy jabs with ver dagger towards Mebi when suddenly a new figure comes hurtling in from above, striking the enemy with incredible force.

Pinning the enemy beneath ver feet, Zi swiftly renders the fose unconscious with a thorn.

One of the adversaries wrestling with Miya also falls unconscious, followed shortly by another. I glance up to see a small ship descending from the darkness. Tai peeks over the ledge of the ship, raining darts down on the remaining hostiles. Zi tackles the last foe off Miya and proceeds to incapacitate them just before two more atu enemies emerge from below deck.

When the smaller ship descends to hover just overhead, Hari jumps down holding a chunk of metal and extends a hand to Zi. "I've got you!" ve shouts.

Zi charges into battle against the two new enemies, grabbing the blade of one's dagger and forcefully driving ver head into their face. The enemy staggers back, but the other foe seizes the opportunity to tackle Zi to the ground, engaging in grappling, searching for chokes or opportunities to break joints.

The first enemy quickly recovers and moves to assist their ally. However, they suddenly fall flat on their face, struggling to lift their own body. Suki has one hand extended towards a nearby cannon and another towards the struggling enemy.

Amidst the chaos, I notice an ingot-tall ragdoll sprinting past me. It seems Buso was successful in retrieving Powa from ver fall and Powa has once again made the tea-soaked cloak into a makeshift body. Powa charges forward and body slams the enemy, who is struggling to lift verself. The foe gasps for air as the potent toxins of the blulip take effect.

Tai, still positioned on the hovering ship above, launches another thorn toward Zi's ongoing struggle. The thorn inadvertently bounces off Zi's impenetrable skin, and Zi releases a rough chokehold on the enemy to swiftly snatch the falling dart, then ve uses it to render the struggling foe unconscious.

With the enemies eliminated, Suki releases ver concentration and rushes to tend to the wounded.

Jove, while still in a bit of a haze, has begun to stir.

Suki moves first to heal Mebi, and once Mebi is stable ve heals Shibi, then ve moves on to Kidu.

"Shit! No!" Suki yells. After a moment's grief ve looks instead to Jove who is slowly becoming more aware.

"Okay, look at me," Suki says to Jove, "I'm going to help you, alright?"

Suki extends a hand toward Jove and another toward the unconscious enemy who attacked ver. Soon, the enemy begins to bleed as Jove's wound is transferred over. Suki looks at Jove and says with tears welling up in ver eyes, "You've lost a lot of blood. You need to rest."

"Forget about me. Help Kidu!" Jove demands.

"I tried. It's too late," Suki says.

"No!" Jove weakly crawls over to Kidu. "Kidu! Kidu, listen to me, damn it! You can't leave me. I can't bear losing any more family. I just can't. Kidu! Damn you! Damn you..." Jove breaks down.

Jove spots Buso perched nearby and stares daggers at ver, "What the hase were you doing abandoning us like that!"

"I- I'm sorry, I just-" Buso stammers.

"Fuck you!" Jove cuts in, "The odds of your notu friend landing alive on an island below were pretty good, meanwhile leaving two unarmed civilians and some pups to fight an armed and trained officer. One of us was bound to die!"

Buso falls silent as Jove tells ver off, likely feeling burdened with guilt. Jove attempts to stand and walk over to get in Buso's face, but ve faints from ver low blood levels and Suki catches ver.

Meanwhile, Hari transfers Miya's injuries to an enemy and then moves to kneel next to Hari. Hari looks at Kidu with sorrow which suddenly turns to rage as ve kicks one of the enemy bodies in frustration. "Damn it with the fucking decoy! Jo, how many survived?"

"Just these few. You don't want to go below deck..." Jomira says solemnly as ve glides down from the ship above.

"Please don't hurt these bodies any more than necessary!" Suki bites. "Odds are these are stolen bodies. Let's try to minimize injuries and casualties in our wound swapping. Odds are some unfortunate bitu will have to live with trying to recover from whatever injuries we deposit, so let's be sparing."

"I'm pretty sure one of the dead ones over there was my coworker!" Powa shouts, pointing to one of the first enemies to die from blulip toxins.

"Ritu, do you really think that's our Tatu?" Suki remarks.

"That's the name that one yelled when ve died," Powa says matter-of-factly, pointing to the first one Zi knocked out.

"Tatu... Damn it." Suki remarks.

"What?" Powa asks. "Ve was a jerk."

"I don't know. I had always kind of hoped ve would turn things around," Suki sighs. "First things first," Suki looks at me, "Do you have any injuries?"

"None that you aren't already aware of." I say.

"Okay… I'm sorry for your loss." Suki says.

I reflect a bit on our loss. I hardly knew Kidu. I only saw ver in short spans over the last several deposits and the few times we really interacted ve was either dissociating and so was not mentally and emotionally present, or ve was high strung and volatile. I cannot help but think of those few times ve seemed present and nurturing. Might ve have been that way more often under better circumstances? Perhaps Kidu never really got a chance to get to know verself either. The thought breaks my heart, and it hurts even more when I reflect on the loss to the pups and Jove.

Additionally, a weak feeling of guilt also grips my heart. I killed two vetu just now. So much for valuing all vetu life. Though one could argue that we were all acting in self defense. Which still might not necessarily fly with ministry members, depending on who you ask, but that would be only one of many things I have done that might not fly with the ministry.

The only death that might have been avoidable was the one Powa caused with the blulip toxins, and maybe the ones I splashed with the tea… Though had I not done that, we would certainly be dead right now. My mind begins to spiral as it tries to ethically assess what just happened. Though one thing is certain, if these bodies were stolen, the loss for those they were stolen from is a tragedy. That reality makes me regret killing them more than anything else.

"Kidu is a painful loss… But mostly for the pups and Jove. Our interactions with ver were mostly limited to brief exchanges in the wage between sleep and ver going or returning from work. So unfortunately we hardly knew ver," I say.

"Okay..." Suki says solemnly, "Not to move on so quickly, but" Suki then looks to Jomira's crew, "who are you people?"

Jomira answers, "We were the ones who used to help people escape Hosudiha."

"Wait," Miya interjects, "Are you the ones we saved from Makali a few deposits back?"

Jomira's crew looks at Miya and me in confusion. They do not know who we are given our Bitu bodies, and it occurs to me that Miya has never actually seen these people before, ve has only ever known their biosignatures.

"Sorry, I don't believe we have ever met..." Jomira says, "But given you know what happened to us a few moons ago..."

"Let me guess," Zi cuts in, "You are that Rirmevu duo from a while back and, just as I said ve would, Makali figured out it was you and didn't only find someone else to transfer your punishment to, but also transferred you into the bodies of the ones ve found."

"Yeah, pretty much." Miya affirms.

"So deductive of you," I say with a glare, "Do you want a medal?"

Zi seems to take a moment to check verself, "Sorry, I shouldn't gloat. I imagine you two have been through hase and I really shouldn't take joy in that."

"I forgive you," I say, "I honestly needed the reality check this whole experience gave me."

I recall the degrading words I had for Sho last we met, and the recollection causes me to glance Sho's way. Ve appears to be listening into the conversation with interest, but upon noticing my attention ve looks off and seems to pretend that ve hadn't actually been all that interested.

"Anyway," Jomira continues, "I'm glad our paths have crossed again. We will do our best to help you going forward. Also, I have something for you Dima, though it is not on my person presently."

There is only one thing that could be. My vedi's blade. Ve really intends to keep ver word, and I cannot say I am surprised.

"So where have you guys been all of this time?" Miya asks.

"We had to take some time to recover and resupply after suffering our losses a few moons ago." Jomira continues, "We still aren't fully supplied, and we were only able to rent out that small ship." ve gestures to the ship above with ver wing, "Anyway, we were looking to get back to work freeing people when we caught wind that someone else had taken over our operation. We learned about two separate pick-up zones, which seemed suspicious that they would divide the people into two groups. So we went to investigate. We checked up on the first group and found a small crowd of about twenty people just waiting. So we quickly traveled to this pick-up zone. When we detected that bodies were dropping, we sprang into action. Now that we know the danger, we had best move quickly back to the other pick-up zone before anyone there gets hurt."

"Come on, we need to toss these bodies overboard quickly," Zi commands. "We are taking this ship."

"Including the ones below deck? They may be covered in blulip's toxins," Miya says.

"We will leave those for now, and be careful with the ones up here. Hey you," Zi points to Powa, "What's your name?"

"Powa at your service," Powa says quietly.

"Powa, can I put you in charge of cleaning up the blulip toxins since you are immune?" Zi asks.

"Sure." Powa says.

I cannot tell if Powa is being solemn or if this is just more intensity issues.

Hari manages to wrap up Kidu's corpse just before the pups come to. Shibi proceeds to run to Kidu's side, but Mebi has to take things more slowly having suffered a fair amount of blood loss.

"Vedi!" Shibi yells.

"I'm so sorry. Ve is dead," Hari confesses.

Their eyes widen. Shibi breaks down in tears, but Mebi holds ver's back long enough to ask, "And Jove?"

"Alive. Asleep for now. Ve will recover," Hari places comforting hands on the pups. Mebi leans into Hari to grieve, but Shibi breaks away and runs over to me. I don't know what to say, so I just wrap my arms around ver and let ver weep. Soon Mebi asks to join us and Hari helps ver over. Miya also comes to embrace the group in an encompassing hug. We huddle together while the others work around us. We may not actually be Mebi and Shibi's vedira, but it certainly feels like we are.

After a moment, Miya hoists me up onto ver back and we guide the pups to a nearby ship cabin where they can rest and grieve. We also move Jove into the same cabin.

Jove stirs awake shortly after being laid down, "Kidu, where is Kidu?" Ve asks weakly.

"Ve is dead," Mebi, who is laying down beside Jove, says while holding Jove's paw.

"Where? I need to see ver," Jove insists and tries to rise.

"Take it easy," Miya says as ve tries to lay Jove back down. Jove is too weak from ver wounds to resist, "You've lost a lot of blood."

"Bring ver here!" Jove demands.

"We can't," I say.

"Why the hase not?"

"Ve is... Messy." Miya says.

At this, Jove begins to cry again and the pups follow suit. I punch Miya on the arm for making such an insensitive comment.

"What was that for?" Miya mutters.

I ignore Miya's question and speak instead to Jove, "I am sorry for your loss. We will give you all some space to grieve."

With that, we leave the cabin.

"Don't tell them Kidu's corpse is messy!" I say.

"What, that was the truth. What was I supposed to say?" Miya says.

"You could have said 'It's just not possible right now, I am sorry for your loss'" I scold as we go to try to make ourselves useful.

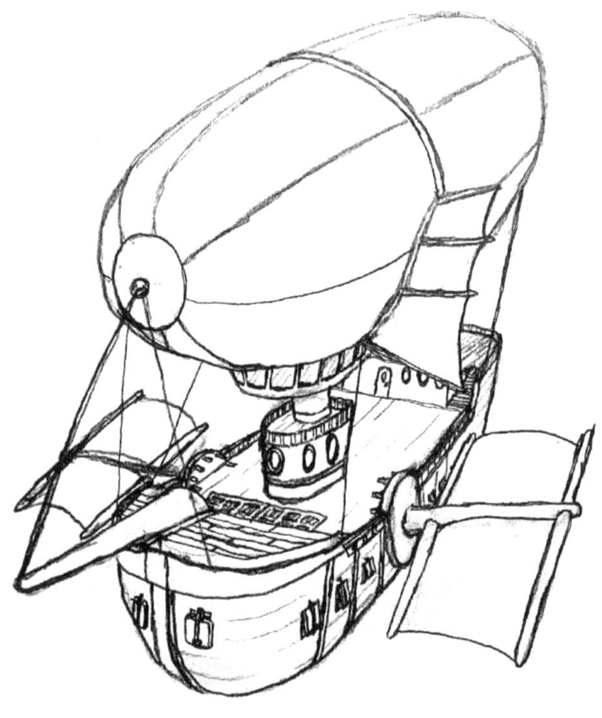

Chapter 24: Mysteries

All who are able-bodied work together to pilot the ship towards the other pick-up location. Among them is Sho, who was piloting the smaller ship during the combat. The small ship is now being towed behind our new acquisition, connected by a sturdy rope. It seems that the team has taken both Tai and Sho under their wing. I have no idea why they would permit Tai to keep tagging along on such a dangerous mission, but ve is here and is receiving Rirmevu-style training from Jomira, while Sho is learning how to pilot ships from Zi.

Once the sails are set such that they may not need adjusting for a moment, Hari approaches Miya and me.

"I'm not sure how long, but I have a moment to chat about the parts of your past that were taken from you if you are okay with potentially getting interrupted." Hari says.

Miya and I give Hari a confused look.

"Sorry, I don't know what you are talking about." Miya says.

"Sorry, not you, I was talking to Dima," Hari clarifies.

"I also don't know what you are talking about..." I say.

"Hmm... Either I am remembering a conversation we didn't have or you two had your minds wiped of it at some point."

"Minds wiped? Don't tell me that is another mind magic thing." I say.

"Unfortunately yes, and I think your memory of our conversation may have gone along with your knowledge of that aspect of mind magic. Anyway, recall the story of how you got caught up in the trafficking mess with Lise. I believe your memory of that time may have been corrupted at some point."

Intrigued, I say, "Go on."

"As I recall, we were both attending the same theatrical production. I had just gotten bullied and ran off to the alleyway because I was afraid of what others might think of me and what they might do to me. Someone tried to assault me in the alley and I was able to buy myself some time using magic. Then seemingly out of nowhere, you showed up, knocked out my assailant, and gave me a dress to replace my stained outfit. However, instead of going back into the theater I went running after you. When I caught up you said you were running away from Rirbuseha. You didn't say exactly why but I think it had something to do with your parents being detestable."

"Sorry, what did you just say?"

"Um, I remember you saying you didn't like your parents in contrast to my wanting to go back to mine."

"I mean yeah I didn't like my parents, but that wasn't why I was... Did you say I was running away? I don't remember running away. I remember just going with Lise because my parents had died."

"No," Hari says, "I think that may be a hole in your memory because I specifically remember you saying you weren't an orphan. I don't remember how that came up but I remember that learning that you weren't an orphan had some sort of memorable impact on me."

The rest of the world feels as though it has faded from existence. It is as though my mind has decided to reject everything I think I knew and everything about present reality. I am afloat in a void of emotion and thought for a while before I permit my mind to think about what I just heard. My parents may still be alive, and someone doesn't want me to know that. It's all too easy to believe that one of them is the someone who replaced my memories of that time. Though I have no evidence beyond it just sounding like something they would do.

"Are you alright?" Hari asks, snapping me back into reality.

"No," I say, "But I'm honestly not sure what I am right now. I don't know how to feel about this. Thank you for sharing though."

"Who do you think made you forget your parents?" Miya asks as we leave Hari to ver work.

"Probably my parents honestly." I say.

"Wow, you really think they would do that to you?" Miya asks.

"I wouldn't put it past them."

"What are you going to do about it?"

"I don't know." I say as I stare off, still trying to gather my illusive feelings, "Right now there is just so much else to worry about."

As we approach the second pick-up zone, we see that the small crowd remains gathered, and excitement visibly washes over them when they spot the approaching airship. We assist everyone in boarding the ship and ask them to gather towards the center. Some individuals sniff the air nervously, trying to distinguish the smell of death from the ever-present smell of sewage.

"Can I have everyone's attention?" Jomira addresses the crowd. The people quiet down and give Jomira their full attention.

"I have some good news and bad news," Jomira begins. The crowd murmurs, and some individuals appear worried. "The good news is that we are here to free all of you. The bad news is that this ship and the rescue operation used to be under government control with malicious intentions."

The crowd looks concerned, and panic seems to be on the verge of erupting. Jomira raises ver voice to overcome the murmurs of concern. "The officers from whom we took this ship intended to kill each of you. Sadly, they managed to kill several individuals who are now lying dead below deck." The crowd falls silent. "Due to the presence of toxins, we will all have to remain on the upper deck for the duration of this journey. Additionally, we will likely be pursued at any moment. If we attempt to head straight into the neighboring nation, we will be overtaken. Therefore, we have no choice but to go up. To Sudihatosema." The crowd appears to be a mix of excitement and confusion.

Someone from the crowd shouts, "Won't they just figure out who we are and send us right back here?"

"Not necessarily," Jomira replies. "I have friends up there who will provide us sanctuary, and we will conceal each of your identities when we arrive. You will have the opportunity to start a new life there or, once the heat on us has dissipated, join us on a voyage to Matuha."

Suddenly, a disheartening thought strikes me, and Miya notices.

"Are you okay?" Miya asks.

"Our bodies..."

"What about them?" Miya thinks for a moment and then looks shaken as ve realizes what I'm onto. "Oh.... They escaped from that port... or died there..."

Miya leans us against the guardrail of the ship as we grapple with the increasing likelihood that our bodies are dead.

"Do you think they are... below deck?" I ask.

"I doubt it. They probably clean out the bodies between their killing sprees. How else would they get a crowd of people who can smell death to willingly go down there?" Miya says.

"Good point."

"Well... as much as I hate to admit it, living the rest of our lives in these bodies isn't too bad." Miya says.

"True... but how long can Jove go on wondering what happened to ver siblings?" I ask.

"Also a good point... So, we are heading back to our hometown," Miya changes the subject.

"What do you think are the odds of us being able to get into our house?" Miya asks.

I chuckle. "Not great, I imagine. Do you think we could sneak onto the base to visit the spa?"

"We could certainly try. It would only cost us our lives if we got caught," Miya jokes.

"I'm not sure if it's worth it. Our lives might actually be worth living soon." I say.

"Do you really think so?" Miya asks, "I've been grappling with that question myself. Where do we go after all of this? What's the purpose of our lives once this is over?"

Miya's question is a good one. Where do we go from here? Do we go to Matuha or stay and try to make a difference in Rirze? Can we even stay here? We're considered outlaws. We would need to find someone to scramble our biosignatures. That would suck. It's disheartening to think that after everything we've been through, we might end up with a part of someone else's body merged with our own. Miya will never be able to fly again. Will ve even want ver old body?

"Are... Are you hoping we don't find our bodies?" I ask.

"No. Why? Are you?" ve responds.

"No, it's just... your wings..."

Silence lingers, and I regret bringing up the topic.

"I already can't fly. Though it will certainly be bittersweet to get my body back and not have them," Miya admits. "Anyways, I don't identify with this body. It's not that I find it ugly or anything, but I hate that it's not mine. I don't feel at home in it. It's almost distressing at times."

I reflect on ver words and I think I understand.

"I think I know what you mean. I feel out of place in this body too. My true identity is deeply rooted in the Atu culture, even though I'm currently biologically a Bitu. I miss seeing things in crisp detail rather than relying so much on my sense of smell. While I appreciate this body for making me as tall as I've always wanted to be and a stronger fighter, it's not who I am. I don't identify with it. I think I have been so focused on longing for my legs that I didn't fully consider how much I yearn for my own body, regardless of its height."

“That is part of how I feel, but in Yetu terms. There is also the feeling that I don’t have complete autonomy so long as I am in and responsible for someone else's body,” Miya concurs.

“Hopefully we can find our bodies. Now that I think about it, I don't know how much longer I can tolerate living in a body that doesn't truly belong to me.” I say.

Chapter 25: Sudihatosema

In order to minimize suspicion, the airship is flown away from Sudihatosema and then turned back around to head towards Rirbuseha, the holiest city in the Shattered Skies. The idea is to make it look like we are coming from Rirbuseha instead of Hosudiha, reducing the likelihood of being stopped and searched. Fortunately, the low-lying clouds work in our favor by blocking the line of sight between us and Sudihatosema below.

I feel overwhelming resentment for my Bitu eyes, which further blur the details I yearn to see again. As we get closer, I squint, hoping for a clearer image. But all too soon, we begin our descent into the gray clouds that drain our surroundings of color and beauty. It feels like we are being cast down from grace once again.

My heart begins to race as an irrational seed of panic begins to germinate within me. We made it out of the darkness. When Ritu refused to exalt us, we exalted ourselves; we built a tower, an act of defiance that surely won't go unpunished. My body anticipates the moment when the tower comes crashing down, when Ritu will confuse our minds and place us where we really deserve to be, captivity...

I can't go back. I can't survive another two salaries of bondage! My breathing begins to shorten.

"Are you okay?" Miya asks.

"No. What are we doing?" I say, "Do we really think we won't get caught? Surely Ritu won't let us get away with this! All roads lead back to slavery Miya! I cannot be a slave again!"

Miya removes me from ver back and sits with me, "I'm not going to let that happen."

"Who are you to make a promise like that? If it's Ritu's will, what hope do we have?"

"Would you rather die?" Miya asks?

"I would." I say.

"Then I will tell you what. If things come to that. I'll kill you before you have to go through that again." Miya says.

The thought of Miya killing me makes me feel ill, "No," I take a deep breath, "That won't be necessary." I say. However, I don't know if I really want to turn down the offer. I start taking some deep breaths.

"Are you going to be alright?"

"Yeah, sorry. The last time I saw Rirbuseha like that was right before Lise trafficked me. I am panicking, but I think I just need some time to come out of it."

"Okay, would you like for me to give you some space?" Miya asks.

"Please don't." I say.

Miya nods, "Alright, I won't talk your ear off, but I do want to remind you that you don't have to believe any of that about Ritu anymore."

I think back to the conversation we had as a family back in Hosudiha, looking for comfort in the memory and finding it. I cannot help but wonder how long these old beliefs will haunt me.

"You're right. Thanks." I say.

Miya then wraps me in ver arms and holds me. Ve may have no combat ability to speak of, but I still feel safe. Breathing deeply, I lean into Miya's embrace and watch through the balusters as the airship descends into a courtyard surrounded on every side by a building shaped like the thick outline of a square. I immediately feel uneasy again as several ministry members exit the building to meet us. However, unlike government-affiliated ministry members who wear varying shades of gray, these clergy members all wear teal robes with golden sashes.

"Welcome to Rirma," Jomira announces, "One of the many sanctuaries of Sudihatosema. I understand that you all may feel distrust of the ministry. However, let me assure you, Rirma has been working with us for decades and has proven itself to be a force of redemption in the midst of all the corruption you may have come to expect.

This will not be like any other ministry effort you have experienced. They aim to help without any expectation from you. Not of your labor, nor of your beliefs, nor of your loyalty. At any time, you can choose to leave Rirma's services without repercussion. They will help you learn how to survive in Sudihatosema, and they will help you acquire capital, a job, and security so that you can support yourself and your family, but they will not indebt you. You will never owe them or us anything.

If you wish to leave, please allow them to help hide your identity so that you are not found out by the authorities. You can choose to settle here in Sudihatosema or in Matuha once we can travel there again without raising suspicion."

The crowd murmurs as they process this information, but soon we all disembark from the ship, receive our keys, and are escorted by various ministers to our assigned rooms to inhabit for as long as we need.

The atu and yetu guiding our group introduce themselves as Mrge, the atu, and Nukalaya, the yetu. They have the unrefined smell all atu and yetu seem to have—natural body odor along with a spritz of perfume. Though, being outside of Hosudiha, one can hardly pay any mind to it. The further we are from the ship's smell of death, the more Sudihatosema's beautiful world of scents emerges.

We enter a room with a window overlooking the courtyard, and I watch as the ship departs. What are they going to do with the ship and the many corpses inside? Kidu's body was already removed, as we knew ver. Kidu's body will be cleaned and preserved as best as it can be, so we can give ver a proper burial in whatever location we choose to reside.

We come to a stop in the room, and Nukalaya, stark white in color, dismounts Mrge who turns to face us but stands quietly as Nukalaya begins to speak, "Your residences are in the corridor just ahead. You will find a door numbered the same as your key. While you are in Sudihatosema there are a number of things to keep in mind so that you don't draw unwanted attention to yourselves or accidentally out yourselves as residents of Hosudiha. First, try your best to refrain from the use of profanity. Second, do not ask for variations of woods or coals to burn. There is only one option of each that residents are permitted to burn, and my apologies, but I have been told they are some of the worst options. You cannot even burn any other woods or coals you may have brought with you. Burning other wood or coal options is illegal and can land you a twenty labor or twenty jug fine..."

I can hardly bear to stand idly by as Nukalaya goes on to explain how practically every aspect of bitu culture is either deemed low class or is illegal. The more I think about it, I remember being a little upset when I arrived in Sudihatosema for the first time with Lise. Ve told me about why certain firewoods and coal were illegal. At first I thought it was just the wealthy hoarding resources, though now I see it for what it is, an attack on bitu culture. Another pipe added beside law, the market, and religion all pulling vetu of dark complexion towards one of many forms of slavery.

Nukalaya goes on, "We have a magical ability to swap certain body parts between two targets. We can use this ability to ensure no one will be able to recognize you. You can choose whether or not you would like us to disguise you in this way. Mrge will keep a record of the swaps made so that we can return what is yours to you should you desire it or choose to depart from our services. Please ensure you choose to swap with someone you trust to minimize the risk of someone running off with your body parts."

Miya and I easily decide to scramble our bodies with each other. We are not particularly attached to our bodies anyway. As for everyone else, it's a harder choice to make.

Jove chooses not to scramble ver body. "Who is going to notice me up here in a place I have never been? I think I'll be fine." ve argues.

The pups follow ver lead.

Mrge and Nukalaya offer to swap with Suki and Buso, and they accept the offer. In the end, only a few swaps are made before we begin to disperse to our respective rooms.

"Dima, Miya?" Shibi asks.

"Yeah?" I respond.

"Would ya stay wit us?" Shibi asks.

Jove cuts in, "Enough of that. I'm sure Miya and Dima have had quite enough of us. They are not your vedira, even if they possess their bodies."

"No, it's fine," Miya speaks up. "We would actually prefer to share a room. Right?"

"Yeah. I actually think I require Mebi's snoring to get any shut-eye at this point," I joke.

The three of them smile at our response. I can tell Jove was hoping we would join them as well.

"Excuse me, Nukalaya," Miya says.

"Yes?"

"Can we exchange our keys for the same room as theirs?"

"Oh, certainly. Please hand your keys over to Mrge, and I'll make sure two new keys are delivered to your room along with a wheelchair."

The room exudes luxury, with a soft burgundy carpet covering the floor, light green walls decorated with some pattern which may appear more detailed with atu eyes, a fireplace, and a separate warm brown-tiled area housing the toilet and bath. Two decent-sized burgundy beds stand apart, evoking the most excitement.

"Ah call dat one!" Mebi quickly claims, running to the nearest bed and jumping onto it and exclaiming, "Wah, ah feel woozy."

"Nu-uh, ya don get yer own bed!" Shibi scolds as ve runs over to contest the same bed. I half expect them to start fighting over it when Shibi freezes and takes a deep whiff of the bed.

"Dese aren stuffed wit bitu fur, dat's kuvohedi fur." Shibi exclaims.

Mebi face-plants into the bed possibly from lightheadedness due to low blood count, or in an effort to smell it too. "Jojos' a no-good liar,"

Mebi concludes. A split alm of grief crosses ver face at the memory of ver left behind friend before ve recovers, "Now get off'a my bed!"

"Ya don get ta sleep on dat bed all yerself!" Shibi argues.

"Shibi is right," Jove declares. "In fact, get off of that bed, and everyone help push them together."

"Aww, come on," Mebi complains.

"I don't want to hear it," says Jove.

Shibi and Mebi prepare to get off the bed, and Mebi catches Shibi's eye, whispering bitterly, "Dis is yer fault."

Jove smacks Mebi on the back of the head. "Enough of that. We would be doing this regardless. Now come on."

Those of us who can, split into two teams and push the beds toward each other, creating one massive bed in the center of the room.

"There, we'll all sleep together just like home..." Jove's voice trails off as grief washes over ver. "Damn it, Kidu."

Jove kneels on the floor and begins to weep into the bed. Empathy fills the room, and we all gather around ver. Kidu never experienced such luxury—these beds, this clean and richly scented air. Ve was so close to experiencing the exaltation of ver family that ve had always dreamed ver hard work would achieve.

"I always wondered who Kidu and I would be if we had more than a measly two moments a labor to be with each other between work and sleep. Maybe we wouldn't have hated each other as much. Hase, maybe we would have discovered what this whole love thing is supposed to be about." Jove says.

"You never loved ver?" Miya asks.

"How could I? There was never any time. I may have never had the chance to love ver, but at least I wasn't alone."

"We're here," Mebi says tearfully.

"I appreciate you two. I really do, but I need another adult to navigate through life with, and those two won't be sticking around forever." Jove says as ve gestures to Miya and me.

"We're not going anywhere," I assure Jove.

"Oh, really? What about your families and friends? You had lives before you landed in the slums with us, did you not?"

"Well... I didn't have much of a family to speak of, apart from mentors in the ministry," I say. "I don't think I can go back to the ministry, so I don't really have anyone apart from Miya and all of you now."

"Yeah... and I think it's pretty safe to assume I'll be disowned if I ever show a glint of who I am these labors around my family," Miya adds.

Our solemn reality settles upon us for a moment. I don't know about Miya, but I assume we both realize how little we have left of our old lives to look forward to.

Early the next morning, all I can think about is going for a stroll down to the four sanctuaries. Once everyone's grievances have settled a little, Miya and I excuse ourselves to go on that stroll. We would invite the family to come with us, but Jove is still recovering from blood loss, and I'm not sure the holy site would have the same positive effect on Jove and the pups as it has on Miya and me.

"We will be back as soon as we can." Miya assures the family.

"Arlight, make sure you two keep your heads down while you are out!" Jove says.

Miya pulls out the wheelchair. I am not sure how I feel about it. It is made of wood. There is no cushion, which I guess is fine, I cannot feel my butt anyway. The wheels are also made of wood and lined in a protective leather.

Miya lowers me down into it. There is a strap that I assume goes across my lap. So I fasten it around me.

"How's it feel?" Shibi asks.

"I mean. I guess it's fine." I say as I rock the wheels back and forth to get a feel for the motion.

"Are you ready to get going?" Miya asks.

"Sure, let's do it." I say and begin to roll my way out of the room while Miya holds the door.

As I roll down the hallway beside Miya, I cannot help but feel a sense of excitement at the ability to move myself so efficiently. However, we are not even to the sanctuary lobby before my arms are exhausted. Driving a wheelchair must work different muscles than crawling does. I try to ignore the pain, and push on. However, knowing how far we have to go, I have no choice.

"Hey Miya?"

"Yeah?"

"My arm muscles are not yet cut out for this... Could you push me?" I ask.

"Oh, are you sure?"

"Yeah."

"Alright then."

Miya pushes me the rest of the way through the sanctuary before we run into our second obstacle.

Stairs.

Only five steps from the door down to the street.

Miya and I hardly have a moment to problem solve before a clergy member is behind us.

"Here, let me help you." the clergy member says. Though something about the way ve said it, and the way ve only seems to look at Miya, it makes me feel like an inanimate object.

"Oh, uh. Thanks." Miya responds.

"Yeah, thank you." I say with an emphasis to see if it garners me any attention from the clergy member.

Without making eye contact with me, the clergy member moves to the front and grabs hold of the chair. They lift me up and carry me down the stairs without a word. Panic fills me as a small gust threatens to blow up my robe and expose me while I am being hoisted through the air. My hands have to choose between instinctually holding onto the chair and pushing down my robe to preserve my decency and I manage to choose the latter. Then, once I am safely at the bottom of the stairs, the clergy member looks at Miya.

"Enjoy your walk." Ve says and then ve returns to the building.

I wait for a moment before speaking, "Did that feel awkward to you?" I ask Miya.

"No... Though I understand why it might have felt awkward to you being lifted up and all like that." Miya says.

"It was more than that. It was like ve didn't want to acknowledge my existence." I say.

"Huh, I hadn't noticed. Though thinking back on it... Yeah, I don't think ve ever talked to you directly. That's odd."

"Right... That has never happened to me before. The only difference between us is that I am in a wheelchair. Maybe that made ver uncomfortable? Oh no! Maybe ve assumes I murdered someone!" I exclaim.

"Shhh..." Miya says, "That might not be the wisest thing to say so loudly." Miya suggests.

Suddenly I feel extremely nervous at how many people might assume I am a murderer.

"Hey," Miya cuts into my spiral, "We're going to be alright. Not everyone is ignorant of all of the reasons someone might need a wheelchair."

"Yeah, but I certainly used to believe people with disabilities or any kind of hardship had done something to deserve it. Hase, any time enough things would go wrong in my life I would wonder what I had done to incur Ritu's wrath. Or I would assume Ritu was telling me I was doing something wrong. Or-"

"Yes, there are people as ignorant as you once were, and I have your back." Miya assures me.

My hands crave some knitting needles, but for lack of them, I search for something else to distract my mind when suddenly I catch a whiff of some freshly baked bread.

"You smell that?" I ask.

"I'm already taking us that way." Miya says.

As Miya pushes me along the chair jostles about in a way that irritates my lower back and makes me wonder if this walk will really be worth it. One thing is for sure, I am going to get a cushion for this thing as soon as possible.

"Hello, welcome to... oh... um... How can I help you?" asks the baker.

"May we please have two slices of bread and butter?" I ask.

"Do you have the coin for it?"

Strange, I've never been asked if I could afford something I wanted to buy before. Maybe ve asks because I am squinting to read the prices. Regardless, the sanctuary gave everyone some money to buy food, supplies, and a little extra for any other needs or just to enjoy our stay.

"Yes, of course. Six alms total?" I ask.

"Eight."

I squint at the price sign again. It clearly says three alms a slice. Maybe tax is no longer being included in the prices?

"Oh, I'm sorry. Of course." I say.

Miya hands over our payment, and we wait for a moment.

"Here." The baker hands us two slices of less-than-fresh bread, but I can hardly mind as I am compelled to bite into it straight away. The gluten is a delight to the taste buds, but the stale texture is far from the pillowy softness I was hoping for.

"Um... Sorry to be a nuisance, but there is no butter," Miya says, "May we have some-"

"Scram." The baker scolds.

"Geez, fine," Miya says as we move along.

"What the heck was that all about?" I ponder aloud, "Ve didn't seem to like either one of us."

"I have no idea. Maybe ve is just a jerk or something."

"It's a wonder anyone gives ver business with that attitude." I say.

We move along, finishing our bread just as we approach one of the stained glass archways.

"Oh Miya, I just realized that you have never gotten to see this with eyes before! This is going to be a whole new experience for you."

"Yeah, you're right. Though I wonder if it will be as you remember it."

"Why? Do you think they might have changed things all of a sudden?"

"No, it's not that." We come to a stop just before the arch, "Does that look the way you remember it?"

I look up, and all I can see is a blur of colors that fade into darkness as my eyes pan right.

"Oh, that's what you mean." I say.

"Yeah, still pretty though. Even if it's blurry, I've never seen such an array of colors, and if I squint I can sort of make out the details."

"Yeah..." I say.

I no longer feel compelled to pass through the archway only to be disappointed by a sea of blurry colors.

"Excuse me," says a sudden voice from behind us. We turn to find a couple of regular officers approaching us. "We are going to need to see proof of purchase for that bread you just ate."

Proof of purchase? Since when do we stop random people and demand proof that they bought some bread?

"What exactly would that be, officer?" I ask.

"If you have no proof of purchase, then I'm afraid we are going to have to place you under arrest."

My heart begins to race as panic once again sets in. There is no way this ends anywhere but slavery.

"Wait, hold on," Miya says.

"What? Are you scared? Have something to hide?" an officer asks, "That one looks particularly nervous." The officer gestures to me as I fail to hide my panic.

"No, if you want, we could take you to the vendor who sold us the bread." Miya says.

"Who do you think set us onto you? Ve said you two were a danger to this community and sent us to make sure you don't hurt anyone."

"Wait, are you arresting us for theft or for disturbing the peace? I can assure you we haven't done either." Miya says.

"Yeah, sure, as if you would admit to it. You look nervous. Are you thinking about trying to roll away?" The officer asks me.

"No, I-"

"'Cause if you do," the officer pulls out a dart gun, "I will knock your ass out. Do you hear me?"

"I'm not running!" I shout.

The officer grabs me by my shirt and pulls me out of my wheelchair, close to ver face. "Don't you get aggressive with me!" ve yells.

Miya tries to pry us apart. "Hey, calm down! That's uncalled-"

The other officer strikes Miya on the head with the butt of ver gun, and Miya falls down with ver arm raised in surrender and defense.

"Assault! You are under arrest for assaulting an officer!" The officer yells as ve starts kicking and hitting Miya repeatedly.

The officer holding me then throws me down onto Miya, sending a wave of pain through my lower back. Ve rears back to kick me.

"Hey!" A new and familiar voice calls out, "Officers Suki, Buso, and Powa of Regiment Four! Get the hase off of them!"

The officers look to see Suki holding up ver and Buso's badges, and Powa holding up vers. They back away. "These two are guilty of theft, disturbing the peace, and assaulting an officer!" one of the officers shouts defensively.

"As your superiors, we will be taking over from here." Suki says.

"Now get your asses back to the station!" Powa orders.

The two officers look at each other and then back at their superiors. "Yes, Minister," they say before starting to walk away.

"Double time!" Buso orders, "and I will know if you stop booking it!"

At that, the two officers pick up the pace and jog out of view.

"Alright, they are a ways off now. Are you two alright?" Buso says.

"Yeah, I'm only a little hurt," Miya remarks.

Suki helps Miya back to ver feet, and Powa wraps ver clay around my body.

"Here," Powa says, "I'll help you get back in your chair. I would offer to be your legs for a bit, but the last time we did that I learned that it drains me of energy pretty fast." Powa says.

"You're fine. You don't have to be my legs." I say as I come down from my state of panic. Powa lowers me back down into the chair. The strap buckle that was securing me seems to have gotten bent out of shape when that damn officer grabbed me. So I just tie a knot for the time being.

"That was bizarre," I comment in bewilderment. "Those officers need to be reported. They are just looking to cause trouble."

"I wonder if they were really officers or just thugs with stolen uniforms," Miya ponders.

"I can assure you that you two will need to be extra careful with those bodies while up here," Buso says. "Fami and I may not have talked much, but I still traveled these streets with ver a lot. Folks around here don't take too kindly to vetu of dark complexion."

"Extra careful?" I ask. "All we did was buy and eat some bread!"

"Just try your best to minimize interactions. Pack your own food, and whatever you do, don't make a scene or draw any attention to yourself. The less visible you are, the better."

"That's insane. How are darker vetu supposed to survive in this place?" Miya asks.

"Many don't," Buso says flatly.

That reality hangs in the air for a moment as another piece of the pipeline to slavery clicks into place.

Existence.

I've been through some shit; life hasn't been easy for me. However, even in the most difficult of times as a pale-skinned atu, society wasn't rigged against me simply because of my species or the color of my skin. Meanwhile with a dark-furred bitu body, and a disabled one at that, the pull towards slavery feels as prevalent as gravity. So long as I possess a dark-furred bitu body, what hope is there for my future apart from the hope that I am lucky enough to not draw attention to myself?

It is possible to survive. To do alright for yourself. I think back on Joho, Hari, even Fami. But I know better than to ignore the heaps of luck it takes. Or maybe Ritu's favor? I don't know. Whatever the case of fate, it's just hard to be optimistic. Matuha feels like the only chance we have at a better life, and I am incredibly fortunate to potentially have passage there.

"Anyway, I see you two decided to make the walk as well," Buso remarks.

"Yeah..." I sigh back. "Not quite the same experience through bitu eyes, I'm afraid."

"Nor in these bodies in general," Miya adds as ve rubs at the bruise on ver head.

"Oh? Well, uh, why don't we go get you some glasses?" Suki suggests. "It should be a safer experience with us there with you."

Why hadn't I thought of that? Probably because I had given up on the prospect while in Hosudiha, where glasses were a luxury few could afford. Suddenly, I start to feel excited again.

"Honestly, that sounds great!" I exclaim.

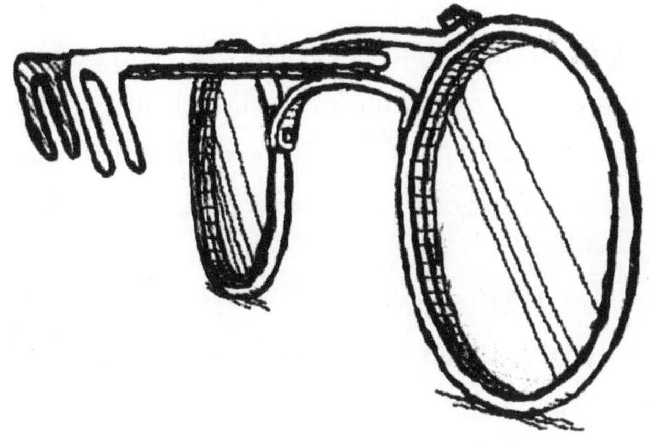

Chapter 26: Sights and Smells

"Oh some dark bitu!" The optician exclaims as we enter the shop. Ve is a light-gray furred bitu wearing brown trousers and an off-white button-up shirt, with a pair of circular eyeglasses resting on ver snout. Ve wears a smile that disarms me and simultaneously makes me worry that ve might make the conversation uncomfortably personal. "You are my favorite kind of customer! Come in, come in. My name is Demo. Let me be of service to you!"

The sudden shift in tone from the vitriol of the officers to the enthusiasm of Demo is quite jarring. I'm not sure if I appreciate it or if it's a bit too much.

The store is clean and well-built, likely receiving government grants since its services are a matter of healthcare. However, it is still privately owned, so there will be a price for whatever glasses we choose. Nonetheless, the extra funds are probably what allows the store to have an indoor space with a large window that lets in light. There are several dozen spectacles adorning the walls, and a counter displaying a large wheel of lenses.

We approach the counter, and Demo hurriedly grabs an incense stick and lights it using the fire from an overhead lantern. "Allow me to make you a bit more comfortable. I know how you like these sorts of smells."

The scent wafting from the incense stick smells somewhat like cheap firewood.

"Uh, thanks," Miya remarks.

"I appreciate your kindness," I say, "but please treat us like any other customer."

"Oh, of course." Demo says.

"It's okay." I say.

"No, you're right. We really are all the same." Demo says.

"Right." I say.

"We all work hard to get to where we are. I'm sure you have worked just as hard as I have and have weathered similar trials." Demo says confidently.

"Right..." I say.

"Why do you sound so uncertain about that?" asks Demo, "Don't listen to anyone who tells you that you are lesser than or otherwise disadvantaged just because your fur is dark. You are living proof that if you work hard, you can rise out of poverty. Besides, dark vetu are not the only ones who reside in Hosudiha."

"Okay, thanks." I say sharply, trying to let on that I would really rather stop talking about this.

"No, I'm serious." Demo says, "Racists will always try to tell you that you are lesser or somehow disadvantaged. They will tell you it's the fault of the light vetu and that light vetu should be ashamed of being what they are despite having no choice in their complexion. They only divide us and encourage dark vetu to give up, perpetuating the stereotype. Now, would you please put your head here and let me know which looks clearer?"

I place my head against the crazy wheel of lenses.

"I'm sorry," Miya cuts in, "but there are some differences between the experiences of vetu of lighter complexions and vetu of darker complexions..."

"There, you see. You have bought into the racist propaganda. Tell me, what difference does complexion really make?" Demo continues to go back and forth between the conversation and testing our vision as do we.

"I mean, it makes no biological difference. Honestly, I think you are right about a couple of things, but I disagree with what you seem to believe we should do about it. I agree that race is ultimately a mechanism invented to divide and control us." Miya says.

"Exactly, it is an illusion," Demo asserts, "and the sooner people stop seeing race, the sooner dark vetu will stop giving up and populating Hosudiha disproportionately."

"I wouldn't call it an illusion. It is a very real tool used to create systems which determine who should be oppressed and who should not." Miya says.

"No," Demo cuts in again, "See you are just proving my point. Race is nothing more than an attempt to make vetu give up and be comfortable in their victimhood."

"I don't know about that," Miya says, "A person can be a victim in need of help and still be strong, competent, and motivated. You also seem to have forgotten the bit about division. While it's certainly not a valid mechanism of division. Race is a real mechanism of division which calls upon real things like complexion, language, grammar, hygiene, culture, and more in an attempt to arbitrarily define this made up thing called race."

"Right, it is made up. So if we as a society could just agree that it is made up, then the issue would be resolved." Demo says.

"Okay... but that wouldn't..."Miya starts, but before ve can get too far I reach over and give Miya's leg a squeeze, attempting to discreetly suggest ve end the conversation or change the topic.

"Hey, what was that for?" Miya asks.

Eyes fall on me, and I am overwhelmed with embarrassment. What should I say? Damn it, Miya, you don't just ask why someone discreetly squeezed your leg!

Miya notices my silent panic and says, "Oh, um, that's right, um, I forgot to ask... How much will this cost us..." I can't tell if Miya actually picked up on what I was trying to communicate or if ve really thought I wanted to know the prices. Either way, I'm annoyed with ver but relieved that the conversation seems to be shifting.

"Hmm... About eighty coins per bifocal, so a purse and six coins should cover it," Demo replies.

I feel a bit disheartened as that is much more than we were given to spend.

"We'll cover it," Suki offers.

"Oh, uh, thank you," I say. I hate that we have to depend on them for this. I don't want to take on any debts, but it would be too awkward to go through this whole process only to turn them down and walk out with nothing.

Demo finishes assessing our eyes and goes off to browse ver selection of bifocals, returning shortly thereafter with two sets. "These should do the trick."

Miya and I put on the glasses. Unlike atu glasses which secure themselves to one's face by wrapping behind an atu's ears, these glasses have comb teeth meant to stick into the fur of a bitu snout and secure the glasses to a bitu's face. The feeling of the combs on either side of my snout is uncomfortable, but hopefully this body will learn to ignore it with time. Once the glasses are secured the world goes from blurry to... still blurry.

Seeing our confusion, Demo plucks the glasses from our faces. "Oh, sorry, my mistake." Then Demo gives Miya the pair I had and me the pair Miya had.

When I put the glasses on again, the way the world sharpens somehow makes me feel more present in this space. It's a subtle but soothing feeling.

"Well, how does it feel to see the world for the first time?" Demo asks, unaware that this isn't my first time, although atu vision is even better. Also, something about the insinuation that we haven't really seen the world just because we haven't had glasses up to this point makes me feel a bit annoyed.

"This is amazing!" Miya exclaims as ve experiences focused vision for the first time.

I piggyback off of Miya's wonder. "So much better. Thank you!"

Suki pays Demo for ver services, and we prepare to leave the shop.

"Thank you for coming by! I hope you love the world you see, and remember, you are capable of anything!" Demo calls out as we exit.

"Why did you squeeze my leg?" Miya asks almost as soon as we step outside to start our walk back to the sanctuary.

"Because you were only going to paint us as the sort of racists ve thinks are out to divide and destroy society. I don't think it was a conversation worth risking." I say.

"Honestly, I think that was a good call," Buso backs me up.

"But if no one has that conversation with ver, then how will they ever learn that ignoring race does nothing to dismantle the systems which leverage it? Nor does it do anything to correct the injustices of past systems." Miya says.

"I don't know, but I don't feel like we are safe to have those conversations in these bodies and in that context." I say.

"I see your point," Miya says, "Sorry about that."

"It's all right." I say, "Under different circumstances I don't think I would have intervened."

"From my experience, I wasn't able to overcome that sort of mentality until I experienced the reality of the situation in Hosudiha," Suki adds.

"Fami had a friend who was of that mindset. There was no convincing ver friend of reality, not until ver friend decided to question the narrative ve believed and started to actually listen. I hope ver friend is doing well. I wonder if ve knows what happened to Fami."

A moment of silence hangs in the air as we all reflect on the legacy of Fami.

"So, how are you all settling in?" Buso asks, changing the topic.

"It's a lot," I admit. "The loss of Kidu is hard. The loss of the lives we once had is also tough. I'm sure you all are familiar with that, though."

"A little, but probably not quite in the same way as what you two are going through," Buso says. "I actually have kids and a spouse. We saw this escape coming for quite some time, so they are not living on the base. They are secretly living with a friend on a smaller island town. When all of this blows over, I hope to meet up with them and escape to Matuha."

Suki chimes in. "My parents were supportive of me getting involved with the ministry, but they subtly yet strongly advised against it. I think they were trying to warn about the corruption while also trying to keep themselves and my siblings safe in case I happened to become radical and come after them for their criticisms of the ministry. It's a valid concern. You don't receive permission to study and practice higher levels of magic if you aren't a little extreme in your allegiance to the ministry."

Suki manages a slight smile, "So, they will probably be happy to hear about my decision to abandon the ministry." ver expression darkens again.

"It must feel good to know you have their support," Miya says.

"It would," Suki says, "However, now I can't return to them without putting them in danger. Their support of me is risky for them. I wish we could all escape together, but I don't think they would come with us even if the opportunity presented itself. They are not only dependent on family assistance to survive but also dedicated to being the change they want to see in this country."

Suki looks up towards Rirbuseha, "I don't know how I feel about their dedication to this nation. I admire their intentions, but it has caused me harm."

It is intriguing to me that Suki's parents might have hurt ver through wanting to better this nation in spite of the ministry, one of the greatest sources of harm I've come to recognize as of late. I need to know more. "If you don't mind my asking, in what ways did their dedication to bettering Rirze hurt you?"

Suki's face looks like ve is struggling between feelings of resentment or feelings of compassion, "They don't teach to hate others, quite the contrary. Though I'm not sure they realize how they lay the groundwork for hate."

Something about that statement resonates with me, though I cannot explain why, "In what ways did they lay the groundwork for hate?" I ask.

"They taught me to remain ignorant of other religions or ideologies because such things were not only inferior but also dangerous. They taught me to think in terms of an in-group and an out-group, and that the out-group was fearworthy. From there it doesn't take much for someone to come along and capitalize on that fear by blaming those in the out-group for the plights of our society. Such tactics easily give rise to hate given that groundwork of ignorance and superiority."

"Did they not also teach you the lessons of love and peace in the Holy Scriptures?" Miya asks.

"Lessons of love and peace held back the hate for a while, and while many such lessons never give way, most people have a threshold of fear that will override love." frustration seems to intensify Suki's tone as ve goes on to say, "Then they are driven to either hate or to confuse hate for love when they are permitted to hate transgressions, but those 'transgressions' are identities which cannot be decoupled from people."

Suki takes a deep, calming breath and continues, "Eventually, I was seduced by the extremists who told me to be afraid of those who believed and lived differently from me. They convinced me to do horrible things to those people. I'm worried about my siblings. That they too will fall to extremism if they remain where they are. At the same time, may vedi have indeed made a difference, and nowhere is completely safe from extremist influence. I don't know how to feel. But I do grieve my inability to reconnect with my family."

"I don't know which situation I prefer," Miya says. "In my case, my family's rejection is what keeps me apart from them, whereas in your case, your family's acceptance is what keeps you apart from them. I'm sorry for your losses in all of this."

"I don't have a family!" Powa chimes in. "I woke up in the nearby mountains, walked into Sudihatosema, and the Ministry gave me a job!

You all are the only family I've ever known. So I guess I'm the luckiest to have you all here with me!"

Part of me feels bad for Powa, but such is the life of most notu. Besides, who am I to say that ver life is somehow less fortunate than mine just because it is different. Maybe the same can be said for my life with disabilities.

"You did lose Tatu..." Buso reminds Powa.

"Oh yeah... Yeah, that sucked. I wish Tatu could have been less of a jerk," Powa says flatly.

Now that my vision is sharper, I notice the lingering glances. Almost everyone we pass takes a moment to stare us down. Some even look disgusted at the sight of us. Parents gesture for their kids to come closer, and merchants watch our hands closely when we pass near their stands.

I take off my glasses and put them in my bag.

"What's wrong? Do you think you got the wrong prescription?" Suki asks.

"No, it's just... I don't know. If I have them off, I can at least pretend that no one is watching me."

"Who's watching?" Suki asks.

"Everyone." I say.

"Oh... You think it's because you're a-" Suki starts.

"Yeah." I cut in.

"Ah, sorry about that." Suki says.

"Oh, is that not normal?" Miya asks.

"It's not something I ever noticed as a pale-skinned atu," I say.

I try to immerse myself in my sense of smell to divert my attention from how people might be thinking about me, about this body, and about my disability. Never before have I wanted to escape from this body so badly.

The most prominent scent in the air is that of freshly baked goods. However, it's not just baked goods; there are distinct aromas of different types of bread, treats, flowers, woods, perfumes, and...

"Miya!" I exclaim.

"I smell it too... It's coming from us," Miya confirms.

"Well, I wasn't going to say anything, but yeah... you two could really use a bath," Suki remarks.

"Noted... but we were talking about our original bodies," Miya corrects.

"Oh... I'm so sorry." Suki says meekly.

"Nah, it's fine. We do smell pretty bad," Miya acknowledges.

"Alright, well," I interject, "I guess we'll have to postpone our return to the sanctuary. Let's follow the trail."

"May we come with?" Buso offers. "We might be useful in case of danger."

"Yeah, that would be nice," Miya agrees.

We follow the trail into an alleyway. It appears that the trail takes less crowded routes and passages until we reach a brick wall where it abruptly ends. Suki examines the wall closely, having the keenest eyesight among us.

"There seems to be a gap in the mortar. If I use property magic to make it lighter, we might be able to slide it open. Buso, is it clear on the other side?"

"I don't sense anyone. It seems to be an empty alleyway behind what I believe is the spa. The details are a bit fuzzy, but there are a couple of atu and two..." Buso pauses, realization dawning upon ver.

"What?" Miya asks.

"Two yetu... One of them doesn't seem to have wings."

Hope and excitement surge through me.

"That's Miya!" I exclaim.

"Okay, give me an alm, and then try giving it a push," Suki says, focusing on the slightly ajar portion of the wall and a nearby stone.

Miya gives the wall a push, and sure enough, the section slides free from the rest and Miya moves it out of the way. We all pass through the small opening into an empty alleyway behind the spa. Miya then slides the wall portion back into place to cover our tracks, and we proceed to follow the trail for a short distance until we reach the rear entrance of the spa.

Chapter 27: Who We Are

"Should we knock?" I ask.

"They know we're here," Buso informs me.

Suddenly, the door cracks open, but it remains secured by a chain. An unfamiliar voice speaks, "Can we help you?"

"Yes, are Sodi and Kize here?" I inquire.

"They no longer work here... Can I pass along a message?"

"Yeah..." I respond, slightly disappointed by the news, "Um, we need help. We're from Hosudiha and we're looking for some lost family."

"What are their names?"

"I'm not sure if I can share them, as their names might bring them trouble. But one name starts with 'Hi' and the other starts with 'Vi'."

The stranger seems to eye me for a moment.

"Hold on one second," the stranger says, and the door closes.

"It seems like they're getting the other atu," Buso informs us.

The door opens again, and another unfamiliar voice speaks, "Tell me something you think would mean something to me."

"Um, Kidu," I offer, deeming it the safest name to share given the circumstances.

The door shuts, unlocks, and swings open. Though the scent and face are unfamiliar, the facial features resemble what I imagine a half-sibling of mine would look like, and suddenly everything falls into place. My body's identity got scrambled, intertwined with my crush Sodi...

"Are you Viadu?" I ask.

Ver eyes widen with delight, and ve responds, "Are you Dima?"

I nod vigorously, and Viadu immediately embraces me. Sodi, the other atu, also steps forward and gives me a warm hug.

"Oh, I'm so glad you two are okay!" Sodi exclaims.

Two yetu approach, one of them crawling along the ground, and they embrace Miya.

"Come, come. Let's head inside," one of the yetu, whom I assume is Kize, insists.

Kize and Sodi close up the spa and we gather in one of the lounges.

"As much as I want to catch up," Hinuso, the other yetu, says, "First, can we PLEASE sort out this whole body mess?"

"Absolutely," Suki agrees.

"I can help," Sodi volunteers.

"You know mind magic?" Suki asks.

"Yes, we actually use it to gather information from officers who come to the spa. I'll explain more later," Sodi replies.

Sodi positions verself between Viadu and me and faces ver palms towards us. Suki does the same between Miya and Hinuso.

"Before we begin," I say, "Sodi, I want you to transfer my severed spinal cord over as well."

"Are you sure?" Viadu asks, "I was the one who received the injury. As much as I appreciate it, I think I should have it."

"Yeah, but I was the one who first inflicted it onto Makali who then shifted it onto you." I say, "I no longer believe these sorts of punishments are ethical or at all helpful. Not only because they can be undermined by trait magic, but also because they do nothing to address the circumstances that compel people to transgress in the first place. This is an injury that should have never been inflicted, yet I inflicted it. It should be mine to bear, and mine alone." I say.

The silence to follow conveys understanding.

"Okay, I will do it." Sodi affirms.

"Thank you." Viadu says.

"Seriously, don't mention it. I don't want to spend the rest of my life caught up in thinking of myself as unfortunate just because I'm different and poses uncommon challenges. Speaking of which. You had best go make sure your bowels are empty before we start." I say.

We wait for a moment while Viadu excuses verself. When ve returns ve takes a seat on the floor and speaks up, "So, I- um. I just remembered one more thing. I guess Makali didn't like having bitu genitals. So... ve took yours."

At first the news doesn't bother me much, as if I will be able to feel it anyway. Then my heart begins to sink at the thought of what Makali might do with it. Who ve might violate with my penis. I feel clammy at the thought of Makali having access to my penis. The shit eating worm.

"So... When I get moved back to my body. Could I please have my genitals too?" Viadu asks.

"Yes, of course." I say, and we begin.

Though it is unnecessary, I close my eyes and take a deep breath through my nostrils. The air is rich with the scents of a dozen kinds of flowers, several varieties of tea, and several more varieties of other pleasant scents that I cannot even apply a name to. Sodi smells of perfume and roasted kuvohedi, the rump meat of a common livestock, which ve probably ate recently. Then I breathe out... and in again. The air smells floral. Just floral.

I open my eyes to a sharper resolution of vision than I have experienced in a long while. Chills shoot through me as my body feels colder than one covered in fur all of the time. I look at my hands, well-manicured and soft, with a few new scars. I feel the smoothness of my face, and my broad shoulders. There is a slight excess of weight on my hips, buttocks, and chest that are not mine. Those, among other things, are certainly Sodi's, and upon that realization, I can feel my cheeks warm with a blush of arousal.

Arousal is not a feeling I have felt in quite some time having been in a body that lacked the genitalia which produce most testosterone. While my present body also does not possess those genitals, it did a moment ago, and testosterone has yet to deplete.

"Someone's turning red." Sodi teases. Shoot! I am not used to my blushing being so visible on my face. I look away in embarrassment, "Here, may I help you up onto your chair?"

"Sure." I say timidly.

My arousal persists as Sodi proceeds to lift me like I weigh nothing. Viadu climbs out of my chair and then Sodi gently sets me back down into it.

"SoOo..." My voice cracks, and I clear my throat, "Can someone explain to me how our bodies ended up here?"

"Sure." Kize chimes in, "So we learned all about what you guys had been through the last time you visited deposits ago."

"Wwwiiithh, wit, with miinnnnd maaaagiiic?" Miya attempts to ask using ver old yetu speech organs.

"Hey, you're speech is coming along quickly. Good job." Kize says, "Yes, with mind magic. Anyway-"

"How long had you guys been doing that?" I cut in.

"Ever since we opened this spa, we have been using it to gather intel on what the ministry is up to. Officers come in, we take the thoughts their minds are stressing over, replace them with more relaxing thoughts, and then go write them down. Once the session comes to an end, we put the thoughts back, and no one suspects a thing because nothing is missing, and most officers have no idea that mind magic is possible."

I have no doubt my face is redder than ever as I recall the sort of thoughts Sodi must know I have had about ver. I look away in shame, but I can see Sodi looking at me out of my peripherals. I have to apologize.

I look at Sodi, whose gaze is knowing, "I am so sorry." I say.

"I too would like to give my sincerest apologies." Miya joins.

"Don't mention it." Sodi replies and then gives me a double eyebrow lift that sends me spiraling all the more.

"Yeah, honestly, your thoughts were some of the sweeter ones." Kize remarks, "Most of the time."

I want to die.

Buso, in what feels like a divine act of mercy but is more than likely rooted in deep discomfort, breaks in and asks, "Why are you two collecting the thoughts of the officers? Who are you working for? Are you spies?"

"Sort of." Kize continues, "We help warn people or communities the ministry is intent on attacking or apprehending. Speaking of which, shortly after Dima and Miya's last appointment, we gathered intel about plans to apprehend you two. We tried to warn you, but you were not home, and the officers got to you first. Then we tried to rescue you, but they had already swapped you, and it took a long time before these two were recovered enough to let us know they weren't you. Finally, once they were well enough, we went looking for you two and their family, but their hut had been repossessed, Kidu wasn't at work when we checked ver place of employment, and Jove's work never had a definite location. We kept looking until officer activity started to pick up. We didn't want to get caught, so we retreated back here for the time being."

"Wwwhaat aaabout you twooo?" Hinuso asks, also relearning ver previous speech organs, "Whaat haaappennned to the fam?"

"Jove and the pups are okay," I say solemnly.

"And Kidu?" Viadu questions.

"Kidu recently passed away."

Viadu and Hinuso are both taken aback. Grief starts to come over them.

"Do you need some time-" I start to ask.

"No," Viadu cuts in, "just tell us what happened."

After explaining the details of Kidu's demise Hinuso and Viadu ask for some space to grieve and so Kize directs them to a private room.

"So..." Sodi starts. Oh no, please don't tell me we are going to talk about the thoughts I've had. Nervously, I turn my attention to ver and our eyes meet for only a moment before Sodi looks away bashfully, "I-uh, I imagine you have been through quite a bit and could probably use a- ehm- a massage?"

I hesitate. If I say yes, where might things go? If things go far, will I still be able to enjoy it despite lacking genitals? Compounding my anxieties, I wonder what Viadu might have done with my body while ve had it.

After making the request Sodi turns red and quickly adds, "Uh-massages can be really good for blood circulation when you have a spinal cord injury. Well, I guess it was Viadu's body that was paralyzed up to this point, but uh- I could still- It might still be good to-"

"Sure," I cut in. I don't know if I can bear such an encounter so soon. But I cannot avoid intimacy for the rest of my life, Ritu knows I don't want to, and I certainly cannot let this opportunity pass, "That sounds... really nice."

I try to start maneuvering my wheelchair towards the available massage room. However, my arms now significantly shorter, the task feels even more difficult than before. The way my struggling slows things down feels very awkward.

Suddenly the chair begins to move on its own. Startled out of my embarrassment, I look back to see that Sodi has started to push my chair.

"Oh, uh," Sodi stammers, "Is this alright?"

"Y-yeah." I say.

"Oh Ritu, hurry along and get a room you two." Suki teases.

Now equally embarrassed, Sodi begins to push me and Miya gives me an encouraging nudge as we pass ver, "You've got this." Miya whispers, and Sodi takes me into the other of the two private massage rooms.

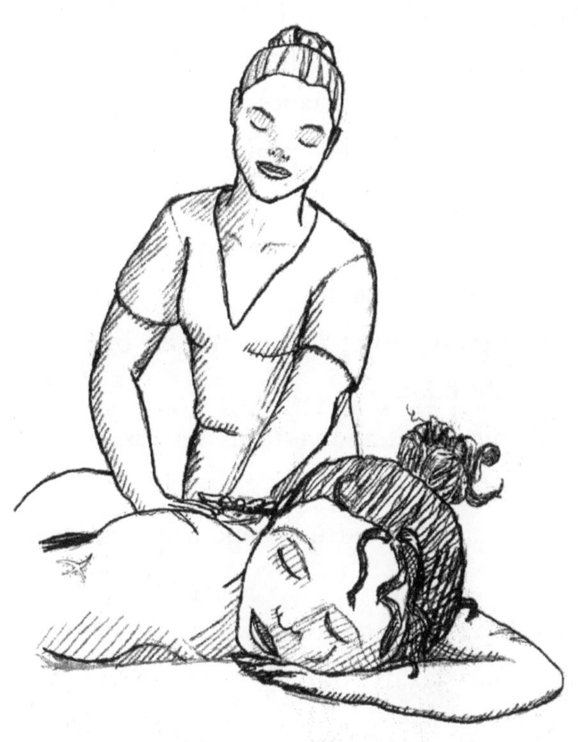

Chapter 28: Catching Up

Once inside, Sodi respectfully turns away to prepare ver tools and to give me a chance to undress with some degree of privacy. I remove my articles of clothing and am filled with delight and arousal to see parts of Sodi's body intermixed with my own. What a bizarre and unique experience to have Sodi as a literal part of me. Gathering my senses, I attempt to climb up atop the bed from my chair. Clawing at the beds cushion in a desperate effort to scale the bed, I find that my upper body strength left me with Viadu's body.

Oh Ritu, please no.

My naked body fully exposed, I grunt and struggle to pull myself up.

"Are you okay?" Sodi asks, still politely turned away.

"Yeah," I grunt, "Just need to get-" Suddenly I lose my grip, slip from the bedside, and fall a short distance before my naked body flops to the floor. Fortunately, I managed to protect my head and only my ego was injured.

After the smack of my body hitting the floor, Sodi spins around and moves to make sure I am alright.

"I'm okay," I grunt just as Sodi rounds the bed to see me naked and sprawled out on the floor.

Sodi's face turns red, and ve turns ver gaze away again, "Are you sure?" Ve asks.

"Yeah... but- um- I could use some help getting onto the bed." I admit.

"Oh, okay. I can do that." Sodi says as ve respectfully grabs a towel to cover me with. Once again effortlessly, ve lifts me up, and then gently sets me onto the massage bed, placing me down such that I am lying on my belly. Then Sodi carefully adjusts my towel so that it is draped reaching from my mid back down to the back of my knees.

Shortly thereafter, Sodi begins to work ver magic on my shoulders.

"I'm not going to be sapping your anxieties away from you as I go this time, so I hope that doesn't worsen your experience." Sodi says.

"Oh, no you're fine. This feels sooo good."

"So tell me what happened to you." Sodi says, and then almost immediately afterwards, "Sorry, I mean in general, not how you got... You know. But, I mean I would like to know that too. If you are comfortable."

"No need to apologize, you're fine," I say, "There is almost too much to recount. One thing is for sure... I am not the same Dima I was when we last met."

"Well as someone who used to know more about you than I had any right to know, I am grateful for this opportunity to get to know you in a more... traditional way."

"Sure. Uh, what do you want to know?"

"Um, what are some of the biggest ways you feel you have changed?"

"Oh vetu, I feel like a completely different person. For one thing, my perspective on the concept of exaltation has been completely devastated. I used to think that a vetu's place in society correlated with the strength of their relationship with Ritu. I thought that people suffered because they deserved it. Then I discovered all manner of exceptions to what I thought was a hard rule."

Sodi begins to work at my neck and the base of my skull, "What sort of exceptions?"

"Well, there are vetu who won't receive help from anyone who hasn't suffered in the same ways they have. Sometimes people need to know they are understood before they can open up. So, it might be that some people need to suffer, not because they deserve it, but because it equips them to reach others who have suffered in similar ways."

Sodi pauses ver work momentarily, "That- that is a really beautiful observation. Sorry," Sodi starts to rub my scalp again, "I just really needed to hear that."

"Oh... Why is that?"

"Ever since I was young I have experienced chronic pains; achy joints, a near constant headache. I cannot tell you how many nights I've spent staring at the ceiling asking Ritu why I have to put up with this."

"Oh. Wow. Maybe I'm the one who should be giving you a massage. Though, I'll admit, it would probably be a rather crummy one, because I don't know the first thing about the practice."

Sodi gives a little laugh, "No, it's okay. It wouldn't help much anyway. I initially got into this line of work because I thought it would help. Eventually that turned into me finding satisfaction in helping relieve other people's aches even though I cannot relieve my own."

"Well I'm glad you found that encouraging... The last person I said it to found it insulting."

"Insulting? How so?"

"They felt like it was vemoizing to reduce people down to tools that Ritu could nonconsensually put through hase just so they could be 'useful'."

"Ah, well when you put it like that. I can see where ve is coming from..."

"Yeah, but that is far from the only exception, it's just the one I was able to make peace with, the one I guess I am still trying to cling to. Though it doesn't explain the ways everything is upside down in Hosudiha. Intervention is rewarded with infection, selflessness with mutilation, and heroics with the threat of financial ruin. Meanwhile, theft saves lives, child labor staves off starvation, and those in power get away with murder. Nothing makes sense anymore. It all feels made up."

Sodi rolls the towel down to expose my mid back and, after applying a bit of oil, gets to work. I experience a sudden surge of sensation racing through my body as one of Sodi's fingers lightly crests the side of my borrowed breast.

"Oh, sorry. I didn't mean to-" Sodi says.

"No no, it's- that was- it's fine." I say, bewildered at the breast's level of sensitivity. My chest was never so sensitive. Is this because I'm not able to feel my arousal elsewhere or are breasts just more sensitive?

"Okay. Sorry. Maybe I should take them back." Sodi says.

"I mean. If you want to," I say.

"Um, do you want me too?" Sodi asks.

"I mean I don't mind them. They actually feel kind of nice. Erm, sorry. I don't want you to feel awkward." I say.

"No, you're fine." Sodi says.

"They are yours. You should really take them back at some point." I say.

"I mean, I don't mind the bit of relief on my lower back." Sodi says.

"Oh... alright." I say. I have always wanted breasts, often trying to create the illusion of having them since I was young. Never in my wildest dreams had I imagined having real ones, and from my crush no less. There is something novel about having breasts and no penis or testicles, but I have never had an issue with my penis or testicles. I would like them back. Though the breasts are welcome to stay for as long as Sodi lets me have them.

Sodi continues the massage, and now I am not sure if the occasional crest is quite so accidental.

"Personally," Sodi says, "I think we have the whole exaltation thing backwards. The ministry puts the rovo before the cart so to speak."

"What do you mean backwards?"

"The expectation is that vetu will receive Ritu, and that reception will produce virtues, and those virtues will lead to blessings being multiplied and social status being elevated. However, like you said, an environment of extreme poverty has a tendency to reward vice, and punish virtue. Interestingly, the same goes for those in an environment of extreme wealth. The greedier they are, the more power they accumulate. Whereas the more generous they are, the further they fall behind in the race for power against their peers."

I struggle to recall examples of Sodi's observations of the upper class. My childhood memories feel fuzzy and I blame whichever of my parent's screwed with my mind. Assuming that stranger really was one of my parents, it would make sense that ve would want to take away the sort of memories I am trying to recall. However, I do remember the way employers take advantage of the desperate situation of the poor back in Hosudiha.

"I get what you mean." I say, "We teach people to be generous, hard working, and non confrontational in a context where workers need jobs, but the jobs don't need them. So the employers abuse and exploit their workers, and the workers have no power to do anything about it. Either the workers put up with the abuse, or they starve."

"Yes! That is another perfect example." Sodi affirms.

Sodi rolls the towel down to my lower back. At this point my mind is struggling to hold a cohesive conversation. My head is feeling a deficit of blood as it rushes to new places in the absence of a penis.

"The ministry's idea of exaltation isn't even in the picture," Sodi adds, "and the employers are incentivized to keep it that way. They need desperate people to uphold a system of abuse that lines their pockets. If the people are not desperate, then they don't have to put up with the abuse, and the employers have to spend money to make their jobs more appealing. It must be cheaper to keep the people desperate."

I assume Sodi moves onto my lower half now. I can only really feel the occasional tug on my torso. However, I do feel blood circulating more to my cheeks, breasts, and other notable zones along my back and neck.

"Yeah..." I say, trying to think of something insightful to add, but all I can think about is this damn towel. Go away, you blasted garment. Sodi seems to work on my legs for a moment while I try not to lose myself. Ritu damn it. I need Sodi. Ver hands are heavenly, but I want more of ver skin, I want to feel it against mine. I don't know if sex is possible for me right now, but I don't care. I just want to be in Sodi's embrace.

After a long while of trying to exercise self control and trying to think of something to say, my oxygen deprived brain finally thinks of something, "If we are operating with the mentality that exaltation ought to only be achievable through Ritu's virtues, why wouldn't we as a society make it nearly impossible for vetu to exalt themselves through hard work? If people had the power to better their own circumstances, there wouldn't be as many people depending on the ministry, giving it power... I wonder if this is exactly the way the ministries want society to be..."

Sodi stops suddenly. A moment passes and I begin to wonder why. I feel like an air balloon that nearly had enough hot air to fly, only for the hatch to be yanked open to let all of the air out. I sit up and shoot Sodi a confused and pitiful look.

Ve looks back at me and smiles, "I was considering it. Though it is almost like you and I have only just met. Let's not rush into things."

RITU DAMN IT! I get it, and I respect ver decision, but COME ON! I may never have this much testosterone again. I feel so pitiful.

"Anyways," Sodi continues, "I'm sure it is that way for some people working in 'ministries'. However, let's not go on assuming all ministries are exploitative. Take mine for example."

I take a deep breath to try to clear the fog from my mind, "You're right. About both things. I respect your decision, appreciate it even. Though I won't say I'm not a bit disappointed."

"I'm sorry-"

"No, don't be. Never feel sorry for saying no or backing out. I'm sorry for saying I was disappointed. You probably already knew I was, and you didn't need me to make you feel bad for expressing your boundaries." I say.

"It's okay... Thank you for apologizing. I appreciate that you are so aware of that. I honestly hadn't thought much of what you said as being an attempt to guilt trip me. The fact that you were the one to catch yourself and apologize. That means a lot to me." Sodi says.

We smile at each other for a moment before Sodi adds, "I'll give you this though." Sodi leans in, and in my surprise I start to pucker my lips until I realize my lips are not ver target, ver kiss lands upon my cheek and it sends static throughout my body.

"Uh- um. Thank- ehm- thank you." I say.

Sodi smiles sweetly.

"Anyway, I don't consider my ministry here to be exploitative at all." Sodi says.

"No, of course not. Though speaking of exploitation. One other thing I have come to learn is just how alive and well slavery is." I say.

"Oh? How so?" Sodi asks.

"Well there are two forms of slavery where the master provides food and shelter in exchange for labor. Those would be the prisons and some of the 'ministries for the homeless'. Then there is the exploitation of low wage workers, making them paramount to wage slaves. Which might be worse than livestock slavery because the 'masters' don't even have to worry about whether or not your wage is sufficient for food and shelter." I say.

"And the abolition laws don't account for those loopholes do they?" Sodi asks.

"On the contrary. They explicitly list indentured servitude as an exception to the abolition. As for wage slavery, I don't think it technically falls under the legal definition of slavery. A lawsuit may be possible for suing the 'homeless shelters'. Though who is going to go around suing homeless shelters when the public perception of them is that they are the good vetu. You would also be making an enemy of the ministry. Something needs to be done. Speaking of which you said we have things backwards, cart before the rovo. What does it look like to have the rovo before the cart?"

"Well, we need to create an environment where virtues are rewarded and vices only hurt. No extreme poverty, no extreme wealth. Though I have no idea what such a place would look like."

"Actually, I don't think vices should only hurt. We vetu learn through failure, but only if we have hope. So sure, if we hand out free resources to those in poverty they may not use it responsibly at first, but over time they will learn to be more responsible. Of course you don't want to give so many resources that they have no incentive to learn good management skills because poor management is inconsequential. But you don't want to give so little that failure to manage the resources results in people feeling hopeless. You also don't want to make free resources conditioned upon a vetu's success in managing them, because again we learn through failure."

"Sounds like you have actually put a lot of thought into this." Sodi says.

"Maybe a bit, but really I'm just thinking through what I've experienced and learned." I say.

"I've read enough minds to know that when people don't feel free to learn from their failures they are more likely to use what little resources they have to buy substances that drown away the feelings of hopelessness. Then there is the added obstacle of addictions hopeless people form." Sodi says.

"Yeah, addiction may compel vetu to continue to abuse their resources even under the best circumstances. Though if resources are not conditioned on being addiction free then eventually those addictions will pass given a few generations." I say.

A moment of silence passes as Sodi does a final pass over my body.

"Thank you for catching me up a bit. I really enjoyed our conversation." Sodi says.

"Me too." I say.

Having concluded the massage, Sodi gives me some unwanted privacy to redress myself. I feel much closer to Sodi than I ever have. Maybe fate, or Ritu, has brought our life paths in parallel so that something more may develop between us. As sexually frustrated as I am, this was a really pleasant experience.

After we all reconvene in the lounge Hinuso and Viadu request that we take them to see Jove and the pups. So we set out right away.

We are traversing a long alleyway when suddenly Kize speaks quietly to Miya, who is riding Sodi's back as Sodi pushes my chair, "I can tell you're not feeling all too well. What is wrong?"

"It's nothing," Miya remarks, "Don't worry about me. I'm just happy to finally be back in my body."

"But it's not all of your body. That's what's bothering you, isn't it?" Kize asks.

Miya remains silent for a moment before ve continues, "Earlier, Dima said ve doesn't want to spend the rest of ver life caught up in thinking of verself as unfortunate just because ve is different and poses uncommon challenges. I don't want to get caught up in those thoughts either. Though it is hard not to."

"So... It probably wouldn't be helpful if I were to magic my wings onto you would it?" Kize asks.

"That sounds nice, but yeah... They wouldn't be my wings. They would go back to you at the end of the labor and just leave me feeling... I don't know." Miya says.

"Well... What if I were to..." Kize says as ve crawls from Viadu's back to Miya's side on Sodi's back, "May I get on your back?"

"Dima." Miya says.

"Yeah?" I ask.

"Unfasten yourself from your chair." Miya says, "Sorry, Kize, are you okay if Dima joins us?"

"I wouldn't have it any other way." Kize says.

With that we decide it makes the most sense for Kize to mount onto my back and Miya on my chest.

When we finally exit the alley into an open street, Kize begins to beat ver wings.

"Let's fly," Kize says.

With that, Kize holds me tight and lifts us into the sky. I cannot help but smile. I close my eyes to focus on the feeling of the air rushing past us. At this moment, everything feels as though it has returned to the way it had been. I know it's not, but it feels so good to pretend. I find further joy in knowing that Miya is probably delighted.

I open my eyes to look out over the magnificent city.

"Oh no," I utter.

"What?" Miya and Kize seem to ask in unison.

"No no no. The sanctuary is under attack." I say.

"WHAT?"

"The sanctuary is under attack!" I yell loud enough to draw the attention of our allies below and a few bystanders, "Go!" I command Kize.

"No," Miya cuts in, "We are going to help, but, I hate to say it, we cannot be of any help without our friends."

I grit my teeth, "Fine. Everyone, let's book it!"

Forming a triangle around the sanctuary are two small Sudihatosema strike ships and one larger Hosudiha prisoner transport ship.

My mind starts to race in an effort to make sense of how they could have found us out so quickly. Images come to mind of the one other Hosudiha resident who was above deck with us the other labor when the officers attempted to murder us. Miya's words from that labor come echoing through my mind, suggesting that officers could be among the passengers as well. A spy. Damn it, we should have guessed!

"I'm not detecting any yetu on the Hosudiha ship..." Miya speaks up as the ships come within ver range, "If my theory is correct, that must mean they have malicious intentions that a yetu wouldn't let them get away with..."

My heart sinks. Do they really intend to dispose of everyone in that sanctuary?

Shibi, Mebi, Jove!

What kind of monsters has Ritu let come to power? Why the hase would Ve be letting this happen?

We fly overhead as our allies dart in and out of alleyways. Sodi seems to start to lag behind as ve tries ver best to wrangle the wheelchair and dodge foot traffic on the roads between alleys.

"Leave it!" I shout down to ver.

"Are you sure?" Sodi shouts back.

As much as a pain the chair had been, it was my one viable option for independent mobility. So, while I hate to see it go, it has to go, and I hope I can find another one soon.

"I'll find another one. Dump it!" I yell.

Sodi abandons the wheelchair, but after a few more blocks of running, Buso, who flew ahead a little to scout, comes back and says , They are departing... We are too late."

Despair looks to settle in when Buso breaks the silence again, "Wait. I'm picking up some others headed our way... It's Jomira and ver crew!"

At this news, we find a clearing to stop in. Soon the crew's small ship crests over the buildings and pulls a crazy maneuver to halt momentum and barely land in the clearing.

"Get on!" Sho calls out to us, and we quickly clamber aboard.

"I'm glad I spotted you all just before we turned back," Jomira exclaims.

"Turned back?" Miya questions.

"Yes, we had just determined that it is too late and risky to strike them—"

"So we aren't going to do anything? Fuck that, let us down!" Hinuso exclaims.

"On the contrary," Jomira engages, "We suspect we know where they are headed, and we are going to strike them when they are at their most vulnerable and with the least access to backup."

"Are they headed for the cliffs?" Miya guesses.

"That seems most likely," Jomira affirms, "We will strike when the Sudihatosema forces depart, and we are under the cover of darkness, with the element of surprise ever so slightly on our side. They will likely be expecting us, but they won't know when nor where we will strike."

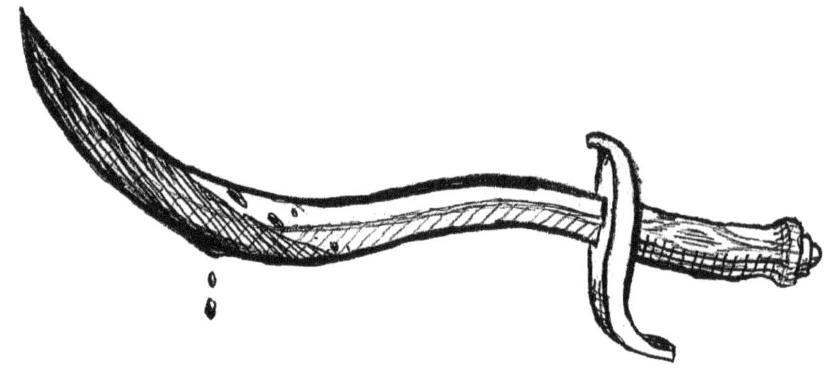

Chapter 29: Renegades

Sho is focused on piloting our ship, following the prisoner transport covertly, when I have Miya place me down near ver.

"Please, don't distract me. I need to focus," Sho says as soon as ve realizes I want to talk to ver.

"I won't take up much of your time. I just wanted to apologize."

"Apologize? I don't even know who you are."

"I'm the one who watched from the rafters at the tavern several deposits ago..."

Sho pauses and gives me a quick look, "Did you switch bodies again or something?"

"Yeah, we found our original bodies. Though right now my body is scrambled with someone else's body." I say.

"Ah, that explains things. So... Are you the one who told me I deserved to die in Hosudiha? Is that what you're apologizing for?"

"I didn't say... Well, I understand. It might as well have been what I said. Yes, I'm sorry for saying that. I'm sorry for looking down on you, for judging you as unworthy. I know better now. I want you to know that you are more worthy than I am to be blessed with good things." bringing up the matter of my worthiness stirs something within me, but I ignore it for now, "Thank you for coming to our rescue."

My words halt the flow of our conversation. I see tears welling up in Sho's eyes. Ve sniffs, "Your welcome... and thanks. I don't know why, but that means a lot... Now, please go away. I appreciate it, but you're distracting me."

"Okay," I respond.

I look around for Miya, but it seems ve has found other work to do.

"Still can't walk?" Sho asks.

"Yeah... I'll just... Go on my own." I say as I awkwardly crawl away to be available to help someone pull on a rope or something.

Before the Hosudiha ship can reach the edge of the island, we swiftly change our position and descend over a different ledge.

"Jo! I'll need your help with this part!" Sho shouts. Jomira flies over to perch beside ver. "Let me know when we're directly underneath the Hosudiha ship."

"You got it!" Jomira confirms and starts directing ver flying, everyone finds something to hold onto as we descend rapidly to get beneath the island which dips twice as deep into the depths as it reaches up into the sky.

We emerge from beneath the island. "Alright," Jomira says, "We're directly underneath them."

"Good," Sho declares, "We'll descend and stay as close as possible to being directly beneath them. They won't see us if we're right under their noses."

"Great thinking!" Zi exclaims, giving a thumbs-up to ver student as ve hurriedly manages the necessary ropes for Sho's maneuvering.

Sho returns the thumbs-up with a grin.

"Hey, everyone, Powa wants to start putting together a plan," Suki announces, speaking on behalf of Powa, who isn't speaking loudly at the moment. "Do we have an update on the situation aboard the prisoner ship?"

"Sure," Buso begins, "There are thirty-four sedated prisoners below deck, likely still alive because they were under the watch of Sudihatosema officers."

"Do you think they'll kill them now that the officers are gone?" Viadu asks, sounding deeply concerned.

"No, they'll remain unconscious for about a wage, and their intention is probably to toss the prisoners over the cliffs before they wake. There's no need for them to spend additional resources and time to kill them before then. Anyway, there are eight officers plus an unknown number of notu. Given the ship's size, I think it's reasonable to expect a few..."

Jomira and I are on our way back to the others having just successfully performed a reconnaissance mission to determine the number of present notu. There is one on the quarter deck and another on the main deck.

As we fly in relative silence, Jomira takes this opportunity to strike up a conversation with me.

"Sho told me about what you said. You've been through a lot, haven't you?" Jomira asks.

"That's an understatement." I say.

"I'm sure. I won't interrogate you too much. It's clear to me that you've chosen to value all vetu life, even when you lack a good reason to. And even if you have a good reason to take it, I just wanted to let you know," one of Jomira's legs moves to reach into a small bag Jomira has fastened to ver body. Ver leg returns from the bag with my rirmevu blade clenched tightly in ver tarsus (the moth equivalent of a hand or foot), "I trust you."

"Even after what I did with the blulips tea?" I ask.

"I don't hold that against you. You were afraid, it could be argued that you acted in self defense and in defense of innocents, and clearly you didn't take joy from it given that you wouldn't have mentioned it had it not been weighing on your mind. Go on, take it."

I take hold of the small tool, the pommel now hollow and cool. I am a little annoyed that Jomira would choose now to give this to me, given that we are flying over a black void. So I take care to hold the blade tightly.

"Thank you." I say. The guilt of the lives I took alleviated a little. "I trust you too. And I'm sorry for what I said back then, calling you agents of Ribe. I choose to believe that you are a force for good."

"A force for good? Do you mean agents of Ritu?"

"I... I don't know. I wonder if Ritu is a force for good now..." I say, looking into the cavity in my blade that used to hold a notu slave.

"Do you? Are you sure you're Dima?"

"I'm more Dima than I've been in quite a while," I laugh. "Though, in many ways, I guess you could say I'm a different Dima than I was back then. And that's not just because some of my body isn't mine."

"In my opinion, you're a better Dima. You've grown. I can't be certain if Ritu is purely good either, but I choose to believe that Ritu is somehow a force for good. Perhaps not a perfect one, perhaps as fallible as the rest of us. Maybe ve is growing too. Who knows?"

"I... I think that's worth believing." I say.

"And it might not be the only thing worth believing." Jomira says.

"Yeah... Thank you. For everything. For giving me so many chances, even when I turned them down."

"It's the least I could do. Besides, I wouldn't be who I am this sun if a good friend of mine hadn't given me twice as many chances to grow."

"Is- is the notu okay?" I ask.

"Ve is recovering. For all of ver life up to recently ve only thought of verself as heat. It's like raising a child. Ve will be alright."

We swoop down onto the deck and give our report. Powa finalizes the plan and everyone gets to work preparing.

Hari distributes dart guns, daggers, and slings.

I take a dart gun and a sling but decline the dagger.

"Are you sure you don't want it, just in case?" Hari asks.

"No, it's fine. It would be useless in my hands." I say, "Not only am I still not sure how I feel about killing, but I also have no training with such a weapon."

"Suit yourself." Hari says.

"It is almost time for us to attack!" Suki yells, "Everyone get with your battle buddy and prepare to strike!"

Shrouded in darkness, seven of us fly in a large arch out from underneath the transport ship, our eyes set on attacking the quarterdeck. Jomira carries Tai, Buso carries me, Kize carries Zi, and Powa rides along in my clenched fist. This leaves Miya back on the ship with the others who will be attacking the maindeck.

Zi's body mass has been distributed between the three of us bipeds so that Kize can lift ver. We each also carry a small shield to catch darts with.

I speak into my fist to Powa, "Are you sure this will work."

"Absolutely," Powa says, "No notu can resist throwing more clay than they can probably afford to."

"Alright, I trust you." I say uneasily. If this goes poorly, I'll be out of the fight before it starts.

As we coast towards our target, Sho lifts our ship up beside the enemy ship to launch the attack on the maindeck. Hopefully distracting our foes enough for us to knock some of them out before they can have a chance to fight. However, just as the veil of darkness thins enough to grant us visibility of our foes on the quarterdeck, it also grants them visibility of us.

"Incoming attackers off the quarterdeck!" yells one of the officers.

My heart begins to pound rapidly in my chest.

Ve is here.

Sergeant Makali locks the wheel and turns to prepare for a fight. With Makali, there are two bitu shield bearers with dart guns, one atu mage, and the one notu on the quarterdeck. The two bitu stand before Makali with shields ready to defend, and the mage stands behind Makali performing a spell.

"Boarding party off the main deck!" Another officer shouts from out of sight. Shit, our timing was off.

"Form two groups! Attack and defend together!" Makali yells.

"Yes, sarge!"

I let loose a dart, as does Tai. While the dart still flies I bag my dart gun and ready my sling and Powa. My dart soars towards the mage but Makali grabs hold of one of the bitu shield bearers and lifts ver up to catch it. The shieldbearer, confused by the sudden lift, flails ver shield outward, taking the dart to the chest and falling unconscious. Makali, looking disappointed in the officer, grabs the shield as it falls and then tosses ver unconscious ally aside.

The other dart strikes Makali's arm but simply bounces off harmlessly, thanks to the Mage's spell.

Once it is clear that we will reach the quarterdeck by momentum alone, I feel my muscle mass shrink as Kize returns it to Zi. The remaining shieldbearer launches a dart up at us, and the notu begins hurling balls of clay. I catch the dart with my shield and then quickly extend Powa towards the incoming clay balls. Just before smacking into me, each of the clay ball's trajectories takes an unnatural shift to the right and they enter into an orbit around Buso, Powa, and me. Before the enemy notu can realize what is happening, ve has already flung a significant portion of ver body mass up at us only to be caught by Powa's magical reach.

All of the clay balls orbiting us slow to a stop in a ring around us, the ring then shrinks until it makes contact with my body. The clay spreads across me taking the shape of a malleable sort of clay armor that is concentrated more on my legs than anywhere else.

Powa and I's weight now too much for Buso to carry, Buso drops Powa and I to the deck where Powa takes control of my otherwise limp legs and brings me to my feet to square off with the enemy notu.

"Tai has been struck with a dart. We are pulling out!" Jomira risks informing us before attempting to pull away to get Tai to safety.

Makali's eyes lock onto Jomira and ve throws ver circular shield, striking Jomira's wing and sending ver crashing to the deck with Tai. Kize releases Zi, who promptly drops to the deck, grabs the shield of the other bearer, and twists it to break the bearer's arm. Zi then kicks the now-screaming bearer off of the shield.

Meanwhile, Buso pulls away, probably until ve can find an opening to attack or defend.

"Did you come all this way just to fight me again?" Makali asks Zi.

"Oh, you know, your ass was just so fun to kick last time." Zi replies.

"I think you will find this fight to be far more challenging." Makali says.

I waste no time and sling a stone towards the enemy Notu who promptly attempts to intercept the stone with some clay. However, Powa thrusts us forward such that ve can contest the enemy notu's control over the intercepting clay enough to move it slightly out of the way. The stone still nicks the edge of the clay both slowing it and sending it off course enough to only graze the notu's gem.

Stunned from the hit, the enemy notu's body deforms slightly and Powa takes the opportunity to steal some of the enemy's clay for verself, and I take the opportunity to throw a punch at the now exposed gem only for an atu hand to take hold of my wrist and deflect my fist away from its target.

My eyes dart to the side to see a new atu officer. Ve must have come up here from the main deck at some point.

Powa quickly moves some clay along my arm and attempts to jab a thorn into the new arrivals wrists, however the atu is quick to retract ver hand, and the enemy notu gains ver wits enough to mount the enemy atu, forming into the same sort of living armor as Powa.

Before I can recover a stable fighting stance, the enemy atu launches a knee into my gut, Powa is quick to shift into the way of the attack, absorbing most of the impact, but, betrayed by my small stature, we are still thrown back against the poop deck wall. The impact forcibly expels the air from my lungs, weakening my grip and sending my sling clattering to the floor. Powa lands us on my feet and I work to catch my breath as I palm a dart from my bag.

"What are they doing sending a couple of children up here?" the enemy atu mocks, drawing a dagger and taking a more cautious fighting stance. We each pace circularly, looking for an opening. Meanwhile, Zi and Makali are locked in a seemingly even exchange of strikes and parries. Neither can seem to land many solid hits and those few that do land are dampened by magically toughened skin. So long as the mages can maintain their spells, Zi and Makali's blades remain uselessly sheathed.

Suddenly Zi blocks a hit that seems to defy physics as it sends ver cartwheeling to the side until ve is flung overboard. The enemy mage must have temporarily shifted ver focus away from giving Makali armored skin to giving Zi the mass of a small stone.

"Shit! Help!" Kize yells now helplessly exposed and trying to take off.

Powa attempts to take advantage of Makali's vulnerability and starts throwing dart laden clay at ver. However, Makali dexterously dodges the clay as ve quickly closes the distance between ver and Kize. At nearly imperceptible speed, Makali draws ver curved blade. Kize attempts to dodge the attack, only managing to avoid a strike to ver body to instead take the strike such that Makali's blade cleanly servers off one of ver wings.

My foe takes advantage of Powa's diverted attention and lunges for me. I swing my shield to knock ver dagger-wielding arm aside, only to be struck in the gut by the officer's other clay coated fist.

The clay shatters on impact, leaving behind a dart sticking out from my chest. My consciousness plunges into a sea of darkness. Colossal waves of exhaustion threaten to sever me from the waking world, when suddenly I somehow perceive Kize descend upon me, to pull me from the waves.

I wake, still propped up by Powa who must have removed the thorn from my chest at some point and is trying ver best to protect my once limp body from our opponent's ongoing assault. Powa seems to have used clay to keep my grip on my shield to use as a bit of additional protection.

Taking control of my arms, I manage to catch our foe by surprise as I thrust with my shield and strike the enemy notu's gem located at the center of the atu's chest. The atu stumbles backwards from my strike and ver notu armor begins to fall from ver body as my strike would seem to have knocked the notu out. Powa is quick to follow up my strike with a thorn ball to the enemy atu's chest, knocking ver unconscious.

Suddenly Makali comes skittering across the floor between us and our defeated foe. I look over to see that Buso has returned Zi to the fight. Kize lays at Zi's feet, hopefully alive after ve took the risk of giving me ver consciousness while helplessly lying at the feet of Makali.

"Get Tai, and Kize out of here!" The wounded Jomira order's Buso, and Buso is quick to obey, moving to gather the wounded.

Makali is quick to roll back to ver feet and the enemy mage attempts to pin Zi to the ground by swapping Zi's mass with something heavy. Powa sends a clay ball towards the mage which finds its mark, but while ver focus is on the mage, Makali charges us. I attempt to thrust my shield into ver charge but ve takes hold of my shield with one hand and my hair with the other. Then ve painfully yanks me from Powa's grasp and throws me over towards the edge of the ship.

"Dima!" Powa cries out.

I am quick to reach out and grab hold of the railing as I pass over. Pivoting at my grip, my body swings over and slams into the railing's balusters. I hold on for dear life. Buso's legs are full, so there would be no saving me if I fall.

Lacking the upper body strength to pull myself back up, along with the inability to use my legs in the effort, I am left watching helplessly as I see Makali strike Powa with my shield, knocking ver out. Makali then scoops up ver blade from the ground and Zi draws ver dagger.

"You seem less confident in yourself all of a sudden." Makali mocks Zi, "Are your skills with a blade not on par with your unarmed prowess?"

"Don't be so sure of yourself," Zi says, "I know my way with a blade. This fight is far from over."

"We shall see about that." Makali says as ve lunges forward with a strike equal parts an attack on Zi's neck and a block against the position of Zi's blade. Zi brings ver dagger up to catch the swing, but as ve does Makali uses ver blade's guard to trap Zi's blade and stab for Zi's face. Zi is quick to jump back and avoid a lethal skewer, but Makali does not let up as ve presses into Zi keeping ver on the back foot.

While Zi is skilled enough to hold Makali off, it becomes clear that ve is out classed in ver armed combat abilities. I start looking for a way to help. I could scoot my way over to the stairs where the railing dips down. Perhaps then I'll be able to pull myself back over.

My plan now established, I begin to work my way along the railing, and I look over to check on Zi only to see ver falling.

Headless...

Fear petrifies me.

"So... Dima, was it?" Makali says as I catch ver eye, "Is it just coincidental, or are you the backslider I dealt with a few deposits ago?"

Adrenaline vanquishes my fear-stricken petrification, and I lock eyes with Makali.

Makali, who nearly doubles my height, walks up to me and watches me dangle in amusement. "Are you really just going to hang there while I stab you? You know, Dima, whether you are the backslider I dealt with a while ago or not, you are vemo, that much is clear. Hmm… maybe I won't stab you. I'll make you a deal. Drop all of your silly darts and I'll spare you so you can be my pet."

"I would rather die." I say, and I am just about to release my grip and embrace death when Makali's arms suddenly get clamped to ver sides by Miya's legs which seemed to come out of nowhere to grapple the giant.

I release one of my hands from the railing to fish out a thorn from my bag, then I let go with my other hand as well. Mid fall, I hook my arm through the balusters and jab through them with my other arm, bringing the thorn down, through Makali's boot and into ver foot.

Fear is a seed that needs not be watered to grow into hatred.

Yet there are many who will water it.

Hatred is a weed that consumes life and sows yet more seeds of fear.

The giant falls… and my fear blossoms into hatred.

Miya jumps from Makali's back mid-fall and helps pull me back over the railing.

My mind turns primal as my hatred compels me to crawl to Makali's side. The coolness of the handle of my rirmevu blade seeps the warmth from my hand. I know not how it ended up in my grasp, and I care not. I remember not how I came to be positioned over Makali's motionless body, and I care not. I care only for the power these things grant me.

I raise my blade, ready to spill the blood demanded by the Shattered Skies. But a flying stone strikes the hand brandishing my blade, the pain causing me to release it instinctually, sparing the monster's life.

My rage seeks a new target. Sho, holding an empty sling, stands on the small ship nearby behind where Jomira grieves over Zi's body.

"Sho!" I shout, filled with hatred.

"Dima!" Jomira calls out attempting to divert my attention, "If you choose to kill Makali, I will not judge you. I may even find pleasure in it. But let me remind you that ve and ver victims are victims of those who spread lies. Just as we were victims at one point. How many people do you think would seek to claim your life if given the chance?"

The question freezes me with guilt. How many have I punished needlessly? How many lives were lost to the infections of wounds that I inflicted? All in the name of Ritu. At least I never raped anyone... but I have non-consentually castrated the genitals of more vetu than I can count. Is that okay just because they were all rapists? It feels okay. It feels like justice. Though why wouldn't Makali feel the same way about everything ve has done. From what I recall, Makali believes everything ve does to those ve deems vemo is justified or at the very least morally neutral. I have mutilated hundreds of vetu, everything I did, I had justified because I had deemed them slaves of vice. I have done horrible things thinking I was saving people from themselves. Makali has done horrible things thinking ve was saving society from incurable ideological diseases.

Jomira continues, "The part of you that many would despise has died, and you are better for it, even if you remain just as guilty. You, Makali, and I... We must make amends, and we can do so more effectively alive than dead. If you kill Makali, someone else will take ver place. However, if Makali can change, ve can inspire change in those who take ver place. Those who are products of the same system that created ver. The same system that created me. The same system that created you..."

Jomira lets that last sentence loom in the air for a moment, causing me to reflect on the system which manipulated me into committing atrocities. I am filled with resentment. Both for the ministry and myself. How could I have let them control me like that? How could I have let myself go along with all of this? Sure, I may be a victim of a system of manipulation, but I was also complicit. I could have stood opposed to the ministry, but I didn't. No matter how much of a victim I am, I am also a villain. I have hurt and killed countless people.

Jomira goes on, "The prisons in Matuha are designed to facilitate change and enable individuals to seek recompense. It is why many of my crew have turned their lives around. As much as it pains me to admit, Makali is one of us."

I pick my blade back up and sit, poised to end Makali's life, only for the question to stain my mind. How many might be justified in killing me?

The sound of conflict from the deck below subsides. Miya calmly places a leg on my back. Ver peace tells me that our boarding party must have triumphed. Still I sit in shock. Footsteps come from below as the boarding party comes up to check on us.

Grief over Zi's demise spreads through those who knew ver best as they discover Zi's fate and compassion spreads through the rest.

Sodi spots me and approaches tactfully.

"Are you okay?" Sodi asks.

"No," I reply. "I hate myself. I don't deserve to be alive right now! I've caused so much harm!"

Sodi places an arm on my back beside Miya's but remains silent.

"You wouldn't touch me if you knew the things I've done," I confess. "I've mutilated children Sodi! People who were just desperate to survive in a system that not only failed them but actively worked against them.

I've robbed families of their loved ones, causing their deaths from infected wounds—wounds that I inflicted! I've done it to hundreds, maybe thousands! I might be worse than Makali in the lives I've claimed! I want to slit my throat as much as I want to slit ver's!"

My words hang heavily in the air, suffocating any other sound. I bury my face in my hands and squeeze my head until it hurts, and then squeeze some more.

"Yes, you are awful," Sodi affirms. "But don't forget that I have read many of your thoughts. You have a lot to do, and you can never fully make up for the harm you've caused. You may never earn the forgiveness of those who will never owe it to you. But you're doing what you must. You're doing the difficult and painful work, and I trust that you will continue. It's not your place to seek recognition but to recognize and empower others, and I believe you understand that. So, despite your past, I am willing to embrace your future."

At this, Sodi gives me an entirely undeserved hug, the rirmevu blade drops from my grasp, and I break into a mess of angry weeping.

Chapter 30: Matuha

All enemy mages are placed in a single cell and are to remain sedated throughout the duration of the voyage. Only one is permitted to be awake at a time so they can eat and take care of needs under intense supervision. Enemy notu have been restrained in the small wooden boxes built for that purpose, and every other enemy has been given their own cell.

With the sanctuary's occupancy now fully awake, the ship has become crowded. We have to work hard to ensure everyone gets a chance to come above deck for fresh air, and we must ration food carefully.

I feel bad for Sho. Ve hasn't had a solid chance to grieve the loss of ver mentor, as ve has been busy directing inexperienced sanctuary members on how to fly the ship.

Everyone involved in the rescue effort now rests atop the ship helping one another process and recover from what just happened. I have been set atop a barrel so that I can be at eye level with everyone.

Suddenly Makali's voice starts to ring out from below deck, "You are a bunch of vemo! You think you know better than Ritu? How foolish. You were never truly loyal to Ver. If you were, you would know better than to question Ver judgment. Those who question Ritu's judgment will suffer by it! You hear me? You are all destined for Hase! Repent of your ways! Maybe if you turn back and submit yourselves to Ritu, Ve will honor your act of humility and exalt you!"

"I am willing to volunteer my body to shut ver up," Buso offers.

"No, I'll do it," Miya insists. "I have been in a bitu body recently. Dima was able to get the hang of a bitu body pretty easily coming from an atu one. So I think I may be able to actually use the body, whereas it would leave you incapacitated."

"That sounds lovely," Suki says. "Hey everyone! Attention, please! I am going to put Miya here into Makali's body. So when you see Makali walking around, don't panic."

Suki works ver way around to a number of individuals to explain the details of what ve meant and informs everyone who is below deck as well.

Finally, Makali's preaching is replaced with a bunch of nonsensical sounds.

The two atu to emerge from below deck don't look like Makali and Suki, but they do resemble them. Kize, with ver bandaged wing nub, is riding the back of the one I presume is Miya.

"I figured it would be easier for everyone if Miya was not easily recognizable as Makali, so I scrambled us," Suki explains from ver partially familiar body. "I also explained that anyone else caught preaching would be met with the same punishment. So hopefully, the rest of the voyage will be a peaceful one."

"How do you feel, Miya?" I ask.

"Odd. Atu sight is cool but weird. If I had gone from a bitu body to this one, I would say it's like my nose and eyes switched roles slightly."

"Yeah, sounds about right," I affirm.

As much as I don't want to, I am too unsure of my life choices to not reflect on Makali's preaching.

Do I think I know better than Ritu?

No, it's more that I don't trust myself to know what is from Ritu and what is not. I humbly recognize my fallibility, and so I have opened myself up to question anything and everything that warrants it. Though I will say that includes questioning if Ritu really is a being of perfect judgment. Perhaps ve is, perhaps ve isn't. My judgment is not perfect enough to determine one way or the other. So no, I am not founding my new beliefs in pride. In fact, I am founding them in humble recognition of my limits and faults.

Was I ever truly loyal to Ritu? Yes, at least, I think I was as loyal as anyone could be. I was loyal to the understanding of Ritu I had been given. Now I recognize that I would have to ignore the fallibility of myself and other vetu in order to conclude that any vetu understanding of Ritu is absolutely correct.

Now I recognize that the best I can do is conditionally lean upon what my convictions and the evidence tell me is good and true. Conditionally because my convictions are certainly fallible, as is my ability to understand and interpret evidence. They always have been, even when my convictions were more faith based I still had to lean upon my fallible intuition to determine what was worthy of putting my faith into. So I will always have to leave room for correction in the inevitable event that I am wrong.

If Ritu is good and true, then I trust that I am still loyal to Ver, and Ve will draw me closer to Ver through correction and other guidance. I am doing what I must to be receptive to Ritu, assuming Ritu wants anything to do with me. If Ritu is not good or true, then I think I would rather be loyal to whatever is, even if it is lesser in power to Ritu.

Am I destined for Hase?

If I am, I'm not sure there is anything I can do about it. Besides, Makali's idea of Hase is far from being worthy of my hope. What sense does it make that Ritu would clue us in on the existence of such a place if Ver desire is for us to choose Ver out of a genuine desire for Ver? It makes no sense that Ritu would provide a fear-based incentive for the choice. There is so much Ritu doesn't tell us about the afterlife, so why tell us about Hase? I prefer Jomira's idea, if there even is a Hase. I could be wrong, but being wrong is an inevitability, and I choose to trust that Ritu will have grace for that.

Though, what is the point of all of this suffering and injustice? What does it accomplish? What point is it meant to bring us to, and why couldn't we have just started at that point? Are we meant to learn from this suffering? Ritu could have just made us have whatever knowledge we need to not produce suffering from the get-go. We don't have to intentionally learn how to breathe! Why do we have to learn how to not cause ourselves and the world harm?

Maybe Ritu is just incompetent, evil, or somehow doesn't exist, and there is some other explanation for magic.

Maybe Ritu and the spirits are actually just powerful beings from the stars with redundant bodies that they can move between in the event of one body dying.

Maybe we are all characters in a book Ritu or someone else authored, and some portion of our lives has just been playing out in the imagination of a reader.

Maybe there are a number of valid possibilities, and it is up to each of us to settle on whatever we prefer to hope for, if anything, while leaving room for the eventuality that we are wrong.

Maybe we are meant to work together to weed out possibilities that are clearly wrong but respect the hope anyone may have for any possibilities that remain.

Sure, some possibilities may be more likely than others, but each meets different needs. So long as no one possibility is being forced onto other people, maybe we ought to let people hope for whatever they want, as long as it's reasonably possible, open to correction, and not harmful to others.

One way or another, reality is what it is. Perhaps it is less important that I fixate on hypothetical divine reasons for why problems are permitted to exist, and instead focus on the present material reasons such problems exist; the reasons that I can do something about. Having made peace with my present beliefs, I check back into reality.

"...and I'm not used to being this tall yet. I hit my head a few times while I was below deck. It might swell up pretty good here in a bit," Miya goes on to explain.

"Well, thank you for taking one for the team," I say, pretending that I had been listening to ver the whole time.

"Honestly, the benefit of not having to listen to Makali drone on and on makes up for it tenfold." Miya says before suddenly looking at me, "Hey, can I speak privately with you?"

"Um, sure, I'll climb on your back and we can try to find somewhere. Though I think we will be hard pressed to find anywhere super private at the moment." I say.

"That's fine." Miya says as I climb on ver back.

Miya takes me somewhere away from people we know, sets me down, and then sits close as ve speaks in hushed tones, "So I have your dick."

I am a bit jarred by Miya's bluntness, and am not sure how to feel about the news.

Miya continues, "A while back there you went on about how you were going to remain paralyzed because you never should have been inflicting those sorts of punishments on people to begin with and-"

"I think I see what you are getting at." I cut in, "The question is, if I am going to give Makali my spine, should I also give Makali my dick..."

"Yeah..."

"Shit, I don't know." I say as I bury my face into my hands, "I don't know if I will be able to sleep at night knowing that Makali has, and can abuse having, my dick when I could have done something about it at this moment. Though can't the same be said for my spine?"

"I don't know either. Something about it feels different. Like, personally, I would judge you more for letting Makali keep your dick than I would for letting ver keep your spine."

"I know what you mean, though I can't necessarily explain how it is different. It just feels different." I say.

"So... Do you want to get Suki or Kize to make the switch? Or would you rather Sodi..."

I can feel my whole face turn red, "Great, another dilemma. Of the options, I would only really feel comfortable with Sodi concentrating on my dick so much, but talk about awkward. I also don't know how Sodi would feel if I asked Suki to do it. Then there is Kize. Kize would be less awkward than Sodi, no potential jealousy because we have no prospect of a romantic relationship, and more inconspicuous spell casting since Kize won't have to point an appendage at our groins."

"Kize it is then?"

"Kize it is."

On our way to make my quiet request of Kize, my eyes catch a glimpse of Jove and the pups as they come topside for the first time. Hinuso and Viadu recognize them immediately and run to them. The pups and Jove see them and receive their embrace.

"Dima! Miya! We are so glad you two are okay!" Jove exclaims.

Hinuso pulls back a bit, "Dima? Miya? Those two are over there." Hinuso jabs a thumb over at us. We wave back.

The jaws of Jove and the pups fall open, and tears begin to pour down their cheeks. "You mean..." Jove squeaks.

"It's us, vera."

At that, the pack of bitu collapses joyfully into a pile of tearful embraces.

"I thought I would never smell you two assholes again!" Jove weeps.

"Nah, Ritu isn't that merciful," Viadu teases, earning a solid punch to the arm followed by more hugs.

Smiles light up our faces. This scene makes all of the pain feel worth it.

The voyage is long, and we make several stops for supplies. As we fly in silence, everyone overcrowds the deck in an attempt to see through the mist that surrounds us. Finally, the mist gives way to a land of deep greens blanketed in sunlight and a thin morning mist that stretches out before us. Rising from the mist there is an odd looking mountain, standing defiantly above the rolling hills around it. The forest rests on a massive island floating above nothing but darkness. Ordinarily, this island would be a middle island with just as many land masses above it as below, but somehow this island floats with the skies above it and beneath it clear of floating rock.

As we approach the forest, the greenery begins to look just as structured as it is wild. At first glance, it looks like a city overrun with nature. Though, upon closer inspection, nature and industry do not seem to be in contest with one another. However, the city is anything but primitive, even the smallest and lowest quality building seems like something you would see in Sudihatosema, just more integrated with nature. From that baseline, the other buildings look even more extravagant and dreamlike. Then there is the mountain, which upon closer inspection is no mountain at all. It is a tower.

The incomplete Tower of Matuha.

Miya, Jove, Shibi, Mebi, Hinuso, Viadu, and I wait in a clean room on the second floor of a records office. All passengers were divided into groups to be processed for census purposes and cultural education. I was given a new wheelchair that is superior to the last one in every way. The seat is fabric and cushioned, the wheels seem to absorb bumps better, and there is an additional rim attached to the wheels so I don't have to push myself by the wheels directly.

Gathering around some large windows, we all peer out in wonder at the whimsical city that blends industry and nature.

"As much as I love being a yetu, I'm glad I get to experience this through atu eyes," Miya remarks.

"I don't know about sights, but the scent is incredible!" Jove exclaims, and we all inhale deeply, savoring the fragrance of fresh air made rich with the contributions of plant life.

Suddenly, there's a knock at the door.

"Come in," Jove invites.

An atu enters the room, holding a book and pencil. "Hello, Welcome to Fariha of the great nation of Matuha. My name is Leraki, and I'm here to register you and provide information on the next steps. May I have your names and how many cycles old you are?"

"Cycles?" I ask.

"Sorry, basins or salaries depending on your city of origin. I just got back from a break and have gotten rusty with the different vernacular. They are pretty much the same thing so please just tell me how old you are."

"I'm Miya, twenty-seven uh salaries old."

"I'm Dima, twenty-six."

"I'm Jove, thirty-two. These two are Shibi, six basins old, and Mebi, nine."

"Ah coulda told ver dat," Mebi interjects, sounding annoyed.

"Me too," Shibi agrees.

Jove playfully nips at them. "Next time."

"Hinuso, thirty-six."

"Viadu, thirty-eight."

"As I understand it, you may have undergone biological changes. If you plan to return to a vetu type different from your current one, please let me know."

"I intend to return to a yetu body," Miya informs.

"I am an atu," I state.

"The rest of us are bitu," Jove adds.

"Will you all be staying together?"

I look at Jove. "If you're all okay with it."

"Yes," Jove affirms, "Yes, we'll be staying together."

Viadu raises a paw and questions, "Really?"

"Yes," Jove asserts firmly.

Leraki notes down our housing arrangement. "Alright, now let's move on to the educational part. Here in Matuha, our government ensures that housing, healthcare, food, and water are freely provided based on each family's needs. Anyone running for a position of power in the government is required to live under these programs without any additional sources of income or access to pre-existing wealth. This ensures that our officials are dedicated to making these government programs sustainable and livable.

Labor is also treated as a product that employees sell to an employer. As such, every employee sets their own terms of labor. Terms of labor include the price for their labor and when they work including when they take paid time off. Employers can only hire or fire an employee. These market regulations, backed with our welfare system, empower workers so that they don't have to choose between survival and being exploited for their labor, making our economy the closest thing to a free market economy where companies compete with each other to sell products and workers compete with each other for employment with the minimum asking price for labor being the value of a livable welfare."

Miya raises a hand, "So... I could just choose not to work?"

Leraki goes on to explain, "Yes and no. If an able-bodied individual is unemployed and reliant on government welfare, their name is entered into a lottery. If there's an essential job that cannot be filled, a name may be drawn from the lottery to train someone for that position. The person chosen will receive triple the cost of their government welfare services as compensation, either for a four-basin term or until a willing replacement can be trained."

Viadu raises a paw and asks, "What if someone is assigned to a job but refuses to do it?"

"In most cases, we find that there's an underlying reason why an individual might struggle with a particular position. If someone refuses to work, they'll be required to go through a rehabilitation program where their physical and psychological well-being will be assessed. They'll receive the necessary support to empower them for their job. If it's determined that they are unable to fill the position, their file will be updated with the reason, and they'll be returned to their previous life while a new name is drawn. If their name is drawn again in the future, they'll undergo another assessment, taking into account any new knowledge or understanding we've gained since their last evaluation."

Mebi raises a paw and asks, "But what if de're just lazy?"

"More often than not, we discover underlying reasons behind an individual's struggle to work. In rare cases where no reason can be determined, it suggests that we haven't fully understood or discovered the underlying cause yet. In such instances, the individual is allowed to return to their previous life, and a new name is drawn. If their name is chosen again, they'll undergo another assessment process to identify the reason, using the knowledge and insights gained since their last evaluation."

I raise my hand and inquire, "What is law enforcement like here?"

"If someone commits a crime, they'll be apprehended and required to submit themselves to a rehabilitation center, where they'll receive assistance in their rehabilitation process. Once they're deemed capable, they'll be expected to provide recompense either through legally defined means or by proposing an alternative form of compensation, which will need to be approved by the victim or a jury. If someone wishes to rectify a wrong they've done or address any crimes they've committed, they can voluntarily enter the judicial process at a rehabilitation center. Criminals are only detained in the rehabilitation center if they're considered dangerous or pose a flight risk."

Leraki concludes, "If you have any further questions, please feel free to ask. Otherwise, we hope you enjoy your time here in Matuha."

"I have one last question. Though, it's a little, I don't know... Nevermind it might be offensive." I say.

"No go on, I promise not to take offense." Leraki says.

"With how prosperous this nation appears to be, why does the tower still remain incomplete?" I ask.

"What do you mean by 'incomplete'?" Leraki asks.

"I mean- um, wasn't it supposed to reach the clouds?" I ask.

"That was the original intention. Yes. Those who don't know the history consider it incomplete." Leraki says.

"Can you give me the short of it?" I ask.

"Sure. The tower started out as a vanity project to boost the ego of the ruler at the time. When that leader passed, ver heir Veturi Lezu Segu, the first dark-skinned atu to rise to power in our nation, which is a whole story in and of itself, saw the cost of the project on the people. So ve had the project halted at the soonest structurally sound point, and poured the rest of the resources into restructuring our society to become what it is this sun, erm, labor. So while some people like to mock the tower as being incomplete and a symbol of Ritu's disapproval of our way of life, we who live here know it is exactly as it needs to be, a symbol of the good in all vetu kind."

Having heard that, I sit back in my wheelchair, feeling more complete than ever.

Zi's body, ver head reattached, lies in a deep hole beside a tree. This hole appears to have been dug and maintained for so long that the roots of the neighboring tree have grown around it. In each of Zi's paws, there are wooden effigies representing Fami and Kidu, whose bodies were lost in the nation of Rirze. Many vetu have gathered to grieve the loss of their loved ones, but especially Zi who was well known within the community.

"Zi is the reason I stand here this sun," Hari begins speaking aloud for all to hear. "After the ministry arrested me for prostitution, I was being transported to an airship that would take me to a Hosudiha prison when Zi caught sight of me. Ve couldn't stand to see a child taken into custody like that. So ve convinced Jomira and ver crew to take a risk. They attacked the airship that was carrying me and others, they liberated us that sun. When-"

Hari seems to pause for a moment as tears choke ver, "When we learned of my family's demise, Jomira and ver crew took me in. They brought me here to Matuha until I was ready to contribute towards their liberation efforts. From the beginning Zi has been like a big vera to me." Hari cannot seem to continue and so steps back.

Sho steps forward. "I didn't know Zi for very long. I too was robbed of my family. One vedi lost to the Rirze prison industry and the other taken by illness after I too was apprehended. Ve never really agreed to fill the void left by the loss of my family, but ve was like a vera to me as well in the short time I knew ver, and I wish ve could still be here to fill that role."

Sho steps back and Jomira steps forward. "Zi and I met when my old crew, may they rest in peace, and I busted a vetu trafficking scheme in the nation of Mefadi. Ve was only a teenager who never had a chance to be a pup. Raised by ver slavers for gladiatorial combat. We brought Zi back here, and ve thrived. Many of you know Zi for ver community work. Though ve was passionate about Fariha, ver future lover was determined to join my crew, and once Zi had sufficiently fought ver demons, ve insisted on joining too. They were some of the best I have ever worked with. I thought I knew empathy, but they showed me just how deep empathy can reach."

Jomira finishes and Jove steps forward. "Kidu was the vedi to my pups. Though the life we shared was practically nonexistent, I know neither I nor my pups would be here if not for the work Kidu put in for our survival. I wish we had actually been able to share a life together. I would have loved to love the bitu who cared so deeply to enable this life we now have."

Jove steps back and Buso steps forward. "Fami tried harder than anyone I had ever known to make the Rirmevu profession a moral one. We were all uncomfortable with the system, but Fami was the first among us who was willing to challenge it. Ver efforts proved that it was impossible to be a good officer in a system that only armed us with tools of harm, in a system that couldn't distinguish between those who needed help and those who needed to be stopped.

We are here this labor because of the selflessness of Fami. Fami, who was always willing to risk ver own safety and reputation to help those in need. Ve shall live forever as an example for us to aspire to as we work to make amends."

The stories and respects fill our hearts for a few wages. It feels like a shame for it to ever end, but eventually, it does, and when it does, I know what I need to do.

"Miya," I say, "You don't have to come with me, but I'm going to offer myself to Jomira's crew."

"I was actually feeling the need to do that myself. I'd happily go with you," Miya says.

Miya and I find ourselves awkwardly among Suki, Buso, Powa, and Kize, all having approached Jomira at the same time after the burial. We all look around at each other.

"Uh, sorry," Suki says.

"Yeah, um, we can wait over here," I start to say.

"We want to join your crew!" Powa shouts to Jomira.

"Oh... well, uh, us too," I stammer.

"Count me in as well. I'm not ready to stop helping the citizens of Rirze," Kize states.

"And the rest of you want to join to make amends, I take it?" Jomira assumes, receiving a bunch of nods in return. "As much as I hate to replace Zi so soon, I think ve would want this. Also, it makes things a bit easier for me. I don't have to post positions and wait for applicants. However, you will all still need to register at a rehabilitation center. They won't permit you to join me until they determine that you are mentally, physically, and emotionally well enough. So go ahead and get to that. Besides, I need some time to rework some details – our headquarters, methods to avoid detection, and the like."

"We could use the spa as our headquarters. Every enemy who knows about Sodi and my allegiances is under Fariha's rehabilitation custody. So the spa should still be a safe place to hunker down."

"I'm not sure about having our headquarters on a ministry base. We may have to work out some details and eventually move, but it will do for now. Will Sodi be joining us?" Jomira asks.

"No, ve has expressed a desire to settle down and start a new life. Ve mentioned that ve might join some labor, but not now." Kize says.

"Very well. Everyone, go register and focus on your recovery. Take the time you need. Don't rush your healing process. I want you at your best, and I guarantee you will encounter unexpected traumas to work through. While you're recovering, you may find that it would be better for you to make amends in a different way. If you discover that to be the case, remember that it is perfectly fine. You owe me nothing. I do what I do to pay my own recompense, but even if I had no transgressions to atone for, this is not something we do for recognition, payment, or any other external reason. This is a mission of love for all vetu kind. This is a mission that may demand your life, as it has taken many others. I am honestly surprised I have lived as long as I have. No matter what you decide in the end. Thank you all for your help, and for your futures."

I turn my wheelchair to return to our bitu family, and upon seeing them I recall a promise Miya and I had made. In my heightened emotional state I had almost forgotten.

"Actually, Jomira," I say and then turn back to face Jomira, "Sorry I just remembered a promise I had made. I would still like to be of any help that I can, but I cannot leave Jove and the pups. I believe sticking with them is the best way I can make amends. Though I'll admit, it doesn't feel right for me to do all of the things I've done only to resign to a life in such a peaceful place as this."

"Hmm... Right" Miya says, "I too made that promise. I think my place is also with the family."

"That is perfectly okay," Jomira affirms, "Not every recompense needs to be some widespread, grandiose, and life endangering thing. Widespread change is often shallow, focusing your efforts into loving this particular family will create a much deeper and lasting impact which is arguably just as important if not more important than what my crew and I do. We need both approaches if we ever hope to see change in this world. Besides, I'm sure you will find that Fariha has its own unique issues."

Suki and I sit at the table in Geni's tavern, observing the patrons as they come and go. The last time I sat here, my whole life took a turn for what felt like the worst at the time, but ultimately worked out for the better.

Thanks to the information gathered by Hari and Kize from the spa's customers, we know that one of the individuals in here is to be apprehended for blasphemy, although we're uncertain of their identity. So, for now, all we can do is wait for the arrest to commence. While we could have gathered more information, we understand that Hari is doing ver best under Kize's mentorship.

"Are you sure you are ready for this Sho?" Suki asks.

"Absolutely." I respond.

Jomira and Buso are positioned on nearby rooftops, trying to maintain a low profile but remaining ready to intervene if things go awry.

As the tavern door swings open, a Rirkase duo enters. The room falls silent, with all except one, turning to assess the situation. The Rirkase approach a bitu sitting at the bar who's back remains turned towards them. Soon after it is clear what is about to happen, most everyone turns a blind eye and some even leave the tavern.

"Modu, you are under arrest for blaspheming Ritu. I kindly request that you come with me quietly and without resistance," the Rirkase atu states.

Modu takes a long sip of ver mead and responds defiantly, "I didn't do it. So go fuck yourself."

"Well, at the very least, I can arrest you for insulting Ritu's shield," the officer retorts.

"I had no idea an inanimate object could be insulted," the bitu quips.

The officer sighs, while ver notu partner discreetly prepares a dart in ver hand. The officer moves to strike the bitu, but one of my darts finds its mark in ver neck first, causing ver to collapse. The notu, who had taken the form of living armor, shifts into a mid-sized biped and turns to face Suki and me.

Suki extends ver hand towards the gem, and suddenly, the body can no longer support its weight. Gravity pulls it through the clay form, securing it to the floor, allowing me to swiftly sling a stone at it.

The notu's clay form crumples into an unconscious pile on the floor.

"Hello, Modu," I speak from behind my newly adorned featureless mask, the symbol of the Tower of Matuha painted upon it.

"We are here to exalt you."

Biology/Form Of Vetu

The following section contains information that is not crucial to the story's plot but may interest those curious about the creatures inhabiting the Shattered Skies.

Notu

Notu are sentient gemstones, classified as non-biological entities. Each notu gem possesses a unique combination of shape, color, and size, ranging from the dimensions of a single nine-volt battery to the size of two nine-volt batteries placed side by side. They weigh approximately the same as these batteries (Note: In the context of the story, batteries have not yet been invented in the Shattered Skies and are mentioned here for reader convenience).

Notu have the ability to use magic to shape malleable substances, creating what is known as their "extended body." This extended body can take on almost any form, as long as it remains within six ingots of the gemstone.

Consciousness in notu beings resides within their gem. Striking a notu gem can stun or incapacitate the notu, the effect varying depending on the force of the strike. A powerful enough strike can shatter the gemstone, killing the notu.

Notu perceive their surroundings through their gem, possessing vision that surpasses that of a Bitu but falls short of an Atu's visual acuity.

Communication for Notu involves vibrating their gem, allowing them to produce sounds. They also receive auditory input through vibrations that reach their gem. Consequently, Notu cannot hear sounds that are quieter than the volume of their own voice. While they can create a wide range of sounds through gem vibrations, their produced sounds tend to have a tinny quality.

Notu lack the senses of smell and taste.

Notu replenish energy through sun exposure. The more intense the sunlight the quicker their energy can replenish. An active Notu residing in a low light environment can burn through all of their energy in a deposit. Once depleted the notu might migrate to someplace sunny to recharge fully within a quarter-deposit of time or require up to a deposit to hibernate in low sunlight, doing nothing, to become charged enough to perform meaningful actions. Notu who deplete their energy in an area with no light will enter into a sort of coma, and if they remain in this state for around three deposits they can die permanently.

Apart from their solar needs, the needs of a notu vary depending on the material it chooses for its extended body. A commonly used material is a special clay that has been chemically treated to retain moisture for longer periods compared to ordinary clay. This clay requires occasional watering to prevent drying out. It is favored due to its low energy maintenance requirements. However, in higher society where energy conservation is less of a concern and the standards for cleanliness are higher, the use of water as a material for the notu's extended body is more popular.

As non-biological entities, notu do not possess biological sex and do not reproduce. It appears that notu simply awaken whenever Ritu requires them to fulfill a specific purpose, awakening in the absence of others.

Yetu

Yetu are a species of giant moth that often resemble a large fur-ball with wings. Their "fur" is comprised of flexible scales, similar to other fuzzy moths. Normally, Yetu weigh between 20 and 30 purses.

The body of a Yetu consists of an ovular shape, approximately the size of an adult human's back which is the same size as an average adult atu or bitu's back. (Note: Humans do not exist in the Shattered Skies; this is merely a point of reference for reader convenience).

Located on the front of their bodies, Yetu have subtle mandibles for eating and drinking. Just behind their mandibles, on the top of their bodies, there is a loose patch of skin that they can vibrate to produce sounds, capable of replicating a wide range of noises with practice.

On each side of the speech skin, there are two small orifices that serve as their hearing organs. Positioned at the rear of their bodies, there are orifices for waste expulsion and reproduction.

Six strong legs protrude from the sides of their bodies, capable of supporting weights up to 200 purses. Additionally, two wings extend from the top of their bodies, with a wingspan ranging between 18 and 20 ingots. These wings enable them to carry their own weight and an additional 100 purses of weight.

On either side of their hearing orifices, Yetu possess feather-like antennas that they use for smelling and tapping into the fabric of creation, allowing them to extract detailed information about living biological beings and limited information about non-living or inanimate objects within a thirty-six block radius.

Yetu lack eyes, but due to the rapidity with which they read and interpret information using their antennas, they are able to create a mental representation of their surroundings, akin to sight.

The biological sex of Yetu individuals changes based on their relationship with their partners. One partner will adapt female sex organs, while the other will adapt male sex organs. This can change if the nature of the relationship evolves, similar to how the sex of a clownfish can change over time in our world.

Atu

Atu are a species that share many similarities with humans. They have a human-like appearance, sound like humans, and go through a similar process of maturation and growth, reaching an average size and weight comparable to humans.

Similar to humans, the biological sex of Atu is determined by various factors, including hormones, chromosomes, gametes, genomes, primary sex organs, secondary sex organs, brain structure, and others. While there are common characteristics associated with the two predominant sexes, there is no consistent combination of sex characteristics shared within each sex. In terms of primary sex organs, most Atu have either two external testicles and a penis or a clitoris, vulva, vagina, womb, and ovaries.

Like humans, different sex characteristics can influence an Atu's behavioral inclinations, and changes in these characteristics can lead to corresponding changes in behavior. For example, higher levels of testosterone in an Atu can facilitate easier access to emotions like anger while making it more difficult to experience emotions like sadness and empathy. This may increase the likelihood of violent tendencies or engaging in violent hobbies, though these behaviors can be expressed safely, when handled poorly, it can result in harm to self and/or others. However, some Atu with higher testosterone levels may dislike the effects it has on their body and behavior. In such cases, they may seek hormonal treatment to align their mind and body for a happier life. This is just one example among many where an Atu's sex characteristics may develop in conflicting ways, similar to problematic developments in the human body. There is no universal solution to resolve every instance of conflict between different biological sex components.

In most nations, the resolution is based on the desires of the Atu seeking assistance, as they are responsible for the risks associated with their own bodies. For minors, input from guardians and medical professionals is taken into consideration. In some cases, medical professionals and guardians may need to undergo psychological evaluations conducted by a diverse jury of professionals and parents to ensure they are suitable physicians or guardians for the minor, free from abusive, neglectful, or harmful traits, and capable of contributing to decisions regarding the minor's health and well-being.

When an Atu's body is not aligned, they can seek two types of assistance in most nations: psychiatric assistance for those struggling to love and accept their body due to societal pressures or other external factors, and medical or magical assistance for those whose sex characteristics are misaligned to the extent that psychiatric assistance is ineffective or for those who simply desire to change their own bodies for personal reasons.

Aside from the similarities to humans, there are several distinct characteristics that Ritu designed Atu to possess:

- ❖ Atu have an orifice at the base of their skull, similar to a whale's blowhole, which allows them to breathe if something gets lodged in their throat, virtually eliminating the risk of choking or infant suffocation during co-sleeping.

- ❖ Unlike humans, Atu can synthesize vitamin C within their bodies, making their immune systems stronger in the absence of external sources of vitamin C and less susceptible to scurvy.
- ❖ The distance between an Atu's reproductive system and waste systems is spread out in a way that makes them less prone to infections compared to humans.
- ❖ Atu do not experience the overcrowding of teeth caused by a third molar, reducing the likelihood of severe mouth pain as they age and eliminating the need for surgical removal.
- ❖ Atu can regrow teeth indefinitely to replace damaged ones.
- ❖ Atu have knee joints more akin to a ball and socket, making them less susceptible to knee injuries.
- ❖ Unlike humans, Atu have clearer eyesight with fewer blind spots since their retinas are not needlessly obscured by blood and tissue. The likelihood of retinal detachment causing blindness is also reduced thanks to this difference.
- ❖ The recurrent laryngeal nerve, responsible for speaking and swallowing functions, remains in the head and neck of Atu, rather than being needlessly dragged into the chest like it does in humans. This positioning makes it less vulnerable to damage from blunt strikes to the torso.
- ❖ Atu have wider pelvises compared to humans, facilitating quicker and less fatal childbirth processes.
- ❖ Atu have spinal columns intentionally designed to suit bipedal life, reducing common pains associated with pinched nerves and similar issues experienced by humans.
- ❖ Unlike humans, Atu feet lack unnecessary bones, making them less susceptible to ankle sprains, plantar fasciitis, Achilles tendonitis, shin splints, and broken ankles.

- The maxillary sinuses of Atu drain downwards, minimizing the buildup of fluids and mucus and reducing the likelihood of related infections.

Bitu

Bitu are bipedal mammals that share many advantages over humans, similar to the Atu, with one notable exception: their eyesight. Unlike Atu, Bitu have nearsighted vision. However, they compensate for this with a superior sense of smell, surpassing both humans and other Vetu.

Bitu undergo similar maturation and growth rates as Atu, reaching comparable average weights and heights.

In terms of appearance, Bitu have distinct aesthetic differences compared to Atu. They possess fur-covered bodies, faces that taper into a shallow snout, spade-shaped ears positioned atop their heads, a long puffy tail extending from their lower back, and claw-tipped paws equipped with opposable thumbs.

One intriguing aspect of Bitu is their remarkable diversity of biological sexes. They exhibit a total of twenty-four distinct sexes, with the majority being born with a combination of an external testicle, a penis, a vulva, a vagina, a womb, and an internal ovary. This wide array of sexes primarily stems from genetic variation within their genomes, with secondary sex characteristics also influencing their sexual identities. This concept mirrors the diversity observed in certain species of fungi in our world, where thousands of biological sexes contribute to greater genetic diversity, ultimately fostering healthier populations compared to species with fewer biological sexes.

The Magic Of The Shattered Skies

Notu Magic

Notu possess a unique ability to manipulate and shape malleable inorganic material within a range of approximately six ingots from their gemstone. This ability is primarily used by notu to mold a malleable material around their gemstone into the form of a body, enabling them to move and defend themselves. However, there are certain limitations to a notu's ability, including:

1. Inability to bend rigid materials: Notu are unable to manipulate materials that are inherently rigid and inflexible.
2. Inability to bend or manipulate biological or otherwise organic materials.
3. Inability to bend or manipulate malleable materials that are encased in biological or otherwise organic materials like internal sweat, urine, spit, and tears.
    a. Notu can bend external sweat but there is rarely enough of it to enable substantial manipulation or restriction of a creature.
    b. Notu can also irritate the water on the open eyes of a creature, temporarily obscuring vision until the target blinks. Goggles are often employed as a defensive measure against this sort of attack.
4. Inability to manipulate malleable materials when encased in a rigid material or otherwise obstructed by a substantial rigid obstacle.
    a. If a malleable material is within six ingots and behind a large wall, but one of the edges of the wall is also within six ingots, the malleable material can be bent.

   b. If a malleable material is within six ingots and behind a large wall, the edges of which are not within six ingots, the malleable material cannot be bent.

5. Limited capacity to increase the rigidity of malleable materials: A notu can only make a malleable material as rigid as thick clay or a similar level of solidity. For instance, they can make a substance like water feel as solid as clay, but not as solid as rock.
6. Susceptibility to fragmentation: When a notu's malleable body is struck by a solid object or used to strike a more solid surface, there is a tendency for those parts of their body to break into pieces.

These limitations define the boundaries within which a notu can utilize their manipulative abilities.

Yetu Magic

Yetu possess a unique ability granted by their antennae, which allows them to tap into the fabric of creation. Through this connection, they can extract precise and detailed biological and locational information about living biological organisms within a range of up to thirty-six blocks. Additionally, Yetu can obtain an approximate understanding of the location of inorganic/non-living materials from the fabric. However, it is important to note that while a Yetu can gather information from great distances, their spell casting abilities are subject to the same limitations as any other vetu.

A limitation with respect to yetu senses is their capacity to process information. Similar to someone with eyes looking at a complex painting, while they can look at the whole painting in a glance, they might not notice particular details until they more closely observe it, likewise a person within a yetu's perceptive range is not likely to be perceived or identified until the yetu puts in more effort to intentionally observe the individual more closely.

Additionally, similar to the way one person with eyes can see where another person with eyes is looking, one yetu can determine where another yetu is focusing their perceptive attention when using the fabric of creation to see.

Vetu Magic

Cliff Notes:

This summary contains information about the magic system in the Shattered Skies universe. The information in these cliffs notes is helpful to understand the story but not essential. It might even spoil some plot points. So read at your own discretion.

There are four schools of magic that all vetu can learn and use to cast various spells. These schools, listed from least to most difficult, are as follows:

1. Property magic
    a. Involves swapping inorganic properties like mass.
2. Trait magic
    a. Involves swapping organic properties like organs or wounds.
3. Mind magic
    a. Involves swapping thoughts and memories.
4. Enchantment magic
    a. Involves making the effects of a property spell permanent.

Except for enchantment magic, which has only one level of difficulty, each school of magic is further divided into two levels marked by whether the mage includes themselves as a target (a vessel spell) or not (a channel spell).

Vessel magic, where the mage is a target of their own spell, is easier to perform than channel magic, where the mage's targets are both separate entities from verself.

There are several limitations that apply to all schools of vetu magic. Here are the general limitations:

- All spells require at least two targets.
- The maximum casting distance is twelve ingots.
- The strength of a spell diminishes with increased distance between the mage and the target(s).
- The difficulty of a spell increases with the distance between the mage and the target(s).
- The difficulty of a spell increases with the mass of the target(s), even if the mass is spread among many smaller units.
- The difficulty of a spell increases with the number of factors the mage must consider to cast the spell.
- Committing the act of casting a particular spell to a sort of muscle memory is required for the spell to be useful in time-sensitive or high-stress situations.
- Only property magic requires the mage to maintain concentration for the spell's effects to persist.

There are four schools of magic that all vetu can learn and use to cast various spells. Each school of magic requires extensive knowledge in a specific field of study to be practiced effectively.

In order from least difficult to most, these schools and their corresponding fields of study are as follows:

1. Property magic
    a. Field of study: Physics
2. Trait magic
    a. Field of study: Biology
3. Mind magic
    a. Field of study: Psychology
4. Enchantment magic
    a. Fields of study: Physics and Psychology

Except for enchantment magic, which has only one level of difficulty, each school of magic is further divided into two levels marked by whether the mage includes themselves as a target (a vessel spell) or not (a channel spell).

Vessel magic, where the mage is a target of their own spell, is easier to perform than channel magic, where the mage's targets are both separate entities from verself.

Each school of magic has specific limitations, although some limitations are unique to certain schools. Here are the limitations that apply to all schools of vetu magic:

- ❖ All magic requires a minimum of two targets.
- ❖ Spells cannot be cast on targets more than twelve ingots away.
- ❖ The strength of a spell diminishes with increased distance between the mage and the target(s).
- ❖ The difficulty of a spell increases with the distance between the mage and the target(s).
- ❖ The difficulty of a spell increases with the mass of the target(s), even if the mass is distributed among smaller units.

- The difficulty of a spell increases with the number of factors the mage needs to consider for the spell to be cast successfully.
- Committing the act of casting a particular spell to a sort of muscle memory is required for the spell to be useful in time-sensitive or high-stress situations.

To cast a spell, one must speak or think of the word "Shuni" with the intention of entering the fabric of creation. Once within the fabric, a spell can be cast by issuing a command. Forming this command is akin to constructing a coherent sentence with one's thoughts, using the language of creation. The command must demonstrate a proper understanding of relevant concepts related to the type of spell being cast. If the mage employs improper syntax or lacks understanding of concepts while in the fabric, they will be expelled from the fabric.

When the mage is ready to exit the fabric, they can think or say the word "Shube".

Property magic

Property magic involves spells that swap inorganic properties between two targets. The properties that can be swapped include:

- Heat
- Speed
- Mass
- Malleability
- Color
- Viscosity
- Luminosity

When a mage casts a property spell no consciousness is taken into account even if the properties are being swapped between two conscious targets. Scholars believe this phenomenon has something to do with a disconnect of sorts in the relationship between consciousness and physical properties. As a result of this, the life of the spell becomes dependent upon the consciousness and continuous concentration of the mage performing the spell.

In other words, among the schools of magic, property magic is unique in that it requires the mage to maintain concentration throughout the duration of the spell. Once the mage's concentration is broken, the properties return to their original sources immediately.

Another quirk which pertains only to property magic is the mysterious locking of a property.

For example, if a property spell swaps the heat of a molten ball of metal with that of a cool ball of metal the resulting heat of each ball will lock at their respective temperatures until the spell breaks. In other words, where in nature a molten hot metal ball will cool over time until it reaches room temperature, a ball heated with property magic will not cool, putting off what appears to be an endless supply of heat up until the spell ends. There is a lot of debate surrounding where the generated heat originates, but most people simply believe Ritu or some other higher power creates it.

Trait Magic

Trait magic involves spells that swap biological traits between two living targets. These traits can range from health conditions to entire organs. Highly proficient mages in trait magic can achieve a degree of body swapping within the same species. However, when it comes to swapping between different species, due to differences in skull shapes among other factors, mind magic is necessary.

Limitations to consider when using trait magic:

- ❖ Wounds can only be transferred between equivalent or closely equivalent organs. For instance, a wing injury can only be transferred to another wing. A wing injury cannot be transferred to a head or a heart.
- ❖ An injury can be swapped between beings even if both targets are of a different species.
    - ➢ Example: A leg injury can be swapped between a bitu leg and a yetu leg.
- ❖ Mages must take into account the autoimmune systems of their different targets. Transferring organs in a way that avoids triggering an autoimmune response is a challenging and dangerous aspect of trait magic. Sometimes trait magic is used offensively with the intent of triggering an autoimmune response. Such an attack can easily be remedied by any mage skilled in trait magic. However, in the absence of a benevolent mage, such an attack is often deadly.

Unlike property magic, trait magic does not require the mage to maintain concentration for the effects of the spell to persist. This is because the inclusion of two conscious targets creates what is known as a "complete trade".

This "complete trade" seems to take place in the subconscious of the two targets because spells can persist between two targets even if one target is unconscious at the time of the spell. Once a trade is made the altered fabric goes on existing in its new state despite the magic of the spell completing its life cycle. This means that even if the target of a trait spell dies, so long as the spell was completed, the effects of the trait spell will remain in place.

Mind Magic

Mind magic involves spells that swap thoughts, memories, and consciousness between two thinking targets. When performing a mind spell, a mage initiates the spell and, while maintaining concentration, captures the thoughts of a target from the moment the spell begins. Once the spell is concluded, the recent thoughts of one target are swapped with the other target's recent thoughts.

Skilled mages can both swap recent thoughts and also the memories associated with those thoughts.

Masters of mind magic can achieve a complete swap of all memories between two targets, regardless of their species, effectively causing them to switch bodies.

In order to target specific memories, a mage needs to find a way to get their target to think of the memories they intend to target. However, when performing a complete mind swap, no such coxing is necessary.

In the same ways as trait magic, and for the same reasons, the effects of mind magic do not require the mage to maintain concentration for them to persist.

Enchantment Magic

Enchantment magic is not technically a distinct school of magic, although it is commonly marketed as such. Achieving an enchantment involves a specific process. A young notu's gem needs to be encased in a rigid material, and Then its consciousness must be groomed using mind magic to identify with the property one wishes for it to concentrate on. When property magic is applied to the notu gem, it assumes the responsibility of concentration, thereby maintaining the effects of the property magic indefinitely.

Enchantment magic is widely considered an abuse of the magical arts and a violation of the autonomy and sacristy of notu life. However, in some nations, such as Rirze, the true nature of enchantments is kept secret from the public and lower ranking government officials.

The Theology of the Shattered Skies

Ritufani

Belief systems which posit the existence of a singular, greatest, divine, creator being often known as Ritu.

Nifani

Nifani is a denomination of Ritufani. Nifani members believe that Ritu is goodness, truth, and the journey towards goodness and truth. Nifani also believe that vetu are fallible in their ability to identify goodness and truth. This implies that no vetu can claim, with absolute confidence, that any being, spirit, or media is Ritu, is of Ritu, or is inspired by Ritu.

In fact, Nifani consider claims of absolute knowledge to be viceful and consider the acknowledgement of potentially flawed or incomplete knowledge to be virtuous.

Therefore, the pursuit of Ritu is a humble search for truth and goodness.

Nifani will often operate as though the best working theory on a matter were truth. While theories are never posited as absolute truth, theories do exist in a hierarchy where some theories are considered more likely to be true than others. This hierarchy can shift in light of new information and not every nifani agrees on how the hierarchy should be arranged.

Similarly, while ethical ideas are never posited as absolute good, ethical ideas also exist in a hierarchy which can shift and over which there may be disagreement and discussion.

Ultimately, the Nifani church has set hierarchies dictating various theories as being the best for a given topic, and various ethical ideas as being best for certain situations. Congregations operate on the set of hierarchies defined by the church in their functions, however, individuals have a right to hold their own personal hierarchies. The hierarchies of the church can be changed, though doing so requires a board of representatives to hear arguments and come to a decision.

Below are two widely repeated slogans among nifani:

"All goodness and truth are Ritu's goodness and truth."

"All vetu knowledge is potentially flawed or incomplete. Therefore we must do the best we can with the best knowledge we have acquired at that time."

The Nifani mission is to gain knowledge, sharpen knowledge, and heal brokenness while simultaneously combating misinformation, manipulation, injustice, and sources of suffering and death. They believe the pursuit of knowledge is an eternal purpose guiding them ever closer to Ritu. The mission is all about the journey, because the destination of absolute knowledge and truth is widely assumed to be impossible for vetu to reach.

Vefani

Vefani is a denomination of Ritufani. Vefani members believe that the original relationship between Ritu and vetu was such that Ritu was the definer of vice and virtue while the vetu were to abide by Ritu's definitions and co-rule over the world with Ritu.

It would come to pass that the vetu decided that they wanted to define vice and virtue for themselves. Thus the vetu entered into rebellion against Ritu which would ultimately lead to the shattering of the land and the plunging of all vetu into darkness. In the darkness the notu, as the vetu who were least rebellious, would fall dormant and the other vetu would fall into depravity and begin to view each other as vemo, resulting in much bloodshed.

Ritu never gave up on the vetu. Ve slowly worked with select tribes of each vetu kind to incrementally steer them back into adopting Verself as their definer of virtue and vice. These chosen tribes would one labor be tasked with bringing Ritu's teachings to all other tribes of vetu.

Ritu's work was slow and gentle so as not to cause another rebellion. However, Ritu's gentleness would come at the cost of many misconceptions among vetu regarding Ritu's nature and intentions. Additionally, due to the many raging wars and what many would call a plague of transgressions, many would come to believe death and vice to be powers which are equal to, if not greater than, Ritu.

So Ritu took on flesh, and came among each chosen tribe in the form of their respective vetu kind. Now among Ver creation Ritu would challenge the misconceptions of high ranking ministers and work to correct the understandings of anyone who was humble enough to accept that, in spite of all of their studies or all that they had been taught or come to assume, they were wrong about Ritu.

As for those vetu who clung to their misconceptions, they would leverage various means of contributing to the deaths of Ritu's many vetu forms. Once vanquished, it appeared to many, even to a number of Ritu's closest followers, that death and vice were in fact powers which exceeded even Ritu.

However, Ritu would set into motion Ver plan to undermine the perceived superior power of death and vice. On the third labor following Ver death, Ritu would raise Ver various forms back to life. Proving to anyone who was receptive to Ritu's vetu forms, that Ritu is who Ve claims to be and assuring the promise that while death will consume all vetu life, death will not be the end of Ritu's followers. For all will be raised to life and once again be given the chance to live in a world without death should they receive Ritu as the definer of vice and virtue.

The Vefani mission is to bring Ritu's teachings to all vetu so that virtues can flourish and the relationship between individual vetu and Ritu can be mended granting vetu Ritu's promise of eternal life.

Venifani

Venifani is a denomination of Ritufani which sort of hybridizes Vefani and Nifani in that they operate by a similar Ritu seeking philosophy to that of Nifani, and they believe the story of Ritu as posited by the Vefani is the best truth and goodness when it comes to describing the relationship vetu have and have had with Ritu over time. Venifani also uphold the Holy Scriptures of the Vefani as being more densely filled with truth and goodness than any other claimed holy text.

Rirafani

Belief systems which posit the existence of many divine higher powers, or celestials, of various names. While some denominations of Rirafani posit a greatest divine being, the greatest being is not often regarded as having power which far exceeds other celestials such that enough celestials working together could challenge/contest the greatest celestial.

Lidifani

Lidifani is a denomination of Rirafani. Lidifani members believe there is a vast number of higher powers which exist above or apart from the world of the vetu. Whether they are star dwellers or exist in a reality which encompasses the world of the vetu.

Most of these higher powers are believed to be indifferent to the reality of the vetu, however, some engage in the vetu world through a variety of mediums.

Some engage through acts of creation, others consume information about the vetu for entertainment, and still others might take on vetu avatars through which they can walk among the vetu and engage with vetu in a number of ways.

There are three predominant sub-denominations which fall under Lidifani. They are the Zelidi, the Relidi, and the Ulidi.

Zelidi

Zelidi is a sub-denomination of Lidifani. The Zelidi mission is to identify and enhance the experience of any celestial avatars even at personal cost. Zelidi believe their mission is in alignment with their purpose for existing.

Relidi

Relidi is a sub-denomination of Lidifani. The Relidi mission is to identify and ruin the experience of any celestial avatars. Relidi find the existence of vetu to be a rather cruel reality, and so they loathe higher powers for creating their reality or otherwise using it for entertainment. Relidi aim to undermine and contest the enjoyment of higher powers in whatever way they can.

Ulidi

Ulidi is a sub-denomination of Lidifani. The Ulidi mission is to appease higher powers explicitly for personal gain. Ulidi attempt to study the nature and intent of individual higher powers in an effort to determine how they might work with them to their advantage. Some attempt to manipulate higher powers into running errands and others attempt to manipulate higher powers into toppling government powers among other things.

Venafani

Belief systems which posit that all vetu are fragments of a single consciousness. Vefani believe that all vetu experiences will be compiled together to form a being composed of every vetu's best attributes. As for the worst aspects of vetu, such attributes will be pruned from the united vetu and wiped from existence in a similar fashion to the way a vetu might shed a negative aspect of verself as ve grows as a person.

The venafani mission is for each individual and community to work hard to grow and better themselves in virtues. Venafani take lessons such as "treat others the way you want to be treated" and "love your enemy as yourself" very seriously because they believe other people are simply different instances of themselves.

The venafani belief system is not exclusive to other belief systems and is often held by vetu in tandem with other belief systems.

Glossary

Atu

/ətü/

ah-too

noun

1. Typically biped vetu with thin body hair, except for concentrated regions on top of their head, in the armpits, and around the crotch (some are capable of growing facial hair as well). They have a face ending in a nose and ape-like ears positioned at the sides of their head. They have nail-tipped fingers and toes, with opposable thumbed hands. They possess a poor sense of smell but have superior vision compared to other vetu. Atu also have a breathing hole at the base of their skull in conjunction with their ability to breath through their nose and mouth. This makes it nearly impossible for an atu to choke on food.

Bitu

/bētü/

bee-too

noun

1. Typically biped vetu covered in fur, featuring a face that ends in a shallow snout. They have spade-shaped ears on top of their head, a long ringed tail extending from their lower back, and claw-tipped paws. Their upper paws have opposable thumbs. They have poor eyesight but possess a superior sense of smell compared to other vetu. Bitu also have a breathing hole at the base of their skull in conjunction with their ability to breath

through their nose and mouth. This makes it nearly impossible for a bitu to choke on food.

Butushoselimo

/bütükwōselēmô/

boo-too-shoh-se-lee-moh

noun

1. A large arachnid with two jumping legs and six webbed legs used for gliding.

Fose

/fōs/

fohs

noun

1. Derogatory term in reference to someone as a low life or as being poor.
   "My nerdy sibling is such a fose."
2. To be the sort of person who would make a secret known to the public.
   "Don't let Momo know, ve is a fose."
3. Short for foselitu.

verb

1. To make a secret known.
   "Don't let Momo know, ve will fose on us."

Foselitu

/fōselētü/

fohs-se-lee-too

noun

1. A small mammal with black fur and striking blue wings. Often considered the lowest form of life.

Hase

/has/

hahs

noun

1. Believed to be a place of eternal conscious torment for those who reject particular understandings of Ritu.
2. A tool meant to scare vetu into blind obedience and loyalty to a particular paradigm of thought.
3. A place where the worst attributes of vetu go to be eradicated throughout the refining/growing process of each vetu.

Hosudiha

/hōsüdēhə/

hos-soo-dee-hah

noun

1. Believed to be the rung of society where the laziest and most morally deprived individuals come to reside.
2. A city with a history rooted in the slavery vetu of dark complexion. While slavery has been "abolished", residents, which are predominantly vetu of dark complexion, are kept systematically poor and desperate to limit upwards mobility and maintain a population that can be exploited for free prison labor or otherwise cheap wage labor.

Jufida

/jüfēdə/

joo-fee-dah

noun

1. A small fur-covered mammal, bigger than a foselitu, that is commonly kept by vetu as a pet.

Jubu

/jübü/

joo-boo

noun

1. An insect similar to a cricket. These insects are known to start chirping on the same sun every salary.

Kuvohedi

/küvōhedē/

koo-voh-he-dee

noun

1. A hoofed mammal that is widely used as the most common form of livestock.

Lidifani

/lēdēfənē/

lee-dee-fah-nee

noun

1. A denomination of Rirafani wherein members believe there are a vast number of higher powers which exist above or apart from the reality vetu live in whether they are star dwellers or exist in a reality which encompasses the reality of the vetu.
2. A vetu who holds beliefs in congruence with the Lidifani belief system.

Matuha

/mətühə/

ma-too-hah

noun

1. A welfare state or social democracy that is dedicated both to the welfare of its citizens and the coexistence of nature and industry.

Mefadi

/mefədē/

me-fah-dee

noun

1. A specific nation which is run as a theocratic dictatorship.

Notu

/nōtü/

noh-too

noun

1. A sentient gemstone that is capable of using magic to shape malleable substances into a body that can take on almost any form so long as it remains within six ingots of the gem. Notu consciousness resides in its gemstone. Striking a notu gemstone can stun or knock the notu out depending on the quality of the

strike. Notu also see, hear, and speak through their gem with vision that is better than that of a bitu and worse than an atu. A notu's needs depend on the material it chooses to use for its body. A special clay is a common body material that only requires an occasional douse of water to keep from drying out. Notu are the only vetu that do not reproduce. It is believed that notu simply wake up when no one is around every now and again.

Nifani

/nēfənē/

nee-fah-nee

noun

1. A denomination of Ritufani wherein members believe that Ritu is goodness, truth, and the journey towards goodness and truth. Members also believe that vetu are fallible in their ability to identify goodness and truth. This implies that no vetu can claim, with absolute confidence, that any being, spirit, or media is Ritu, is of Ritu, or is inspired by Ritu.
2. A vetu who holds beliefs in congruence with the Nifani belief system.

-R

/r/

r

Determiner

1. Added to the end of nouns and pronouns to communicate belonging to or association with the noun or pronoun.

ve-r
"Rama forgot ver notebook"
2. used in titles.
"Ver Royal Highness"
3. used in names.
Ri-r-ha
Literal translation: Divinity's Place
Common translation: Ritu's Temple
4. ARCHAIC•DIALECT
ve-r-self
"Ve knew verself very well"

Relidi

/relēdē/

re-lee-dee

noun

1. Relidi is a sub-denomination of Lidifani wherein members are on a mission to identify and ruin the experience of any celestial avatars.
2. A vetu who holds beliefs in congruence with the Relidi belief system.

Ribe

/rēb/

ree-b

noun

1. Believed to be a deceptive spirit in rebellion against Ritu.
2. A cheap and easy way to make an enemy of anyone by declaring their allegiance to the deceptive spirit.

Riberha

/rēberhə/

ree-ber-hah

noun

1. The largest wormwood island of the nation of Rirze. Positioned directly over Hosudiha and a primary cause of the pollution of Hosudiha's water supply followed by the waste of those who inhabit the small town Susehatosema.

Rirsudi

/rērsüdē/

reer-soo-dee

noun

1. Believed to be Ritu's eternal nation where vetu who accepted particular understandings of Ritu are believed to live their afterlives.
2. The mind of you, the reader, where the contents of this book are remembered and influence your life.

Rirmevu

/rērmevü/

reer-me-voo

noun

1. Believed to be Ritu's moral hand.
2. A law enforcement team consisting of a yetu and either an atu or a bitu.

3. A tool used by powerful people to maintain a desperate population of people to be exploited for free or otherwise cheap labor.

Rirkase

/rērkəse/

reer-kah-se

noun

1. Believed to be Retu's shield.
2. A law enforcement team consisting of a notu and either an atu or a bitu.
3. A tool used by powerful people to maintain a desperate population of people to be exploited for free or otherwise cheap labor.

Rirze

/rērz/

reer-z

noun

1. A theocratic sudo-democratic nation.

Rirha

/rērhə/

reer-hah

noun

1. Believed to be the holiest place where Ritu verself comes to reside periodically.
2. A largely empty palace where some powerful elite vetu live in luxury.

Rirbuseha

/rērbüsehə/

reer-boo-se-hah

noun

1. Believed to be the rung of society where the hardest working and most morally upright vetu reside.
2. A nepotistic city where the same families have lived in unearned inherited power and luxury that requires relatively little work to maintain. Most work that is done by residents of this city aims to ensure the social fabric remains undisturbed and their power uncontested.

Ritu

/rētü/

ree-too

noun

1. Believed to be the greatest divine being above whom there is none greater.
2. Whoever happens to be creating a story set in the Shattered Skies universe.

Rirafani

/rērafanē/

reer-ah-fah-nee

noun

1. Belief systems which posit the existence of many divine higher powers, or celestials, of various names.

2. A vetu who holds beliefs in congruence with the Rirafani belief system.

Ritufani

/rētüfanē/

ree-too-fah-nee

noun

1. Belief systems which posit the existence of a singular, greatest, divine being often known as Ritu.
2. A vetu who holds beliefs in congruence with the Ritufani belief system.

Rovo

/rōvō/

roh-voh

noun

1. A creature with ten long legs protruding from its long exoskeletal body. Commonly used to pull carts and wagons.

Sudihatosema

/südēhətōsemə/

soo-dee-hah-toh-se-mah

noun

1. Believed to be the rung of society where average quality vetu workers and citizens come to reside.
2. A city full of citizens who dream of upward mobility but are more likely to move downward or not at all. These citizens serve to maintain an illusion of achievable upward mobility to reduce the odds of an uprising. Citizens are permitted to have just

enough to be unwilling to risk what they have to upset or permit others to upset the social fabric. This serves to empower and defend upper society.

Susehatosema

/süsehətēsemə/

soo-se-hah-toh-se-mah

noun

1. One of many small town extensions of Sudihatosema.

Tafose

/təfōse/

ta-foh-se

noun

1. Polluted black water that falls from wormwood islands.
2. The water of death.
   "The waters that fall from wormwood islands are tafose."

Ulidi

/yo͞olədə/

oo-lee-dee

noun

1. A sub-denomination of Lidifani wherein members are on a mission to appease higher powers explicitly for personal gain.
2. A vetu who holds beliefs in congruence with the Ulidi belief system.

Ve

/ve/

ve

Pronoun

1. Used as the object of a verb or preposition to refer to an implied sentient being.
   "Ve is a good person"

noun

1. Used to classify beings as sentient.
   ve-tu
   "You may be a yetu and I may be an atu, but we are both vetu."
2. Used to indicate lesser sentience.
   ve-mo
   "Those who find joy in the suffering of others are vemo."
   Translation: Those who find joy in the suffering of others are of lesser sentience.

Vedi

/vedē/

ve-dee

noun

1. The parent of a being.
   "They are ver vedi and ve is their child."

Vedidi

/vedēdē/

ve-dee-dee

noun

1. The grandparent of a being.
   "They are ver parents and ver children's vedidi."
2. 'di's can be added to express levels of great grands.

Vedidira

/vedērə/

ve-dee-dee-rah

noun

1. The sibling of the grandparent of a being.
   "They are ver grandparent's sibling making them ver vedidira."

Vedira

/vedērə/

ve-dee-rah

noun

1. The sibling of the parent of a being.
   "They are ver parent's sibling making them ver vedira."

Vefani

/vefanē/

ve-fah-nee

noun

1. A denomination of Ritufani which believes Ritu is the creator of all things and ultimately took on vetu forms to rescue all vetu kinds from the fruits of their vices.
2. A vetu who holds beliefs in congruence with the Vefani belief system.

Venifani

/venēfanē/

ve-nee-fah-nee

noun

1. A denomination of Ritufani which sort of hybridizes Vefani and Nifani.
2. A vetu who holds beliefs in congruence with the Venifani belief system.

Venafani

/venafanē/

ve-nah-fah-nee

noun

1. Belief systems which posit that all vetu are fragments of a single consciousness.
2. A vetu who holds beliefs in congruence with the Venafani belief system.

Vemo

/vemô/

ve-moh

noun

1. A being of lesser sentience.
   "Those who find joy in the suffering of others are vemo."

Vemoize

/vemô/

ve-moh-eyez

verb

1. To consider or speak of a vetu as though they were a being of lesser sentience.
   "When people say bitu are feral, they vemoize bitu."

noun

1. The process of making a target vetu or group of vetu out to be of lesser sentience.
   ve-mo-ization
   "Those in upper society are prone to the vemoization of those beneath their socioeconomic status."

Vera

/verə/

ve-rah

noun

1. The sibling of a being.
   "Ve is their child, and so am I, making us vera."

Vese

/vese/

ve-se

noun

1. The offspring of a being.
   "They are ver parents and ve is their vese."

Vesese

/vesese/

ve-se-se

noun

1. The grandchild of a being.
   "They are their parent's children and their grandparent's vesese."
2. 'se's can be added to express levels of great grands.

Vetu

/vetü/

ve-too

noun

1. A being of higher sentience; a bitu, atu, yetu, or notu. All vetu have the same capacity for intelligence. None of the species of vetu are more prone to any particular set of emotions or behaviors (no vetu are more prone to anger and criminal activity on grounds of nature/biology. Yetu, however, do tend to be more empathetic creatures due to their enhanced ability to perceive the experiences of other vetu due to the way they perceive the world). These qualities are true and have always been true of the various vetu species. Differences in temperament or criminal activity are purely the result of circumstance; divisions in social class, ratios of needs to needs met, among other environmental factors. There are those, however, who peddle and believe lies about underlying differences between the vetu species, resulting in widespread harm and oppression.
   "You may be a yetu and I may be an atu, but we are both vetu."

Vetura

/vetürə/

ve-too-rah

noun

1. The spouse of a being.
   "We are married, making us vetura."

Wormwood Islands

/ˈwərm-ˌwu̇d ˈī-lənds/

wohrm-wud-ai-luhnd

noun

1. Islands that are home to a diverse array of deadly mutant plant life. These islands are characterized by a covering of black moss, giving them the appearance of floating masses of coal. The origins of these islands can be traced back to the devastating war that shattered the skies, during which they were bombarded with bio-weapons derived from forgotten technologies of ancient times.

Yetu

/yetü/

ye-too

noun

1. An insectoid vetu normally with an ovular body covered in fur-like scales. Their body is about the size of an adult atu's back and they have moth-like wings spanning between 18-20 ingots. Yetu have two feather-like antennas protruding from the top of their body with which they can tap into the fabric of creation to read detailed information about living biological beings and sparse information about non-living or inanimate objects within thirty six blocks of them. Yetu speak by vibrating a loose piece of skin on their backs. Some yetu are highly skilled at using this speech organ to replicate any sound or voice.

Zelidi

/zelēdē/

ze-lee-dee

noun

1. A sub-denomination of Lidifani wherein the members are on a mission to identify and enhance the experience of any celestial avatars they identify even at personal cost.
2. A vetu who holds beliefs in congruence with the Zelidi belief system.

Special Thank You!

- My wife
- My family
- Ritika (Sensitivity reader on Fiverr)
- Arianna Krzyzkowski
- Colton Nelson (Author of the Wyvern Trilogy)
- K. C. Norton (Author of Tale of the Hidden Village)
- Anna D (Sensitivity reader on Fiverr)

Check out my website for author updates, merch, and more!

www.RituVediAuthor.com

Milton Keynes UK
Ingram Content Group UK Ltd.
UKHW012030110124
435898UK00016B/242/J

9 798989 683918